A BOAT FOR A GOAT

A KENNEDY REEVES MYSTERY

MJ MAC

This novel is entirely a work of fiction. The names, characters, and incidents portrayed are a work of the author's imagination. Any resemblance to actual persons, living or dead is entirely coincidental. Although real life places are depicted in settings, all situations and people related to those places are fictional.

Paperback Edition 2022
ISBN: 979-8-9870479-1-0

E-Reader Edition 2022
ISBN: 979-8-9870479-0-3

To Dan, for believing.

Sunny Dayz Cruise Line

THE HELIO

DAY 1: DEPART PORT CANAVERAL, USA

DAY 2: NASSAU, BAHAMAS

DAY 3: GRAND TURK, TURKS AND CAICOS ISLANDS

DAY 4: PUNTA CANA, DOMINICAN REPUBLIC

DAY 5: AT SEA

DAY 6: ARRIVE IN PORT CANAVERAL, USA

Kennedy Reeves was sitting on the dock at the back of her home overlooking the Stono River in Charleston, flipping through another mindless magazine, when her phone chirped. Seeing Mila's name on the screen, she smiled as she answered.

"WE'RE GOING BACK TO WORK!" her best friend screamed into her ear. "Check your email!"

"What?" Kennedy exclaimed. "Hold on, let me see." She looked at her phone, but it didn't show any new messages. "Mila, I haven't gotten anything yet," she said disappointedly.

Mila was puzzled. Surely, if the corporate office had contacted her, they would have contacted Kennedy as well. "Hang up with me and reboot your phone because we are going back to work!" she chattered.

Kennedy's mind raced. While she hadn't received a message, one had to be on its way. "I'll call you right back," she promised. *Please, let there be a note from Alfred.* She exhaled and pressed the reset button on her phone while she uncrossed her legs, stood up, and began pacing the length of the dock as the phone reset. *Good Lord, how long does it take to reboot?* Her phone buzzed with a message: YOUR PHONE REQUIRES AN UPDATE. PLEASE STAND BY.

"Are you kidding me?" she huffed at the phone. "This is only my life we have on hold. Wasn't there a better time to do this?" Kennedy stood still and placed a hand over her eyes. "Breathe in, breathe out. Don't look at the phone. Wait for the stupid chime to tell you that it's finished." *Let's just see where we are.* She peeked through her fingers at the screen. "Nine percent?" She stuck her tongue out and placed the phone on the bench. "What kind of update is this? A new operating system?"

The five minutes it took to reboot felt like five days as Kennedy tapped her foot, paced the dock, walked back to the bench to check the update's progress, and continued the maddening cycle. Then, finally, she heard a chime. *"Now, may I check my email?"* Kennedy said with sarcasm as the phone's icons began to repopulate. She touched the email symbol at the exact moment her phone rang. It was Mila.

"Anything?"

"I'll call you back. It took a while to reboot," Kennedy said and hung up.

She tapped the email symbol again and was prompted to enter her password. Kennedy closed her eyes in aggravation and punched in the information. The app opened, and with a hopeful heart, Kennedy searched for a note from her boss. Not finding one, her heart *and* her stomach dropped. *Maybe it went to the junk folder.* She clicked on the folder and scanned it for Alfred's name but found no messages from him. Sweat popped on her forehead and down her back as she realized she wasn't being asked to return to work on the *Helio*. The only email she had received was an invitation from her sister, Willie, for an event she had no desire to attend. *They picked someone else. It's fine.*

Kennedy dialed Mila's number. "Nothing from Alfred. What's going on?"

Mila hesitated. She didn't know how to respond without hurting her best friend's feelings. "Well," she swallowed, "we've all, or almost all, been called back to the ship. The *Helio* is going out again."

"Everyone?"

Mila was hesitant again, anxious about how much information she should share. She didn't want to be unkind. "Franklin and Rosemary have known for a few weeks. I've been working on the spa renovations but hadn't been told an official date, only to complete the revamp. I got a notice a few minutes ago and called you. There must be a mistake, Kennedy," she said, perplexed. "Have you heard from Omar or Tony?"

Kennedy sighed. "No, not at all, but congratulations. This is big news." She tried to brighten her tone. "When is the *Helio* going back out? I can't believe it. We're finally returning to work—well, all of you are, I'm not. She paused as the reality of the situation sunk in. "Oh, God, Mila, I can't stay here much longer. I'm not going to make it. I wonder if I can get a job as one of the cast members or as a social hostess. I could do that again. I could—"

"Kennedy, relax." Mila interrupted. "You are the best cruise director in the industry. I'm willing to bet your email got hung up somewhere. You know how corporate screws things up. Breathe."

Kennedy inhaled deeply. "Okay, okay, breathing." Suddenly she was anxious again. "Mila, I just can't. I can't be here a minute longer. One more mindless magazine or reorganization of my closet, and I may go over the edge."

"And we are now changing the subject," Mila said cheerily. "How are things at Casa del Reeves? Is Lolly driving you nuts? Who is she fixing you up with this week? And most importantly, are we planning your wedding yet?" She giggled.

"You are an evil, evil woman." Kennedy blew out a big breath of air. "Last week was dinner with one of the new associates from my father's bank. The man was beige."

"Beige?" Mila queried. "As in the color?"

Kennedy sighed. "Beige suit, beige loafers, beige hair, even his conversation was beige. I had to sit there, smile, and make small talk when all I wanted to do was scream." Kennedy's voice began to rise. "Scream like I want to do now because I haven't received a message to tell me that I'm going back to work." The words came out in a rush.

Mila used what she called her spa voice as she tried to reel Kennedy back in. "Kennedy, tell me about the beige man. What was his name?"

Kennedy answered slowly as if in a daze. "His name? His name." She paused, racking her brain. She could see the man's face but could not recall his name. "I have completely blanked. He was so nondescript." She gave a nervous laugh. "Mila, I cannot remember his name." She pounded the post on the dock. "Wait a minute. It was something normal, not preppy." She shook her head. "It's no use. I can't remember. The whole evening was so dull I must have blanked it out." Kennedy sighed. "I wish I hadn't been forced to ask Lolly and Richard for their help with the property taxes, but I was strapped. And *of course*, the loan came with strings: three command performances per week."

"Three?"

"Oh, yes," Kennedy answered. "One is for Lolly's and Richard's social gatherings. Then there is the weekly family meal with Willie the Perfect and her family and Carter, *if,* he remembers. And then lunch with Lolly, my least favorite." She watched as an alligator sunning itself on the bank of the river slid into the murky water. "That is a special one. My mother picks one of her favorite restaurants and spends the meal eviscerating me in public while smiling at everyone in the room. It's an interesting form of torture that even the Spanish Inquisition was afraid to try."

"Let's go back to the beige guy," Mila said. "He wasn't really that bad, was he? I mean, if Lolly invited him, he had to have some social ranking, and from what you have told me, invitees must also be able to hold an intelligent conversation.

Kennedy lightly pounded her forehead with her fist. "Mila, it's no use. This guy has completely escaped my—" she stopped talking. "Hold on. My phone is buzzing," she said excitedly. She tapped on the email symbol and saw a piece of junk mail. "Nothing important," she said gloomily.

"Okay, back to Mr. Personality," Mila said. "What was he like, other than beige?"

"Mila, there have been at least thirty different men my parents have attempted to set me up with since I have been home. They all are forgettable."

"You must remember something from the evening."

"Mr. Beige, as we shall refer to him, works in risk assessment at the bank with my father. The evening was like all the others: cocktails on the patio, my mother playing the hostess version of twenty questions while giving me *the look* because she felt I wasn't chatty or witty enough. I did smile a lot, but then again, I was on my second martini. Then, magically, as I was finishing my drink, it was time for dinner. And thank goodness for that because, number one, I was running out of things to say, and number two, I was starving, afraid that my growling stomach would upset Lolly. Noisy stomachs rate a zero on the social behavior scale," she chattered.

"Lolly had set the table perfectly. The silverware gleamed, the crystal glasses were spotless, the china flawless, and the peonies in the cut glass bowl complemented not only each other but didn't have a scent and wouldn't compete with the aroma of our dinner. It was all…quite perfect." Kennedy took a breath. "My mother had made an arugula salad with balsamic dressing, sautéed mushrooms, and wild rice, and there was a cherry and red wine sauce that I want you to know that I managed *not* to spill on the snowy white tablecloth. The wine sauce was for the roast quail and— DAN!" Kennedy blurted out. "His name was Daniel."

Mila felt as if she had been on an amusement park ride. "How did we go from how the table looked and the dinner menu to the beige man's name? I'm bewildered."

Kennedy was puzzled. "Seriously, Mila? Dan Quayle, forty-fourth vice president? Famous for misspelling the word *potato*? The early 1990s? Everyone, even elementary school children, roasted the poor man. I am rolling my eyes at you right now."

"Excuse me. I lived in Poland at that time. I was busy taking tickets and performing in the family circus," Mila said smugly.

"Oh, there you go again, using the Polish family circus excuse." Kennedy smiled sadly. "Thanks for trying to help me find a reason to smile." Kennedy snapped her fingers. "I just had a crazy idea. What if I used these dinner disasters in one of my after-hours shows if I ever get to go back to work? I could call it 'Dating: The Good, The Bad, and Wow What Was I Thinking?' I can talk about Mr. Beige and some of the others, too. I told you about the warlock, right?"

Mila sputtered. "A warlock? No, I believe I missed that one, Kennedy. I can't wait to hear about it. You have such a colorful way of telling stories."

Kennedy chuckled. "Shortly after I returned to Charleston, I went on a blind date set up by Willie the Perfect and her husband, Paul. The guy was a friend of Paul's. We got to the restaurant, the introductions were made, and everything seemed fine. After the waiter took our drink order, Willie's phone rang. One of the girls was having a teenage crisis. Willie excused herself and beckoned Paul to go with her, leaving me sitting with this guy I had never met before. We made awkward, strange small talk and found some things we had in common. I thought things were going well." She took a deep breath. "And that was when he informed me that he was not only a stockbroker but also a warlock."

"Excuse me? A what? A warlock as in male witch?"

"Yep," Kennedy said slowly. She saw the night replayed in her mind. "He sat across from me and told me he was a warlock with a perfectly straight face."

"Kennedy, you aren't serious."

"Oh, I am quite serious. Mila, this is what my life has become, but it gets better. Please let me continue. This man, we'll call him Brian, went into great detail about how he uses his warlock powers to buy and sell stocks. I kept looking around to see if Willie and Paul were nearby, and this was a practical joke, but when I didn't see them, I realized he was serious."

"What did you do?" Mila was trying hard to stifle the laughter bubbling up.

The date was a moment that Kennedy would never forget. "Well, he finished telling me about his warlock powers and asked what I thought. I blurted out the only thing I could think of. I said, 'I'm so very sorry, Brian, but I'm Episcopalian, and I just don't think this will work out.'"

Mila was laughing hard now as she pictured a man in a hooded robe sitting across from Kennedy, having a first-date conversation. The image was hard to get out of her head. She tried to catch her breath. "What happened next? Where were Willie and Paul?" she asked.

"Well, there was an awkward silence, and then the waiter showed up with our drinks, and Willie and Paul were behind him. They sat down, and the conversation turned to the yacht club, new restaurants, and events in town. Not another word was said about using mystical powers to trade stocks. I wouldn't have believed it myself if I hadn't been the one it happened to. Willie asked me a week later if I wanted to double-date again, and I fibbed, telling her I was afraid I had caught something and thought it best to stay home."

"I can't believe that you had to go through the entire dinner," Mila said, and a maniacal giggle escaped as the image of Kennedy and the warlock seated at dinner popped into her head again.

Kennedy sniffed haughtily. "Now, Mila, what would Lolly say? Of course, I had to go through with the dinner. My family would have disowned me if I had been so crass as to end a date over something as trivial as a man professing to be a warlock. I *might* have been able to get out of it if he'd been a zombie or a vampire. No, Willie would have made sure to tell my mother, and Lolly would have died of shame. I can just hear her." She mimicked her mother's voice, "He's a perfectly fine gentleman, Kennedy. Don't look a gift horse in the mouth. You can overlook his curious little hobby. You aren't exactly getting any younger. Tick-tock."

Mila let out another burst of laughter at Kennedy's impersonation of her mother. "Okay, that one goes in the new show you are talking about. The story is so crazy and funny, and only something that would happen to you." She became quiet. "So, what will you do with yourself, my friend?"

"I'm going to keep busy. Maybe I'll start writing that dating monologue. I'm fine, I promise, but I'm running out of patience." She changed the subject, "Where is the cruise going?"

Mila was quiet.

"Come on, Mila," Kennedy said. "I'm not going to fall apart."

"Our old route. We leave Port Canaveral, one day in Nassau, one day in Grand Turk, one day in Punta Cana, a day at sea, and then we return the passengers to reality."

"That sounds like heaven," Kennedy said wistfully. She smacked her forehead with her hand. "Mila, I am so sorry. I am so wrapped up in my pity party I haven't asked you about the spa! How is the transformation coming along?"

Mila let out a big breath, and Kennedy could imagine Mila blowing it up into her bangs. "It's good. It's just a never-ending list of things to be done or checked. And I'm sorry to do this, but I've got to fly. The plumbers have arrived to install some of the equipment." She paused. "I am certain you will be on the cruise with us, Kennedy. This is a mix-up by the corporate office. I'm sure of it," she said with conviction. "Now, I've got to get this spa up and running before the first cruise. I made a lot of promises, and I need to hold up my end of the bargain. And don't worry, Alfred probably thought he sent you the first email and can't figure out why you haven't responded yet. He's undoubtedly freaking out, believing another cruise line has snapped you up. You know he is your number one fan. I'm willing to bet he typed your email address wrong."

Kennedy sighed and looked out at the water. The alligator was climbing back on the bank again to bask in the sun. "I just don't know what I will do if I don't get asked."

Mila chuckled. "Well, you could marry someone named Briggs or Stratton or something suitable like that, give Lolly a wedding to plan, have two perfect blue-eyed children, live in a fabulous mansion in Charleston, and for fun, visit old friends like me on a dilapidated cruise ship and drunkenly reminisce about the good old days."

"I'm hanging up now, Mila. I love you."

"I love you too, Kennedy, and don't worry. It will be okay. And if not," she said flippantly, "you can begin looking for cotton candy pink lace bridesmaids' dresses. As maid of honor, I would prefer mine with a large bow on the back," she said flippantly. "Bye!"

Kennedy stared at the phone, her mouth hanging open, as a laughing Mila hung up on her. Mila had gotten in the last word and had left Kennedy feeling hopeful and light.

She walked up the dock toward the house. Casa del Reeves, as she referred to it, was unusual from other Charleston properties. The original house was a 1950s-style brick cottage that her grandparents, Robert and Maggie

Spencer, had built. Shortly before Kennedy was born, Robert and Maggie had deeded the adjacent acreage to her parents, who built a larger, more modern home. As the years passed, a breezeway connecting the two homes was built and later enlarged and enclosed. The glass enclosure, the solarium as Lolly liked to call it to her society friends (or the solemn room as Kennedy and her grandmother would call it in sarcastic whispers), was where the family could gather each morning for breakfast and then again at night during the colder months to toast the sunset. They would sit on the dock or the patio for cocktails in the warmer months.

Cocktail hour had always been a lively affair as Kennedy was growing up. Friends and business associates would often drop by. When her grandparents were alive, there were games of badminton or croquet on the side lawn, marathon bridge or canasta tournaments, or a friend with a guitar. In those days, gaiety and laughter filled the air, and when Robert and Maggie died, a void filled that space. Now, when people came by the house for cocktails, it was to hammer out a business deal or gossip about the latest scandal.

Her grandparents and her parents had been at opposite ends of the spectrum. Kennedy often wondered if her mother had been left on their doorstep. While her parents strove for academic and social perfection in their children, her grandparents focused on ensuring their grandchildren experienced what life had to offer. Only one child followed the path set forth by Richard and Lolly, her sister Willie. Or, as Kennedy called her, Willie the Perfect. Willie was married to a handsome lawyer who worked with her father at the bank. Society had set her membership in the Junior League on the day she drew her first breath, and with her marriage to Paul, the doors of the yacht club and country club were quickly opened. Two perfect children arrived at the proper time, and the picture was complete. Willie *was* perfect, just like her mother, Lolly. They both had the same head of flawlessly straight blonde hair, which was cut and touched up every three weeks. While Lolly had the house on the Stono River, Willie had a beautiful brick home in a fashionable

Charleston neighborhood, and both homes always looked ready for a photo shoot. When it came to her brother-in-law, Paul, the only thing Kennedy could say was that he made a great martini. When Willie had told her mother she was marrying Paul Rose, she said, "He's handsome, he has manners, he's a lawyer, you and Daddy like him, and he has the same last initial as ours, so I won't have to change my monogram." Twelve months later, wearing her mother's lace gown with cathedral train and the proper six bridesmaids, Willie became Mrs. Paul Rose.

Kennedy and Carter, her younger brother, were the disappointing children of Lolly and Richard. Kennedy, for not following in her sister's footsteps, scandalously breaking off an engagement, and running away to work on a cruise ship. Carter, for continuing to make questionable choices that occasionally landed him in hot water from time to time, but Lolly overlooked this. Kennedy had helped him at one point get a job on the *Helio* to get out of Charleston for a while.

To the shock and dismay of Kennedy's parents and siblings, Maggie Spencer bequeathed the 1950s brick cottage to Kennedy when she died. Like her grandfather, Robert, Kennedy was a sea gypsy. As each cruise contract lasted six months, with six weeks off, having the cottage gave Kennedy the ability to have homes on and off the sea. Unfortunately, having a house connected to her parents came at a price, and this last year, without work, the price had been high.

Kennedy walked up the brick path from the dock to the house and saw her mother cutting peonies for the dining room arrangement. "Oh, Lord, another dinner tonight," she said under her breath.

Kennedy and Lolly's relationship had always been rocky, even in the best times. Kennedy joked that it started before she could speak. Kennedy and her mother didn't have pleasant conversations like Lolly and Willie. Instead, Lolly and Kennedy had caustic verbal sword fights, each trying in vain to get in as many sarcastic slashes as possible. Even as a child, if Lolly had wanted one thing, Kennedy would automatically go in the opposite direction. A direction that often led her in tears into the arms of her grandparents.

"Kennedy," her mother looked up as she cut the head of another peony from its stem, "don't forget we have dinner tonight. Your father is bringing home someone interesting he and Paul met at the yacht club," she said in a flat tone.

"Great," Kennedy replied with false enthusiasm.

Lolly returned to decapitating the flowers in front of her. "Oh, and you received another package. You get so many of them. Perhaps you would have had the money to pay the property taxes on your house if you had spent a little less on yourself. Maybe whatever you bought this time will fill the empty void in your life."

Kennedy counted silently to ten and then to twenty. "It's probably something for work, Mother," she said defensively.

Lolly turned slowly to look at Kennedy. "Oh, the work that you don't have?" She decapitated another flower.

Kennedy didn't want to get into an argument, but she couldn't allow her mother to have the last word. "No, Mother, the job I will return to shortly when cruise ships are allowed back out at sea. The world's governments shut down the cruise industry. If you remember, they shut down a lot of things."

Lolly clucked and put a flower in the basket beside her. "It's such a shame. If you had stuck with interior design and married Joe, you could still be working. Perhaps renovating someone's beach house or a nursery for a new mother."

Normally, Kennedy would have smiled and allowed Lolly to get in the last dig, but she felt defensive. Knowing that her friends were returning to work made Kennedy more vulnerable than usual. "Mother," she said in defeat, "could you please stop picking on me? Per our agreement, I will be at dinner tonight, sociable and charming, per your conditions."

She started up the path to her house and had only taken ten steps before Lolly spoke again. "Could you try not to yawn during dinner tonight? It would be an improvement over the last dinner," she said acidly. "Honestly, I don't know what was worse, your yawning or the stories you told. I was mortified."

Kennedy stopped and turned around slowly. "I am sorry I am such a disappointment to you. You asked that I contribute to the conversation at dinner. The reverend asked me for a crazy cruise story, and I shared the senior swinger's cruise. He seemed to have enjoyed it," she said tartly.

Lolly slammed the peony she had just cut into her basket and stood up. "You can be so exasperating, Kennedy. I think you do these things on purpose to push my buttons." She picked up the basket of flowers. "Please put on something decent and try to do something with your hair if it isn't too much trouble. You do own a hairbrush, don't you? Try to use it. You look like a wild hooligan."

Kennedy was suddenly ten years old again. "I suppose as I don't know what a hooligan looks like, I will have to find a picture so that I know how my hair offends you this time. Do you let people know before they come over that wild hooligan hair upsets you? Is it in the invitation?"

Lolly began turning a dangerous shade of red as she stamped her foot. "Kennedy!" she pointed a finger at her. "Do not push me. I am not in the mood for your sarcasm." Lolly took a deep breath to calm down. "Your father's dinners are important for his job and our social standing, and may I remind you that these dinners were a part of the deal you made with us when you needed money because you had no job. I will expect you in the solarium for cocktails at seven. Do not be late, arrive with your hair combed and makeup on, in a nice dress, and please have POLITE conversation prepared to make our guest feel at home. Got it?"

"Yes, Mother," Kennedy replied and quietly walked up the brick path. She kicked herself for the one-hundredth time for making a deal with her parents and prayed that a note from Alfred would magically appear, asking her to return to work.

At precisely thirty minutes before seven, with no email from Alfred, Kennedy donned a black sleeveless dress and pearl earrings. She pulled her hair back into a suitable chignon, dabbed on some lipstick, and ran the mascara wand across her eyelashes while trying to think of polite, suitable conversational topics. When she was on the ship, she had no problem chatting with the guests. However, while passengers wrote in their comment cards that talking with Kennedy was like speaking to a dear friend, it was always difficult when her mother was in the room. Lolly would judge and bait her, seeking a way to twist her words, and Kennedy could never pass up the challenge.

Her mother, father, and another of Charleston's most eligible bachelors were in the solarium. "Martini, Kennedy?" her father asked as she entered.

"Yes, please, Dad," Kennedy said with false enthusiasm.

He turned from the bar cart and handed her a martini. "Kennedy, I'd like to introduce you to Briggs Branson. Briggs is a fellow yacht club member, and I thought he would enjoy one of your mother's home-cooked meals." It was all Kennedy could do to bite her lower lip and push her nails into the palm of her hand as she shook Briggs's hand with her other one.

"Briggs, what an unusual name. Do you have a brother named Stratton?" she asked, sitting down.

The man looked at her strangely. "It's a family name," he said, smiling faintly as her mother and father looked daggers at her. *This can't be real. Mila is not going to believe this.* Drinks led to dinner, and over the clanking of the silverware on the china, the typical mundane conversations that had become a part of her weekly obligation began.

"Kennedy, I read today that some cruise ships will go out soon. Have you heard anything?" her father queried.

Kennedy perked up. "Funny you should ask, Dad. The *Helio* is going on its first cruise soon. I haven't heard anything yet."

"Just remember, dear," Lolly said, her voice dripping with sarcasm and nodding her head ever so slightly toward the man seated across from Kennedy, "when God closes a door, He opens a window. Perhaps not being asked to return to work is a door telling you to try something different."

Kennedy knew she would regret what was getting ready to come out of her mouth, and she could hear a little whisper say, *don't do it, don't say it,* but she plunged forward. "Hoisting myself up to that window isn't as easy as you seem to think."

Lolly's eyes narrowed. "You certainly didn't have any problems hoisting yourself out of a window as a teenager, did you?" She turned to Briggs, who was concentrating on his dinner plate. "I need to apologize, Briggs. You must think that we have no manners, but Kennedy has always been the rulebreaker of the family. It will make her an excellent mother someday." Lolly smiled sweetly at Briggs, and Kennedy began to cough. Lolly looked from Briggs to Kennedy and then back at Briggs. "You know, I believe being home with us this year might be turning Kennedy away from her nomad life. We might be able to convince her to settle down and stay in Charleston."

At that moment, Kennedy's phone buzzed. She had
put the phone in her lap when she sat at the dining room
table, so she would know if an email came through. Trying to
look nonchalantly at the screen without being noticed, she hit
the icon.

"Kennedy!" Lolly admonished her. "We do not use
our cellphones at the table. It is terribly impolite." She turned
to Briggs. "I do apologize, Briggs."

Briggs offered Lolly an easy smile. "Nothing to
worry about, Lolly. I've been alone on my boat for so long
that I've forgotten the rules of society. Unfortunately, we
seem to have become conditioned to respond to the chirp of a
telephone." His voice boomed around the wood-paneled
dining room.

Kennedy looked down at the message. *I goofed.
Email address screw up. Sorry. I need you on
the* Helio *ASAP. Alfred.*

Lolly snapped her fingers in Kennedy's face. "Hello?
Kennedy, did you hear me?" she was speaking very loudly.

"If you can tear yourself away from whatever is so riveting, would you please help me clear the table so I can serve coffee and dessert?"

Kennedy beamed at her mother, who looked at her like she had two heads. "Of course, Mother, I would love nothing more than to help you."

The next few days were a flurry as Kennedy frantically tried to put six months of clothes, shoes, and toiletries into two suitcases. "Mila, nothing fits!" she wailed into her phone.

"What do you mean nothing fits?" Mila questioned. "What exactly doesn't fit?"

Kennedy huffed. "Not a single evening gown, dress, or skirt in my closet," she cried. "I've been wearing yoga pants or pajamas for a year. What am I going to do?"

Mila, always the practical friend, asked, "How much do they not fit? A little? Or is it more drastic? I've only seen you on a computer screen lately. Do you need to buy new clothes?"

"Just a little," said Kennedy meekly.

"Easy fix," Mila said with a cheerful tone. "Go buy some shapewear and double them until you lose the weight walking the ship. With all the steps we walk in a day, you will be back in your clothes before the passengers arrive. Now, hurry up and get down here. I need you. And don't forget to get your health test."

Kennedy realized she had a lot to get done in a ridiculously small amount of time. "Right, okay, I need to make a list. I've got to go, Mila," she said, hanging up the phone.

Kennedy searched her house for a notebook but couldn't find one. She was usually tidy, but in her frantic trying-on of clothes and shoes, it looked like a tornado had passed through it. Finally, giving up, she walked through the solarium and into her mother's house. "Mother, do you have a spare notebook or legal pad I can borrow?" she yelled.

"Kennedy, honestly, one does not enter someone's home yelling unless there is a fire or some other type of calamity," Lolly reprimanded, looking over her reading glasses at Kennedy from where she sat in the living room reading the newspaper.

"This is a calamity, Mother. I have exactly two days to pack, get a health test, fly to Florida, and get on a ship for six months. I believe this does, in fact, fall under the calamity column," Kennedy snapped.

"Whatever," Lolly said, shutting her eyes as if a migraine had suddenly come upon her. "I cannot believe you are returning to that ship after how they treated you. Furloughing you for a year without any notice, never checking to see how you were, cutting off your health insurance, and then suddenly they snap their fingers and tell you that you have a week to report, and you jump. What kind of people are these, Kennedy?" she asked incredulously.

"People who pay me money to do what I do, and well," Kennedy replied, looking around her mother's living room. It looked as if a photo shoot for a home décor catalog could take place at any moment, a far cry from her own house with clothes flung across the furniture.

"Go check your father's office," Lolly sighed. Kennedy made a beeline for her father's study, and Lolly trailed close behind her. "You know if you would just give up this insane idea and stay here, I am sure you could—"

Kennedy interrupted her. "Mom, please don't say it. Please say, 'I'm happy for you, Kennedy. I am glad that you are going back to the ship and going back to work.' Say something like, 'I am happy that you are happy, Kennedy. I know this has been a frustrating time for you.'" She sighed heavily. "But, please, Mother, please do not tell me to stay here, give up my career, and get married. I have no interest in that. Remember? I tried, and it didn't work. Someone placed a ring on my finger, and I fled in the middle of the night in a panic." She gave her mother a beseeching look. "Now, I need a notebook to make a list. I'm going to the department store, the drugstore, and the grocery store. Is there anything I may pick up for you while I am out?"

Lolly feigned a smile. "No, but before you go, may I please ask that you at least put on lipstick and some mascara? I'm sure eyelashes would be too much trouble. And would you please change into something suitable? You may not care who sees you, but I care, Kennedy. While you may do whatever you want on the ship when you are here in Charleston, you are still my daughter and a reflection on me," she said with an irritated tone.

Kennedy picked up a legal pad lying on her father's desk. She had known what Lolly would say, and she thought for a moment before she said her next words. She smiled sweetly at her mother. "Yes, Mother, I can do those things, but why bother with the lipstick? No one can see my lips because we are still wearing masks."

Lolly stared at Kennedy and threw her hands up in the air. "Kennedy, you make me want to scream. I cannot wait for you to leave so my life may return to its normal routine and not this ongoing battle I seem to have with you at every turn. The next two days will not go fast enough! Go!" she yelled.

Kennedy made an about-face and stormed through the solarium and into her own house. She grabbed her keys, purse, and phone. *I'll make the damn list in the parking lot, anything to get away from this asylum. I swear, regardless of the subject, I am always wrong in my mother's eyes. Please let this contract be for a year and not six months. Two years would be even better.*

Kennedy drove into town mentally changing gears from the verbal battle with her mother and began making a list in her head of what she would need for the next six months. Usually, she had a target date of when to report and could gather items during her six weeks off. Getting the news last night now meant a mad dash. Needing outfits for each day and evening for the length of her contract had made Kennedy learn how to hone her workwear choices. During the day, she wore an ensemble consisting of a jacket and sheath dress in several colors, and for evening wear, an elegant black evening gown and a few long black skirts paired with a sequined or taffeta top took care of her needs. Shoes were the next hurdle as Kennedy walked at least ten miles per day, and many times the shoes she had put on in the morning were still on her feet when she finally got to her cabin at the end of a long day. Kennedy had found a fantastic pair of comfortable pumps and bought three pairs in nude and black. The last difficulty was the trivial things most people took for granted: hair products, hose, makeup, and pain reliever. One could pick these items up in port, but the expense was not worth the luxury. The first time a new staff member said, "Oh, I'll just grab something in port," the others would have a silent chuckle, having once been in their shoes and learned the hard way.

Kennedy completed her errands quickly and efficiently. She decided she would go through her list one last time tonight and pack tomorrow. There was one final family dinner tomorrow night, and she would fly to Orlando the following morning. Mila would meet her there, and life would return to normal. *Well, normal for me*, she thought.

Dinner the following night was stilted, and the silverware clinking on the china was the only consistent noise. Willie and Carter had tried several times to start a conversation during the meal, but Lolly, angry at Kennedy

for leaving, shut down any attempts for a pleasant

conversation.

"Ken, tell everyone I said hello," her brother, Carter,

said. "This gig with the marine engineering team is good, and

the money is solid. I want to wait and make sure that cruising

is back to normal before I go back."

Carter Reeves, Kennedy's younger brother, had been

a water sports instructor for the cruise line. His good looks,

boyish grin, curly brown hair, and a tattoo on his left

shoulder made ladies young and old flock to try out surfing

or parasailing. Women who had never been seen with wet

hair outside their hair salon or bathroom suddenly wanted to

learn how to snorkel after seeing Carter.

Lolly eyed Kennedy. "That is what she should do.

She should wait until she knows for sure—"

Kennedy interrupted her mother, causing her two

siblings to stare at her—you did not interrupt Lolly unless

you were on fire. "Mom, please, I'm going. My bags are

packed, and my flight leaves tomorrow morning. Could we please have a nice dinner and not fight?" she pleaded. "I want to have a happy memory of my last dinner with all of you, and right now, I am struggling to find anything happy." Clearing his throat, Kennedy's father asked her if she needed a ride to the airport. Thankful for the diversion, Kennedy turned to her father. "Yes, Dad, a ride would be great."

"I'll meet you at the car at eight o'clock sharp." He nodded at Paul and Carter. "If the two of you will please put any of her suitcases that are ready in the car, I would appreciate it." He stood up and excused himself, telling them he had some work to review. He pecked Willie on the top of the head and Lolly on her cheek. "Dinner was wonderful as always, dear," and he walked out of the dining room and to his study.

Willie and Paul exchanged relieved looks. "Well, it looks like we are off as well, Mother." She walked over and kissed her mother's cheek. "Dinner was delicious as always. Would you like to have lunch tomorrow?"

Lolly first looked at Kennedy and then at Willie. She gave a small sigh and nodded her head. "That would be lovely, dear. Palmetto Café at one?" Willie nodded, and she and Paul walked quickly out of the dining room.

Carter stood up as well and bused his mother's cheek. "Mom, I've got to go too. I'm meeting someone," he said.

"Oh? A girl?" Lolly asked hopefully, her eyes lighting up.

"Nope, my bookie," he yelled and ran out of the dining room, trying to catch up with Willie and Paul as they made their way to the front door.

"Carter, you need to get a haircut. You look like a hooligan," Lolly called out lovingly.

It amazed Kennedy how one word could be said so derisively to one child and yet so affectionately to another. Kennedy began to clear the table. "Would you like help with the dishes, Mother?"

"No, I'll take care of it," Lolly said in her martyr-like voice. "I'm sure you have plenty of last-minute things to do. I'll be fine. Don't worry about me."

Kennedy gritted her teeth. She hated when Lolly pulled the martyr card. It made Kennedy feel both guilty and irritated. Lolly only played that card when she didn't get her way.

Lolly turned and looked at Kennedy. "I suppose we should say our goodbyes now as I'll be at the gym before you and your father leave." She noisily placed silverware on a platter. "Goodbye, Kennedy, have a safe trip. Let us know when you will return so I can have the house aired out. We may need to use it while you are gone, but I'll have it cleaned before you return." She looked around the empty dining room and cocked her head. "It looks like you will need to get your suitcases into the car alone since Carter and Paul have left, but I'm sure you can manage it alone. You prefer it that way, after all." Lolly walked over and gave Kennedy what she called Lolly's church hug. It was a hug by the dictionary's definition, but it was stiff and over within a second. Lolly reserved it for people she felt obligated to hug.

"Well," Kennedy stammered, "I hope you have a good workout, Mom. I'll see you in a few months." She began to leave the dining room, wiping a tear that had stung her eye. She turned to say something to her mother but saw Lolly had picked up her phone. *She's probably calling Willie. Well, at least I've given them a year's supply of things to dissect.*

Kennedy walked through the solarium toward her house, deciding that a last walk on the grounds was in order for her final evening. She looked around. Every spot held a memory: parties with paper lanterns that hung from the trees, Carter racing by on water skis, fierce croquet matches where the object was to knock your opponent's ball into the river and not to win, and dinners on the patio with her grandfather at the grill gazing at his wife while momentarily forgetting his grilling responsibilities and burning the meat. Finally, Kennedy walked onto the dock to smell the pluff mud's sharp sting and hear the river's symphony. She listened to the deep bellows of the alligators, the loons crying back their mournful song, the chirping of the crickets, and the taffeta-like rustle of the palmettos as a breeze blew through their fronds. She knew she would miss nature's orchestra, but it would be here when she returned. Kennedy had a different symphony on the ship, one that she conducted: the chatter of the passengers, the bawl of the ship's horn, the staccato of shoes coming quickly down the steps, and the steel drums playing in the background. There was always a symphony around you, her grandmother had once told her, but you had to be still to hear it.

The following morning, Kennedy's father dropped her off at the airport. As he parked at the curb, Kennedy got out and pulled out the first of her two suitcases and put it at the outside queue for check-in. "Going somewhere exciting, miss?" the porter asked, his eyes widening as he put her suitcase on the scale. "Wow! This is going to cost a lot."

Kennedy smiled, handing him her passport, confirmation information, and credit card. "Oh, yes, I'm going back to work, and it's worth any amount of money."

Richard brought her second suitcase up to the porter, and he put it on the scale. Kennedy turned and hugged her father. "Thanks for the ride, Dad," she said, misting up.

Richard cleared his throat. "Kennedy, your mother means well." He paused, looking for the right words, "You two have always been oil and water." He chuckled and then cleared his throat again. "She doesn't understand the choices you have made. I don't understand them either, but I respect them. Willie followed the path your mother knew. But you chose a different one. A path she doesn't and may never understand. Things will smooth out in time, I promise."

Kennedy wiped her eyes. "Thanks, Dad, I appreciate it. Working on a cruise ship is my life, and I'm happy with my choice. I tried to go down Mom's path, but it didn't work out, and fortunately, the fact that it didn't work out put me where I was supposed to be. If I had not panicked and run away when Joe proposed, I would have never become a cruise director, so it wasn't a total loss," she said ruefully.

"Have a good trip, Kennedy," her father said, embracing her warmly. "We'll see you in a few months."

Richard got into his car and pulled away while Kennedy waved goodbye.

The porter handed her back her credit card, boarding pass, and baggage claim tickets. "Good luck!" he said. Kennedy walked through the double doors and smiled. She was going back to her world.

Mila was waiting for Kennedy in the Orlando airport's baggage claim area. She jumped up and down when she saw her friend clapping her hands. "Wow, you really missed me," Kennedy said as the two women embraced. It had been a long time since they had been face to face. Phone calls, texts, and video chats were good, but to see your best friend in person after so long was priceless.

Mila looked wonderful. The year working on the spa renovation seemed to have invigorated her. Mila was slim and tall with long, ash-brown hair that fell in beautiful waves down her back. Kennedy was surprised it was still hanging down. Usually, by mid-morning, she would have pinned it up in a top knot. Dressed in a pair of beige linen loose trousers, a creamy sleeveless top, and bohemian jewelry, Mila received second looks from both men and women as she hugged her friend.

"So, what happened?" she asked in her accented English. "I got a text that said, 'You were right! Alfred had a bogus email address. Will you please pick me up at the Orlando Airport in baggage claim at noon in three days?' We had one quick telephone call about not fitting into your clothes, one about your flight information, and that was the last I heard from you."

"You won't believe this," Kennedy said, rolling her eyes, "but while we were on furlough, corporate decided to update our personnel files and whoever typed in my email address typed Kennedy Reese instead of Kennedy Reeves." She shrugged her shoulders. "Easy mistake, but boy, am I glad you checked with Alfred to see what was going on. I was at one of the mandatory Lolly dinners when his text came through, and it took everything in me not to jump up from my chair and dance on the table."

Mila grinned. "I believe Lolly would have frowned on that," she said flatly.

Kennedy waved a finger. "Frowns cause wrinkles, Mila. We don't frown," Kennedy said, laughing. It felt so good to laugh freely again.

Kennedy's suitcases came around the baggage carousel, and they lifted them onto a cart. "That's it," she pointed at the bags, "my life for six months crammed into two pieces of luggage."

"These are heavy," Mila whined. "What did you pack? Rocks?" They laughed, walking toward the parking garage.

"So, here I am. What is going on? Who is back? What are the protocols? And can we please stop by Tradewinds? I need to say hello and pick up some packages from Mr. and Mrs. Papadopoulos. I have missed them so much. They were so good to me during the worst time of my life."

Mila unlocked the trunk of the car. "I stopped by to see George and Helen on my way to pick you up and grabbed your boxes," she said, heaving one suitcase into the trunk. "We have to be on the ship by three. I knew we wouldn't make it out in time if we stopped to see them. I'll drop you off at the cruise terminal, let you get checked in, and we can meet up later, okay?"

"Aye, aye, captain," Kennedy saluted her friend and maneuvered the second piece of luggage into the trunk. They got into the car. "I am sorry I won't get to see George and Helen," she said, turning to Mila.

Mila started the car. "They send their love but are being careful. The pandemic scared them, and you know how superstitious George can be. He isn't taking any chances. We'll find a time to see them between cruises," Mila chirped. "You'll see everyone tonight!" She looked at Kennedy with alarm. "You have your paperwork, right?"

Kennedy patted her bag. "Right here. What do I need to be prepared for when I get to the terminal?"

Mila explained that she would need to keep her paperwork handy as she would show it at various stations. Then, before boarding the ship, someone in a hazmat suit would collect her paperwork and give her a master key and cabin assignment. "We start classes tomorrow morning at the unholy hour of eight o'clock. Welcome back!" she cackled.

The two women talked the rest of the way to Port Canaveral, interrupting each other, laughing, and catching up as if they had not been apart for the last year. "Did you hear from Omar during the furlough?" Mila asked innocently.

Kennedy answered cautiously. "Here and there, but then he went to Switzerland to visit his family, and I didn't want to intrude. But, to answer your question, yes, we kept in touch."

"And?" Mila questioned, looking at Kennedy.

"And nothing," Kennedy replied briskly, staring at the windshield. "We tried to flirt, but it's difficult to start a relationship when you are in separate countries. And dating through a computer screen has its challenges, especially when they freeze up. The computer always seems to capture your worst facial expression." Kennedy stopped speaking and turned her head to stare at Mila. She poked her on the shoulder. "You know something. I can see that you are trying not to smile. What do you know?" she asked excitedly.

Mila turned and looked at Kennedy with a wide smile. "Oh, only that he's been thinking about you and has asked me a thousand questions. He even called Alfred to make sure you were coming back. He kept pestering me, wanting to know what day and time you were arriving. I believe things may pick up where they left off, my friend. Just don't let him slip away. He's an amazing man who seems to be falling for you." She paused for a moment and then plunged forward. "Kennedy, you are my best friend, and I know you will try to find one hundred reasons to keep it light and not get involved."

Kennedy's face turned pink. "Yes, but…" Then, realizing they were at the cruise terminal, she knew that opening her door was the best choice to avoid this particular conversation. Mila jumped out and helped Kennedy with her suitcases.

She patted her friend on the shoulder. "Just give it some thought. It's only flirting. See where it goes. Let it happen. Unscrew that very tight lid on the cookie jar!"

Kennedy dropped off her bags at the baggage handling area and made her way to the first of two testing tents, where she presented her passport and health certificate to a person in a yellow hazmat suit. She wasn't sure if the person was a man or a woman, as the face mask made it hard to see. Upon closer inspection, Kennedy realized the person in the yellow suit was a woman. The woman took Kennedy's temperature, pricked her finger, and gave her a nasal swab. She began making lists of things she needed to do to pass the time. She needed to find out which cast members would be on the ship and figure out what they could pull together for entertainment. She wondered when the first manifest would be available for review. She switched gears, walking through all the decks of the *Helio* in her mind. Getting herself organized helped as a distraction.

"Kennedy Reeves, you may proceed," said the voice behind the helmet. "Here is your paperwork. Please continue to the gangway."

Kennedy made the long walk to the pier and forced herself not to run. Her heart began to beat faster as she got closer to the gangway. It had been an eternity, and she couldn't wait to get back to work.

"HALT!" A tall person wearing a white hazmat suit came outside a tent and pointed at the entrance. "Please turn around and stand at the entry." The person walked back into the tent from a side entrance.

Kennedy walked back and stood on the large footprints at the tent's entry. She deduced that the person was a man this time. He handed her two plastic bags. "Place your paperwork and passport in the first bag and seal it. Place your personal item in the second one. Your personal belongings and luggage will be delivered to your cabin after they have been sanitized. May I please have your name and title?"

"Kennedy Reeves, Cruise Director," she said, sliding the bags toward him. He motioned for her to come further inside the tent for another blood test and thermal scan. She waited patiently for another fifteen minutes and received the green light to board the ship. The man handed her an instruction card and her keys. The instruction card contained essential information she would need immediately and her cabin number. She read the instructions, which told her to go directly to her cabin, where she would stay until all staff members and crew arriving that day were on board. Once she had entered her room, she could remove her mask. The note said that her bags would be delivered outside her cabin, and when she heard a knock on her door, she was to count to thirty before opening it to retrieve her luggage. When it was time for dinner, she would again follow the same directions as she had for her luggage. Further information would be waiting for her in the cabin.

Kennedy opened the door to her cabin on deck seven and looked around. It was good to be home. She went inside and saw a packet sitting on the desk, but before she could open it, there was a knock at her door. Out of habit, she automatically opened the door, already forgetting the rules to count to thirty. Standing in the doorway was Omar Meier, Director of Security. Kennedy felt a shiver of excitement as she and Omar locked eyes on each other.

"Welcome home, Kennedy Reeves." He gave her a million-watt smile. "Seeing your lovely smile after so long brings me immense joy." Kennedy noticed that Omar had not changed much in the time since she last saw him. He was of medium height with black hair, which she noticed was turning silver at the temples since she last saw him. His swarthy dark looks and graceful manner were compliments of his mother, who was Malaysian. His European mannerisms and accent were courtesy of his father, who was Swiss. Suave, polished, and never with a hair out of place, Omar exuded elegance from his cufflinks to his perfectly polished shoes. Franklin Blaas, the chief engineer on the ship, would not play poker with Omar because he had no tell and would only smile devilishly as he took Franklin's money.

"How did you know I was here?" Kennedy asked.

"I am the director of security, Kennedy. I have a little pull," he said in his accented English. He took her hand in his. "I am so glad to see you, my friend. It has been too long, and seeing your beautiful face makes my soul happy." He put a finger on her lips so that she wouldn't speak. "Now, before we get into trouble, I will bid you adieu and see you after dinner." He pulled his hands away from hers reluctantly and winked at her. "I believe you have an email from Alfred and a packet to read before we gather." He turned and began to walk down the corridor.

Kennedy stood in the doorway of her cabin in a daze and then shook her head. She had a ton to get done before dinner. Turning on her computer and logging in, she pulled up her messages. The note from Alfred was brief and told her to read the packet and to stay in her cabin until the ship's horn blew. After the horn sounded, she was to make her way to the Solstice Theater for a short meeting. Twenty minutes later, she heard three raps on her door, and a voice called out to tell her that her baggage was sitting outside. Remembering this time to count to thirty, she opened her door and brought her suitcases in. "Well, I better get started. These bags are not going to unpack themselves," she said to the room, and as she unpacked, her phone began to buzz with messages from friends on the ship welcoming her back home. Franklin, Rosemary, Tony, and Chef Michèle sent welcome messages, each referencing the meeting and then a catch-up in their regular spot.

At precisely fifteen minutes before seven, the ship's horn blew, and Kennedy made her way from her cabin to the Solstice Theater, located at the aft end of the fifth deck and served as the location where the main shows were performed. They were all there: Rosemary Flores, the executive housekeeper; Franklin Blaas, the chief engineer; Tony Gano, the dining room manager; Luke Harris, the beverage manager; Chef Michèle, Omar, and Mila, as well as the captain and senior officers.

The captain walked to the center of the stage. "Good evening, everyone," he said. "As you can tell, it's a strange new world, and life as we knew it has changed." He looked around the room. "The staff and crew we have brought back are all team members you have worked with over the years. With the many changes in our protocols, we thought it best to bring back a strong team. Tonight, I want to give you an overview of what the next two weeks will look like. In addition to brush-ups on customer service, we will take classes in CPR, first aid, and fire safety. Rosemary Flores will review the new cleaning protocols and familiarize you with the hand sanitizing and hand washing stations we have added around the ship. We are all responsible for keeping the *Helio* virus free." He pointed at Franklin. "Chief Engineer Blass has installed a new air filtration system, and he will go over how it works so that you may explain it to a passenger if asked. Much of what we will learn will make you knowledgeable about our new procedures so that you may share them with a guest to make them more comfortable as they return to cruising."

He stopped and looked around the room. "I could read all of this," he said, holding a stack of papers in his hands, "but you are all adults. It's a lot to take in, people, and we have a lot of information to learn in a short amount of time. I don't know about all of you, but I am thrilled to be back. While it was wonderful to spend time at home with my wife and four teenagers, it was also pure hell." He chuckled, and the audience laughed with him, nodding in agreement. They had all had difficulties with the forced time at home. "I will now turn over the medical portion of tonight's discussion to Doctor Craig, but before I do, I want to tell you all something." He took a deep breath as he looked at the faces in the chairs in front of him. "Welcome back, team. It is certainly good to see each of you. I have missed all of you, and I know that if there is any group that can get this company back to cruising, it is the one in this room. We'll see you all tomorrow morning, bright and early."

"Hail, hail, the gang's all here," boomed Franklin as their little group gathered later on the promenade deck. "Damn, I'm glad to see all of you!"

"Same here. It feels like old times," Luke said. "Being at home with my mom was making me stir crazy. I love her, don't get me wrong, but you would have sworn I was thirteen years old again, the way she acted."

Mila rolled her eyes at Luke. "What? No bevy of beauties to snuggle up with? I guess that would have been difficult with your mom there," Mila said wryly.

Luke blushed good-naturedly, he was known for always having a beautiful woman waiting for him when the ship docked for the six-week break, and it was never the same woman twice. "Just waiting for you to say yes, Mila." He gave her a wink.

"Rosemary, how was your time away?" asked Kennedy.

"It was sad," Rosemary said solemnly. "I could not go home to the Philippines to see my family, but we were able to talk by video. Thank goodness I have younger cousins who could set things up for them. My older family members were worried that it was witchcraft when they saw me on the screen. I worry about my mother and my aunties. They believe in the old ways and don't trust doctors and science."

"Tony?" Franklin asked. "The last thing I remember was you leaving the ship when we docked in Puerto Rico after the earthquake."

Tony winced and squeezed his side in a gesture that Kennedy recognized. Tony was in a constant state of stress which manifested in his back. "Gosh, I guess that's right. We docked in Puerto Rico, and I left on emergency leave. My parents' home had a lot of damage because of the earthquake. I stayed for a little while to help them rebuild, and then the world turned upside down. So, I decided to stay in Puerto Rico and ended up rebuilding my hometown."

Franklin looked at Tony in disbelief. "Tony, do you even know which end of the hammer to hold?" he teased. "Wine keys, peppermills, your crumb catcher, yes. But I've never seen you use a hand tool," he chuckled.

"Ha, ha, Franklin," Tony chuckled. "It was good to be home, although my mother decided that my being home allowed her to nag me about settling down. Every Sunday after church, another lady had been invited for lunch."

Mila stifled a giggle. "Hmmm, sounds like Kennedy's mother, are they related?"

Kennedy rolled her eyes at Mila. Tony continued, "I stayed in touch with Alfred, and as soon as he knew we were coming back to the ship, he told me to hustle back to Florida. So, I contacted Mr. Papadopoulos at Tradewinds, and here I am."

"Well, someone around here was busy," Kennedy said, changing the subject. "Mila, when do we get to see the spa?" she asked.

Mila's eyes danced. "Soon, I promise. I want it to be perfect when I show it to you. I am so proud of Oaza, and I want my best friends to see it, but not until it is perfect." Mila wrapped her arms around herself. "There is so much riding on this renovation. I have called in every favor I had and made promises I hope I can keep. I promised the corporate office strong sales. Speaking of corporate, they set up an interview for me tomorrow. It sounds like this woman drove them nuts to get one. She must be desperate to get back to work. She's jumped through every one of their hoops."

"Has anyone heard if any other ships are going out?" Kennedy asked.

Mila responded slowly, "We are the only ship at this time from Sunny Dayz. I have heard that if all goes well with our initial cruises, the other ships will be phased in, but it is all based on how we do. Our success is imperative for the company to survive." The group was silent as they digested this information.

The Sunny Dayz Cruise Line was a family-owned company formed in 1880 with one ship. Over the years, slowly and steadily, the company had added more ships to its small fleet. During times of war, Sunny Dayz offered their ships to transport troops. The little company grew, staying small and quietly attending to the needs of its guests. Then, in the late 1970s, the cruise industry took off like a rocket due to television. Cruising became a popular and exciting way to vacation. The company bought older ships and refurbished them, realizing that they would never be able to compete with the more prominent cruise lines but could offer more personalized customer service.

The cruise line now had seven ships, each with her own eclectic charm. The *Eldora* and *Oriana* cruised the Greek Islands and the Mediterranean, while the *Malina*, a new ship to the fleet, took passengers through Alaska. The others called the waters of the Caribbean and Mexico home. New technology and modern conveniences were added as each ship was updated, but the ships did not have the flashy glitz and glamour offered by larger cruise lines. What they did offer was a comfortable charm that kept their clientele coming back year after year. There had been discussions about buying a private island to provide an additional port of call in the Caribbean, but those plans had fallen through when tourism plummeted.

Kennedy yawned. "I'm exhausted. It's been a whirlwind of a day, and I'm drained mentally and physically." She looked around at her friends. "I'll see you all bright and early tomorrow morning for class." Then, hesitating for a second, she looked at Omar. "Would you like to walk a lady home?"

Omar swallowed. "I wish I could, Kennedy. But, unfortunately, with fewer security staff, I must take the next patrol," he said awkwardly.

Kennedy was suddenly embarrassed. She thought she must have misunderstood what Mila said and misread Omar's visit to her cabin when she arrived. "Oh, that's okay," she said quickly.

"But I promise I will see you tomorrow morning," he said with a wink and walked away from the group.

"Hmmm," Franklin said smugly, "am I missing a part of the story?"

Fanning himself with his hand Luke said teasingly, "Franklin, I do believe that was our fair Kennedy was flirting outrageously with Mr. Meier."

Tony couldn't help but join in the fun. "I'm shocked at her brazenness," he said, mockingly shaking his head. "Her mother raised a hussy."

Kennedy looked at the three men. "All of you can stuff it! I was simply asking for an escort home." She turned to Mila. "Mila, will you walk me home?" And linking arms, the two women departed giggling.

The following day everyone on the ship began taking the mandatory trainings designated by the corporate office. Rosemary taught classes on the new cleaning procedures. She had spent an exhausting two months preparing for the return. Rosemary spent the first month learning about the latest products and protocols to be used, finding and buying equipment, and walking through the ship daily to note the changes needed to maintain guest and staff safety. The following month she trained her staff in an empty warehouse, creating mock cabins and public spaces so every team member could watch and critique each other. The training encompassed more than cleaning rooms. Her staff took refresher courses on guest satisfaction and back-of-the-house protocols and spent a week learning multiple towel designs for the passengers to find each day in their cabin. In the end, her team was exhausted and overloaded but happy.

While everyone else on the ship was busy with refresher courses and new protocols, Mila sat in a coffee shop waiting for her interview. Mila, generally, got her technicians from two nearby spa schools. She had been successful with the candidates she hired, so it was unusual for a candidate to apply directly through the corporate offices. Trying to stay on the corporate office's good side, Mila felt it best to interview the candidate. Opening the file, Mila looked at the headshot and cover letter fastened to the inside cover. The candidate had an impressive resume. Mila was surprised to see the number of techniques she was versed in, as well as scheduling and bookkeeping. Mila scanned the coffee shop but did not see anyone resembling the woman in the headshot. She sent a message to her friend who owned a nearby spa to confirm her use of one of their treatment rooms. After Mila interviewed a potential candidate, she would personally assess the applicant's techniques, paying close attention to their speech, modulation of their voice, and body language. A masseuse with a voice like nails on a chalkboard could undo the relaxation expected from a massage.

"Excuse me, are you Mila Casimir?" asked an angular woman with short, white, spiky hair. "I'm Sara West." She held out her hand to shake Mila's. "I believe we have an interview."

Mila was taken aback. She had expected a round-faced woman with sandy brown, shoulder-length hair from the headshot. "You certainly don't look like your headshot," she said with a chuckle.

Sara offered her a tight smile. "Sometimes you need to make a drastic change, and it's only hair, after all. It grows." Mila motioned for Sara to sit down. "Let's chat and then go to the salon next door. I booked a room so you can show me your techniques."

Ninety minutes later, the two women were back in the coffee shop. "Sara, you are certainly enthusiastic and performed your facial flawlessly." Mila hesitated. "May I ask why you want to work on a cruise ship? It can be difficult if you haven't experienced it."

Sara looked down at her hands and then up at Mila. "Ms. Casimir, I don't have a life anymore, and I want to be upfront with you. Two years ago, I was wrongfully terminated from a job I loved and could not find work because the person who fired me had spread a false rumor." She took a deep breath and looked steadily at Mila. "He and I had been in a relationship, and I broke it off. He fired me shortly after the breakup." Sara told Mila that the only job she could find in the area was as a spa receptionist. "But I wanted to learn, Ms. Casimir. I knew I could find a way to use my talents in the spa world. So, I learned how to book appointments without causing backups and went to classes at night to get my certifications." She smiled. "I even learned bookkeeping. I wanted to know everything to keep improving at my job." She looked down at her hands again and then back up at Mila. "It's been a decent job, but I need to move on. I have always wanted to work on a cruise ship, and I thought if I could get my foot in the door in a ship's spa, I could work up the ladder."

Mila stood up, holding out her hand to shake Sara's. "Well, get your bags packed. You have a passport, right? You will need that and a health screening before you can come on board."

Sara smiled widely, looking relieved. "Already have them," she said. "I wanted to be prepared in case our interview went well. I've been updating my health screenings every month. The people at the clinic think I'm crazy, but they keep taking my money."

Mila nodded her head. "We will see you tomorrow. Meet me at the Port Canaveral Cruise Terminal at noon, and welcome to the *Helio* family."

Sara beamed. "Thank you so much, Ms. Casimir. You won't regret this!" she said happily and shook Mila's hand again. Then, Sara gathered her portfolio and walked out of the shop, but not before turning around again to wave to Mila.

Mila sat back down, pulled out her phone, and called Kennedy. "Well, I hired the girl on the spot."

"Who?"

"The one who applied through the corporate office," Mila answered. "She looks nothing like her headshot—a completely different person," she said. "She's everything I could want. An excellent technician, pleasant voice, has her certifications, knows bookkeeping and scheduling…" Mila trailed off.

"What's wrong, Mila?" asked Kennedy. "You seem unsure."

Mila shrugged. "I'm sure it's nothing."

Kennedy could hear hesitancy in her friend's voice but knew Mila was prone to overanalyze every decision. "Mila, she didn't come from your regular source. Everything's been shut down. How else was she going to get an interview? She's eager, and you said she is enthusiastic and has learned to pivot and learn everything she can to make herself versatile." She paused and added softly, "Remember, we all have a story about why we fled to work on a ship. You have a story; I have a story. Every single one of us has a reason we work on the ship, and none of them fits in a nice square box with a bow. It's the one thing that glues us all together. When you hear hoofbeats, think horses…"

Mila looked up at the ceiling of the coffee shop. "Not zebras," she finished. "You're right, and you know that I always overthink every decision I make. Remember the wall tile?" she laughed at herself and gave a slight shrug. "If she doesn't work out, I'll find someone new."

The next wave of staff arrived the following morning, including Bert, the ship's photographer; Sara and the other spa technicians; Billy, the lead bellman; the entertainment cast; and others.

"Bert, it's so good to see you, but it looks like you are losing a battle with your equipment," Kennedy said as she bent down beside the ship's photographer. Bert was sitting on the floor. His shoelaces were untied, and his cameras and equipment bag straps were wrapped around him in a tangled mess around his middle and shoulders. "How did this…never mind. Let's get you standing again."

"Thanks, Kennedy," Bert sighed. "A year away, and I'm still a klutz." The first day he and Kennedy had met, he had almost strangled himself to death when the strap of his camera had gotten hung up on a handrail. When Kennedy came upon him, he was almost purple. She quickly released the strap and sat him down so he could catch his breath. Ever since that day, Bert had been Kennedy's number one fan, and Kennedy had a soft spot for Bert. He meant well but had a knack for finding trouble. When she had asked him why he chose to work on a cruise ship, he admitted he had previously worked for a small-town newspaper and had published a photo of a couple in an embrace, unaware that the image would cause a scandal. When the dust settled, two couples were divorced, the newspaper had been sued by everyone involved, and Bert had lost his job. The only people who had come out of the courtroom happy were the attorneys. Bert's troubles had followed him onto the ship as well. He had a knack for taking the wrong picture at the wrong time. After a few mishaps early in his career on the ship, he made of point of sending Kennedy the proofs of any candid shots before posting them in the lobby for purchase.

"I've got to set up my computer and start on the photos of the spa," he said as he got to his feet. "The corporate office has asked me to take them for the website. This could be it, Kennedy," he said excitedly. "I could work for the marketing department instead of taking canned photos of people that will reside, sadly, in some dusty photo album." He took a breath. "This is my chance!"

"Bert, this is wonderful news," Kennedy said, genuinely happy for her friend who was hanging the last camera strap on his shoulder.

"I also got this," he said, fishing a pocket recorder out of his camera bag. "I'm going to use it when I take the photos of the passengers to help remind me who they are. This way, if a passenger buys a photo, I can remind them about the others I took. I'm really going to take things more seriously now."

"That's great, Bert," Kennedy said, impressed. "I hope it increases your sales."

"Thanks, well, I'd better go," and he walked away.

Standing there, watching Bert leave, she sent up a wish for his success. He was sweet but also known for not following through on a project or procrastinating to the point that he missed his chance. She had fervently hoped that he would get it together.

The days flew by. Kennedy and Omar found time to flirt with each other to the delight of their colleagues who watched them. There were also trainings, and more trainings, while everyone relearned their jobs. Along with lifeboat and fire drills, everyone was required to be certified by Safety Officer Tully in first aid, CPR, and fire safety. Part of Tully's job was also to perform daily safety walks to check that no one had tampered with the lifeboats, flotation devices, and fire extinguishers. Everyone took fire safety very seriously, as dialing for help was not an option when they were a hundred miles from land.

The night before the ship took on its first cruise, a small party occurred in the spa. Mila's friends stood in wonder at the beauty that she had created. The spa was breathtaking. The muted colors of the fabrics complemented the rich woodwork, and the shimmer of the mother-of-pearl mosaic tile that graced the walls played off the metallic flecks in the dark blue floor tiles. Overhead, a stunning ring chandelier seemed to float in the air.

"Mila, this is beautiful, but I see that I am going to have my hands full with repairs," Franklin groaned. "Couldn't you have used wallpaper that looked like mother-of-pearl? Did you have to get *real* mother-of-pearl tiles? My guys will never be able to do work this delicate. They are as graceful as Bert," he grumbled.

"Speaking of Bert," Kennedy turned to Mila, "did he make it to the spa to take the photos he promised to corporate?"

Mila shook her head. "No, he didn't, and I'm not going to mother him." There was a touch of irritation in her voice. "He spent most of his time chatting up the cast, and when he wasn't chatting up the cast, he was flirting with the servers when they were in the employee lounge. He just cannot be trusted to do what he says he will do, Kennedy."

Kennedy was dismayed. "That's too bad. He seemed so excited. I had hoped he had turned over a new leaf."

"Mila, may I ask a question," asked Omar. "Why did you name it Oaza?"

Mila explained that Oaza in Polish meant oasis, which was what she had wanted to create. An oasis on the sea for the passengers. It had taken some convincing, but once she had walked the corporate team through the entire plan and the design, they were on board and began taking credit for the spa's new name.

Kennedy looked around at the oasis her friend had created. She raised her glass. "To Oaza and the beautiful Mila," she said as everyone clinked glasses. "I hate to drink and run, but I have an early morning tomorrow and a million things to do before the passengers arrive. I should receive the final manifest at the ungodly hour of five in the morning," she laughed. "Plenty of time for me to review, scramble, and pivot."

"Plenty of time?" echoed Franklin. "One quick question before you leave, dear. I believe you have received some draft manifests. Are there any passengers that I should be made aware of, Kennedy? Any names you would like to share?"

"Why, Franklin," Kennedy said breathlessly, fluttering her eyes, "I don't know what you are talking about. But if I were you, I would put on my dancing shoes for the Captain's Dinner as a certain group of ladies who can't take their eyes off the silver fox of the *Helio* will be joining us," she cooed.

"Nooo," groaned Franklin, "not the ladies from the retirement village, not them. One of those ladies always tries to dance me into a dark corner."

"If they get too fresh, I'll knock them into the pool,"

Rosemary said grumpily, "but I may torture you and make

you dance with them for a little while."

Sunny Dayz Cruise Line

THE HELIO

DAY ONE

DEPARTURE FROM PORT CANAVERAL, USA

BOARDING BEGINS AT 2:00 P.M.

Every member of the staff and crew was eager to set sail. A feeling of excitement, the kind you felt the day before Christmas, was in the air. Rosemary was in a corridor happily scolding her staff for minor mistakes as she inspected the cabins.

"Mer, have you checked the VIP staterooms on deck eight? Those are yours. Mrs. Jameson will be here, and she is very particular."

"Do you mean Mrs. Snappy Snappy? She's on the ship?" Mer asked. He snapped his fingers to imitate Mrs. Jameson and laughed. "Well, if that is the case, I left a black banana peel in her closet, the trashcans are full of stinky old eggs, and I made the bed with dirty sheets, Auntie," he said mirthfully.

Rosemary looked down her glasses at Mer. "You may think that you are my favorite nephew—" she started, but Mer interrupted her.

"Relax, Auntie. I took care of the rooms. They are perfect and ready for you to inspect."

"The towels are in the shape of the sun?" Rosemary barked.

"Yes, Auntie," Mer answered her sulkily. "I made the silly towels into the shape of the sun." Then, before she could pepper him with more questions, he added, "And the bed is triple-sheeted and tucked correctly, the bathrooms are spotless, the mirrors sparkle, and there is no dust on any furniture."

"No water spots on the faucets?" she queried.

"Oh man, I knew I forgot something!" He chuckled, seeing her face. "Auntie, you know I would not leave water spots on the faucets." This was a game they had played for years.

She shook her finger at Mer. "I don't know, Mer, you can be such an insolent boy. I should check to make sure you did your job right."

"Excuse me, excuse me, coming through," a voice called out from behind a tall stack of towels. Suddenly, towels flew in all directions as one of the housemen collided with a housekeeper coming out of a cabin.

Rosemary looked at the corridor, which was now littered with white terry. *We'll be lucky if we are ready before the passengers arrive,* she thought to herself. But Rosemary had little to worry about. After two months of preparation, her team was ready.

In the various bars throughout the ship, the bar staff was busy stocking glassware, polishing glasses, and cutting fruit for the ship's signature drink. The SunRumbrella had been the creation of the corporate office's marketing team. The rum and fruit juice cocktail was served with a paper umbrella and was the company's signature drink. However, it was Luke's firm belief that the name had come about out of drunken desperation.

Franklin Blaas, Chief Engineer, checked the monitors in his office, ensuring the pool's water temperature, air conditioning, music levels, and new purification systems were all working correctly.

Mila was taking a last moment in Oaza before opening the doors to the passengers. If Oaza proved herself on the *Helio* with dollars, the corporate office had agreed to allow another spa to be renovated. They had also dangled the carrot of overseeing all of the company's spas to Mila if Oaza proved to be a money maker. *Not bad for a girl from Poland who, fifteen years ago, didn't know an orange stick from an emery board,* she thought to herself. She took a last look at Oaza's reception area and smiled.

Kennedy had been at her desk since dawn, reviewing the final passenger manifest and preparing mentally for the cruise. She was delighted and apprehensive at the same time. The Ladies from Harmony Lakes were on this cruise, as were some dear friends Kennedy had nicknamed the Club Diva Boys. "This should be entertaining," she mused aloud, tapping her pencil on the pad of paper. If the two groups hit it off, social media chatter would be immediate as both had large followings.

The Ladies from Harmony Lakes consisted of six widowed women who had met at Harmony Lakes, a fifty-five and over retirement community. When the ladies were not on a cruise, they were planning their next one. They shamelessly plugged the Sunny Dayz cruises to their friends in hopes of special discounts, which they often received. The ladies were harmlessly nosy, always wanting the latest ship gossip. Dolly, the oldest, was comical and one of Kennedy's favorites. She had gotten to an age where there was no filter on what came out of her mouth. "I can't be held responsible for what my face shows when people speak," was her favorite saying.

The Club Diva Boys, a group of men who had met twenty-five years ago working at a drag club, would also be on the cruise. They had been on Kennedy's first cruise as an assistant cruise director. After watching one of her performances, they quickly took her under their wings, coaching her on costuming, onstage presence, and choreography. She believed that if it had not been for them, she would not be in the position she was in now. While only one was still attached to the drag club, as the owner, they got together once or twice a year for a reunion, and usually on a Sunny Dayz cruise ship.

She looked further down the list. "Oh dear," she gulped and said aloud, "Vera Jameson is joining us." Mrs. Vera Jameson could be described in three words: wealthy, opinionated, and imperious. As Kennedy had come up the ranks, she had heard horror stories from other cruise directors about Mrs. Jameson. It was said that she could insult someone and say it with such sweet venom that you took it as a compliment and thanked her, but it was not until later that you realized she had insulted you. Vera was always quick to remind new staff on the ship that she was the college roommate of one of the family board members, and her opinions held weight. A few cruise directors and social hostesses had found themselves without renewed contracts after Vera had called the corporate office.

Kennedy remembered her first challenge with Vera. She had been sent to the *Oriana* to fill in for the regular cruise director, who had gone home to deal with a family emergency. At one of the ports of call, a passenger had boarded with her dog and demanded a separate cabin for the canine. As Kennedy delicately explained to the passenger that the ship had no extra cabins, Mrs. Jameson interrupted the conversation with an outlandish request. Feeling like a ping pong ball between the two women, Kennedy resolutely told the one guest she would have to keep the dog in the cabin or leave at the next port. Next, with her head held high, she looked Mrs. Jameson in the eye. "I am very sorry, Mrs. Jameson, but we cannot meet your request today. However, I have a compromise I would like to share with you." It was a turning point for the two women. Vera silently applauded Kennedy for having a backbone, something she had not encountered before with the other cruise directors. Vera did not often hear words such as no and compromise, and from Kennedy's honesty and courage, mutual respect blossomed between the two women.

Over the years, Vera had made many ridiculous requests to see how Kennedy would handle them. She requested deviled quail eggs, pigs in a blanket made into a Christmas wreath, and Kennedy's all-time favorite, a holiday dish she called frosted pâté—which Vera insisted Chef Michèle make especially for her. When Kennedy brought Chef Michèle the recipe Vera had given her, his face began to turn purple, and he threw the card down on the stainless-steel counter and screamed, "I am a chef, not a 1950s housewife!" He stormed out of the kitchen but, a few hours later, presented Vera with the pureed liverwurst, mayonnaise, and cream cheese concoction in a crystal bowl. Vera was delighted and ate it greedily on club crackers. Vera also had a penchant for smoking cigars in her room. To cover up the odor, she would commandeer one of the ship's floral arrangements, which only worsened the smell. Kennedy shook her head at the memories and wondered what Vera would do on this trip.

She reviewed the other VIPs for the cruise. In addition to Mrs. Jameson were four additional names: Jones and Terri Butler, Mr. Bart Phillips, and Gunner Owen Atcher. Mr. and Mrs. Butler, the notes read, were the former owners of a fast-food chain that had recently been sold for millions of dollars. Kennedy knew that Mr. Bart Phillips was a member of the company's board of directors and his being on the cruise surprised her. Still, she surmised he was either taking the cruise to report his observations of the maiden voyage for the next board meeting or was taking one of the complimentary cruises he got each year. The last VIP passenger had no notes, simply the name Gunner Owen Atcher. Kennedy thought it was strange that there were no other notes, only the letters VIP beside his name. Her fingers flew across her keyboard to discern who the man could be. While there were still hundreds of things to be done before the passengers boarded, Kennedy had a nagging tickle.

She typed in his name as it appeared on the manifest, and there was only one hit. Clicking on the link took her to a page citing a biography of the man. Unfortunately, there was no photo. Instead, words like consultant, hotel operations mastermind, strategy specialist, reorganizational expert, and operations architect popped out. The more she read, the more worried she got. "What did you just tell Mila?" she scolded herself. "When you hear hoofbeats, don't think of zebras," she said to her empty cabin. Kennedy convinced herself that this man was most likely a friend of one of the shareholders as the reservation had been made by the corporate office, who often struggled to give the teams information they needed for reservations they had booked. She straightened her papers and placed them on her clipboard to head down to the pier.

She descended the gangway to the pier to ensure that the entry looked inviting. A red carpet had been rolled out, and potted palms had been attractively grouped to form an aisle. Tall cocktail tables stood on either side of the rug, soon to be laden with cold bottles of water and SunRumbrellas for the passengers to take as they boarded. A tented area had comfortable lounge furniture in case someone wanted to sit. The steel drum band was set up nearby. Close enough to help put the passengers in the mood but far enough away so conversations could still be held. She stood back and grinned. While Sunny Dayz was not one of the big boys in the cruise industry, she felt that the little things, the potted palms, the red carpet, live music, and the specialty drink, made their passengers feel welcomed. Then, as she turned one of the plants to a more attractive side, she heard voices behind her. She looked at her watch. It was too early for passengers to arrive, but two men walked up the carpet. Kennedy was curious. One man was short and thin with an ashen complexion and a dark receding hairline. His face was wet with sweat, and he mopped it with a white handkerchief. Kennedy assumed he was sweating because of the dark blue wool suit he was wearing in the hot Florida sun.

"Good afternoon," he said briskly, stashing his handkerchief in his pocket and extending his hand. "I am Mr. Bart Phillips, from the board of directors. I believe I am on your arrival list?"

Kennedy was startled. "Of course, Mr. Phillips, we weren't expecting you quite so early, but, please, welcome aboard the *Helio*," she said. "I'm Kennedy Reeves, your cruise director."

She turned to the other man. He was tall and slender with pointy features. His black hair made little triangles as it stood up from his scalp. He wore a white linen suit and white eyeglasses. He kept squinting at her and blinking his eyes together. His pointy features and squinting reminded her of a weasel coming out of a hole in the ground. Kennedy turned to him. "And you are, sir?"

"Well, I should think it's clear who I am, as I am here with Mr. Phillips. I am Gunner Owen Atcher," he said curtly. "I am certain I am on your list as well, as there must have been several emails from the corporate office announcing my arrival." Kennedy looked at him bewildered. He sniffed. "I am a soon-to-be-named vice president of the cruise line, and I must say that I am amazed that you are not prepared for us, nor is there anyone here to greet us but a junior staff member." He looked disdainfully from Kennedy to Mr. Phillips, who was mopping his forehead again. "I expected the entire senior staff to be here when we arrived," he said indignantly.

Kennedy quickly gathered her composure. "I am quite sorry, Mr. Atcher, I…*we* were not given any information by the corporate office. We received an email that Mr. Phillips would join us, but we were not given a time." She smiled brightly and extended her hand. "But we are delighted that you will be traveling with us on our first voyage." Gunner pointedly ignored her outstretched hand, and she quickly dropped it. "After the long hiatus, the staff and crew are excited to go out to sea again. Please allow me to show you both to your cabins."

Gunner began to push past her toward the gangway. "That won't be necessary," he said irritably. "I'll find it later. Please show me where I will be greeting the passengers."

Kennedy was at a loss. "Oh, Mr. Atcher, we don't want to put you out. The senior staff will be in the lobby to help the passengers find their cabins."

Gunner turned to face her. "Miss Reeves, I believe I just told you that I would be greeting the passengers as the future vice president of the Sunny Dayz Cruise Line. I am certain it is not difficult to show people where they need to go," he snapped.

Kennedy swallowed. "Yes, sir, I understand, but as you have not been on the ship—"

Gunner interrupted her, holding up his hand, "Miss Reeves," he took off his glasses and squinted at her, "this ship is no more complex than any hotel or resort that I have run in the past, and in my time running many, many five-star resorts, I have had no problem directing people to where they need to go. I have reviewed the diagram on the company website, and as someone of extreme intelligence, I feel certain that I can direct the passengers accordingly." He pinched his fingers between his eyes. "Please inform the captain that he will greet the passengers with me," he said arrogantly. "I am certain that he and I, the senior ranking officials on this ship, will be able to manage things."

"Yes, but—"

He waved a hand dismissively at Kennedy. "Now, run along to do whatever it is that you do," he said with an impatient tone of voice. "I hope you are a little more prepared and gracious to the guests who are about to board the ship. Our arrival experience was subpar. Perhaps your time off has made you a bit rusty in the customer service department."

Kennedy was speechless at the man's words.

He looked down at the bag in his hand and placed it on the ground. "Please take this to my cabin," he motioned to a leather bag. "It holds my skincare items. I don't usually allow them to leave my side. I assume you can handle the delivery?" he asked and brushed past her, walking up the gangway. "I'm going to tour the ship."

He had only taken a few steps when he turned to speak. "Bart, I will see you in the lobby shortly, and bring your notepad." He rested his eyes on Kennedy. "I can tell we have our work cut out for us." He marched up the gangway, leaving Kennedy and Mr. Phillips alone on the pier.

Kennedy stood there processing her first impression of Gunner Owen Atcher. She could use many words to describe him, and none of them were ladylike. Dealing with him for six days was not going to be easy. She decided she would not share his demand with the captain. He would be busy enough getting the ship underway. Captains directing passengers to their cabins was something only seen on television.

Kennedy turned and looked at Mr. Phillips. "Well, Mr. Phillips," she said brightly, "it appears Mr. Atcher has left us. May I show you to your cabin and deliver Mr. Atcher's bag to his room?" She picked up the leather duffle bag.

Mr. Phillips nodded his head quickly. "That will be fine," he said quietly.

By two o'clock, Kennedy and the other senior staff members were on the main deck while the junior staff members were on the pier awaiting their guests. There was a buzz of excitement in the air. Usually, greeting and directing the passengers was considered a chore, but today, the level of enthusiasm was genuine. The scene was perfect for arrival. A gentle breeze rustled the leaves of the potted palms. Bottles of water and SunRumbrellas glistened on the trays, and the red carpet was ready to whisk the passengers away from reality. Taking a deep breath, Kennedy prayed that the cruise would go well. So much depended upon it.

"Kennedy, thank goodness you are here. I need to share something with you," said Billy, the lead bellman. Billy had been with the ship for five years and was still as nervous as he had been on his first day. He was also known for blurting things out at the most inopportune time, which made Kennedy motion him to the side. She smiled warmly at him.

"What's up, Billy?" she asked.

Billy looked around. "You know our special VIPs that came on board early?" Kennedy nodded her head. "I just took their luggage to their cabins, and that man in the white suit has five suitcases. Five." He held out his hand so Kennedy could see his fingers. "And the bags are huge," he exclaimed, holding his arms out to mimic their size.

Kennedy interrupted him, "Shhhh, Billy. Let's remember our customer service refresher class we just took. Remember, it's our job to make our guests feel welcome. We are here to make their cruise special and meaningful. This is not a judgment zone, and we are not here to gossip about them. Our job is to make sure their time with us is sunny and bright," she said in a sing-song voice.

"But Kennedy—"

Kennedy interrupted him again, "Billy, I am sure there is more luggage for you to begin taking to our VIP cabins. Mrs. Jameson will be joining us. Do you remember her?" Billy nodded his head. "And you know that she will have many bags to be taken to her stateroom." Kennedy put her hand on his forearm. "Would you help me by keeping an eye out for her? I'd like her arrival to be flawless," she said. "We also need to remember that Mr. Atcher and Mr. Phillips are with the company, so we want to keep our conversations to ourselves and not discuss them in the crew bar, right?"

Billy nodded. "Yes, ma'am."

"Thanks, Billy. I know you get excited," Kennedy said kindly. "Let's just make sure to be a little cautious, okay?"

As Billy left for the baggage area, the passengers began to arrive. Smiling and helping the guests to find their cabins, the way to the promenade deck, and the pool helped Kennedy keep busy. Although there was a smile on her face, her stomach was in knots over what she felt was to come.

The first group of familiar faces Kennedy saw in the lobby were the Ladies from Harmony Lakes. She broke out in a grin and greeted them all warmly. Kennedy chuckled inside as she watched Marilyn scan the lobby looking for Omar, Franklin, or her brother, Carter. "Ladies, it is so good to see all of you," she gushed. She looked at each of them. "Laura, you look lovely as always. And Dolly, I still don't think you are old enough to be Laura's mother. Marilyn, please, remember that our staff and crew are off limits. Louise, good to see you," she stopped and looked around, "Where is Beth?" she asked. Beth, the loveable but ditzy member of the group, came up hurriedly.

"Oh, my goodness, I thought I lost all of you," she said out of breath, jogging up to them.

"No such luck," said Dolly drolly.

"I was sitting on a bench, and I got distracted—"

"You got distracted?" Dolly chortled. "You can get distracted by a butterfly floating by."

Beth continued, not having heard Dolly, "There is a couple that will be on our ship, and let me tell you, the outfit she was wearing was scandalous." She looked around. "She looked like a lady of the evening, you know, a H-O-O-K-E-R," and she spelled out the word primly but in a loud whisper. Marilyn and Louise rolled their eyes at each other. "Thank goodness for the red carpet to get me here. It was like I was following the yellow brick road in *The Wizard of Oz.*"

"Too bad you didn't find your way back to Kansas," quipped Dolly.

Beth knit her eyebrows together in confusion. "I'm from Oklahoma, Dolly, you know that. I've told you so many times. You must be getting forgetful in your old age."

Dolly sighed. "I keep trying to forget you, and you keep coming back like a bad case of heartburn."

"So, first things first," Louise interrupted, looking at Kennedy. "Hold up your hand." Kennedy playfully held up her right hand, smiling as she knew what Louise had wanted her to do. "The other one," she said testily. Kennedy held up her left hand. "Ringless, I see," she sighed dramatically. "Did you not meet anyone while you were in Charleston? Surely there are tons of available men there. I'm sorry, Kennedy, but your mother must be so disappointed," Louise scolded.

Always ready for Louise's pointed barbs, Kennedy had her reply ready. "Oh, Louise, my mother is so used to being disappointed by me that she now catalogs her disappointments and can bring them up alphabetically, chronologically, or by subject, as befits the moment."

Marilyn pushed her way forward and purred, "And how is your very handsome brother? Is he on the ship this time?" She turned her neck to look around the lobby for the young man. Marilyn had met Carter on a previous cruise and had tried to corner him in a few dark spaces, hoping he would fall for what she called her "sexy but seasoned" act. Instead, Carter, ever the gentleman who had been cornered before by more than one of his mother's friends, let her down easily, saying it was against company policy for him to entertain the idea of a relationship with a passenger. But, as much as he hated it, rules were rules.

"Oh, he's fine but has decided to stay in Charleston," Kennedy said. Then, seeing Marilyn's pout, she quickly changed the subject. "Tell me what you ladies have done for the last year with no cruises to take," she asked brightly.

"NOTHING!" Dolly spat out. "Which is why we had to take the first cruise we could get. If we hadn't," she looked daggers at Beth, "some of us would have ended up in a jumpsuit and handcuffs." She turned and looked at Marilyn shaking her finger. "And I know what you are thinking, Marilyn; you have a monogrammed set of handcuffs in your drawer."

Beth chimed in, "I took the time to make sure I saw life as a glass half full. So, I always had something pleasant to think about."

Dolly snorted loudly. "Half empty, half full, just drink the damn glass of wine and keep pouring them to get through the day."

Laura stammered, blushing, and turned to Kennedy. "Please forgive my mother. We seem to have forgotten how to behave in polite society. I am thankful you are a friend and can overlook my mother's peculiarities."

Kennedy looked down at her clipboard. "Well, ladies, you are here on deck five as always, so I will let you go on your way. Don't forget the Captain's Dinner and show tonight. The cast has been working very hard, and I am sure you will not want to miss it."

Dolly put her hands on her hips. "Are you doing your after-hours show, too?" she asked. "I love that show. Sometimes the things that come out of your mouth remind me of myself. I can help you put a little more sass in your show, you know."

Kennedy giggled. "Oh, just wait, Dolly, that is, if you can stay up that late," she winked.

The ladies were turning to leave when Bert hustled over. "Excuse me, ladies," he said, "would you like to step over to the photo area and have your picture taken? It's the first one of the cruise."

Marilyn quickly answered, "Well, of course, we do, sugar, just make sure you get my good side," she said seductively, putting her hand on her hip.

"Exactly what side would that be?" Louise asked dryly.

"All of my sides are my good side," Marilyn huffed. "Just ask any of the men who have had the pleasure of dating me."

"One million served, isn't it?" Laura and Louise had to stifle a laugh at Dolly's comment.

Beth looked puzzled. "I don't understand. She doesn't work in a restaurant."

Laura put her arm around Beth. "Never mind, honey, let's just get our photo taken, okay?"

They walked over to the photo area and got in position for Bert to take their picture. Kennedy saw Bert pick up his recorder, say a few words, and then take several photographs. Kennedy watched them bickering and laughing as they left Bert and went to the elevators. It was good to have friends to get you through the rough times.

The next group of familiar faces brought a huge smile to Kennedy's face. John and Don spied Kennedy as they entered the lobby and rushed over to her, quickly followed by Robert, Dave, Steve, and Phil. They formed a large circle around her. "Are we still allowed to hug? Do we fist bump? What do we do? I am so confused," Dave cried.

"Air hug," Robert called out quickly.

"How are you all here? I was surprised to see your names on the manifest," Kennedy said excitedly.

John waved his hand at her, took off his white rhinestone sunglasses, and pushed them over his thinning dark blond hair. "Oh, honey, it's easy now," he said. "We each got an email from the reservations department about the cruise, and thirty minutes later, we were on a video call and had booked our trip before we ended the call."

"So, tell me," Kennedy queried, "what's new with all of you? I only see so much on social media. I think the last thing I saw was Phil ranting about a true crime series involving a man with an exotic animal zoo. Something about tigers."

Phil turned scarlet. "Oh my God," he wailed, "to think I wasted sixteen hours of my life watching that insanity."

Kennedy was puzzled. "Sixteen hours? Wasn't it only eight episodes?"

Phil looked down at his shoes. "Well, yes," he said sheepishly, "if you only watch it once, but honestly, I had to go back and watch it again because it was just a train wreck," he said in his south Louisiana patois. "It was worse than any dramedy we had in New Orleans."

Robert interjected, "And let's face it, some of us watched it for the outfits. They were…bold."

"Hmmm, bold, beautiful, sexy," John mused, "with the right dance moves, I could have that guy booked in the club and laugh all the way to the bank," he said mirthfully.

"But enough about us, what happened to you, sugar?" he asked.

Don chimed in. "Yes, how was time at home with your darling mother?" he cackled sarcastically. Don had met Lolly once and had told the others that Kennedy had not exaggerated about her mother.

"Did the delicious Joe come back into the picture? Are we planning a trousseau?" Robert asked.

Kennedy made them wait for a few seconds. "Well…" she said, rolling her eyes, "let's just say that I had to make a deal with the devil while I was home, and the interest payment was a once-a-week dinner, which became known as the dating game. My parents invited every socially prominent bachelor under seventy-five to the house under the guise of a home-cooked meal." They burst out into laughter. "It was dreadful and too much to chat about now," she said.

"What are the shows for this trip, Kennedy? Everything said TBD except for the seventies night, and it said we could come dressed as our favorite seventies television character," asked Steve, the quiet one of the group.

"Oh, the seventies, to have been me in the seventies," John said mournfully. "So free and crazy, and the outfits I could have pulled off."

Dave took off his sunglasses and looked at John. "Could have pulled off? I think you are still wearing some of them, John," he said snidely.

Kennedy shared the show schedule, explaining that the compressed rehearsal meant a few of the shows were repeats from previous years. "Tonight, is our tribute to *Mama Mia*," she said and changed the subject. "So, enough about me, what happened in your worlds while things were turned upside down?"

Phil, always the chatterbox, spoke up first, "Accounting never stops, and since we were not allowed to be in the office, we had to set up shop at home. I had to keep my house clean all the time just so that I wouldn't be embarrassed doing a video call." Although he always looked like he stepped out of a magazine, Phil was also a notorious slob. "I also had to make sure that any," and he held up two fingers making quotation marks, "visitors were gone early in case of a morning call. I didn't need any unexpected walk-ons while on camera." He sighed heavily. "New Orleans has just up and died, Kennedy. No parades, bars closed…a string of second street bands and floats couldn't liven up that town right now."

Steve piped up, "I guess I am next. Like Phil, the law never closes, either. I worked from home and continued to bill by the minute. My clients were happy, and the partners in the law firm were happy with my billable hours. I was more productive at home and didn't miss the office distractions."

Dave shared that while everything was shut down, he had reworked the travel guidebooks he wrote. "Getting a room was easy, and because restaurants and bars were empty, I could take time to describe the places I went and the food I tried. I also did some freelance articles, which opened a new avenue for me."

John interrupted him, "He might have found a whole new avenue, but for the entertainment business, it was like someone threw up concrete barriers on a Los Angeles highway. We had to close the doors to Club Diva," he said sadly. "I'll have to start all over putting a show together based upon the talent I can find, that is, if I can find it again." He smiled at everyone. "But thank goodness for good friends and good years. Because of these two," he pointed to Phil and Steve, "the rainy-day fund they forced me to set up kept me afloat because boy has it been raining! I felt like Noah!" he said, laughing. "But I also had time to think about reopening, and I believe," he said with a twinkle in his eye, "that I have hit upon a honey of an idea—bachelorette brunches and baby showers." Kennedy looked at him, bemused. "Brunch is the hot thing these days," he said with an air of authority. "Pair it with the right talent on stage, hunky half-dressed servers, and alcohol. I could be back up and in the green in a matter of months. Especially now that my good friend Robert is helping me to book groups –"

Robert interrupted John, "I guess this is where I come in," and he shared that the last year had been challenging for him. He had been laid off as a sales director for a hotel when it had closed its doors. At loose ends, he went to visit John, and a night of cocktails and writing on the back of some napkins had ended with Robert moving back to Florida to help John reopen the club. "We'll market the brunch through the local channels. I've partnered with a few hotels already to see how we can make some package deals. So, we'll see where it takes us," he began fanning himself. "But thank goodness for this cruise because I am dying for some fun!"

Kennedy smiled and turned to Don. "Well, last but not least, dearest Don, how is the shoe business treating you?"

Don owned five shoe stores in Georgia. "Since you asked," he said, his accent as thick as molasses, "the shoe business has been as cold as my Aunt Matilda." He continued in his thick lazy drawl. "Which meant that I had to change my way of thinking. And like John said, thanks to these marvelous creatures," he put an arm around Phil and Steve,

"I opened an online store, Mr. Donnie's Shoes. We realized that many of our friends who perform have difficulty getting great shoes. So, Mr. Donnie's Shoes was born, and we now have a website for those looking for a size six or a size thirteen-D red satin pump," he said proudly.

Kennedy smiled, looking at her dear friends. "I'm so glad you are all here and getting some much-deserved time off. It sounds like you needed to get out and let the wind blow through your hair and allow the creativity to flow." She turned to John. "When do you think you will have the club back up and running?" she asked sweetly.

John arched an eyebrow and shook a finger at her. "So that you can steal my material, you naughty girl? Don't think for a second that I am unaware of your scheming. I know how you operate." He grinned at her and put a hand on his hip. "Let's see how your show is tonight and how much you have pilfered already."

Kennedy looked John straight in the eye and raised an eyebrow. "Hmmm, is it me stealing your lines, or are you stealing mine, John?" she asked archly.

"Well," he said somewhat sheepishly, "I did borrow the whole thing about Lolly, didn't I?"

"And?" Kennedy prodded.

"Okay, and the bit about your sister and the Junior League," he said, blushing.

Dave interrupted the two of them. "Sorry to break this up, but I am dying to know, is the spa open? I want to treat these guys to some spa time. I am so desperate for a pedicure. I swear I am one step away from having hooves."

Kennedy nodded her head. "The spa is open, renovated, and beautiful! Dave, you may even want to think about writing it up in your travel guide at some point. Mila poured her soul into it. You should probably book something right now because it is sure to fill up if it isn't already." She looked down at her watch. "Gentlemen, I am so sorry, but I must go and help some of the other passengers. It was so wonderful to catch up with all of you. Don't forget about the Captain's Dinner tonight." She turned to leave.

"Kennedy, before you go, who is that?" Phil asked, nodding his head to the side. "He acts as if he owns the place, and the hate bombs he keeps throwing this way should have blown us to smithereens." Gunner was standing in the center of the lobby glowering at Kennedy. "Does he realize that he looks like Mr. Rourke from *Fantasy Island*?"

"And who is the nerdy little guy beside him? A pasty Tattoo?" asked Don.

Kennedy swallowed and smiled. "Well, the 'nerdy' one is one of our board members, and the other one is the soon-to-be-named vice president sent from the corporate office to observe the cruise and see what changes we may need to make for a better guest experience," she said anxiously.

"His strutting around makes him look like a constipated rooster, but, then again, most people from corporate offices look like that. I call it the 'I need to validate myself and the enormous salary I make' look," Steve said. "I used to see it every day." Phil nodded his head in agreement.

Don looked back over at Gunner and then at Kennedy. "He keeps looking over here and gesticulating. I think he's trying to get your attention."

"Do you want us to do something to get you out of going over there?" Dave asked.

Kennedy sighed sadly. "He's probably found something else that I have done wrong."

"Do you want us to beat him up?" Steve asked. "We can corner him, beat him up, and leave him on the pier."

Robert laughed. "I bet we can even do it and look macho."

Kennedy looked at each of them. "You are kind, but this is someone I need to play nicely within the sandbox if I want to keep my job," she said.

"All right, darling, we get the hint, but remember, we love you like the sister we stole clothes from, and we will do anything you need us to," said John speaking for the group. He put his white rhinestone sunglasses back on, and they all blew kisses to her as they left for their cabins.

Kennedy walked over to Gunner. "Mr. Atcher, how may I assist you?"

Gunner sniffed. "Why is there only one way onto the ship? There should be several points of arrival."

Kennedy took a moment to understand his question. "Mr. Atcher, this is how the passengers arrive and depart the ship," she explained. "Like an airplane, one way on, one way off, unless there is an evacuation. It's how the ship was built."

Gunner huffed. "That is ridiculous. This will be at the top of my list to discuss with the board when I return. There should be multiple ways for the passengers to get on and off the ship. The way it is now is far too restrictive. Second, the way you are greeting the passengers is unacceptable." He pulled a stopwatch from his pants pocket. "I have seen you greeting guests and spending far too long speaking with them. Moving forward, you will stand behind a podium and have a determined amount of time to spend with each guest. There is no time for chatting and friendliness. It's all about time efficiency," he said, pointing to his stopwatch.

Kennedy was perplexed. "Actually, Mr. Atcher, that is my job. I ensure that the passengers have a relaxing and comfortable trip." She continued, "One of the guests you saw me speaking with booked his trip through a friend in the corporate office. I was asked to look out for him. Two other groups I welcomed post a great deal on social media and encourage others to book their cruises with the cruise line. Again, I was instructed by the corporate office to look after these groups personally."

Gunner huffed. "You probably won't need to worry about things like that in the future," he said. "I have written new standards of efficiency that I will give you to review. I have also taken the time to diagram a new chain of command. It would be in your best interest to thoroughly understand the new standards and hierarchy as your job will depend on this information." He turned and looked at Mr. Phillips. "Am I right, Mr. Phillips?"

Mr. Phillips, in a high nasal voice, looked at Kennedy and squeaked, "It would behoove you to follow Mr. Atcher's guidance on this cruise. I will be sharing his comments and suggestions with the board."

At that precise moment, an uproar overtook the lobby as a slim woman with shoulder-length silver hair in a black and orange three-piece silk suit entered the space. Vera Jameson strode through the room as if she owned it. The rows of gold necklaces and pearls swayed with each purposeful step she took, and her laser-like eyes scanned the lobby for Kennedy. Then, seeing her, Vera snapped her fingers at Billy the bellman to follow her as she locked her eyes on Kennedy and marched toward her.

Billy, bags wrapped around him on either side, struggled with a trolley full of luggage. He tried in vain to keep up with Mrs. Jameson, but unfortunately, tangled between the bags and the bell cart, he tripped and fell to the ground.

"Honestly," Vera sighed tiredly and rolled her eyes.

Gunner seeing the commotion, walked quickly towards Vera, believing her to be an important guest he should greet personally. He looked with disdain at the bellman who struggled to get to his feet. "Why wasn't this guest's luggage put through the new protocols and taken directly to her cabin?" he asked. Kennedy hastened over to help Billy to his feet.

Billy shuffled, nervous and uncomfortable. "I-I-I t-tr-tried to tell her, the port officials tried to tell her," he stammered. "But Mrs. Jameson did not want her bags touched by anyone other than me." He looked at Kennedy. "I tried to tell her, Kennedy, I promise," he said earnestly.

Vera interrupted him. "Kennedy, if I may break up this little tête-à-tête may I remind you that I am not just any passenger, I am THE passenger, and I WILL NOT be treated like a cow being pushed through a slaughterhouse chute to go on a cruise."

Gunner interrupted, holding out his hand to Vera. "Mrs. .... I'm sorry, we have not been properly introduced. I am Gunner Owen Atcher, the future vice president of the cruise line, and I would like to personally guarantee you that I will be at your beck and call during this cruise. In my years in hospitality, I have been privileged to assist some of the finest names in the world. In fact, when I was at…"

Gunner droned on, oblivious to the expression on Vera Jameson's face. She looked at him as though he were a garden slug that had crawled onto the tip of her expensive orange silk sandal and was making its way towards her perfectly pedicured toe. She looked down at Gunner's still outstretched hand. "I am neither interested in who nor what you are," she said frostily. I need to discuss MY boarding process, MY suite, and MY itinerary with Kennedy and ONLY Kennedy, as she has assisted me for years without issue."

She arched an eyebrow at Gunner. "As to your being vice president of the cruise line," she gave him a thin smile, "well, that remains to be seen. The company puts a great deal of stock in my opinion, and I have no trouble giving it. Now Kennedy and I need to discuss a private matter. Excuse us." Vera tapped her foot as she waited for Gunner to leave, but he stood there, groping for something more to say. Finally, she arched an eyebrow at him. "I'm quickly running out of patience. Please go and take your overblown, exhausting manner with you. And please," she added, looking at him in disgust, "find a handkerchief to wipe your forehead. You are positively dripping." She dismissed him with a shooing motion of her hands. "I am sure there is someone on this ship you can impress with your self-importance. Good day, Mr., what was your name again?"

"Atcher," Kennedy whispered.

"Ah, yes, Atcher. You may leave."

Gunner blinked his eyes rapidly as he turned a dangerous shade of red. Humiliated by Vera's dismissal, he made an about-face and stalked off, gesturing wildly at any staff member in his path. Mr. Phillips trotted close behind, writing frantically in his notebook. Kennedy, always on edge for Mrs. Jameson's arrival, was silently grateful for the demanding woman's presence. Vera had cut Gunner off and dismissed him in a way Kennedy was sure he had never experienced.

Vera turned her attention to Kennedy. "My dear, who was that dreadful man? Please tell me I will be nowhere near him or his little shadow for this jaunt. I cannot bear a person who thinks they are better than anyone else simply because of a title. He didn't even offer to help this poor man up," she said, nodding at Billy. She took Kennedy's arm under hers and began to stroll about the lobby. "Generally, I find that men who feel the need to tout their titles are the biggest frauds in the room. Boorish behavior is simply uncouth." She locked her eyes narrowly on Kennedy and dropped her arm. "So, if you are here, I can infer that you did not marry while you were away?" she asked curtly.

"No, ma'am," Kennedy replied.

"Good. You need a man that will be worthy of you, although you are getting a little long in the tooth. I expect your dance card is not as full as it once was." She smiled, and her eyes crinkled. "When I was a young woman, there was a line of suitors at my house every evening, and my father would come out onto the porch at ten o'clock with a shotgun to tell them to go home." She gave Kennedy a knowing look.

"But I knew he was secretly *pleased* with the number of gentlemen callers."

Billy had been following at a discreet distance with the luggage cart. He rolled his eyes and snickered quietly at Vera's story. Vera whipped around. You there, I believe you can find your way to my cabin if you have half of a brain. Please go now and watch that you don't manhandle my luggage. I do not want to find any scuffs or scrapes on it. Do we understand each other?" she asked, narrowing her eyes at the young man. Billy gulped and nodded, quickly rolling the cart away from the two women toward the elevators.

She turned back to Kennedy. "I simply must talk to you about the boarding process. It is quite dreadful. There must be something you can do so people like me aren't forced to suffer the indignities I had to endure today."

Kennedy nodded. "Yes, ma'am, I will look into this, but as the process is controlled by the–"

Vera cut her off. "I am not interested in who controls what. I simply need to see what you *personally* can do." She continued. "Next–" She stopped abruptly as she spied Bert walking toward them with his camera around his neck. "IF YOU DON'T MIND!" she hissed and pointed a bejeweled finger at him. "Let's be clear right now. You do not have my permission to take my photograph. You people are worse than parasites, always trying to take a photo at the most indiscrete time and then selling it to a newspaper." Kennedy nodded at Bert, who turned around abruptly, searching for another passenger to photograph. At that moment, Kennedy became distracted by a middle-aged couple who walked into the lobby looking lost.

The man was slender, with greying black hair brushed back from his forehead in a pompadour. Cherry-red sunglasses sat on his head and matched the roses that were embroidered on the jacket he wore over his white T-shirt and bleached jeans. Red cowboy boots and an unlit cigar the man was chomping on completed the ensemble.

Vera swiveled her eyes in the direction of Kennedy's stare. "Oh, dear Lord," she blurted out, causing several people nearby to turn around and look at her. "*What* is that woman wearing? Are we now allowing prostitutes on the ship?"

"Shhhh, Mrs. Jameson," but Vera was not a woman easily silenced.

"I believe she purchased her outfit from an adult novelty store," Vera said scornfully, pointing at the couple, "and he looks like her pimp," she barked. "Kennedy, what on *Earth* are we allowing on this ship?"

Kennedy searched the lobby to see how she could remove Vera quickly and make it seem inviting. She saw Franklin walking through the lobby and caught his eye. She waved wildly at him, beckoning him to come over as Vera gave her a strange look. When Franklin reached the two women, Kennedy said, "Mrs. Jameson, have you met our Chief Engineer, Franklin Blaas? He is the man behind the machine, and he asked me earlier if he could be allowed to escort you to your cabin when you arrived. I have told him so much about you," Kennedy smiled prettily at her friend and pleaded at Franklin with her eyes.

Vera looked Franklin up and down, appraising him like a thoroughbred. Then, finally, she turned back to Kennedy. "Well, isn't he a tall, silver hunk of man?" Kennedy breathed a sigh of relief. "Yes, I believe this will do, Kennedy. You should go help that couple," she said, pointing again at the newcomers, "they appear to be lost. Maybe they got on the wrong ship. And if not, perhaps you could help them make some selections from the ship's store for some proper attire. I suggest finding something more suitable to cover body parts that should not be so cheaply advertised," Vera said, her voice dripping with sarcasm.

She turned to Franklin and offered him a wide smile. "Now, Mr. Blaas," Vera linked her arm into a stunned Franklin's. "Would you please be a dear and escort a gentle lady such as myself to my stateroom," she purred.

As Vera sauntered off with Franklin, Kennedy walked over to greet the new passengers who were having their photos taken by Bert. The man stepped down, but the woman stayed to have more photos taken, changing her pose with each click of Bert's shutter. She was thin with a deep tan that complimented her shoulder-length, sun-kissed caramel hair. The couple looked familiar, but Kennedy could not place them. She was sure she had seen them before. The woman held up her hand to Bert, silently asking him to stop, as she realized her skirt had ridden up her legs. She frantically yanked it to mid-thigh. "Shucks, Terri, don't worry about showing your legs. I like seeing them!" her husband boomed.

"Good afternoon," Kennedy said amiably to the man. "Welcome to the *Helio*. I'm Kennedy Reeves, your cruise director, and you are the –"

The man answered, heartily shaking Kennedy's proffered hand. "We are Mr. and Mrs. Jones Butler of Mississippi," he said with a thick, deep southern twang. "You may have heard about us recently on the news, we just sold our little restaurant chain, Buck-A-Cluck, to some fast-food conglomerate, and they gave us so much money we aren't sure how we will spend it all, are we, Sweetsie?" Jones took Terri's hand as she stepped carefully away from Bert's photo setup.

A lightbulb went off in Kennedy's brain as she suddenly realized who the Butlers were. She had seen their names on the manifest but had not made the connection until he mentioned the sale. One evening at dinner, her father had shared the details of the Buck-A-Cluck deal. It had been a very lucrative transaction, her father said, and Mr. Jones, while appearing to be a country bumpkin, was actually a very savvy businessman. Buck-A-Cluck's littered the South, Midwest, and East Coast at every truck stop or gas station on every interstate and highway. With the sale, they had joined a list of other recent mega-millionaires. Kennedy saw the company logo in her mind: a cartoon chicken on a blue background with his wing in the air, seeming to give the viewer a thumbs up. Her father also shared that the restaurants could go worldwide, and a portion of the proceeds from every new restaurant built would go into the Butlers' pockets.

"Yep, it was the opportunity of a lifetime," Jones continued, just loud enough for anyone around them to hear him. "When that big company with their fancy lawyers made me the offer, I couldn't say no, although I played hard to get. People just love my fried chicken." He whispered behind his hand. "Don't tell anyone, but it's the grease," he said with a wink. Kennedy could do nothing more than nod her head. "So, Kennedy," he drawled, "as the person who probably knows everything, can you help me out? I can make it worth your while." He pulled his billfold, attached by a chain to his belt loop, out of his back pocket. He flashed a ten-dollar bill at her. "Do you think you could get us upgraded to a nicer room? I want to make this a trip to remember for Terri. She started as a cashier at one of my truck stop restaurants. The moment I saw her, I knew she was the one for me." He gave Terri a side hug, and Kennedy looked down at her clipboard. "Mr. and Mrs. Butler, I am sure you will be happy in your stateroom. It boasts lovely views and—"

Jones interrupted her. "But is it the *best*? I want the absolute best of everything on this trip, and if you have any way of making that happen, I can make it worth your while." He flashed a ten-dollar bill in front of Kennedy.

"Mr. Butler, please put your money away. According to the manifest, you are in our Owner's Suite. Why don't I escort you to the room as this is your first time on the *Helio*?" Kennedy began to make her way to the elevators but checked her pace when she realized Terri was having difficulty keeping up. The tight dress and four-inch sandals only allowed Terri to take small steps. Making their way through the lobby to the elevators, passengers, staff, and crew members stared open-mouthed at the parade. Kennedy walked the Butlers to their stateroom, explaining the ship's layout and safety protocols along the way. Passengers would watch a safety video in their cabin and receive a personal tour of their muster station.

"A mustard station? What's that? A place to get things for your hotdog?" Terri asked cocking her head to the side. Her expression reminded Kennedy of a dog hearing a high-pitched noise.

"Muster," Jones repeated. "It's where we go in case we hit an iceberg. Like they did in that movie you love."

Terri looked at Jones with pure fright in her eyes. "Will there really be icebergs? I thought those were only up North where penguins live. Jonesy, aren't we going on a Caribbean cruise?" she squeaked in her high-pitched, breathless voice.

"Yes, ma'am," Kennedy answered in a calm, soothing voice. "We're going to the Caribbean. "Sun, sand, and no icebergs. But we are required to make sure everyone knows where to go in case of an emergency."

Terri swallowed and stared at Kennedy in apprehension. "But what happens if there are pirates? I've seen the news! What do we do then? Jonesy, I don't know if this is a good idea. We could just go and forget about taking the cruise."

Kennedy realized she needed to calm the situation down at once. Mrs. Butler looked like a deer ready to run. "Mrs. Butler," she said sweetly, "we don't foresee any icebergs, pirates, or problems. I want you to think of the muster station like the seat belt in your car. You know where it is, and you put it on *just in case* there's an emergency, but you don't get into the car intending to get into an accident."

Terri pondered Kennedy's explanation. "Well, hearing it put that way makes perfect sense."

They arrived at the Owner's Suite, and Kennedy took out her key to open the door, reminding herself not to cringe visibly. The Owner's Suite was unique, which was the only polite way to describe it. Designed by the wife of a board member who touted that she had a "natural talent" for decorating, passengers rarely booked the suite, and if they did, they quickly demanded a different stateroom. And one look inside explained why. Kennedy had gone to school for interior design, and entering the room was a painful chore.

As you opened the door, the first thing to catch your eye was the black and tan zebra-striped carpet. Next, your eyes might trail over to the black granite wet bar with gold faucets and glass shelves, making you wonder if Hugh Hefner had lent a hand in the design work. However, when you saw the emerald-green trim and gold and white filigree wallpaper, your next thought was to step back quickly towards the door and slam it shut in horror. If you had decided to stay in the room at that point, you would finally notice the round, ivory velvet settee in the center of the room. It was a commanding piece but one you would expect to see in a Las Vegas casino lobby rather than the middle of the suite's living room. Kennedy turned to look at the Butlers. From their expressions, she wasn't sure if they were appalled or in love. Mouths agape, they walked around the living area, turning slowly in circles. Terri tried to pick up a black and gold Grecian vase but couldn't lift it. "Oh," Kennedy laughed gently, "it won't come up. We put special putty on them so they don't fall over if we have rough seas."

Terri squealed and began jumping up and down. "Oh Jonesy, this is perfect! Do you think we could find out who did the decorating? I would love to have them do our new place back home."

Jones nodded his head. "You read my mind, Sweetsie. I bet Kennedy here can find out who it is, and we can fly them to the house as soon as we get home."

Kennedy smiled weakly. She walked to the bedroom doorway and, having never seen it, shuddered. The living room had always been painful enough to see. She stepped into the bedroom. The bed, of course, was the focal point of the room. The headboard consisted of a large, ornate gold frame bolted to the wall with tufted black leather and zebra-striped fabric. The bed's coverlet was black satin, and a zebra-striped bed scarf lay across the foot of the bed. On either side of the bed were black nightstands with a gold crackle overlay. Hanging from the ceiling over the nightstands were zebra print pendant lamps, and the walls had been papered in a red, black, and gold thinly striped wallpaper. Looking around, Kennedy wondered if Elvis had worked on the design for the bedroom while Hugh Hefner designed the living room.

"Oh, Jonesy," Terri said, "I feel like a queen." She twirled around the bedroom and fell back on the bed.

Kennedy walked toward the bathroom. To leave at this point would be silly, and she was curious if Hugh and Elvis had collaborated to design it. She was surprised to see that the room was quite tasteful. Large black tiles lay on the floors, and the walls were papered in black and gold wallpaper. The countertops were black granite flecked with gold mica, and two large black sinks sat on the countertop under gold faucets. Kennedy noticed that a housekeeping staff member had placed a large sun made out of towels between the two sinks. A massive gold slipper bathtub sat in the middle of the room. The shower was large with black and gold tiles which, to Kennedy, resembled a Gustav Klimt painting. Compared to the other spaces, the bathroom was not terrible despite its ornateness.

"Jonesy, are you thinking what I'm thinking?"

He nodded as he scanned the room, noting the finishes. "I am, Sweetsie. This setup would be perfect for the master bathroom. We'll get started right away." He pulled her two hands to his lips and kissed them. "But, first, I want to relax and enjoy my time with you." He winked at Terri, and she blushed.

Kennedy took this moment as her cue to leave. "Don't forget to watch the safety video," she called out as she walked out of the suite. "One of the crew members will be by shortly to escort you to your muster station."

As the guests were all on board, getting settled in their cabins, watching their safety videos, or touring the muster stations, Kennedy went to her cabin to take care of the thousands of minute details that were part of her job. However, she decided first to check her phone messages. There was a call from Vera Jameson politely demanding that Director of Security Omar Meier escort her for cocktails, the Captain's Dinner, and the show in the Solstice Theater that evening.

"Kennedy, please don't let him think that he will elude me on this trip," Vera said crisply. "He may have slipped away with some excuse of an emergency on other cruises, but tonight I want him as my escort. And you can tell him that this is not a request," she repeated.

Kennedy chuckled. It sounded as if Franklin had whispered something in Vera's ear about the ship's director of security. Kennedy contemplated how to break the news. Omar hated all things pretentious, and Kennedy knew she would pay dearly for not getting him out of squiring Mrs. Jameson about. *I'll remind him that all staff members are required to socialize with the passengers per the corporate directives,* she thought to herself. As Vera was one of the company's VIPs and a friend not only to the family but a former roommate to one of the board members, her requests were not taken lightly.

The following message was from Jones Butler. "Kennedy, don't forget we need the name of the designer who did our room. We want to fly them out to our house as soon as the cruise ends." Kennedy felt she knew what his next words would be and silently chuckled when she heard them. "And if you could get me their number ASAP, there will be a little something extra for you," he said. Shaking her head, Kennedy giggled.

The last call brought her high spirits down as if a bucket of ice-cold water had been thrown on her. It was from Gunner Atcher, who wanted to see Kennedy at once in his cabin. His message stated he was very displeased with the accommodations he had received and wanted to see her before he unpacked. Kennedy sighed and got up, walking quickly to Cabin 823.

Kennedy knocked on the door, and Gunner opened it quickly, beckoning Kennedy into the room. "Can you explain why I was given this room?" he threw out his arms. "I'm shocked that you consider something like this worthy of the future vice president of the cruise line." He walked around the room and then stopped and turned to her. "I expected better of you, Kennedy. The minute you met me and understood who I was, you should have upgraded me to one of the larger suites, but instead, you gave me this." He threw his hands up in disgust. While not as opulent as Vera Jameson's suite, Gunner's stateroom was luxurious and on the upper tier of the *Helio's* room type, just below the luxury staterooms. The room featured a separate bedroom, a seating area with a couch and chairs, a sliding door to a private veranda, a spacious bathroom, a large closet, and a writing desk. In her opinion, Gunner's accommodations were on par with a four or five-star hotel suite.

Kennedy stammered, unsure of what to say. "Mr. Atcher, I apologize that you are unhappy." She continued, "But we are sold out, and I do not have another cabin to assign to you."

Looking around the room in contempt, Gunner squeezed his eyes shut and pinched the bridge of his nose with his fingers. "This is simply not acceptable. We have an Owner's Suite. Why was I not put in there? I should have a room that reflects my position. A vice president is as close as one can get to being an owner."

Kennedy knew she needed to be delicate, and she felt that her job hung upon her next words. "Mr. Atcher," she said thoughtfully, "I am deeply sorry for this inconvenience, and if there were a luxury suite available, I would certainly have you moved. Unfortunately, as I explained, we are sold out for this cruise, and the Owner's Suite is occupied." She swallowed hard. "I will, however, make a note in your profile that for future cruises, a stateroom that is more suitable for you and your status be selected."

Gunner glared at her. "Are you getting smart with me, young lady?" he snarled.

Kennedy paled and shook her head. "No, sir, not at all. I only want to ensure that we take wonderful care of you and make the proper adjustments for your future journeys."

"Just remember," he said, walking up to her, "this foul-up will be in my notes. I am furious that you allowed my accommodations to be this lacking, especially after you learned who I am." He gave her a long look. "It makes me wonder what else is lacking, as your attention to detail leaves drastic room for improvement," he said scornfully.

Kennedy was on the verge of tears. She had just gotten her job back, and this man was threatening her before the ship had even left port. "Mr. Atcher," she said sincerely, "again, please accept my apologies for this error. If you will, please excuse me. I must attend to other areas of the ship before we depart."

She walked out of Gunner's stateroom and shut the door, looking up at the ceiling to blink back the tears threatening her eyes. She took a deep breath and straightened her shoulders before she walked down the corridor.

Kennedy took the back steps and went down to deck six. She wanted to peek into the spa to see the passengers' reactions to the new look. When Kennedy walked in, she was thrilled to see a beehive of activity as passengers booked appointments and looked at the items for sale in the retail area. She saw Sara, Mila's new associate, helping Dave and Phil find an open block so the group could have their treatments together. Kennedy waved to them. *That should be some nice revenue*, she mused to herself and walked through the door that led to the private treatment rooms and Mila's office. As she got close to Mila's office, she heard Bert complaining.

"Mila," Bert whined, "You know I need to take pictures for the corporate office. How am I supposed to get my work done with so many people in here?"

Mila looked at him from across the desk. She had just come from the reception area. "Bert, my spa is full of people booking appointments, and I am over the moon right now. I don't care when you do the photo shoot. Do the shoot at midnight when the spa is closed for all I care." She stood up and crossed her arms. "You had ample time before we set sail, but you were too busy hanging out in the crew bar and sunning yourself on the deck to be bothered with taking the photos," she lectured. He looked at her sullenly. "The solution is for you to shoot the spa when we dock in one of the ports. The passengers will be ashore and won't be in the spa. Or," she held up a finger, "you can do the shoot after midnight."

Bert sighed grumpily and left Mila's office, walking down the back corridor. He knew Mila was right. He had procrastinated again, but this time she was not going to bail him out as she had in the past.

"Poor Bert," Kennedy said, popping her head into Mila's office and then nodded at Bert's departing figure.

Mila rolled her eyes and came out from behind her desk. "Poor, poor, Bert," she said sarcastically and smiled at her friend. "I wish I could chat, Kennedy, but the spa is hopping, and I need to help with the appointments. I only came here to talk to Bert, so we didn't have an unpleasant conversation in the reception area where the passengers could overhear it. Anna Marie and Sara are swamped, and I don't want to chance losing business. Sara is handling things well, but I don't want her to run away before we even leave port." She beamed. "What a wonderful feeling to be so busy."

Kennedy smiled at her friend. "I am so happy for you, Mila, the spa is fabulous, and you should be proud of your hard work." She hesitated for a moment. "Before you go, have you met the soon-to-be vice president of the company, Mr. Atcher?"

Mila shook her head slowly. "No, I haven't had the pleasure yet. How did we not know that he would be on the ship? What is he like?" Kennedy's face began to crumble. "What's wrong, Ken?"

Kennedy leaned against the door jamb and closed her eyes. She bit her lip, trying to regain her composure. "Trouble. I think he is big, big trouble."

Mila was torn, she knew her friend needed her, but she also knew she needed to help Anna Marie and Sara. "Ken, I wish I could talk now, but I've got to go and help. Can we talk more tonight?" Kennedy nodded, and Mila stepped around her and into the corridor. She placed a warm hand on Kennedy's arm. "Come to my cabin after your show, and we will have a glass of wine and talk this out. I promise you'll have my undivided attention. Now give me a smile before I leave." Kennedy gave her a wan smile and gave her a thumbs up. "That's better. Hey, one more thing, have you…" Mila made a circular motion with her finger in the air. "We all promised we would do our part."

Kennedy slapped her head. "No! I'm on my way. I can't believe I forgot!" She left the spa through the employee entrance, took the back staircase to deck five, and walked down the staff corridor. She opened the door and found herself in the back of the ship's main theater. After toasting the new spa, Franklin sternly reminded everyone to do their part to ensure good luck on the cruise. Superstitions were common on the ship, and no one dared to make fun of another's belief. Franklin, she knew, threw a shoe overboard before every cruise. She had wondered where he got them until Rosemary explained she had a collection from lost and found. Luke poured a shot of rum, raised it to the sky, and poured the alcohol into the ocean right before the passengers arrived. Rosemary always wore the same gold earrings on the first day, and Omar would walk off the ship, turn around and place his right foot on the gangway step before the first passenger arrived.

Kennedy's superstition was more personal. She would go into the main theater, walk out onto center stage, and turn slowly in place. She had done this before every cruise for as long as she could remember, and Kennedy couldn't believe she had neglected to do it today. She wondered if it was the reason why things had gotten off to a rocky start with Mr. Atcher. The empty stage was a place to gather her thoughts before the next crisis appeared, and there always seemed to be a crisis of some kind. The key, Kennedy had learned, was to take a deep breath, smile, and find a solution while on her feet. She had learned early in her career that smiling and moving forward was the only way to survive working on a cruise ship. Kennedy closed her eyes and took a deep breath. She pictured her grandparents in her mind, and an instant calm washed over her. They had supported her choice to work on the ship and understood her in a way her parents never had. It was because of Robert and Maggie that she had a love of the sea and entertaining.

Robert Spencer, a naval officer, locked eyes on Margaret "Maggie" Callahan, an entertainer for the USO, on board a ship returning to the United States from Europe. It was love at first sight. They were seldom apart in their sixty years of marriage, and you could tell they were more in love each day simply by being in their presence. Their marriage gave Kennedy hope, but it also made her realize that a love like theirs might be unobtainable for her. She drew in a deep breath and exhaled. "Okay, buttercup, put your sea legs on. It's showtime."

Kennedy trotted up the back staircase to deck nine, where the pool was located. She smiled as she saw cast members helping the passengers get into the spirit of the cruise by dancing with them to the Caribbean music emanating from the speakers. Luke and his team of bartenders, dressed in bright tropical print shirts and wearing palm frond hats, were busy mixing more batches of the SunRumbrella punch and serving them to the thirsty passengers. With each sip, the passengers seemed to slough off the psychological baggage that weighed on their shoulders.

SUNNY DAYZ SUNRUMBRELLA

2 PARTS PINEAPPLE JUICE

2 PARTS ORANGE JUICE

1 1/2 PARTS RUM

LIME JUICE

GRENADINE SYRUP

CITRUS SLICES

CRUSHED ICE

COMBINE ALL INGREDIENTS IN A LARGE CONTAINER. POUR OVER CRUSHED ICE. GARNISH WITH CITRUS SLICES AND PAPER UMBRELLAS

Kennedy walked to one end of the deck and saw that the limbo and golf putting contests and a rousing game of ping pong were already in full swing at one end of the deck, and it appeared that many passengers were already vying for the Sun Trophy. She shook her head. The trophy was a golden cruise ship sitting on a bed of blue acrylic waves. Someone in the Sunny Dayz corporate office had seen another cruise line giving away trophies to passengers on their cruises for participating in events on the ship, and they quickly copied the idea. The passengers loved it, and many rebooked cruises so they could have another chance to win the coveted trophy.

Walking to the other end of the deck, Kennedy saw that a conga line had formed. She was not surprised to see the Ladies from Harmony Lakes were at the front of the line, and she was delighted that the Club Diva Boys had joined them. Kennedy wondered how long Marilyn would flirt with them before she realized it was futile. She looked around and saw groups posing for Bert, who was happily snapping photos to be posted later in the lobby. *It's what it's all about*, she smiled to herself, *making memories. We help make the memories that carry people through the tough times.*

A few moments later, the loudspeaker came on as the captain announced that the *Helio* would soon pull anchor and depart for the islands. Kennedy watched the passengers walk quickly to the railings, waving goodbye to the world and reality for a few days. However, her smile quickly faded when she saw Gunner and Mr. Phillips standing above on the promenade deck overlooking the pool. Kennedy observed Gunner as he pointed in various directions, and Mr. Phillips would nod his head in agreement and write in his notebook.

Gunner and Mr. Phillips looked down at the pool deck. They saw a gray-haired group of people, happy to recline in their lounge chairs and sip on complimentary drinks. This was not the wild party crowd either man had envisioned. The guests were not young and fashionable but older and more conservative, except for Mrs. Terri Butler, who lay reclined on a lounge chair in a whisper of a red tropical print bikini. Gunner looked meaningfully at Mr. Phillips. "When I take over, I intend to change our target demographic, and I'm depending on you to help me sway the board members to this line of thinking. This shift will be hard for them to wrap around. They've been doing it the same way for decades."

Mr. Phillips cleared his throat. Changing the board's mind would not be easy. The company was quite comfortable with its way of doing things, and the clientele, which was not the young and wild drunken cruisers Gunner had in mind, were mature guests who were content to sit back and relax on their cruise.

Gunner pointed at the passengers below. "What I see here is stale and stagnant." He pointed at the conga line. "Nothing more than a floating retirement village." Gunner motioned Mr. Phillips over to the railing and explained his vision for the new Sunny Dayz Cruise Line. "I see this as an eternal spring break on the water," he said. "We would station a rock band up here while down there," he pointed at the pool, "young women wearing tiny bikinis will lounge around or be tossed into the pool." He touched his chin with his forefinger. "And alcohol, Mr. Phillips," he looked at the short, balding man beside him, "lots and lots of alcohol. The more alcohol they consume, the less they will care about spending money. When they get their credit card bill the following month, they'll pay it remembering the exciting time they had on the cruise and will book another. We can also eliminate the formal dining room and turn it into a casual restaurant that sells burgers, chicken wings, and sandwiches. This new demographic doesn't want the stuffy dinners their parents have on their cruises, which will save us a ton of money with labor and food costs. We should also think about changing the evening entertainment. We need to have music concerts. B listers, of course. We can't afford the big acts, but if we could find B listers or cover bands, we could offer it to them as a working vacation. A little sun and sand, a concert or two, sell some T-shirts, and take home a check. This will be fantastic!" He clapped his hands.

Mr. Phillips kept nodding and wrote down every word Gunner said, excitement coursing through his blood as he daydreamed about the change in the passengers. It would mean that he, of course, would have to help oversee these changes, and he was already planning how he would tell his wife that he would have to take these cruises alone. "How do we start?" he squeaked.

"With the senior staff, I need to make them understand who and what I am to their future," Gunner said ominously.

The senior staff met in the conference room shortly after the ship was underway. In the past, this had been a quick ten-minute meeting to share information about passengers, notes from the captain, and any schedule changes. Information from this meeting would then be quickly conveyed to all other teams on an as-needed basis. Kennedy entered the conference room and saw Franklin, Mila, Rosemary, Chef Michèle, Omar, and Tony sitting around the conference table.

Kennedy took the empty seat beside Omar. "Omar," she said sweetly, "I have a huge favor to ask, and unfortunately, it's not a request but a demand from Mrs. Jameson."

"Now, Kennedy—" Omar remonstrated, but she quickly cut him off.

"Mrs. Jameson has requested that you serve as her escort this evening: cocktails, dinner, and the main show."

"Hahaha," Franklin chortled. "Kennedy may have suckered me into ushering Her Highness to her stateroom, but *you* have to spend an entire evening with her." Franklin wiped tears from the corner of his eyes. "This is great! You laughed at me when we passed in the corridor, Omar, and now I get to have the last laugh."

Kennedy turned her eyes to Franklin. "If you aren't careful, I may suggest she request you for the following night. I can do that, you know." Hearing her words, Franklin swallowed his laughter and looked bleak.

"Hey, does anyone know anything about this guy who is on board? Gunner Owen Atcher? He's a VIP according to the manifest, but there were no notes," Tony asked the group.

"He's got quite a name." They all shook their heads except Kennedy and Mila, who exchanged glances.

Kennedy cleared her throat. She decided she would share who Gunner Atcher was after they had gotten through the critical information. "All right, team, let's get started. It appears that we—" Suddenly, the door flew open, and Gunner and Mr. Phillips walked into the room.

"Excuse me, but I believe this is my meeting, not yours," Gunner interrupted with a condescending tone. Kennedy looked at him bewildered.

"Begging your pardon, sir," Franklin spoke in an authoritative voice. "First, who are you, and second, why have you barged into our meeting?"

Gunner placed his hands behind his back and walked around the table, finally stopping at the head of it. "I am Gunner Owen Atcher, and moving forward, these will be my meetings." He held up his hand. "We need to set some ground rules. There are three times that you may speak in this meeting." He held up his first finger. "If I speak to you

153

directly." He held up his next finger. "When it is your turn to share information," and holding up a third finger, he said, "or if you can answer a question when asked. These meetings will run my way when I am on board." He motioned to Mr. Phillips, who was standing in the corner. "Now, Mr. Phillips, if you will, please formally announce me to those in this room. Word of my arrival was either missed or ignored by this group, which we gathered when a junior staff member greeted us."

Mr. Phillips stood and mopped his forehead with a handkerchief. "Good afternoon, everyone," he said nervously. "As many of you know, I am Mr. Phillips, one of the independent board members of the cruise line." He motioned at Gunner. "The man at the head of the table is Gunner Owen Atcher, who will soon be named as vice president—" He began coughing hard, and the words following president were obliterated in the noise. Rosemary jumped up and handed him a bottle of water, and he took a long drink. "Thank you," he said gratefully. "I am sure that it goes without saying that Mr. Atcher should be treated like any other high-ranking member of our company while on the cruise. At present, he is here as a consultant and will share his observations and recommendations with the board after this cruise. He has been given the authority to make on-the-spot revisions to standards and protocols and will make all necessary changes to ensure that our guest satisfaction scores are high." He looked around at the blank faces that stared back at him and stammered, "H-h-he will be formally named upon our return to Port Canaveral." Mr. Phillips swallowed as everyone looked at him in disbelief. "Mr. Atcher comes to us from the Sun Piper Resort Company, and while his background is not in cruises, he is one of the foremost experts in hospitality, having authored several standards used throughout the hotel industry. He is also well versed in cost-cutting measures and time efficiency. And as we know, efficiency equals profitability. So, please, let's give Mr. Atcher a warm Sunny Dayz welcome. I believe some applause is in order," and he began to clap profusely to the silent room. Coming out of shock, the team exchanged looks and began to applaud slowly at the news they had just heard.

Gunner clapped his hands together and rubbed them back and forth. "Thank you, Mr. Phillips." He looked around at the faces at the table. "Team, and that is how I want us to think of ourselves here, and while there is no I in team, there is me." He pointed a thumb at his chest. "Get it? Me? Just a little joke to start us off." Franklin quickly caught Kennedy's eye and gave her a look as if to say *is this guy for real?*

Gunner took off his glasses and wiped them with his handkerchief. Kennedy noticed the frames had changed from white to pale blue to match his shirt. "We will move forward as one team with one voice, and from now on, that voice will be mine." He looked around the room. "Always," he said with emphasis. "I am here to bring this cruise line to the top of its class, and with my help and years of experience in hospitality, we will turn this tired retirement home cruise line around and make it number one in the market. We will change our marketing demographic to go after a new customer. A customer programmed to spend money now and pay for it later when their bill arrives."

He paced the room. "There may be changes that you don't like or disagree with, and I will tell you now that, quite simply, you have two choices. You can accept the changes and do things the new way, or you can turn in your resignation and leave the ship at any time." He looked at each of them. "It does not matter to me if you leave," he said and continued, "there are plenty of people who can do your jobs. Not one of you is special, I can assure you." Everyone began to shift in their seats uncomfortably. This meeting was not going the way they had expected, and they exchanged quick worried looks between them.

"First and foremost, some of the things you will hear in this room and during my individual meetings with you over the next few days will be painful to hear." He looked pointedly at Kennedy. "I have observed enough today to see that time away from the industry has made most of you very rusty." His eyes then went to Mila and Rosemary. "Ladies, if you cannot handle what you hear in this room, I suggest you rethink your place at this table. In this room, we will not have feelings. If you are the kind of person who gets their feelings hurt easily, this will not be the company for you to work for moving forward." He slammed his hand down on the table, causing everyone to jump. "This is the big boy table. The commentary may sometimes be rough, and I don't want to see any tear-stained faces."

He looked at each of them. "The board will give me their full backing to make any staff changes I see necessary once I am named vice president." He chuckled. "It seems they value my observations and opinions more than yours." He clapped his hands together. "It's my way or the highway, people, and you can choose to stay or leave. It is your decision. If you can't take the heat or the criticism, you know where the door is." He pointed at the door and then looked back, locking eyes with each person in the room. "If you choose to complain to anyone in the corporate office, be prepared to find excellence with another cruise line because I will find out," he said threateningly. He rubbed his hands together. "I'll give you a moment to allow my words to sink in." Every person in the room, except for Mr. Phillips and Gunner, looked pale and drawn.

Gunner began to pace the room again. "Let's talk about my first observations today, and it concerns the ladies on the ship." He looked at Kennedy, Mila, and Rosemary. "Ladies, you and your fellow lady workers need to smile more. You have relatively decent faces. A cheery smile would be an improvement over what I saw today. Remember," he stopped and said cocking his head, "a smile is an inexpensive facelift." He chuckled and went back to pacing. "Gentlemen, keep doing what you're doing. Guests like to see a man in control with a strong, serious face. It gives them a sense of security. Secondly, men, moving forward, the ladies will escort the guests to their cabins if needed. I saw one of you playing tour guide earlier today, and it is not a job for us." Gunner punched one hand into the ball of his other one. Our job is to command the ship."

"That's not going to go over well with the captain," Franklin muttered under his breath,

Gunner's eyes lasered in on Franklin. "I'm sorry. Did you have something you wanted to share with the group, Mr.

Blaas?" he asked. When Franklin looked down and shook his head, Gunner smiled widely. "I didn't think so."

"Now, where is our executive housekeeper, Rosie Flowers?" he asked. "Interesting name."

"I am here, sir, but it is Rosemary or Miss Flores, please," she said amiably and stood up. "I do not like being called Rosie, and my last name is—"

"Well then, Rosie," he interrupted, smiling. His teeth glistened in the overhead lights. "I don't see a need for you to be in these meetings. Your place is keeping the ship clean, so why don't you scoot down to housekeeping and make sure that things are ship-shape?" He laughed out loud, but no one joined him. "Oh, and Rosie, I plan to go over your department with a fine-tooth comb. I'm sure that you will want to make it proper before my inspection. We will also discuss guest room cleanliness. I know you took some classes and did some homegrown teaching with your staff, Rosie, but I am here now to set the standards. There were also a few issues in my room that we will discuss." He looked at her and waved his hands as if he were shooing an annoying dog away. "Run along now," he said, and with those words, Rosemary, a senior member of the team for over a decade, was summarily dismissed. Lips pursed, Rosemary made an about-face and walked out, glancing at Franklin, whose face was almost purple with rage.

Gunner rapped the table with his knuckles to get everyone's attention as they had all been distracted by Rosemary's exit from the room. "Now to our little beauty shop director, Millie Casino." Kennedy thought Gunner's behavior was strange. He knew who Kennedy was, and Rosemary had just been dismissed, which only left Mila. "Mille, where are you?"

"It's Mila Casimir," Mila said, looking defiantly at him.

"Ah yes, right," Gunner said and smirked. "Millie, dear, there is no reason for you to be here either, is there? You aren't exactly operations, are you?" He cocked his head. "Your little beauty parlor is more like the sprinkles on a cupcake." He gave her a sick smile. "Nice, but not necessary, although I look forward to my complimentary spa treatments while on board. And you should know that I intend to try them all. I need to ensure our guests are receiving their money's worth, after all," he said self-importantly.

Mila spoke up hesitantly, "But Mr. Atcher—"

"Gunner, please call me Gunner," he said, chuckling, "after all, there won't be much of me you won't see after my manscaping." Mila blanched, and Franklin and the other men looked as if they were going to be sick.

Mila recovered and sat up straight, looking at her spreadsheet. "Gunner, I am sorry, but the spa is booked solid, I am pleased to say. As of departure, every time slot has been taken by paying guests." She looked him in the eye. "I guess people on this cruise like sprinkles on their cupcakes," she said frostily. "I don't know when I can fit you in for one treatment, let alone several."

"Oh, Millie," his chuckle sounded almost threatening. "I'm sure you can, and you will find openings. Because if I don't get to try out the spa, there may be no reason to have one at all." He held her gaze. "I'll stop by later, and we can discuss this one-on-one. I believe that once we have had an opportunity to chat, you'll better understand how things will work around here and what an asset I can be to you." Waving his hand, he dismissed her as he had Rosemary. "Now, run along, darling. Off you go to your little beauty shop."

Mila gave him a murderous look. "I suppose I'll run off now," she said sarcastically, looking daggers at Gunner. "Come see me," she mouthed to Kennedy and stalked out.

The door slammed shut. Turning back to the group at the table, Gunner rubbed his hands together. "As it appears that the corporate office did not send my bio or you chose not to read it, I will share a little about myself." He looked at those left in the room. "I am an expert in all things hospitality. My opinions have been sought out by some of the biggest names in the hotel and resort world. I have been offered many jobs, but I have turned them all down for the challenge of taking this mom-and-pop cruise line from its drab reputation into something spectacular." He became very animated. "Cruisers want excitement," he said. "They want sex and big-name entertainment, not some low-budget version of whatever Broadway musical some high school drama club is putting on." He paused, realizing that Kennedy was still in the room. "Oh, Kennedy, I didn't see you sitting there. Would you be a babe and get us all some coffee? I think this meeting is going to go long. You don't mind, do you?" He pulled off his jacket and stared at her.

Kennedy, initially, did not realize she had been dismissed from the meeting, but his words played through her head as she rose. She stood and walked out of the room with every ounce of dignity she had in her body. Standing in the corridor, shaking with rage but holding her head high, she seethed. "It will be a cold day in hell before I return with any coffee, babe," she hissed.

An hour later, the single word, "ten," went out across the radio. Only those who had been in the meeting knew what it meant. Walking quickly, but not so quickly as to make a guest feel something was wrong, the team met on the forward end of the promenade deck. Years ago, they had chosen this spot as a place to meet. It was far removed from the usual haunts of the passengers, crew, and staff.

"That man is impossible," Omar said, punching his fist into his hand. "I thought I was going to have to place him under arrest for fraud after hearing his stories."

Franklin growled. "How about if I wrap duct tape around his mouth and place him in one of the laundry bags in the boiler room?"

Tony opened the bottle of antacid he kept in his pocket and shook out two tablets. He looked at the three women. "I could not believe how he spoke to all of you," he said. "I thought the days of treating women that way were over."

Franklin shook his head slowly and looked at each of them. "What is the board thinking? I am sure that the way he spoke to us is not how he spoke to them, which concerns me. What kind of picture will he paint of us to the corporate office and the board?"

Kennedy wrapped her arms around herself. "Guys, we heard it from him and Mr. Phillips. He has the backing of the board," she said solemnly. "Which means we have no allies in the corporate office now. The only thing we can do is to take care of our guests the best way we know how."

"And smiling pretty girl sprinkle smiles," Mila said in a high, breathy, sarcastic voice.

Kennedy chewed on her lower lip. "We have to get through this cruise together as a team. When the corporate office launches another ship, he'll be on that one."

"We need to warn the others," Mila said.

"Let's wait a few days," Franklin said cautiously. "Let's see what happens before we say anything to anyone."

Rosemary was still steaming, and it had taken a while for her to calm down enough to speak. "He called me Rosie even after I asked him not to. He said my training was homegrown. I trained with professionals in the industry. And when he told me I needed to go down to my department to make it spic-in-span for his inspection, I wanted to punch his face," she spat out. "Let's go ahead and throw him overboard now."

Franklin was troubled. "I don't care for the way he belittles people. He believes it makes him look powerful." He looked at Mila, Rosemary, and Kennedy. "And count yourselves lucky that you were dismissed. After all of you left, we were forced to listen to him recount every moment of his career. He had the audacity to tell us he was, and this is no exaggeration, 'God's gift to hospitality'."

Omar picked up the conversation. "He just went on and on about himself, oblivious to the fact that we have responsibilities. It's clear he has no level of awareness."

Mila began to giggle, and they all turned to look at her. "Oh, my goodness," she said, laughing uncontrollably. "He's a goat."

"A what?" Tony looked at Mila, who was now doubled over and laughing uncontrollably. "A goat? What are you talking about?"

Mila wiped her eyes as she calmed down. "Listening to you talk about how he shared how great and wonderful he believes himself to be, made me think of a customer we had in Las Vegas. We would write the word GOAT or draw a picture of one next to his name in the appointment book so the others would know who it was. This guy would come into the spa acting self-important, telling us how great he was, how his bosses thought he was the greatest of all time. He believed the company he worked for, a multi-million dollar casino resort, would fold without him." She took a breath. "Thinking about the meeting and listening to you talk about what happened after we left, it hit me. Gunner Owen Atcher believes he is the *greatest of all time*. He's a goat!" Mila began laughing hysterically again.

Tony, who ran the dining room, looked morose and ate a few more antacids. "It's great you can make a joke, Mila, but what are we going to do?" he asked. "He said he has been given carte blanche to fire people. I need every dime I make to send home to my family. I can't have my job threatened because some guy who read an article in a magazine thinks he knows how to run a ship's dining room. A ship's dining room is quite different from a hotel restaurant. It takes finesse."

"None of it's the same," Franklin said. "Yes, hotels and cruise ships are similar, but they are like third cousins. When something happens on the ship, we have to deal with the situation right then and there. There is no calling someone from the outside to help or to pass it off at shift change and go home. We deal with obnoxious guests, harsh weather, faulty equipment, and staff that get off at a port and never come back, twenty-four hours a day, seven days a week, for six months at a time. And we handle it," he snapped his fingers, "like magic. This, my friends, is why some work in the cruise industry and others stay on land." He looked at each of them. "I promise we will get through this one way or another."

"Or," said Omar ominously, "we're going to find new places to work."

"Hey, where is Chef Michèle?" Kennedy asked anxiously. "He's one of us. Why isn't he up here?"

Omar chuckled. "Oh," he said with a mischievous smile, "Mr. Atcher decided that the kitchen was the first department he wanted to visit as he knows everything about the culinary world."

"But we are preparing for the Captain's Dinner! The first one!" Kennedy exclaimed.

"Chef Michèle tried to tell him, but Gunner didn't care."

Rosemary shook her head sadly. "Oh no, that is not going to be pretty. Chef Michèle is volatile on a good day. I had hoped he would mellow some, but he returned feistier."

Kennedy was thoughtful. "Well, he's not the most pleasant person, but *he is* one of us."

Franklin snorted. "I would never use the word pleasant to describe Michèle, but he is an amazing chef. I'll take his hostility for a taste of his bouillabaisse any day. People do not realize that he is a culinary artist and runs his kitchen with an iron hand."

"Only at first," Rosemary said softly. "In the beginning, the staff is petrified of him. He came up the old way, but they stay to learn from him." She smiled. "He's a softy when none of us are around. Behind that gruff exterior

is the heart of an angel."

"An angel?" Tony grunted and twisted his waist back

and forth. "More like a demon from hell. None of you have

to work with him."

Over the protestations of the executive chef, Gunner had

decided his first one-on-one visit would be to the kitchen. He

was, after all, a former food and beverage director and knew

it would not be difficult to find something wrong in the

space. "Sloppy housekeeping around the soup kettles," he

said, running a finger around the kettle's base. He held the

finger up for Mr. Phillips to see, and although Mr. Phillips

could see nothing on Gunner's finger, he dutifully wrote

down the man's words. "We should cut the staff in half to up

our profit margin," Gunner rattled off and then turned around

and looked at Mr. Phillips over the top of his glasses. "The

menu will need to be evaluated for cost-cutting measures. We

should prioritize our idea to get rid of the formal dining

room. The cost savings alone will make the board agree with our plan, and it won't change the guest experience with our new demographic."

Gunner continued his walk, oblivious to the stares of the kitchen staff. He lifted pot lids and sniffed the contents, ran his hand across the stainless-steel countertop, and opened the doors to the walk-in refrigerators and freezers to peer inside. The staff decided Gunner was either very brave or very stupid to be in Chef Michèle's lair without an invitation.

Few dared to come into the galley. Chief Engineer Franklin would only set foot in the kitchen if Chef Michèle personally requested it. The dance between the two men was worthy of an Italian opera. Chef Michèle would first grumble about the length of time it took Franklin to appear. Franklin would ignore him and take his time unpacking his tools, laying each device on a towel. Then Franklin would get a cup of coffee and chat with whatever staff was around. Chef Michèle would yell at Franklin in Haitian, although no one was ever quite sure what he said. Franklin would turn red and roar back and begin to pack up his tools noisily. Michèle would then storm out, howling at the top of his lungs as he left the kitchen. The kitchen staff would count quietly to one hundred, and then one of them would walk over with Franklin's coffee, and he would begin to unpack his tools again. Later, Michèle would slink back in and place a dish near where Franklin was working. Franklin would eye the plate warily and take a bite, and as he chewed, a large smile would break out on his face. Then the two men would laugh and talk while the culinary team exhaled. The only other person tolerated in the space was Kennedy. Her visits always made Michèle smile. She complimented and fussed over his latest creations, telling him how lucky she and the passengers were to have someone with his talent on board. Chef Michèle would bask in the attentiveness, knowing full well that the attention came with a last-minute request, which he would always grant her.

Trying in vain to ignore Gunner and Mr. Phillips as they walked through his kitchen, Chef Michèle's voice got louder and sharper as he barked out his instructions for the Captain's Dinner. The culinary staff noticed that his eyes were beginning to bug out of their sockets, and his nostrils quivered with each breath he took. They looked at each other with nervous eyes as Gunner continued his walk through the kitchen, lecturing loudly to Mr. Phillips while Chef tried to speak over him to his team. Chef Michèle finally could take no more and whipped around to face Gunner and Mr. Phillips. He placed the piece of paper he had been holding on the counter. "May I help you?" he asked in his accented French.

"No, no, we just want to look around and observe, Chef," Gunner said, motioning to the staff standing in line at attention. "Please continue with your instructions."

Chef Michèle gave a curt nod. "Very good." He picked up a meat mallet and turned to face his staff. He smacked the mallet into the palm of his hand. "The chicken breasts for the piccata need to be—"

Gunner interrupted him. "Chef, you know I oversaw the food and beverage department at several of my resorts, right? I mentioned it earlier today in our meeting." He leaned back against the stainless-steel counter, crossing his arms. "In every place I worked, the chefs looked forward to my visits. They would say, 'Gunner, I don't know how we would have gotten through the day without you!' Every single one of them told me how much they looked forward to my visits to their kitchens," he said proudly. He pushed himself off the counter and touched a row of knives hanging on a magnetic bar. "I can give you a few pointers on your techniques."

The staff watched nervously as Michèle's eyes began to get larger, and he began to breathe harder through his nose. He passed the meat mallet quickly from one hand to another.

Gunner continued, "You have gotten down the basics, but you seem to be running this kitchen like a cafeteria, not a proper restaurant," he waved his hand around the room.

"Pardon me? Not a proper restaurant? What do you mean my kitchen isn't run properly?" he snapped defensively. He turned and began beating the chicken breast on the counter with the meat mallet. "I assure you, Mr. Atcher, that I am qualified to run this kitchen, and I run it as a proper ship's kitchen." His nostrils flared as he spoke, and the chicken breast in front of him began to look like a pile of pink mush. "No one, and I repeat, no one, has ever come into my kitchen and said words like these."

Gunner walked over to Chef Michèle, his body blocking the others from the conversation. "We both know that I am closer to being a real chef than you will ever be, aren't I?" he whispered near Michèle's ear. "If my information is correct, you began your career cooking on a cargo ship, and let's face it, it wasn't rocket science to feed that crew beans and rice, was it? You have no formal education of which I am aware. And while you may be able to wow the midlevel cruisers on this ship with your flambés and tableside cooking presentations, haute cuisine is a word you would have to look up in a dictionary, isn't it?" he said with a touch of arrogance. "As I said, the real chefs I have worked with told me every day they couldn't get through an evening without my expertise and assistance." The culinary team stood at attention, fearfully watching the exchange between their boss and the stranger. Gunner walked over to stand in front of them. "Now, I want to review the menu for tonight's dinner. As the future vice president of this company, what comes out of the kitchen will reflect far more on me than it does on you."

Chef Michèle snapped his fingers and pointed at the paper he had left on the counter. Ano, the sous chef, picked it up and handed it to Gunner. He squinted at the paper and pulled it back and forth. "There are so many grease stains on this menu I can barely read it," he complained and sighed disgustedly. "I suppose it will have to do." He looked again at the menu with distaste. "For future reference, this kitchen will have a clean menu posted and ready for my inspection at all times." He sniffed and continued to squint, pulling the menu back and forth. He seemed to be having difficulty reading it. Finally, he pulled out a red pen from his jacket pocket and bent over the stainless-steel countertop to write on the piece of paper. "You know," Gunner said, turning his head to Mr. Phillips while ignoring Chef Michèle, whose eyes were bugging out dangerously, "we may want to think about having a celebrity chef brought on board, someone to liven things up and get the passengers excited." He straightened, moved his eyeglasses to the top of his head, and turned around to face Michèle. "If we decide to go with a celebrity chef, you will share the title of executive chef with them." He paused. "After all, it is only a title. Having a celebrity chef with that designation will be good for marketing purposes."

Gunner began pacing. "Mr. Phillips, I like this idea. We should look at hiring a celebrity chef. Someone with a little scandal in their past…" He began snapping his fingers together. "I've got it! What if we found a music star who cooks and would be willing to do a concert? If they had a cookbook, it would be ideal. We could get them to do book signings, teach a cooking class, and put on a concert during the cruise. It's genius!" he said excitedly. Gunner put his glasses back on his nose and returned his attention to the menu on the counter, scribbling on it. "There," he said, putting the cap back on his red pen. He handed the paper to Chef Michèle. "These are the changes you need to make for tonight's dinner. I suggest you study them, so mistakes like these are not on the next menu." He clapped his hands and looked at the group. "Chop, chop, everyone!"

He leaned in and whispered in Michèle's ear, "I won't tell anyone about these mistakes. We'll keep this between us." He winked at Michèle. "I am sure that, like the others, you will become grateful for my guidance and corrections over time. If you had gone to a culinary school, you would have never made these blunders." He turned to Mr. Phillips. "Let's go to the dining room to see Mr. Gano," he said officiously.

There was stunned silence in the kitchen. The staff, unsure of what to do, stood there, afraid to move or even breathe, awaiting the impending volcanic eruption they were sure would come. Michèle snorted, holding the menu with red scribblings on it. He walked over to a trashcan and dropped the paper inside. "It's a shame it had so much grease on it," he said to the room. "I couldn't read the changes he made," he said with a wide grin. He returned to where the chicken breasts lay on the counter and picked up his meat mallet. After a few violent swings, what was left was another pile of pink mush. He turned and faced his staff. "Why are you all just standing there? We have a Captain's Dinner to prepare for," he said briskly. "You heard the man, chop, chop," he said, clapping his hands and laughing. Realizing he would not erupt, the staff began scurrying to their stations as Michèle barked out orders.

Tony Gano, the dining room manager, had worked himself up into a nervous frenzy as he awaited Gunner's arrival. Gunner had told Tony to expect him for their one-on-one directly after he met with Chef Michèle. Tony paced the dining room and alternated between twisting his torso, flapping his suit coat, grabbing his lower back, and checking his watch. His stomach was doing backflips worthy of an Olympic gymnast, and he popped two antacid tablets into his mouth.

Tony's exhaustive attention to detail meant that the dining room ran flawlessly. He would pore over the manifest with Kennedy as soon as he received it to ensure that the seating chart was perfect. However, even after discussing it with Kennedy, he second-guessed his decisions. Tony felt that he owed a superior experience not only to the guests but also to Chef Michèle and the culinary team. Passengers would quickly forget about the food if the ambiance was poor. Before Tony opened the dining room doors each evening, he would personally inspect every table for spots on the silverware or water glasses. He would line the salt and pepper shakers side by side to ensure that the servers had filled them to the same height and that the linens were spotless. The staff liked teasing him that the antique silver crumb catcher in his jacket pocket had been his favorite toy as a baby, not a rattle.

Gunner entered the dining room through the double doors off the kitchen. He bent over a table and made a face. "Tsk, tsk, Mr. Gano, this room is not ready for guests," he chided, picking up a fork and squinting at it. He threw it back down on the table. "I expected better from you as the dining room manager. As you know, the dining experience is one of the highlights for these unsophisticated cruisers. Your staff has not even finished setting the tables. How did you propose to have them ready for my inspection if you had not checked them yourself?" he scolded. "This is very concerning," he sniffed.

Tony began to speak, "But sir, we are—"

Gunner's face suddenly turned dark red. "Never ever interrupt me! When it is time for you to speak, I will let you know," he thundered. Tony turned pale and fumbled in his pocket for the bottle of antacids he kept there. Gunner began pacing. "Mr. Gano, you will never know when I will inspect your work. It is your responsibility to always be prepared. I gave you ample opportunity to have this room ready, and as it is the first Captain's Dinner, I expected you to take more initiative." Gunner looked at his fingernails. "Although, I may suggest that we change the name to something else. Giving all the credit to the captain is a bit much, don't you think?" He cocked his head to the side. "Maybe we'll call it the President's Dinner."

Gunner sat down at a table and pushed the place setting forward. "I am certain that you have taken the opportunity to read my bio since our initial meeting today. What I told you in the conference room was just a smattering of my accomplishments." Tony came close to speaking, but the sting of Gunner's harsh words kept him silent. Gunner settled into the chair and leaned back. "Did you know I was once asked to be the general manager for a five-star restaurant in New York City?" He waved his hand dismissively. "I turned it down, of course, I had a better opportunity, but they came after me." He picked up the knife in front of him and turned it over on the table. "They wanted me for my attention to detail, reputation, and ability to make people work. In fact, once…" Gunner droned on and began telling Tony a story about another of his accomplishments.

Tony tuned out. He wondered how much longer Gunner would keep him hostage. There was so much to finish before the doors for tonight's dinner were opened, and he began to make a mental list, but suddenly his brain took a detour. He saw a pink slip slide under his cabin door, requesting that he pack his belongings and leave the ship, as he no longer worked for the company. Tony's thoughts raced from one thing to another, and he began to perspire as his heart beat faster. What would he do if he got fired? How would he face his family?

Gunner snapped his fingers in front of Tony's eyes. "Are you daydreaming while I'm here, giving up my valuable time to share vital information with you?" he scoffed. He turned to Mr. Phillips, who was seated at a table nearby. "We will want to note that a change in management may be necessary for this department," he said solemnly. "I, of course, have some ideas of who the replacement should be." He turned back to a visibly shaken Tony. "Please give me the seating chart for tonight. I'm sure there are mistakes as you appear to be very distracted, and some time has passed since you last made one." Gunner took out his red pen, and Tony handed him the clipboard.

Gunner shook his head at Tony. "I'm not sure how you got this position, Tony. Perhaps it's because you have been with the company for so long. I don't think you have the right skill set for the duties required to be a cruise ship dining room manager. Maybe something in a local restaurant would be more your speed." Gunner rambled on, making changes to the seating arrangements. "I will be watching you very closely tonight, Mr. Gano. I might be able to salvage something in you." He sighed heavily and looked at his fingernails. "Conceivably, under my tutelage, and if I have the time, I could perform a miracle, some kind of Pygmalion effect." Gunner handed the clipboard back with the changes he had made.

Tony looked at the seating chart, noting the marks in red. He didn't want to ask the question, but the words came out of his mouth before he could stop them. "Are you certain, sir?" he asked, swallowing hard.

Gunner looked daggers at Tony. "I am quite certain," he said evenly, narrowing his eyes. "And it would be in your best interest not to question me. Get these changes made immediately for all dinner seatings on this cruise." He muttered under his breath, and Tony heard what he said. "Perhaps certain passengers will not dismiss me so readily when they realize the power that I now hold." Tony could feel a cold sweat breaking out at his temples and neck. He ran a finger around the collar of his shirt, and his tie suddenly felt very tight. Gunner had made a war zone of the dining room with his changes. Vera Jameson had been moved to the worst table by the kitchen doors, which was likely to get Tony shot. And he had placed Mr. and Mrs. Butler at the captain's table, which would indeed have Tony walking the proverbial plank at dawn with the captain's sword at his back. It was a well-known fact that the captain rarely had anyone other than his senior staff at his table unless Kennedy cleared it with him.

"Mr. Atcher," Tony stammered, "I don't believe these changes will go over well."

Gunner looked at Tony and said indifferently, "Mr. Gano, I am not interested in your opinion. I am your superior, and I am telling you to make these changes. If you cannot make these adjustments, please tell me now so that we may inform the corporate office and the captain that you have relinquished your duties and that I will be doing your job until I can have your replacement here." He stood up to leave. "One more thing, Mr. Gano, we will not do the processional of servers tonight or ever again."

Tony was flabbergasted. "B-b-but Mr. Atcher, the captain requires that we do the processional. The servers have been practicing, and it's a tradition to do it at the Captain's Dinner. It is a signature of our ship."

"Mr. Gano," he said hotly, "once again, let me remind you of my position versus your position. If I tell you to remove it, you remove it. Surely, you can comprehend that. Don't do it!" He banged his fist on the table, causing the silverware to bounce. Gunner turned on his heel and stormed out of the dining room.

Mr. Phillips stood up quickly and closed his notebook, hurrying with his head down to follow Gunner. Kennedy was entering the dining room and passed Gunner on his way out. She could see he was visibly unhappy, but before she could utter a word, he snarled at her, "Miss Reeves, I have made modifications to tonight's dinner seating. You are not to alter them, do you understand?" He pointed a finger at her and said in a deadly tone, "I am serious. Anything done to reverse my orders will have you removed from the ship at the next port." He strode off, pushing the doors open forcefully.

Kennedy saw Mr. Phillips pass by her. He had heard the exchange between Kennedy and Gunner and kept his eyes forward, not looking at her. She took a few more steps into the dining room and saw Tony rocking back and forth in a chair. He had his arms wrapped around him. "I can't do this, I can't do this," she heard him say in a mantra.

Kennedy reached him and quietly said his name, not wanting to startle the man. "Tony, I just passed Mr. Atcher, and he told me he had made some changes to the seating chart and threatened my job if I did anything to alter it. What happened?"

Tony moaned and began to rock harder. "He's going to fire me!" He began to speak frantically. "My stomach is in knots. He is threatening to replace me with someone he knows if I go against his orders." Tony began to get hysterical and looked at Kennedy with wide eyes. "But on the other hand, if I go through with his changes, the captain will fire me." He laughed maniacally. "Either way, I'm fired!" He began giggling uncontrollably. "Why am I even here? What does it matter?" He cackled again and threw his hands up in the air. Kennedy saw panic and tears in his eyes.

Kennedy was concerned. Tony was a ball of stress on a good day, but it appeared he was going over the edge. She held out her hand and pointed to the clipboard. "Let's see what the changes are." Tony handed her the paper, which had red arrows and writing on it. She tapped her pencil on the clipboard. "Oh dear, I can see why this would be so upsetting." She looked Tony in the eye. "He's made some changes that could have some disastrous effects." She sat down and motioned Tony to sit beside her. "What if we do this," she pointed, "and this? I believe making those two changes will make it so that you won't get into trouble." She looked at him steadily. "If you do, blame me." She handed Tony back the clipboard.

"What about the processional?" he moaned.

Kennedy was confused. "What are you talking about, Tony? We'll do the processional the same as always. Especially tonight, it's the first cruise back."

Tony shook his head and said mournfully, "No, he told me we wouldn't do it anymore. He even said that he wanted to change the name of the Captain's Dinner and call it something else."

Kennedy sucked in a breath and took a moment. "I don't think you need to worry. Once I share this with the captain, he'll veto Mr. Atcher's decision. The parade of servers upholds tradition and is important to our returning guests and staff. And the last time I checked, this was the captain's ship, and his word is final until we hear otherwise from the corporate office."

Tony exhaled, visibly brightening at Kennedy's words. He had stopped rocking in his chair and stood up. "Oh, thank you, thank you. I didn't know how to think through what to do. But, Kennedy, this is only day one, and I'm terrified of what will happen. He keeps threatening my job. Should I get off in Nassau?"

Kennedy hugged Tony. "No! Absolutely not! I think he's just trying to shake us up."

Tony groaned miserably. "Well, he's certainly doing that to me. I'm so upset that I need to get another bottle of my antacids. My stomach is still doing backflips!"

Leaving the dining room, Gunner took the elevator to deck six. He wanted to see the spa he had heard so much about from Mr. Phillips. Gunner had sent Mr. Phillips back to his cabin to document his comments from the meeting with the leadership team and his one-on-ones with the executive chef and dining room manager.

Gunner intended to make his current girlfriend the *Helio's* new spa director. It would cement his relationship with her and allow him to keep tabs on the ship when he was not on board. However, he first needed to find a way to remove Mila. Mr. Phillips had shared that the spa director had been with the company for many years and was well-liked by the corporate office and the board of directors. When she came to them with the idea of renovating the spa, she also brought construction timelines, a budget, revenue projections, and a solid marketing plan. She had also dangled the idea of upgrading the other spas if Oaza turned a profit on time.

Gunner walked into the spa and saw that Oaza was busy with passengers milling about, buying retail items, and looking at the brochure. Although busy, the space exuded a sense of peacefulness. As Gunner walked around the retail area, he casually picked up items and put them down haphazardly. He was so taken aback by the busyness of the spa that he did not notice Sara, Oaza's newest team member, following him and putting back the items he was randomly setting down. Initially, Gunner had thought Mila was being difficult or boastful during the meeting when she told him there were no appointments available. However, looking at the number of passengers in the spa, he realized that Oaza was a moneymaker. It was clear to Gunner that much thought and consideration had gone into making a space that was both chic and tranquil and would make passengers want to spend their hard-earned money for the ultimate in pampering. Seeing a break at the reception desk, he quickly walked up to it.

Anna Marie, who had worked for Mila in the spa for several years, looked up from her computer screen, smiling graciously. "Hi, welcome to Oaza. How may I assist you?"

Gunner gave Anna Marie a devilish smile and leaned onto the countertop in front of her. He looked at her nametag. "Anna Marie is such a lovely name to go with a pretty girl. You must have tons of friends back home," he said in a silky voice. Anna Marie blushed at his words. Gunner smiled broadly. "I wonder, Anna Marie if I could be counted as one of your friends? A new one? And maybe you could get a new friend an appointment for tomorrow?" He gave her a sheepish grin, "I was supposed to make one before I got on board, but I got busy and forgot. And now," he trailed off and sighed sadly, "well, you can feel how desperate I am for a facial." He picked up her hand and rubbed it on his face.

Anna Marie pulled back her hand quickly and looked at her computer screen. She was unnerved that he put her hand on his face. She wanted to help, but Mila had reminded her that backing up appointments was a big problem. Saying no and offering an alternative was the best policy. She looked up at Gunner. "Oh gosh, I am so sorry, but we don't have any availability tomorrow, Mr.?" Anna Marie turned pink. "I'm sorry, I don't believe you told me your name."

"Surely you could find something for me?" Gunner felt his temper begin to flare. "Your new friend?"

"I'm sorry, I-I-I…"

"That's too bad, Anna Marie. As your new friend and one of the VIPs on the ship, I thought you might be a little more accommodating." He pushed himself away from the desk and saw Anna Marie's puzzled look. "Didn't Mila tell you that the company's new vice president was on board?" Anna Marie shook her head. Mila had gone straight to her office after the staff meeting and was now in one of the treatment rooms giving a massage. "You ought to make a point of knowing who the VIPs are on the ship. Mila may not care, but you should. You need to know if one person is more important than another. It would make your job easier, especially when one of them is standing in front of you." A line was forming behind Gunner, and Anna Marie was getting uncomfortable. Sensing her concern over the line behind him, he decided to push the envelope, hoping she would cave in. He pushed back from the desk. "Anna Marie, I'm the new vice president, and now that you understand who I am, why don't you look again? I'm certain you can find an opening for me," he said with a touch of arrogance and poked his forefinger at her computer.

Anna Marie's face went from pink to bright red, making her freckles disappear. "I am very sorry, but I don't have any openings tomorrow; however, may I try to find a suitable time for you another day?" she asked apologetically and looked at him pleadingly.

Gunner shook his head, irritated that the young woman did not understand that she should do what he said. "No, that will not work for me, Anna Marie. Evidently, you don't understand me. As the vice president of the cruise line, if I tell you I need an appointment, you move someone else to fit me in. Got it?" he hissed. The guests in the line were beginning to get impatient at the wait, and several stepped out of line and placed the items they had wanted to purchase down. Anna Marie looked worriedly as they left. Gunner placed his hands on the countertop, not budging. "Let's try this again, Anna Marie, and I'm going to talk slowly so you can understand me. Find me an appointment for tomorrow, and I don't care who gets bumped," he said testily, stabbing a finger on the countertop for emphasis. "And if you don't find an appointment for me, I'll have you sent back to whatever small hick town you call home, and you can find a job there." He glared at her. "Now that you understand how this works, do you think you can find an opening?"

Anna Marie's face began to crumble. Her lower lip quivered, and tears welled in her eyes, making their way down her plump cheeks. "Well?" Gunner asked, and Anna Marie took one more look at Gunner's scowl and fled the reception area. When she reached the door that led to the locker and private treatment rooms, she opened it and ran through it. The door slammed behind her with a loud bang. Mila was quietly closing the door to the room where she had just given a massage when she heard the door slam and saw Anna Marie sobbing against the wall.

"Anna Marie? What's wrong? Why aren't you at the reception desk? Oh, honey, what is wrong?" she asked as Anna Marie's shoulders began to shake.

Anna Marie turned around and looked at Mila. Her ordinarily happy face was blotchy, tear-stained, and miserable. "That man, h-h-he's horrible, Mila," she hiccupped as a fresh batch of tears made tracks down her face.

Mila was confused. "Who's terrible, Anna Marie? Wait, is anyone out at the desk? Who is taking care of the customers?" Mila took a few steps and opened the door to see Sara at the desk with a guest. There were no other men in the spa except Gunner, who was in the retail space. She turned back to Anna Marie, whose shoulders shook as a fresh batch of tears fell from her eyes. Mila was used to Anna Marie's tender feelings, but the young woman had never deserted the desk. "Tell me what happened, Anna Marie," she said soothingly.

"I was nice," Anna Marie hiccupped again. "I apologized, I offered to find another time for him, but he threatened to fire me if I didn't bump someone and give him an appointment. I didn't know he was a VIP!" Tears welled in her eyes. "Please don't let him fire me. Don't let him put me off the ship. I don't know how I would get home, I…"

Mila, hearing Anna Marie's words about being fired, knew that Gunner was the reason for the young woman's tear-stained face. She took long, slow, deep breaths trying to get Anna Marie to imitate her. Mila looked at her receptionist with a calm face. "It's going to be okay. I'm going to go out there and take care of this." She hugged Anna Marie and turned her around. "I want you to go into the restroom to collect yourself and wash your face. Then go to the yoga studio and do some deep breathing exercises. Come back and join me at the desk when you feel recentered."

Anna Marie offered her a weak smile. "Okay," she said. "I'm so sorry, Mila, he was just so awful."

Mila gave her a warm smile. "Go. I'll see you in a few minutes when you feel better."

Mila walked through the door to the reception area and felt that every eye in the spa was on her. Gunner looked up and crooked a finger beckoning her. "Mr. Atcher, I am very sorry. It seems we have a misunderstanding."

Gunner snorted. "No misunderstanding. I told you I needed an appointment, and you ignored me. And for some reason, you haven't explained to your staff who I am," he said self-importantly, not caring that everyone in the reception area could hear him.

Mila did not want the guests to hear the conversation, which was quickly escalating. It was no wonder Anna Marie had fled in tears to the back. While it went against her better nature, she decided it would be best to make an exception. She lowered her voice to a whisper, "Mr. Atcher, I explained earlier that I did not have any openings, but as you seem insistent, it would be my pleasure to move some things around to make room for your appointment. What time would you prefer?"

Gunner waved his hand dismissively. "Just find a time. I will apparently have to work around you, although rearranging my schedule will be inconvenient." He took out

his red pen, scribbled something on one of the brochures, and

thrust it at Mila. He recapped the pen and began to walk out

of the reception area, stopped at the entry, and turned around.

"You may want to explain to your staff that I am grading all

of you. Based upon my impression so far, the entire spa has

an F," he said in a voice loud enough to be heard by everyone

in earshot. "If your spa associates can't manage something as

mundane as an appointment, what else might they be unable

to manage? The good news is that as dismal as the customer

service was today, it can only go up, and I know the perfect

person who can make that happen," he smirked. He walked

back over to Mila and looked down his nose at her. "It

shouldn't be hard to convince the corporate office to hire

her." He then turned his attention to the passengers in the

retail area and locked eyes with a few of them. "It is a shame

to have a beautiful spa but such terrible customer service.

Such a shame," he shook his head and walked out of Oaza.

Mila turned around and plastered a smile on her face.

She walked to the reception desk and tried to make eye

contact with several guests, but they would not meet her eyes. The downcast gazes told her what she already knew. Gunner had just given the spa a public black eye. She smiled lopsidedly. "I'm so sorry, everyone, opening day insanity," she trilled. "Sara, will you get some champagne for everyone? I believe we can get rid of this negativity with some bubbles."

Later that day, after Oaza had closed, Mila and her team met to review the next day's appointments. "Okay," she said, looking down at the book. "That brings us to Mr. Atcher: a men's facial, hydrating mask, and a manicure," Mila laughed uncomfortably, "goodness, that's a lot of spa time. Any volunteers?" she asked, looking around the room. "Anyone?" she asked weakly and sighed. "It's okay, ladies. I understand completely. I will—"

"I will," a voice spoke up. "I'll take care of Mr. Atcher," Sara announced.

Mila exhaled a sigh of relief. "Sara, thank you for volunteering. Are you sure? I'm happy to take care of him. He may be difficult."

Sara shared a look with Anna Marie and then turned her attention to Mila. "I don't have anything to lose. I'm new, and if he fires me, he fires me. I promise it won't be the end of the world for me," she said. "I've been fired before, and the world didn't come to a crashing halt." She realized that her hands were clenched in her lap. She forced them open and patted her thigh.

Mila cleared her throat. "Okay, as Sara volunteered to take care of Mr. Atcher, who will take her shift at the desk?" she asked cheerfully, and several voices piped up.

Promptly at seven o'clock, Director of Security Omar Meier knocked on Mrs. Vera Jameson's cabin door. Kennedy had stressed the need for punctuality as Vera was known for her intolerance of tardiness. Omar smiled and assured Kennedy that he would be at Vera's door at the appointed time. Kennedy was unaware that punctuality had been drilled into him as a young boy in boarding school, where he learned to be on time or face the consequences. He was curious why

Mrs. Jameson had specifically requested him as her companion for the evening. In the past, one of the ship's officers would squire her for cocktails, take her to see the bridge, and then whisk her off to dinner. He asked Kennedy why Mrs. Jameson had requested him for this duty, and she explained that Vera had seen him when she and Franklin had passed in the corridor and had called Kennedy with the request, citing that he had eluded her on previous cruises. Omar believed his friend Franklin had some part in Vera's gentle demand.

Vera answered the door wearing a long, turquoise green, raw silk dress, which hung loosely on her frame. Around her neck were blue-green fire opals, which matched the gown perfectly. Omar noticed the enormous four-carat marquis cut diamond ring she wore on her left hand. "Good, you are prompt, Mr. Meier," she said crisply, "I appreciate that in a person."

Omar smiled and extended his hand to her. "At your service, Mrs. Jameson. I look forward to being your escort this evening."

Vera cackled and motioned for him to come into the cabin. "Oh, let's be frank, Omar, as we will be in each other's company all evening. We both know you aren't looking forward to this at all, but you will do it because it was requested, and being a man with manners instilled in him, you would not deny a request. You are the kind of gentleman who takes great pains to make certain your guest is happy, no matter the personal cost to you."

Omar chuckled; she had him pegged. "Mrs. Jameson, I am at your command. May I help you with your coat?" he motioned to the matching piece on the chair.

"Ever the gallant, Mr. Meier." As he held out the lightweight silk wrap for her to put on, Omar caught the scent of her perfume. It was a curious mixture of sandalwood and citrus, which surprised him. He had figured Vera would use a classic scent, not one as earthy as the one she wore.

Stepping into the corridor, he offered her his arm. "Where would you like to go for our cocktail, Mrs. Jameson?" He began to make suggestions, "We could go up to the observation deck, take in the view and a drink in the Libation Lounge, or—"

"Omar," Vera interrupted, "first, let's dispense with calling me, Mrs. Jameson. I would like not to feel like I am in some Victorian novel." He nodded, and the corners of his lips turned up in amusement. "Next, I'm going to be honest," she said. "I am dying for a cigar. I have not had one since I got on board because I couldn't figure out where to go, and I didn't want to smoke in my stateroom until I saw if there were any lilies in the flower arrangements to take. Is there somewhere an old woman like me can have a cigar and an old-fashioned?" she asked almost pitifully.

Omar was taken aback by her request. "Mrs. Jameson, Vera, I would be happy to escort you to the smoker's lounge and would be delighted to get you an old-fashioned." They walked down the corridor toward the elevators. "I believe Luke, whom you may remember from previous cruises, is working in Vantage Point tonight, and it is near the new smoking lounge."

Vera nodded her head, stepping into the elevator. "That will suffice. When you get my drink, please make certain to tell Lucas it is for me. I'd like to see if he remembers how to make it correctly."

Vera and Omar arrived on deck nine, and he guided her to the back of the ship. They rounded the corner, and Vera stopped in her tracks, gasping at the smoker's lounge standing in their path. "Dear God," she said, aghast. "It looks like a very expensive birdcage!"

The octogen-shaped room was a recent addition to the ship to give passengers a comfortable place to smoke. Oiled teak bars hugged the outside of the structure from the floor up four feet and then started again at ten feet, climbing to the ceiling. The six-foot glass allowed anyone walking around the lounge to see inside. Chestnut brown, buttery-soft leather barstools rimmed the blue-veined quartz bar, which abutted the glass walls on three sides. In the center of the small lounge, plush dark blue velvet swivel chairs sat across from each other, flanked by teak tables. Once Omar heard Vera's description, he could not remove the image of a birdcage from his mind. It was true; passengers would be able to walk by and gape at the occupants, making those inside feel like they were caged birds on display.

"Vera, I will leave you here to allow you some solitude to enjoy your first smoke of the cruise while I fetch your old-fashioned." He bowed and left.

Vera sat in one of the navy-blue swivel chairs and pulled a cigar case and cutter from her beaded purse. She smiled, looking at the two pieces which had been a gift from her late husband. His giving them to her was one of the few times Harvey had gotten the upper hand and stunned Vera into silence.

Vera clipped the end of the cigar and lit it. She savored the aroma as it swirled out of the end of the cigar. The smell took her back to the day Harvey had presented the pieces to her. Vera had been seated at the dining room table, waiting for him to arrive so dinner could be served. Harvey had walked into the room, placed a light kiss on Vera's head, and laid the silver monogrammed case and lighter on her place setting. He continued to his seat, sat down, and drained his water glass. The room was silent as Vera looked from the items in front of her and back at her husband. Finally, she rang the bell for the maid to bring the salads to the table.

After the maid left, Harvey cleared his throat. "I presume these will meet with your needs?" He pointed at the items in front of Vera, and she nodded her head, not daring to speak. She was curious about what was to come. Harvey cleared his throat again and steepled his fingers. He looked directly at Vera. "Very well. In the future, please do not pilfer my cigars. We lost a good gardener last week. I thought he had been the one taking my cigars. I lost my temper and fired him." He chuckled and looked at her shaking his finger. "When more went missing this week, I realized that you were the culprit." His laughter dissolved into a coughing fit, and he took a deep breath. "I went to his home, begged his forgiveness, and presented him with a box of cigars, and I asked that he come back to work. I have to pay him more money, but it is worth it. He's a damn fine gardener." He looked directly at Vera, who still had not said a word. "I shall keep you supplied with your cigars, Vera, but do not take mine," he said soberly. Then he picked up his fork and began to eat his salad while Vera sat there stunned into silence.

Omar returned to the smoker's lounge a few minutes later, carrying two glasses. In one hand, he held a crystal champagne flute with an orange peel floating in the tawny brown liquid. He had a rocks glass with two fingers of the same dark alcohol in his other hand. "Vera, I must ask," Omar said with confusion. "Why the champagne flute? Luke laughed out loud when I told him I needed an old-fashioned specifically for you. When he took down the champagne glass, I was almost afraid to bring you this." He handed her the cocktail.

Vera gave a slow smile as she took the champagne glass. "Well, if you must know," she said with an air of superiority, "I detest the feel of a wet glass, and they are forever getting condensation on them even if the drink is not on the rocks." She shook her head. "It's vulgar," she said distastefully. "And cocktail napkins disintegrate the moment you try to use one, so to keep my hands from having to touch a wet glass, I have this," she said, raising her flute. "It also makes the bartenders remember me," she winked.

<u>VERA'S OLD-FASHIONED</u>

½ TSP SUGAR

3 DASHES OF ORANGE BITTERS

1 TSP WATER

2 OZ BOURBON

ORANGE PEEL

ADD THE SUGAR AND BITTERS TO A ROCKS GLASS, THEN ADD WATER AND STIR UNTIL SUGAR IS NEARLY DISSOLVED. POUR INTO A CHAMPAGNE FLUTE, ADDING BOURBON AND STIRRING GENTLY TO COMBINE. EXPRESS THE OIL OF AN ORANGE PEEL OVER THE GLASS, AND DROP IT IN.

"What shall we drink to, Vera?" Omar asked.

Vera smiled. "I would like to drink to you, Omar," she said. "Beware the quiet man, for while others speak, he watches." She lifted her glass to him. "I don't know who said that, but somehow those words fit you as well as your suits. To you, Omar."

Omar nodded, accepting the compliment. "And, if I may?" Vera raised an eyebrow. "To Europe, where they believe that women get more attractive after thirty-five."

Vera burst out laughing. "Touché, Omar, well played." She clinked his glass with hers. They quietly savored the bourbon as it hit their tongues. The bourbon and the smell of Vera's cigar were a unique bouquet.

Omar broke the silence. "Tonight, Vera, this evening is about you, so let us speak of your company. Kennedy tells me that you are a businesswoman. I only know that you run a successful funeral company, which is quite unusual." He smiled at her disarmingly and sat back in his chair. "Please tell me about what you do."

Vera was surprised. She had not expected this. Far too often, people hid behind mindless small talk. "Some find it vulgar to discuss work, but I thrive on it," she said and sat back in her chair. "My husband inherited a small chain of funeral homes from his father as a young man. The funeral homes were in southern Alabama, and Harvey had learned the business at his father's knee." Vera sighed. "Harvey was a methodical businessman, and the company grew slowly but

steadily. By the time of his death, we had close to forty

funeral homes dotted throughout the South. It was a good

business, but our social life was dreadfully boring. People

shied away from inviting the funeral home director out for

parties, and Harvey was about as exciting as a can of paint.

So, when I first met Harvey and understood the kind of man

he was and the business he was in, I decided I could be

attracted to his money and would overlook his dullness."

Vera chuckled. "It wasn't until we had been married for a

few years that I realized a person could truly die of

boredom."

She looked squarely at Omar, who didn't seem to be

phased by her comment. "After Harvey died, I took over the

company, figuring if someone as dull as Harvey could do it,

someone with my drive could do it better. I had taken care of

the books, but I didn't know a thing about what happened on

the front end. Then, shortly after my second year of taking

the reins, a member of our circle called and asked for a

private meeting with me. He explained that he was battling

terminal cancer and had one last request. He wanted to be buried in the Cadillac he had restored and to be seated in the car's front seat in one of our rooms while his friends and family paid their respects. At first, I was stunned, but my greed for money took over when he told me he would pay top dollar to have his last request followed to the letter. He loved the car. It gave him a sense of purpose when his family had no use for him. She fluttered her eyelashes and shrugged her thin shoulders. "Who was I to say no?"

"A year later, he died, and the hospital contacted the funeral home to collect the body for the funeral preparations. I made sure our attorney was close by when the family arrived. I explained to the new widow that the man had come to us to discuss his arrangements, and, while unorthodox, we were duty-bound to uphold his last wishes. After I had explained what he had paid for, she became enraged and stormed out of the office, threatening lawsuits. Fortunately, her attorney read the contract and agreed it was a legal agreement, having been paid in full, and made in his right mind." Vera took a long drag on the cigar and let out a large puff of smoke. "After the funeral, I was ostracized by my social circle, but I found I didn't care." She leaned forward and looked Omar in the eye. "I had figured out a way to grow the company. Providing people with a funeral based upon their last wishes."

Omar was stunned. He could not believe the words coming from Vera.

"Funerals are funny. People either plan them knowing that death is inevitable, or they put it off, not wanting to confront the end." She waved her cigar. "I allow people to have the last word. We've had car funerals, Viking funerals, a tiki bar with karaoke, a book reading, quite a few cocktail parties, and one unusual one with the ashes of the deceased mixed in with fireworks. That one took some research." Vera held up her hands in supplication. "Death will happen to each of us, and if someone wants an unconventional funeral, why not give them what they want and make a profit? It's supply and demand in a sense."

Omar shook his head. "Do you find this unconventionalism tasteless?" he asked.

Vera knit her eyebrows together. "Who am I to judge?" she asked. "I will admit, I have found some distasteful, but for the most part, they are tame, and money is money. You see, Omar, when confronted with death, people want one last moment of control over something they have no control over. One last time to call the shots. Death visits each of us in its own time. Isn't there a song about being nothing more than dust in the wind? It was one of Harvey's favorite songs. Dreadful, in my opinion. If I happen to hear it on the radio, I quickly turn it off."

"How is the company doing with the options you now offer?" Omar asked, still in shock at her candor.

Vera sat back in her chair and gave him a satisfied smile. "My company is now worth thirty times what it was the day Harvey died, and I have at least one funeral home in every state. The tabloids poke fun at what we offer, but I'm the one who laughs all the way to the bank."

Omar was dumbfounded. Vera had a level to her that he had not been prepared for. He had believed her to be another spoiled, wealthy woman used to getting her way.

Omar knew it was impolite, but he had to ask, "Do you think Harvey is rolling in his grave at the unusual methods you now offer and growing his father's company in a way he never dreamed of?"

Vera smirked. "Oh, Omar, even on his best days, Harvey never gave anything more than a twitch," she cackled.

They sat silently, absorbing the conversation as Vera's cigar smoke swirled around the room. "Tell me something, Omar," she said. "I believe it was Abraham Lincoln who said, 'It has been my experience that those who have no vices have very few virtues'." She stared at him. "What is your vice? You can clearly tell what mine are," she said, pointing to the bourbon and the cigar in the ashtray.

Omar smiled at her devilishly. "Oh, madam, I have both vices and virtues, but as a gentleman, I would not wish to be indiscreet with a lady such as yourself." He sat back and smiled secretively. "Let us continue to enjoy our bourbon, the view, and the company. I fear we only have a brief time alone before I must escort you to dinner."

"There you go with that Victorian prose again," she laughed. "You win."

Twenty minutes later, they stood to leave. Vera placed her hand on Omar's arm. She suddenly seemed quite vulnerable. "Am I inappropriate, Omar? I forget that not everyone is as brash as I can be, and I know I can be off-putting. I'm not often in polite society anymore."

Omar gave her a devilish smile and patted her hand. "Vera, I think you are the perfect amount of inappropriate. Just enough to keep us on our toes." He laughed and opened the door, and they began to walk to the main dining room.

There was a feeling of excitement and anticipation in the air as the passengers entered the main dining room. Bert took photos of the guests and explained where they would find their photos the following day in the lobby. The Captain's Dinner was a long-standing tradition for the cruise line, harkening to the company's first passenger ship. Kennedy never tired of the dinner. She believed the formality of the night gave the cruise an air of sophistication and a touch of romance. Ordinary men looked debonair in their dinner jackets and tuxedos as they escorted elegant women wearing a sea of shimmering and colorful gowns.

Kennedy caught her breath when she entered the dining room. Her mother's dinners were always beautiful, but the room tonight made Lolly's tables seem ordinary. The silverware gleamed in the softened lighting, and the ivory tablecloths and napkins edged in oxford blue set off the dark blue and gold on the china. The room was simply breathtaking. The staff stood at attention, awaiting the arrival of their guests. They, too, were giddy with anticipation and looked impeccable in their ivory dinner jackets trimmed in navy and gold at the lapel to match the china and linens. Kennedy strolled through the dining room, checking place cards to ensure no one had moved them around. The seating of certain guests was critical and placing Vera by the kitchen door would have had disastrous ramifications. Then, feeling confident in the evening, she went to see how Bert was faring with his photography.

The Club Diva Boys had just arrived to take their photos, and Kennedy grinned. Bert spoke into his recorder and motioned for them to step into the photo area. "Gentlemen, you look spectacular, and your outfits are the epitome of sophisticated style." They laughed, lining up for their individual photos.

Don, the shoe store owner, went first. He placed his shoe on the chair and grinned, showing off the leopard print loafers and the fuchsia and gold socks he was wearing. "Aren't these to die for?" Don asked, beaming. "I had to have them the moment I unboxed them in the store and knew that someday I would wear them," he said, laughing. "I just didn't know it would take this long!" Bert captured Don's smile as he depressed the shutter.

Phil was next in line, wearing a gray plaid tuxedo with an aqua and gray checked bow tie. Steve followed in a black jacket, herringbone pants, a mint green socks with flamingos. The group hooted when he showed his socks. "It's only a little flair, and Don insisted," he blushed.

Robert, always the traditionalist, looked like James Bond in a white dinner jacket and leered at the camera as he tugged on his cuffs theatrically. Dave was the last of the group in a black coat and yellow paisley vest.

"Where is John?" Kennedy scanned the area for the last member of the group. "You can't do your group shot without him."

Don waved his hand. "Running late as usual. He loves to make an entrance." He turned to hear several passengers grumble and saw John rushing toward them. "Oh, look, everyone, Mr. Entertainment has arrived, applause please!" They stood together and politely golf clapped as John swaggered up to Bert to have his photo taken. John wore a sapphire blue velvet suit with an orange ascot at his neck. His white rhinestone-studded sunglasses winked in the lights.

"Didn't we see that suit on one of the red-carpet events?" Steve asked.

"Perhaps," John sniffed and pulled down his glasses. "But let's face it, accessorizing it with the orange ascot makes it look trendy rather than dull like the guy who wore it with a black tie." He turned in place. "Admit it. I look so much better in it, don't you think?"

"You might want to reconsider that line of thought," Dave said, looking John up and down.

"It seems that someone has been hitting the SunRumbrellas a little too hard if he believes that," Robert sang out and plucked a pink paper umbrella from John's ear.

"Ladies, ladies, you're all pretty," clucked Phil. "Can we please have Bert take our group shot with Kennedy before the other guests form a mob and throw us overboard?" He pointed his bald head at the line. Kennedy threw her head back laughing and stood in the middle of the group. After Bert took the picture, they walked to the dining room.

"Let's get you seated," she said, looking at the seating chart, and they followed her to their table.

Walking back to the podium, she saw Vera and Omar arriving. Vera looked stunning in her turquoise gown, and Kennedy smiled as they glided past her. "You'll pay for this," Omar mouthed and winked as he guided Vera to her table near the captain's. Kennedy felt a shiver run down her spine.

Once it seemed that all the passengers who were dining were present, per custom, the captain and first officers entered with the stateliness of a king and his knights. They sat down, and Tony looked to the captain, who nodded. The house lights dimmed, and a spotlight hit the dining room doors as exciting music began to play. In the past, when this happened, the dining room doors would burst open, and the servers would parade through the dining room with domed trays on their gloved fingertips to the applause of the passengers. The servers would then go back into the kitchen, pick up the culinary team's appetizer and present it to their tables. However, when the spotlight hit the doors, and the music began, it was not the ivory jacketed staff that stood there as the doors opened, but Mr. and Mrs. Jones Butler, who stood there like lit Christmas trees as the spotlight hit the thousands of rhinestones on their outfits. Each person in the dining room let out a gasp, and Kennedy's stomach dropped to her knees.

"Oh my," Phil said breathlessly.

"Gracious," Steve murmured.

"You go, girl!" John said, guffawing and clapping his hands.

However, it was Vera Jameson who summed up what many were thinking. "Dear God, will someone please ask them to turn off the spotlight? I am almost blind."

Terri was wearing a denim and rhinestone evening gown. The open v at her mid-thigh showed off her tan legs, and encircling her neck was a three-inch high collar made entirely of rhinestones. Jones stood beside her in a red graffiti-splattered dinner jacket, black shirt, and white jeans. Unaware they had broken several social protocols for dinner,

Kennedy sighed inwardly, wondering how to manage the situation. Typically, arriving in the main dining room in denim and after the captain was seated would have had a guest turned away. Fortunately, the captain and Kennedy caught each other's eye, and with a quick nod from him, she walked quickly to the podium.

"Mr. and Mrs. Butler, you look dazzling tonight," Kennedy said with false enthusiasm. "But we need to get you seated right away to start the server's processional and the captain's first toast. I was delighted to see that I am sitting with you tonight." She began to walk them through the dining room.

As they walked, she could hear the murmurs and gasps of the other diners. When Kennedy passed Vera and Omar, she heard Vera say dryly, "I'm not surprised it's bedazzled. In their world, formalwear means that one needs to fire up the hot glue gun."

Terri looked miserable. "I'm so sorry," she whispered as she sat down. "It's the dress. I knew it. That's why they were all whispering and staring as we walked by." She shook her head. "I told Jones this dress was not right for tonight, but he insisted when he saw it in one of the celebrity magazines." Kennedy looked at her sympathetically.

"Sweetsie, I wish you wouldn't worry," Jones drawled loudly. "Those stuffy old biddies wish they looked as good as you. They know it, and I know it." He was drowned out as the spotlight hit the entryway again, and the music began to swell. This time, the *Helio* servers stood ready in the doorway for their parade.

Once the parade ended, the captain walked to the center of the room to give his toast. He welcomed the passengers and thanked them for choosing to spend their holiday on the *Helio*. Kennedy heard a commotion as the captain addressed the audience and saw Gunner speaking noisily to Tony at the podium. Kennedy could deduce through the body language and gesticulations that Gunner was livid about the parade and the seating changes.

"And why did we do the parade?" Gunner hissed loudly, slamming his hand down on the podium, making several guests seated nearby jump. "I specifically told you to remove the parade. It's a joke." The guests sitting near the podium turned their heads to glare at Gunner, as it was clear they could not hear the captain over the commotion he was creating.

"Ahem," the captain cleared his throat. "As I was saying, I want to thank each of you for coming out on the cruise. The staff and crew of the ship are as excited to be here as you are," and as he said those words, a server tripped, and a tray of wine glasses crashed to the floor. "Like I said," the captain laughed weakly, "we are very excited." He lifted his glass. "Please join me in a toast. To a wonderful and uneventful cruise." Kennedy groaned inwardly as she felt words like that were sure to invite trouble.

Dinner was a disaster of epic proportions. The servers who a year earlier had functioned like a well-timed clock were offbeat. Silverware clattered on trays, and glassware rattled as staff tried not to bump into one another. Then, when the soups and salads were being delivered, one of the servers tripped as he walked up the steps. He flew across the aisle, landing himself and a bowl of tomato soup in Marilyn's lap. Marilyn yelped and stood up quickly. "Oh, madam, I am so sorry," he said, mortified as all eyes in the restaurant turned toward Marilyn's white slinky dress that was now a tie-dyed mess of red and white. "I am so deeply sorry. How can I help?" he begged, trying to wipe the soup off her dress but succeeded in only making it worse. Marilyn wanted to weep but forced a smile on her face when she saw that the server was on the verge of tears.

"Well, Marilyn," quipped Dolly, looking around as people stared at their table, "that's one way to get a man to fall into your lap."

"Mother," Laura hissed through clenched teeth, "not another word. That is enough out of you. We don't need to call any more attention to what just happened. There's already been quite a bit of commotion tonight."

Dolly bounced on the banquette as she looked around the room. "Hasn't it been great? So far, it's been a show within a show," Dolly clapped her hands like a child. "The fight at the entry, Marilyn's young man falling for her, and the couple who resembled twin Christmas trees. Whatever

Kennedy has in store for her show tonight better be good because dinner has been a hoot."

To divert everyone's attention from the distractions, the captain decided that now would be the opportune time to introduce the ship's officers. He and the first officers went to the center of the room, where he briefly described what each officer did and allowed them a moment to speak. Generally, after the captain introduced the last officer, Chef Michèle and his staff would come out and take a bow. However, when the last officer stepped back, and the captain moved forward to introduce Chef Michèle, a thunderous crash came from behind the swinging doors. "I will not work with such an imbecile. I quit!" Chef Michèle screamed and threw his hat on the floor. He stormed out of the dining room.

The passengers were stunned and looked at each other. While it was no more than two seconds, it felt like a lifetime. Kennedy, who was to be introduced after Chef Michèle, quickly turned on her microphone. "Ladies and gentlemen, while I have met many of you, I would like to introduce myself formally. I am Kennedy Reeves, your cruise director, and it appears that Chef Michèle is suffering from some stage fright tonight and cannot take his well-deserved bow, but let's give him and his talented culinary crew a huge round of applause." As the applause died away, she continued, "I would like to invite all of you to see our main show tonight. Our entertainers have been working very hard to bring you a stage and song rendition of the musical *Mamma Mia*. For those who do not want to relive ABBA's greatest hits, we have several lounges, including the Vantage Point Lounge, the Lunar Lounge, Keys, our piano bar, and the casino, for your evening's entertainment. On behalf of the members of the *Helio* and the corporate offices of the Sunny Dayz Cruise Line, thank you for cruising with us, and we beg your forgiveness as we get our sea legs back." She waved to the audience, which was the cue for the spotlight to turn off and the house lights to come up. The guests returned to their meals laughing. They seemed to have taken the events at dinner in stride, sharing stories about other funny moments on cruises.

The captain walked through the swinging doors into the kitchen. He pulled Kennedy aside. "Great saves tonight, Kennedy, and thank you," he said earnestly. "You took care of that oddly dressed couple and Chef Michèle's strange blow-up. What is going on tonight? Chef can be volatile, but he's never missed a moment to bask in the applause."

"I have an idea," said Kennedy. "I'll see if I can find him and get him to calm down so the kitchen can get back to normal." She peeked out of the swinging doors. "Captain, so that I can find Chef Michèle, would you have one of the first officers take my place at the Butler's table? I don't want to seem rude."

As Kennedy and the captain were about to leave, two of the cast members burst in from the rear of the kitchen. "Kennedy, we need you. We have a situation."

The look on their faces said it was a matter of urgency and wanting to head off any problems in the show, Kennedy hurried after them. "Don't worry, sir," she called over her shoulder, "I have this under control." She entered backstage and found the dressing room in shambles and the cast members glaring and sniping at each other. Kennedy felt sure it was simply a case of opening night jitters as it had been a year since they had performed in front of a live audience.

After calming down a nervous cast, Kennedy stepped on stage an hour later to introduce the show. She noticed Gunner and Mr. Phillips sitting in the fourth row, center. *Great, something else for Gunner to critique,* Kennedy thought to herself. She squeezed each cast member's hand as they took the stage and went to watch the show from the right rear wing. As the curtains opened and the young woman playing Sofia began her opening song, Gunner decided to sigh dramatically and whisper loudly to Mr. Phillips. The disturbance made several people in the audience turn and glare at them. Louise and the other Ladies from Harmony Lakes sat near them and shushed them loudly. The young woman singing her solo faltered at the commotion but quickly regained her composure.

Watching the rest of the show, Kennedy was pleased. Other than Gunner's disruption, the performance had gone well. There were a few minor mistakes, but these were not noticeable to the passengers, who happily enjoyed the live entertainment. Kennedy left the backstage area quickly when the show ended to thunderous applause as the cast took their bows. She needed to get ready for her after-hours show in the Lunar Lounge.

A few years ago, her boss, Alfred, in the corporate office had asked if she could give some thought to entertainment options after the main show. He explained that the company did not have the funds to pay for another entertainer, but he believed she could come up with something. Kennedy had been able to cobble together a series of after-hours shows: a cabaret/comedy hour, a couples versus newlyweds game show, and her favorite, an improv night using the cast members. The shows were a hit and became a staple for the *Helio*. For the first night back, she had decided to do her cabaret show, which seemed like a great idea at the time. Unfortunately, Gunner's behavior on the cruise so far made her question her decision.

The Lunar Lounge was an intimate jewelry box. Marble high-top tables with barstools littered the back of the room, while low side tables and navy-blue velvet swivel chairs surrounded the small stage, which consisted of a circular wood inset in the dark black and blue tartan carpet. A single barstool stood on the stage next to a microphone and stand.

The captain greeted Kennedy in the staff area behind the lounge. "Did everything go as planned tonight, Kennedy?" he inquired. "The last time I saw you, you were being shanghaied by two of your cast members who were having an emergency."

Kennedy nodded, smiling warmly. "All is well, sir. It was only opening night jitters."

"And Chef Michèle, have you been able to find and sort him out?" he asked hopefully.

Kennedy made a face. "I haven't had time, but I am fairly confident he will be back to himself by morning."

The captain frowned and sighed. "I suppose that is the status quo, which is all I can hope for." He rubbed his hands together. "Now, how do you want me to introduce you?" he asked.

Kennedy gave a slight shrug. "Just a regular introduction, Captain, and thank you for helping me tonight. Your opening plays a big part in one of my first jokes." He raised an eyebrow.

"All in good fun, sir, I promise," she smiled wickedly.

Kennedy looked around the room and noted that the Club Diva Boys and the Ladies from Harmony Lakes had commandeered seats up front so they could watch the show together. *Well, that's a plus. I'll have some friendly faces up front.* As they arrived from the main show, the passengers were in high spirits, and Kennedy prayed for a good performance.

The captain stepped onto the stage and placed a glass of champagne on the barstool. Then, he took the microphone from the stand. "Ladies and Gentlemen," he said in his deep baritone. "I am sure you are all as excited as I am to see the one and only—thank goodness she's the only—Kennedy Reeves." '

Kennedy took a deep breath and burst onto the stage. She was wearing her black-beaded top and long black skirt from dinner but had updated her ensemble with a pair of long red gloves, a large rhinestone bracelet, and dangling earrings. She clapped her hands in front of her. "Welcome, welcome, welcome, and because no remarkable evening ever began with," and using a high, breathy voice, she said, "'Ummm, I'll have a soda.' I ask that you please raise your glass with me as I would like to propose a toast...to your livers." She paced to one side of the stage, holding her glass high in the air.

"I'm serious. I want to toast your livers." The crowd began laughing at the absurdity. "Ladies and gentlemen, let me explain, your livers will be working as hard, if not harder, than those of us working on the ship. I've seen some of you drinking already today, and I am impressed," she said sarcastically. "If drinking were an Olympic sport, we might take home the gold!" She walked to the other side of the stage, still holding her glass up. "Seriously, you should give your livers a little love. Go on, pat them…wait," she looked out at the audience as she walked back to the center of the stage. "None of you know where your liver is, do you?" she asked, laughing along with the audience. "Okay, okay, let's have an anatomy lesson." She pointed a red satin finger at her midriff. "Your liver is here." She was beginning to feel comfortable with the crowd as she connected with them. "Good job! You found it! Well, some of you," she scanned the audience and pointed. John raised his glass in the air to get his server's attention. "Oh, look," she cooed, "he's trying to play catch up." Hearing himself as part of the act, John blushed, chuckling, and raised his glass to her in a salute.

"Oh, my goodness!" she said, horrified. "Did you just toast me with an empty glass? It's bad luck! Although I suppose an empty glass is better than not making eye contact." She looked at the audience. "You know what happens then, right?" They shook their heads. "Oh, in some countries, if you toast without keeping eye contact, it's considered seven years of bad sex. I wonder who I broke eye contact with a few years ago. It would explain so much," she deadpanned. The crowd burst out laughing. "Can we please get this man a drink? And quickly? He may need some luck tonight, and I don't know how he is with eye contact." Again, the audience and John burst into laughter.

Kennedy began pacing the stage again. "I want to thank the captain for his lovely introduction tonight." The audience applauded softly. "Yes," she said in exaggeration, "that is his real voice, and when he's not on the ship, he spends his time as a foghorn." The audience let out a roar of laughter, and Kennedy saw the captain chuckle. "Speaking of the captain," she continued as the guests began to quiet down, "we have several other team members that the captain did not introduce you to this evening at the dinner." She walked over in front of the Ladies from Harmony Lakes and stooped down. "Ladies, the purser is not the man you talk to about where to buy purses and handbags." She stood back up, put her hand to her mouth, and whispered theatrically. "He's the one that keeps the accounts and presents you with the bill at the end of the cruise." She shook her finger at them. "Remember, not the handbag guy, the checkbook guy."

She stood up, pacing again. "The chef de partie is not the party chef," she placed a finger on her temple as if remembering something and looked up at the ceiling. "Although, if memory serves me, he does a fabulous hula dance in the crew bar after a few drinks, complete with coconut bra and grass skirt…and he was not wearing underwear, ladies and gentlemen!" The crowd laughed uproariously.

Kennedy was enjoying herself. She could feel her confidence coming back as she walked to her barstool and picked up the glass of champagne. "Did you enjoy the show tonight? Aren't those entertainers fabulous? Let's give them a big hand," she said, clapping her hands together. "Let me give you a little insider information, the shows are their real job, not playing shuffleboard or holding the stick for the limbo contest." She rolled her eyes. "I just make them do those things to torture them. It's fun." She took a large sip of champagne and held up a gloved finger. "Oh, and a piece of advice. We know that the sea air can make you amorous, but please remember there are cameras everywhere. The guys in security take great delight in watching your greatest," she cocked her head to the side, "or not so greatest moments." The crowd began cheering wildly.

"Did she put that in for you, Marilyn?" Dolly chortled. "You know you've been known to—" Laura and Louise clamped their hands over Dolly's mouth simultaneously.

"Now remember, tonight's show is a cabaret and comedy show, although two hours ago, I thought this was going to be a contortionist act." She breathed into the microphone and placed a hand on her hip. "If you had seen me putting on my shapewear in my cabin, you would have understood." She paused and looked at the audience laughing. "I had no idea I could go into those poses. I even cramped up at one point!" The women in the audience began laughing hysterically as the men looked dumbfounded.

"She is on fire tonight," John whispered to Steve. "If she ever decides to come back on land, I'm going to beg her to come work at the club. She's like a young Joan Rivers."

The audience began to settle down. "Which brings me to my next request. In all seriousness, folks, we ask that you fill out your guest satisfaction cards before the end of the cruise, but please be kind. Every card is sent to our corporate office, where they are reviewed, dissected, and scrutinized...over cocktails. I can only assume this because some of the directives that come back can be a bit personal." She took a few large notecards from the barstool and sat down, placing the microphone in the mic stand. She held out the first notecard. "On one of the last cruises, a passenger wrote, 'The ship is fine but could use some updating. Kennedy is a delight. She is a great cruise director and kept us busy.'" Kennedy raised her thumb to the audience.

"'Should you consider an update?'" Kennedy put the card in her lap and cocked her head, looking quizzically around the room, which had burst into laughter. "He was talking about the ship, right?" she deadpanned slowly. "Now, remember, we don't see these surveys. They go straight to the corporate office."

She waited a few seconds and said with a solemn face, "A month later, I got an email suggesting that during my next time off, I should consider some updating in the form of plastic surgery. I used to think diamonds were a girl's best friend, but I have since realized it's my soon-to-be named plastic surgeon." The audience's laughter was contagious, and Kennedy laughed along with them. She looked around the lounge and saw Omar leaning against the back wall, chuckling, and for a moment, they locked eyes. He gave her a smile and two thumbs up, and she felt her world was perfect.

After the show, she shook hands with several guests who had stayed after to compliment her. Kennedy thanked them and then walked over to see her fan club. Phil stood up and genuflected to her. "I'm not worthy of being in the same room as you, Kennedy."

Dave embraced her. "Honey, you were just spectacular!"

"Fabulous!" trilled John. "Can I use the contortionist part in my show?" he asked quickly. "It is to die for. But I have to know, how on Earth did you come up with that bit?"

Kennedy looked at him. "Have you ever tried to put on two layers of shapewear?" she asked wryly.

"Now *that* should be considered an Olympic sport," Marilyn chimed in.

Kennedy suddenly felt very tired. The adrenaline from the show was beginning to wear off. "I'm so grateful that you all came tonight. It meant the world to me to have some friendly faces out there in case I bombed." She looked at her watch. "I hate to do this, but I need to prepare for tomorrow before it gets here. Will you forgive me?" she begged.

Louise spoke up for the group. "Of course, darling, but there is one thing we want to ask you." She lowered her voice. "Who was the nerdy guy and the man with him who seemed to be everywhere tonight and always causing a stir? We saw them making a scene at dinner, and they kept making rude comments during the main show. The guys tell us that they are with the corporate office. Is that true?" She looked around and whispered confidentially, "And the tall one stared daggers at you during your show. He never laughed, never clapped, nothing. The little one just mops his forehead and writes whatever the other one says in his notebook. Who are they? They were weird and rude. I never knew you could be both at the same time."

Kennedy squirmed uncomfortably as all eyes were on her. She shrugged her shoulders. "They are some of our corporate team members reviewing this cruise to see how we're doing on the first trip out."

Marilyn wiggled her body and looked at Kennedy pointedly. "I want to know what is wrong with the tall guy. I sidled up to him in the bar, thinking he could be a potential conquest, but after two minutes, I was trying desperately to get away." She fanned herself. "All he wanted to do was talk about himself." She placed her hands on either side of her hips. "I mean, *what man* would want to talk about themselves when they can talk about me?" she lamented.

Kennedy smiled graciously. "Marilyn, I'm sure he was just trying to impress you with his accomplishments," she said lightly. "He was probably nervous. You are a lot of woman to handle." She looked at the group and grimaced. "I really have to go," she said desperately. "I think the blood supply to my brain is being cut off by the elastic I am wearing. I'll see you tomorrow!" She left them, walking quickly to the staff area at the back of the lounge.

Kennedy took the back steps to get to her cabin. She changed into comfortable clothes and put a bottle of wine in a tote bag. Then, going back to the staircase used by the staff, Kennedy walked down one flight to Mila's cabin. She knocked on the door softly, and Mila opened it.

"I hope you have a bottle of wine in that tote bag," she said, gesturing to the canvas bag in Kennedy's hand, "because I need a drink or two. After the day I had, I might drink the whole bottle." The two women sat down. Mila opened the drawer beside her and brought out two wine glasses.

Kennedy unscrewed the cap and poured the wine. "First, a toast. To the first day. We survived." She let out a large breath and clinked Mila's glass.

Mila looked at her gloomily. "Barely," she said. "Kennedy, I'm sorry I didn't take you seriously earlier. This guy, Gunner, he's horrible." Tears welled up in her eyes. "First, he said the spa was just sprinkles on a cupcake, and then he was a jerk in the spa in front of passengers." She took a gulp of wine and stood up. She began pacing angrily. "He made me feel worthless in the meeting. The spa is just as important as any other part of the ship. We make money for the company while making the passengers feel great about themselves." She looked at Kennedy and thrust her empty wine glass at her. "I need a refill." She continued, "Having a spa appointment is the ultimate bragging right on a ship." She changed her voice, "'I'm so sorry, I can't go with you, I have a spa appointment,' is like being a part of the cool club." She turned and faced Kennedy. "He made Anna Marie cry today."

Kennedy blinked. "Anna Marie? She's a rock."

Mila nodded. "She's been with me for years. She manages the desk, knows many of the returning passengers, and has a way of maneuvering appointments around so that no one feels slighted when we get backed up." She huffed. "Because I didn't bow down and give that jerk a spa appointment in our meeting, Gunner felt the need to vent his frustrations on her." Mila shared how Gunner came onto Anna Marie, flirting with her, had made her touch his face, and when he didn't get his way, he threatened to fire her. "I've never seen Anna Marie lose her composure in public before, but he hit a nerve. She left the desk unattended she was so upset."

Kennedy was astonished. "What happened next?"

Mila took a deep breath and plowed on. "After being a jerk to my employee and making rude comments in front of my customers, the pompous ass told me he had the perfect person to replace me." Mila looked at Kennedy wiping her eyes. "This spa means so much to me. I poured myself into it. Alfred told me that if we did well with this spa, he would go to the board to ask that we do another one. There was also talk about putting a spa on the private island they were talking about buying."

Kennedy looked at her friend, who was in deep pain. "No more talk about Gunner. We need to find something good that happened today."

Mila was quiet, looking down at the carpet. Suddenly, she raised her head. "Yes, there was a good part of today. Sara, the new spa tech, was amazing. She did everything I asked. She restocked the retail shelves, covered the desk when Anna Marie took off, she even volunteered to do Gunner's treatments tomorrow so no one else would have to be subjected to him. She's an absolute dream and has such a calming presence. I could see her as a general manager of a classy boutique hotel. You look tired, my friend," Mila said warmly. "I had better let you get off to bed."

"Yes, I am tired," Kennedy yawned. "Our friend, Mr. Atcher, did not help matters today. I think his arrival on the ship should have been a warning." She rose to leave. "Did I tell you that he summoned me to his cabin to demand better quarters? His stateroom is one tier below Vera Jameson's, which was not what he felt he deserved." Kennedy laughed. "He had seen that we had an Owner's Suite on the website and demanded to be moved there." She mimicked Gunner's voice, "'As is befitting my place in the company.'" She shook her head. "If the Butlers had not been in love with that suite, I would have personally moved his belongings just to shut him up."

Mila could see the conversation happening in her head and began giggling. "Can you imagine his face when he would have walked into the cabin?"

Kennedy envisioned the pinched look on his face as he saw the zebra carpet and the round couch. She began to giggle. Her giggles turned into deep laughs as she imagined him walking around the stateroom with its eccentricities. She clutched her sides and slowed down her breathing. "Oh, thank you, Mila, I needed that," she said, catching her breath. She suddenly got serious. "I know you were not at dinner, but Gunner upset Chef Michèle so badly tonight that he caused a scene at the Captain's Dinner. I'm sure it will have ramifications."

Mila cocked an eyebrow. "Perhaps Michèle could ask Gunner to help him do inventory in the freezer and accidentally lock him in there for the duration of the cruise."

"Mila!" Kennedy exclaimed.

"Think about it," Mila said. "It seems like Gunner is intentionally trying to do things to make us look bad and make himself look valuable." She sighed heavily. "And having a board member as his lapdog to write down his every thought doesn't help."

Kennedy suddenly felt depressed. "You heard him in the meeting today. Any small slip can mean we are out of a job."

Mila blew out her breath. "The staff meeting was humiliating. I have never been dismissed from a room before. It was demeaning."

Kennedy looked at Mila sadly. "You may have been dismissed, but at least you weren't asked to be a 'babe' and get him some coffee."

Mila realized they were both sinking again. "This guy is bringing such negativity to our world." She took Kennedy's hands in her own. "Remember, we are the glue that holds this team together, and we can't allow this negativity to feed. So, you know what we need to do, right?" she asked.

"Get a piñata, pretend it's Gunner and beat it to death?" Kennedy asked acidly.

Mila shook her head. "Nope, we need to reset ourselves, and a good night's sleep will help," she said with forced optimism.

Kennedy cocked her head to the side. "Are you sure? Because I'm certain I have a piñata in the storeroom," she said. "And I know where Franklin keeps the hammers."

Mila shook her head. "Nope, a good night's sleep. Doctor's orders. I am, after all, your unofficial therapist."

Kennedy hugged her friend. "We smile, move, breathe in, breathe out...and we move on," she said.

Kennedy left Mila's room and made her way to her cabin. There were still a few things to take care of before the morning.

However, as she and Mila prepared for sleep, doubt began to creep into their thoughts as the day replayed. Kennedy fell into a restless slumber. In her dreams, she saw Gunner whispering to Mr. Phillips and Mr. Phillips scribbling frantically, flipping page after page in his notebook.

THE HELIO

DAY TWO

NASSAU, BAHAMAS

ARRIVAL 4:00 A.M.

DEPARTURE 5:00 P.M.

The following day dawned bright and sunny. The ship had reached Nassau while the passengers slept, and many were surprised to see land out of the windows when they woke up. Most had never felt the ship's docking, thanks partly to the captain's and crew's skillful expertise but also due to the number of SunRumbrellas consumed the night before. The port was already bustling with other cruise ships, and the lobby was full of cheerful chatter as the passengers made their plans for departure. Many would make a beeline for the Straw Market, which sold handbags, hats, colorful T-shirts, and other assorted novelties. A discerning few would venture further to Pompey Square, the beach, or Fort Charlotte. Kennedy stood in the lobby watching the passengers leave for the day. The Ladies from Harmony Lakes stopped to say goodbye on their way to town.

"I hope I don't lose Mom today," said Laura facetiously. Kennedy giggled as she took in Dolly's red polka dot pantsuit, white floppy hat, and humungous red sunglasses.

"What?" Dolly hollered. "You've never seen an old lady go out into town?"

"You look positively lively and lovely, Dolly," answered Kennedy. "I only wish I was going with you."

"And how do I look?" Marilyn sashayed in front of Kennedy like a runway model. Always the tropical bird of the group, Marilyn wore a bright floral print dress and high heels while the others wore pants and comfortable walking shoes.

Kennedy made a face as she looked at Marilyn's shoes. "Are you sure about those?" She pointed to Marilyn's bright yellow espadrille wedges. "The sidewalks in Nassau can be tricky, and some of them are dangerously cracked. I would hate for you to get hurt."

"Well, Kennedy," she drawled, "if you're so worried about my getting injured, perhaps you should have a handsome crew member be my escort for the day?" she pouted prettily. "That way, if I twist my ankle, they can come to my rescue and carry me back to the ship," she said with her hand on her hip.

Louise rolled her eyes at Kennedy. "Do you have anyone who could throw a one-hundred-and-fifty-pound sack of potatoes over his shoulder?"

Kennedy stifled a giggle. "What are your plans today, ladies?"

"We're going drinking!" Dolly yelled boisterously. "I bet you didn't expect that, did you?"

Laura interrupted her mother, "We are going to tour a rum distillery, and at the end of the tour, they have a tasting room, Mom. We are not spending the day drinking like some college co-eds."

Dolly chuckled. "You can pretend to taste all you want. I'm going there to drink!"

Laura caught Kennedy's eye. "Do you have any suggestions, Kennedy? We don't want to tire Mom out with the heat and sun, and apparently, she has decided to get drunk at the distillery."

"Is there a problem with having fun and getting drunk as opposed to being drug all over the island?" Dolly snorted.

"Mother, please!" Laura remonstrated. "Go on, Kennedy. As you can tell, she isn't wearing her filter today."

"A trip to the National Art Gallery would be lovely and keep you out of the heat. There is also the crafts center," Kennedy shared. "You can buy some authentic Bahamian art, meet the artists, and watch them work."

Dolly was impatient and waved her arms. She pointed at the oversized watch on her wrist. "Let's go, ladies! I'm leaving without you. I don't have time for idle chit-chat. I don't know how many hours I have left at my age. Let's move it!" She began to shuffle to the gangway, and Laura gave Kennedy an apologetic look.

"Times like these make leaving her on the steps of a retirement home with a note pinned to her chest look better and better," she sighed. "Hold on, Mom, I'm coming."

Not far from where Kennedy stood, Bert was taking photos of Terri Butler. She walked over to them. Terri was wearing a black cotton spaghetti strap romper, high wedge heels, and a thick gold necklace with the word SWEETSIE written in cursive. Jones was wearing an orange print tropical shirt and matching shorts. He lifted the straw hat clamped to his head in greeting. Kennedy noticed the hat was the same one the bartenders wore on the pool deck and wondered which of the bartenders he had given a ten-dollar bill to for the hat. The cigar in his mouth completed the outfit.

"Mr. Butler," Kennedy said in a stern tone. "Do I need to remind you again about our smoking policies? We do not allow any tobacco products outside of the smoker's lounge." Jones pulled the cigar out of his mouth and showed Kennedy. "It's unlit, and I'm sure you could look the other way this time, couldn't you?" Kennedy gave him a hard stare, and seeing the resolute look on her face, he took the cigar out of his mouth and placed it in his shirt pocket.

Much to Bert's chagrin, Terri had finished posing and walked over to where Jones and Kennedy stood. "So, where are you headed off to?" Kennedy asked.

"We're going to swim with the pigs," Terri said in a breathy voice. "Doesn't that sound like fun? They meet you at the boat when you arrive. Little piggies swimming in the water." She wiggled her fingers in the air. "After that, we are going to feed some stingrays." She looked at Jones and hugged him, planting a kiss on his cheek. "I'm so excited."

"Yep," said Jones, "and we better get going. Sorry, Kennedy, there's a speedboat waiting to take us on this tour. It's private, you know." He waggled his eyebrows, took the cigar out of his pocket, and waved it around. "I had a friend of a friend set this up for us," he said conspiratorially. "They said they would even take me to swim with some sharks if I wanted to later today," he bragged.

"That sounds like a lovely day," Kennedy said hesitantly. She wondered to herself which company was taking them. Some tour operators who were not affiliated with the cruise lines would promise anything for the expectation of an expensive and private charter.

"I'm so excited," squealed Terri as she hugged Jones's arm again.

"Well, we're off," he exclaimed and lifted his hat to Kennedy. As they walked through the lobby, he swatted Terri on the backside, and she yelped playfully, tottering on her high heels.

"Dreadful people," Vera sniffed, walking up to Kennedy as they watched Terri and Jones leave. "The necklace was an interesting choice. It reminds me of a dog collar. If she gets lost, she can be returned to her owner," Vera said cynically.

"Mrs. Jameson, please!" Kennedy was trying to suppress the laughter that was bubbling up. "I'm certain you could find one at one of the jewelry shops on Bay Street," she said with a trace of mockery."

"You are a bit cheeky today," Vera said crisply but smiled warmly at Kennedy. "I should tell on you to that nasty Mr. Atcher."

"And what is on your agenda today, Mrs. Jameson?" Kennedy asked.

"I'm off to Graycliff. My husband and I met the owner once, and we stayed there many times after he opened the hotel."

Kennedy couldn't resist prodding Vera. "In 1844?" she mused playfully.

"Are you being smart?" Vera asked sharply, although she was thoroughly enjoying the banter. "For your information, I have an appointment to roll and purchase some fresh cigars and then spend a few hours puffing away to my heart's content in a lovely location which I assure you is unlike the gilded cage on this ship. Later, I will be escorted to a beautifully set table in a gorgeous garden and dine on a lovely filet of sole," she said smugly.

Kennedy nodded. "That certainly sounds like a wonderful day, Mrs. Jameson," she said warmly. "Just be sure to be back in time for departure. The ship leaves at five."

"That, my dear girl," Vera said with emphasis, "you do not need to worry about. My car and driver will bring me back promptly at two o'clock, allowing me plenty of time to avoid the swarm of sweaty passengers clutching their cheap souvenirs and reeking of coconut oil. Honestly, some of them smell like those dreadful coconut snacks that one buys in a vending machine." She paused for a moment. "It will also ensure that I will not run into our friends spending the day with pigs. Odd what people spend their money on." She turned her nose up in the air and walked haughtily down the gangway.

Kennedy watched Vera leave and shook her head slowly. Despite her imperious behavior, she liked Mrs. Jameson. Vera said the very thing you were thinking but didn't have the nerve to say aloud. Kennedy snickered. Watching Vera and her mother Lolly on the same cruise would be a battle of wills. The odds on who would win would set Las Vegas on edge. Looking down at her watch, Kennedy realized she needed to hurry if she was going to get to the staff meeting on time. She wanted to make sure she did not give Gunner any reason to call her out.

The conference room was lively with chatter when she entered, and she took her place at the end as she was the last one to enter the room.

"Franklin, is it possible to have the men's dry sauna door fixed?" Mila asked. "It's sticking from the inside. I thought we had fixed it when we did the renovation, but it's doing it again, and I don't want anyone to get trapped. It could be deadly."

"Deadly?" Franklin asked, raising an eyebrow. "That's a bit overdramatic." Mila opened her mouth to say more, but Franklin held up his hands in supplication. "Put an out-of-order sign on the door, and I'll get one of the guys to look at it today." He looked around. "I sure hope today's meeting is a quick one. I've got a lot to get done while we are in port, and I have a meeting with the goat." The conversations continued as requests were made and information was shared. Then, looking at his watch a few minutes later, Franklin announced, "It's almost ten o'clock, and I've got a ship to take care of and a lot to do." As Franklin finished his sentence, Gunner entered the room wearing a pristine tan linen suit, white shirt, and loafers. Red eyeglasses were perched on his head today. Mr. Phillips followed behind, wearing another dark wool suit, and Kennedy giggled inside, wondering if he owned anything else.

"Well," Gunner said, rubbing his hands together, "to use Mr. Blaas's words, we have a ship to take care of, and I have a lot to talk about, so I suggest that you all settle in." He looked around the room and saw Rosemary and Mila sitting at the table. "Did you not understand yesterday that your presence was unnecessary at these meetings?" He looked directly at both women and sighed. "I suppose you can both stay to hear what I have to say. It won't do any harm *this time*." He put his hands behind his back and began to circle the table. He stopped when he got to Kennedy, sitting at the end of the table, and bent down to speak to her. "Comfortable in your seat, Ms. Reeves?" he asked in a low whisper. "I'm surprised you believe you are qualified to sit there." Kennedy wisely bit her lips together.

Gunner stood up and continued walking around the table. He put his eyeglasses on. "This ship is in bigger trouble than I originally thought, and as senior staff members, I expected better of you. Yesterday's performance was a joke, and while I am sure that the passengers were not aware of the mistakes made," he paused and looked over his eyeglasses at the group, "I was, and we're going to discuss each issue in detail. Please pull out your notebooks because I expect you to all take notes to make the proper changes. It is a shame I am forced to treat you like elementary school children, but it seems that is what is required."

"First, let's begin with the disastrous dinner service. When I was general manager of…" Gunner shuttled between his successful career and criticizing Tony for the errors he felt were made, both real and imaginary. As Gunner droned on, Kennedy could see Tony trying to quietly fish his roll of antacid tablets out of his pocket. Gunner paced back and forth as he spoke and the color on his face got redder with each word. "I hate having to repeat myself," he said and slapped his hand on the table, causing everyone to jump. The slap was so hard that his red eyeglasses tilted on his head, and he needed to right them. "You either didn't understand or didn't care about some of the things I said yesterday, Tony. "If I make a change, *that* is what we will do. There will be no deviation from my directives." He glared at Kennedy and began pacing around the table again. "If you cannot understand that there is only one voice, and the directions I give you are to be followed to the letter, then you are welcome to leave the ship. We are docked, and there is plenty of time for you to pack your belongings and get off the ship. Every single one of you is replaceable," he said in a threatening tone. He stopped and stood behind Tony's seat, looking down at him. "Perhaps I should have some of you replaced today."

Gunner looked around the table and noticed the executive chef was missing. "Where is Chef Michèle? He should be here. His refusal to follow the changes I made to the menu and his public temper tantrum during the Captain's Dinner is inexcusable," Gunner said irately. Tony timidly raised his hand. "Speak," barked Gunner.

"I'm sorry, sir, but he is on the island gathering local produce for the ship."

Gunner snorted. "A stupid reason and a cost issue if I ever heard one." He looked at Mr. Phillips, sitting in the corner of the room. "Mr. Phillips, please make a note for us to look at the food costs. It appears that our executive chef is more interested in grocery shopping in town than attending a mandatory meeting. Let me make this clear to all of you." He looked around the table at each of them. "I expect you to be at any meeting that I call at any time. I don't care if you think something else is more important. My meetings take precedence over everything!" He went to the credenza, took a bottle of water, and guzzled it.

"Now, going back to the Captain's Dinner. Tony, please explain why you went ahead with the parade of servers and did not make the seating changes I made?" The skin from Gunner's neck to his face was turning red again, and he was rapidly blinking his eyes as he walked toward Tony, who had turned pale. "Was I not clear when I told you I wanted the Butlers at the captain's table and that insipid

Jameson woman seated by the kitchen?" He threw his hands up in the air. "She acts as if she owns the ship, and you people bend over backward for her." He slapped his hand on the table inches from where Tony sat, and Kennedy could see Tony's hands shaking. Gunner took a moment and spoke in an icy tone, "People, the Butlers are our new target market and should be given preferential treatment, not some old biddy with one foot in the grave." The only sound in the room was the ticking of the clock on the wall. "Mr. Gano, I'm waiting. Will you explain why you took it upon yourself to undo my changes? Please, I need an answer. Have you suddenly lost the ability to speak?"

"S-s-sir—," Tony stammered. Kennedy could not take Gunner's bullying of Tony for another second.

"It was me, Gunner!" she said, standing up. She looked at Tony and then shifted her stare to Gunner. "I made the changes. As cruise director, the passengers and their happiness are my responsibility. Mrs. Jameson is—"

Gunner's face was a storm of emotions, and he cut her off, slicing the air with his hand. "Excuse me?" he asked, glaring at her as his face turned maroon. "Were you given permission to speak? Did I ask that you answer a question that was directed at Tony? And please, please tell me the exact moment I permitted you to call me by my first name," he hissed. Kennedy stood there mutely. She had never been spoken to in such a manner, and she had never been in a meeting where she felt she had to stick up for one of her coworkers.

Gunner was breathing hard and went back to the credenza, where he took a second bottle of water and drank it, staring at the wall. "Ms. Reeves, I would suggest that you sit in your chair like a good girl and speak only when you are called upon because, don't worry, I have a great deal to discuss with you." He turned around and smiled at her sickly. "In fact, since you feel so talkative, let's switch and discuss your area." He blinked his eyes rapidly. "Not so chatty now? That's okay, I'll start," he said icily.

"We've already discussed the onboarding process, so I won't belabor the issues I saw. I will provide you with detailed instructions before the next cruise. What I saw last night in the theater and the lounge was pitiful. In a nutshell, your entertainers are weak, and your after-hours show is a joke. I will be replacing your show with a trained comedian. What you put on last night was painful to watch. I'm surprised you can show your face after the performance. I suggest you save that for an open mic night at a hotel bar.

Regarding the sad excuse for a cast, I can only assume they are terrible because you selected them." Gunner looked at Kennedy, who was trembling. "Don't worry. I have something else planned to take over the main evening entertainment. Something less homegrown than your little musical production." He placed his hands behind him and began to pace. "Now, onto other more pleasant things. When I was the general manager of..."

Kennedy slowly sat down in her chair, fighting back the tears of rage threatening her vision. For the first time in her life, thoughts of violence ran through her head. She pictured Gunner falling over the railing and into the sea and her standing there waving to him as he fell into the dark water. She closed her eyes to remove the vision. As he was droning on about himself, Kennedy realized Gunner didn't talk about ways to fix things. Instead, he searched for a mistake, real or imaginary, that he could blow out of proportion and use to dismember you publicly in front of your peers. Then, once done ripping you apart, he would quickly change gears and talk about himself, his accomplishments, and how highly valued he was. He was, in his overblown opinion, the *greatest of all time*. Omar caught Kennedy's eye. "I'm sorry," he mouthed, and she gave him a shaky smile.

Having finished his latest story, Gunner walked over to Mila and bent over her. "I do hope today will be a better visit to the spa than what I experienced yesterday," he said in a smug voice. "Just remember, I can have a real spa director here like that," he snapped his fingers in front of her face and straightened up.

He walked over to where Rosemary was sitting. "Rosie, I expect that my visit to housekeeping will be an eye-opening and educational visit for you. While from a passenger's viewpoint, the ship looks sanitary, I am quite certain you are not as well versed in the correct cleaning protocols as you think. The standards that the big ships have are stringent. You are fortunate I am here now." He puffed out his chest. "In fact, I singlehandedly wrote the manual adopted throughout the hospitality industry. There was even an article written about me that called me the King of Clean. My company was so grateful for my hard work and the long hours spent developing it that they paid me a very handsome bonus. You are lucky you can learn from someone like me." Gunner motioned to Mr. Phillips, who pulled a four-inch binder from his briefcase and handed it to him. "I was going to give this to you later, Rosie, but since you are here, you can have it now. A little light reading for you." He dropped the binder in front of Rosemary, and she blanched at the size of the book.

"Thank you," she croaked, looking somewhat overwhelmed at the binder.

The meeting ended an hour and a half later, and everyone quickly left the room to escape Gunner. Franklin was the last person in the room. He tossed a plastic bag containing a new pair of coveralls onto the table near Gunner and another near Mr. Phillips. "You may want to put those on before you come to the shop," he said, pointing to the coveralls.

Gunner looked at the package disdainfully. He sniffed and squinted his eyes at Franklin. "Perhaps, you should put some effort into having a cleaner work area, Mr. Blaas. I am sure we will discuss that subject and many others about your department when I arrive." Franklin stared at Gunner for a moment and then turned and walked out of the conference room.

Franklin was proud of the *Helio* and his team. He had been an orphan growing up in a series of foster homes, and after a stint in the Coast Guard, the Sunny Dayz ships became his first true home. Learning on the job from the older mechanics, Franklin worked his way up the ladder to his current position as chief engineer of the *Helio*. He had never married and owned a small condominium in Ormond Beach, which suited his needs when he was not on the *Helio.* Being on land permanently was not the life Franklin wanted. Strangely, he reveled in the problems that faced the ship, and there were plenty of them, twenty-four hours a day. It was his job to solve them, and he took immense pride in that responsibility. He often solved the more challenging problems he encountered in his sleep as his mind rested and came up with a solution, and in the early hours of the morning, you could find him fixing the very thing that had stymied him the day before.

Franklin thought it would be best to start his meeting with Gunner by showing off the new air circulation and sanitation systems that had been recently installed. He had spent years begging the board for the new technology, but it was not until recent events and the thought of lost profits that the company agreed to install them. When Gunner and Mr. Phillips arrived at the appointed time, Franklin was dismayed to see neither were wearing or carrying the coveralls Franklin had given them at the meeting. He shrugged his shoulders and began to explain how the new system worked and its benefits for everyone on the ship.

After a few minutes, Gunner waved his hands at Franklin to stop him from talking. He took off his glasses. "Mr. Blaas, I already know everything there is to know about these systems," he said tiredly, blowing on his glasses and wiping them off. "I probably know more about it than you do." He put the red eyeglasses back on. "Now, when I was..." He began to speak in a lecturing tone. Franklin leaned against the wall, seething with anger and unable to hear Gunner's discourse. Franklin controlled his temper, reminding himself that the *Helio* had the new systems because he had spent his time off learning everything he could about the recent technology that had become available. He learned how to retrofit the new system into the ship's current setup and then, through shameless lobbying, pleaded to the board and corporate office for the system at every opportunity until, at last, it had been granted.

Gunner stopped speaking and spun around. "I would like to see your office," he said, squinting and sniffing. "I find that seeing someone's office space gives me great insight into their personality." He turned to Mr. Phillips. "I don't think we'll need you down there, Bart. We can discuss the maintenance department changes later today after I have toured it." Franklin bristled at the conversation between Gunner and Mr. Phillips. He found it rude and disrespectful, but so far, most of what Gunner did fell into those categories. Taking Gunner to his office went against his better judgment, but Franklin reasoned it was better than fighting an impossible battle. "I'm not generally in my office, but sure, let's go and see it," he said with false enthusiasm. He led Gunner down to the maintenance shop.

Franklin's office would have made a professional organizer either hang up their label maker in despair or roll up their sleeves in anticipation. His massive desk was a sea of paperwork, hardware pieces, light bulb boxes, and tools. Rolled blueprints sat in a corner and resembled a small forest of birch trees, and a cabin door lay on top of two sawhorses. Binders, manuals, and boxes of nails and screws were scattered across it. Piles of catalogs and instruction manuals were stacked haphazardly throughout the room, some of which had tools strewn across them. Two large garbage containers stood behind his chair, overflowing with papers. It looked like a disaster, but Franklin knew the location of everything. One time, Kennedy and Rosemary had decided to tidy up his office, but Franklin had been alerted by his team and was leaning against the door, smiling and shaking his head, when they arrived. On the wall across from his desk were large monitors he used to view the automated systems on the ship. To the left of the desk, next to the door, was a wall where rows of clipboards hung with paper maintenance requests.

"So, this is the brain?" Gunner asked incredulously as he took out a small camera and began taking pictures. "It's rather antiquated," he said derisively and sniffed. "I developed a program for the last company I worked for. It cut down on manpower and waste in the maintenance department. You could use…" he trailed off, looking at the wall of clipboards in front of him. He looked at Franklin incredulously and then back at the wall of clipboards. "Tell me you don't use paper maintenance requests but a computerized system." He took one of the clipboards down and read it out loud. "MEN'S LOCKER ROOM: DRY SAUNA DOOR REPAIR. STUCK. WILL NOT UNLOCK FROM INSIDE."

Franklin nodded. He was leaning against his desk. "We use a paper system. We switched to a computerized system once, but there were too many issues with the program, and a lot of time was wasted. Computer programs may be fine for some things but not for others. The one we had was a waste of money and time, in my opinion. Each clipboard matches up to one of my guys, and I can assign that person to the job he does best, ensuring we don't waste any manpower or time. We also have radios if we need to dispatch someone quickly. And, as this is my department," he said, folding his arms and drawing himself up to his full towering height, "I don't believe I will be changing my methods anytime soon."

Gunner turned around quickly to face Franklin. "You may not have the luxury of making those decisions in the future, Mr. Blaas," he said scornfully. He looked around the room with an air of disgust. "Well, let us continue with our tour. As Mr. Phillips did not come with me, I will recreate my notes from these photos. They say every picture tells a story, and this one tells me that there is much that needs to be changed." Gunner shut his eyes and rubbed them. "It is so filthy down here; my eyes are drying out." They left Franklin's office and passed several maintenance workers in royal blue coveralls who walked into the office, took clipboards off the wall, and reviewed their assignments.

Franklin held out another bag of coveralls and a pair of rubber non-slip shoe covers to Gunner. "Mr. Atcher, wouldn't you like to put these on before we continue our walk? I would hate for your suit to get dirty."

Huffing at Franklin, Gunner sneered. "If I wanted to look like one of your maintenance men, I would have put it on." He waved at him dismissively. "Now, let us, please, complete our tour. I'm sure there is much more for me to document." Franklin led Gunner through the maintenance area, and Gunner made a point of photographing everything he saw.

"Mr. Atcher," Franklin said, "you shouldn't be back there." Gunner was photographing a collection of pipes that were stacked in a corner.

Gunner shook his head. "I need to document your sloppy habits. There is no need for you to have a collection of pipes and other building materials." He gave Franklin a long look. "And I'll go wherever I please."

Franklin swallowed. "It's not safe for you to be back there, sir, especially as you aren't wearing protective footwear," Franklin motioned for Gunner to come out. Suddenly the ship rose and fell mildly. Gunner swayed and looked at Franklin anxiously.

"It's nothing. It happens when the ship in the next berth starts to prepare to leave port," Franklin offered in explanation. "But you should come out of there. There may be—" Suddenly, the ship moved again. Gunner lost his balance and fell against the stack of pipes. His once pristine suit now bore a long and wide tattoo of dirt and grease.

Franklin held out his arm to Gunner. "Steady there, Mr. Atcher. I did ask that you come out from there and suggested you put on some coveralls. I'm sorry you messed up your nice outfit," he said, trying to swallow back a smile.

Gunner pushed away Franklin's arm as he came out from where he stood. He tried to wipe the grease off with his hands, but when he did, he only made the stain larger. Seeing the dirt and oil on his suit and hearing Franklin's words, Gunner turned scarlet with anger. He stuffed the camera into his pocket. Then, he pointed a shaking finger at Franklin. "You and your department are as disgraceful as your office," he said harshly. "Your people are greasy, dirty, and unkempt, and I will make it my mission to get rid of you and your antiquated ways personally."

Another wave rolled, and Gunner slid on the floor as his loafers were slick on the bottom and had no traction. He fell to his knees. The maintenance workers walking by with their clipboards tried not to smile. The man in the fancy suit had no business being down in the shop without coveralls and the correct footwear. Gunner snarled as he righted himself. "When we return to Florida, I will demand that you begin using the new system I developed. This department needs to be in the current century instead of being on the *Titanic* where you currently are." He pointed a shaking finger at Franklin. "The maintenance department will complete no further repairs until this area is free of grease and grime and is organized in a manner that I find acceptable. If it is not, I will put every member of this team off the ship. I will be down here tomorrow morning with the camera to document what has or has not been completed." He looked around again and said nastily, "This place is nothing short of a pigsty." He strode out of the shop in a huff. Franklin walked to his office and slammed the door so hard the frame shook.

"What do we do now?" asked one of the workers.

"I don't know about any of you," another answered, picking up a broom. "But if the man in the suit said to clean, I'm going to clean. I can't afford to be put off the ship."

Franklin threw himself into his chair, fuming. "I don't need this crap," he muttered out loud. "I'm close to retirement. I could get off the boat tomorrow and not look back. Let this idiot run the ship if he thinks he knows how to do it. Let him figure out the constant repairs, the meager staff, and do it on a nonexistent budget." He closed his eyes and slowed his breathing. He needed to tell Rosemary what to expect and prayed Gunner's inspection of the housekeeping department would not be as frustrating as the one he had just experienced. "If it's as bad as mine, I'll beg her to leave. Screw the company; they don't seem to value us anymore," he said with regret to the empty room. It pained him to say the words as the *Helio* had been his home for so many years. He picked up his radio and told his staff to return to the shop for an important meeting.

Gunner stormed down the corridor and, reaching his cabin, yanked open the door and slammed it behind him. He ripped off the grease-stained jacket and, balling it up in a wad, threw it in the corner of the room. *Franklin did that on purpose. He made sure I would fall into something and get filthy. Sure, he offered coveralls to me in front of people, but he did it on purpose. He wanted to embarrass me by having me look like one of the maintenance men.* He looked at himself in the mirror. "I need to break up this team. What this ship needs is a younger staff that has not formed bonds and only feels loyalty to one person...me."

Rosemary waited for Gunner on deck eight with hopeful expectations as she and her team cleaned cabins and the public spaces while the passengers were in port. She was confident in her staff. Rosemary had spent weeks retraining them before the ship took on passengers so the *Helio* would be safe for everyone. She was quite willing to read the four-inch manual Gunner had given her in the hope that it might teach her something new in addition to refreshing her memory about protocols. When Gunner and Mr. Phillips arrived, Rosemary could tell that Gunner was in a terrible mood and was wearing a different suit than the one he had worn earlier at the staff meeting.

"Good afternoon, Rosie," he said coldly. "Let's hope my visit to your department is better than my visit to maintenance."

Rosemary extended her hand. "Let's start in the game room, Mr. Atcher and Mr. Phillips, so you may see how we clean a public area." She paused and looked at Gunner levelly. "If you don't mind, I go by Rosemary or Ms. Flores, not Rosie," she said firmly but pleasantly in her soft Filipino accent.

Gunner smirked. "And I like Rosie, so Rosie it is," he said flippantly and sniffed.

Rosemary drew in a large breath and swallowed hard. "If you please, this way," she said, opening the door.

Passengers seldom used the game room, and with everyone in port, it was the perfect place to show the two men how the public spaces were cleaned and disinfected. Gunner drilled Rosemary with questions, and she answered each one easily. He was irritated that he had been unable to find any mistakes by Rosemary or her team. "Very well, it appears that you have the public spaces in hand, Rosie, although I am sure you are missing something. Let us go look at the guestrooms next."

Rosemary corrected him. "Sir," she said deferentially, "we call them cabins or staterooms."

Gunner whipped his head around at her. "I'll thank you not to correct me, Rosie, and I'll call them whatever I want," he snapped.

Rosemary bowed her head. "Of course, sir, whatever you wish," she said quietly.

They walked down the corridor, and Gunner allowed Rosemary to get ahead. He pulled Mr. Phillips aside. "I want you to time how long it takes one of them to clean a room," he whispered and handed Mr. Phillips a stopwatch. "If they go over the allotted time, it is something I can use against her to have her removed."

Rosemary stopped. "Here we are," she said proudly. "As you can see, my team cleans each cabin thoroughly while the passengers are ashore."

"I'll be the judge of that," he barked and stepped into the first cabin. He stood in front of a trashcan by the desk and watched as a young woman cleaned the room. As the housekeeper completed her self-inspection, she gathered the bags of trash and placed her cleaning rags in separate bags according to the chemical used and what the rag had cleaned. "I am done, Miss Rosemary," she said softly.

"Are you?" Gunner asked smugly. "It looks like you forgot this." He stepped aside, revealing a trashcan with two luggage tags inside. "Tsk, tsk, Rosie," he said, shaking his head. "Not a very thorough job, is it? It makes one wonder how many other rooms have something incomplete."

Gunner motioned for Mr. Phillips to follow him into the corridor. "I want to time them from start to finish," he said briskly. "Rosie, find a room that has not been cleaned, and we will time the housekeeper. Time means money." Rosemary walked the two men halfway down the corridor, finding a room that a housekeeper was beginning to enter. Rosemary asked her to wait for a moment and explained that she would clean the cabin as usual, but they would be timing her. Rosemary stressed that the young woman should clean the cabin as she usually did. "Well, that should be telling," Gunner said, raising his eyebrows. Mr. Phillips entered the cabin and shut the door. "Go!" Gunner barked and began to follow the housekeeper into the room. Rosemary was behind him, but Gunner shut the door in her face preventing her from entering the cabin.

The young housekeeper had a wild look as she cleaned the cabin frantically. The short man's stopwatch made her nervous, but she was more frustrated that the tall man seemed to be consistently in her way. Rosemary had never timed her housekeepers before. Her emphasis was on the quality of the cleaning, not the amount of time it took, and if someone were dawdling, she would have a conversation with them which usually had the desired effect. While the young woman cleaned, Gunner stayed behind her, commenting loudly on her work. When the housekeeper finished, she was panting and sweaty and looked like she had just run a marathon. "Time!" shouted Gunner. "Thirty-two minutes," he said triumphantly. "Mr. Phillips, please write down the time for our notes. We will want to analyze this information." He opened the door and beckoned for Rosemary to enter. "Rosie, I must say, thirty-two minutes is disappointing and much longer than the industry standard. I wonder why your team is so slow?" He shook his head sadly. "Could it be because you are not concerned with how long it takes to clean a room?" he mused. "When you multiply the number of added minutes against the number of guestrooms, it adds up, doesn't it?"

Rosemary nodded. "Yes, sir, but it does take time to clean and disinfect a cabin properly, and we work as a team to ensure that we finish before the passengers return," she stammered. "In addition, this was a stateroom, so there was more work for the housekeeper to do."

Gunner was not interested in what Rosemary wanted to say. "You need to instruct your team to work faster," he said threateningly. "If they cannot, I am sure I can find housekeepers who will." He looked at her with a fierce stare. "I can also find a new executive housekeeper who will hold them to the allotted time."

Rosemary bowed her head in shame. "I am certain we can make the needed changes," she whispered.

"That's my Rosie," he said, clapping his hand on her back. "You know when I was the general manager at…" Gunner began telling another story of how he had singlehandedly turned around a housekeeping department, sharing that cleaning times under his watch had been taken down to under twenty-six minutes, beating the industry standard. "And we consistently beat that time, Rosie. I ran a tight ship, and if a housekeeper could not finish her work in the allotted time, I replaced her that day. No excuses." He looked at her. "I cannot tolerate a lazy housekeeper. Do we understand each other, Rosie? Now, I'm going to inspect a room alone with Mr. Phillips and prepare a list of what is wrong in the room. I fear I will need to keep a closer eye on this department." He turned to Mr. Phillips, "Let's find a clean room to inspect."

They walked down the corridor, and Rosemary pointed to a cabin ready for inspection. "You will wait here," he said to Rosemary as he and Mr. Phillips walked into the cabin, leaving the door open enough that his comments would carry into the corridor. "Oh dear, Mr. Phillips, please mark this down. Tsk, not to the level of cleanliness I would expect here," he called out. He wanted to make sure Rosemary could hear his comments. "Mr. Phillips, please note this," he remarked and winked at Mr. Phillips as they stood in the center of the cabin. Gunner had no intention of inspecting the room. It was beneath him. "Hmmm, do you see this, Mr. Phillips? It is not acceptable. Please make a note for my report." There was nothing wrong with the cabin. The housekeeper had cleaned it thoroughly. Gunner's running commentary was only to put Rosemary on edge.

He stepped out of the cabin and back into the corridor. "I'm surprised your housekeeper would say this room was ready for inspection. Something as simple as the signature towel design on the bed is missing. How do you explain this?" he asked, surprised. Rosemary motioned for the housekeeper to follow her, and they walked into the cabin together. She, too, was at a loss as to why the towel design was not on the bed, but looking around, she saw nothing else wrong with the room. "Rosie, Rosie, Rosie," he said sadly. "It pains me to say this, but I feel that I should tell you now that after this cruise is over, I will probably take charge of the housekeeping department. I'll keep you on for now, especially as I will most likely need a translator, but it is evident you cannot ensure that rooms are clean for the guests." He pinched the bridge of his nose as if he were in pain. "I find your eye for detail is lacking, Rosie. I wonder if you have allowed the lines to blur in your department, and not wanting to hurt a staff member's feelings, you have allowed things to slide," he mused. "I've heard that some members of your staff are related to you," he said, raising an eyebrow.

Rosemary felt defeated. Gunner seeing the distress on her face, rubbed his hands together. "I gave you a manual to read this morning. When you open it, you will see my name as the author. If you intend to keep your job, you need to memorize it," he said with a touch of self-importance. "If you choose not to," he cocked his head and held his palms up in the air. "Well, I am sure you can find a job as someone's maid." He turned to Mr. Phillips. "I believe we have seen enough here," he said in a crisp tone, "don't you?" He walked out of the cabin with Mr. Phillips close on his heels.

Rosemary's mind was whirling after the two men left her. She walked out of the cabin in a daze. A mixture of emotions was going through her head—shock, confusion, devastation, and anger. She took such pride in her staff and knew the care and attention they gave the ship was as good as her own. The housekeeper, who had cleaned the room Gunner had inspected, had tears running down her face. "Miss Rosemary," she hiccupped, "the guest told me they didn't want the towels made in the design," she sobbed. "They told me to fold them and put them in the bathroom. Should I have done it anyway? I am so sorry! I didn't know!" she cried. "I was only doing as the guest requested."

The housekeeping team gathered around her, chattering. They wondered what would become of them, and if they would have to leave the ship at once, should they start packing now? They asked her how they would make a living if they didn't have a job on the ship. Like Rosemary, a part of their money went home to help their families. Rosemary looked at each of them calmly. "It will be okay," she said reassuringly, taking their hands in hers. Tears smarted Rosemary's eyes, but she blinked them back. She had to be strong for her team. "We will make this work, I promise you."

"Auntie," Mer, her nephew, spoke, "Mr. Squinty Eyes has many face products in his room. What if I go in there and mix some of them with some cleaning chemicals? He could have a bad reaction and go away."

"Mer!" she said harshly. "You need to be quiet. That is not how we get rid of a kontrabida." She looked at each of them. "We must work harder and faster until he leaves or finds something else to look at." She clapped her hands. "Now, everyone, get back to work. We have much to do before the passengers return." It wasn't until later that Rosemary realized that Gunner had never provided her with his list from the inspection.

Gunner's final visit of the day was to Oaza. As promised, Mila had squeezed him in for the three treatments he had requested under the guise of evaluating the spa. Anna Marie was at the reception desk when he arrived. Her face lost color as soon as she saw him, and she began to stammer. "H-h-hello, Mr. At-At-Atcher, welcome to Oaza," she said. "P-p-please don't fire me," she whispered.

Gunner gave her a disarming smile. His teeth gleamed. "Anna Marie, I'm not going to put you off the ship," he said smoothly. "After much thought, I have decided that your behavior yesterday is a direct result of your training, which is painfully lacking. Now, let's put yesterday behind us and get my spa treatments started, shall we?" He spoke to her with veiled sarcasm. "I'm looking forward to the hydrating mask. The wind and sun are playing havoc on my skin." He stroked his cheeks as he spoke, and Anna Marie inwardly shuddered. "What do you think?"

Anna Marie felt uncomfortable. She looked down at her computer, pressed a button on the screen, and the printer spewed out a piece of paper. "Yes, sir, you have a deep cleansing facial, a manicure, and the mask scheduled for today." Anna Marie came out from behind the desk, holding the paper. "If you w-w-will follow me, Mr. Atcher, I will show you to the locker room so you can change into a robe before your treatment," Anna Marie said bravely.

Gunner looked at her as if she had two heads. "I will most certainly not!" he said hotly, his temper flaring. "As I am your future vice president, it would be unseemly for me to appear in a robe. I am only doing these to evaluate the spa services." He took off his glasses. "Just show me to the private lounge where I can wait, although it had better not take too long," he said tersely. Anna Marie nodded meekly and walked Gunner to the private reception lounge, where clients relaxed before going in for their treatments. A few guests were in the lounge, including Vera Jameson and Marilyn and Louise from Harmony Lakes. All three ladies noticed Gunner's arrival but hid it by having their noses stuck deep in their magazines.

After showing Gunner into the lounge, Anna Marie began to leave, but Gunner spoke up tiredly, "Aren't you forgetting something, Anna Marie?" He washed his face with his hands. "Come now, let's think about it for a moment. Go through what you are supposed to do if you can gather enough brain cells," he said mockingly. Anna Marie looked at him blankly. "My beverage order?"

Anna Marie looked like a frightened rabbit. She put her hands on her cheeks, turning red in embarrassment. "Oh, my goodness, I am so sorry, Mr. Atcher. When you said you didn't want to change into a robe, I was afraid to offer you a beverage in case it was the wrong thing to do with your being the new vice president," she babbled. "You see, I take the guest to the locker room and show them the door that will lead them from the locker room to the lounge. I ask them at that point what they would like to drink and have it waiting for them as soon as they sit down. That way, the drink isn't watered down from the ice melting. Then I take this," she held out the paper in her hand, "which has the client's name and the treatments on it, slide it into the frame on the door to their private treatment room, and notify the technician." She finished her apology out of breath and gave him a weak smile.

"Anna Marie," he said through gritted teeth, "I don't care about how you do things now because it will all change. That is, if you are even still here. However, offering me a beverage would have been the right thing to do whether I was wearing a robe or not." He looked at her and cocked his head to the side. "Thinking is not your strong suit, is it? I am genuinely concerned about the impression you leave on our guests," he said with a frown. "If you can manage it, please bring me a spa water, the one with the cucumbers." He waved his hand dismissively.

Flushing, Anna Marie rushed out of the lounge, and the three women in the room lowered their magazines and looked at each other. Gunner either didn't notice that he was not the only one in the room or didn't care. He sighed dramatically and picked up one of the brochures Mila had made sure were scattered throughout the room. She contended that reading about more spa services would guarantee an additional booking, if not on the current cruise, on the next one. He squinted at it and flipped the pages noisily. "The services and the brochure will need a complete revamp. Especially with the new, younger market, we will go after. More extravagant treatments will need to be offered, not these old lady services," he said disgustedly and tossed the brochure on the table like a frisbee. It skittered across the table and landed on the floor. The three women again lowered their magazines at Gunner's words. Their eyes communicated their feelings without uttering a word.

Anna Marie returned with Gunner's drink and shakily set it on the table in front of him. She picked the brochure up from the floor and placed it on another table. Gunner squinted at his watch. "Anna Marie, does Mila or whoever is doing my treatments even know I am here? Have you taken the time to tell them? I had to rearrange my day to accommodate this appointment," he said crisply. He stood and began pacing. "If I need to find my treatment room myself, please let me know. I wouldn't want to overburden you," he snapped.

She looked at him with frightened eyes and said timidly, "I'll check Mr. Atcher. It will be just a moment."

He paced around the lounge, sighing loudly. Then, finally, he saw the door that he assumed took guests back to the treatment rooms and began to move toward it. Suddenly he yelled out as his shin connected with a small marble table near Vera. "Damnit!" he yelled.

Anna Marie heard Gunner's cry and hurried back to the lounge. She found Gunner rubbing his shin and saw a slight smile on Vera's face. It was clear that Vera had moved the table with her feet so Gunner would run into it. "Mr. Atcher, I'm sorry, it will only be a few more minutes." She turned to Vera, "Mrs. Jameson, if you will follow me?" She held the door leading to the private treatment rooms open.

Vera lowered her magazine. "Anna Marie, dear, it's obvious this man is in dire need of a facial," she drawled and looked over at Marilyn and Louise. "Wouldn't you agree?"

She looked from Gunner to Anna Marie and back to Gunner. "From his mottled complexion, it's plain to see that his needs are far greater than ours, even though we are old ladies. I would hate to see what his skin will look like if it continues in its reddened state. By all means, please, take him back if his room is ready. I don't mind waiting. After all, patience is a virtue only some of us have been gifted with." She smiled wickedly and picked up her glass of spa water, toasting Marilyn and Louise.

Gunner looked at Vera with pure venom. It was the second time she had insulted him in front of staff members. He brushed past Anna Marie limping. "I'll find the treatment room myself," he snapped at Anna Marie.

"Dreadful man," Vera said dryly to his retreating back. "A pity Mila doesn't offer services that repair a person's behavior."

Gunner stalked down the hallway of private treatment rooms opening doors furiously and startling several customers in the middle of their treatment. He either did not notice or did not care to read the signs on the doors, typed in large, bold print indicating if the room was vacant or occupied. A second sign noted the client's name and the treatments scheduled. Mila hoped that detailing this information on the doors would curtail interruptions and keep the relaxation flow going. Sara was in the last room and was placing her tray on the counter when Gunner opened the door. Startled at the intrusion, the tray in her hands flew into the air. Mud, gel, and her instruments clattered noisily to the floor, and she stooped to pick them up.

"This is unacceptable," he fumed, looking around the room. "Why is the room not prepared? The lights lowered? Where is the music? Why are we not prepared for the guest? Just disgraceful!" he snarled. He realized Sara was on the ground picking up the items on the floor. "Why are you on the floor?" he demanded.

"Sir, I apologize," she said quietly, picking up the items on the floor. "I was startled by the noise when you came in and dropped the tray. I was on my way to bring you back. Please lay on the chair, and I'll turn down the lights and start the music." She stood up and touched the control panel. The lights dimmed to a comfortable, warm glow and soft, soothing music came through the speakers.

Gunner reclined on the chair and exhaled. "That's more like it. I think I saw you in the spa yesterday. You were stocking the retail shelves."

Sara bent down to pick up the last few items from the floor. "Yes, sir."

"When I first saw you yesterday, I thought you looked like a girl who once had a crush on me for a split second. Now I realize that you look nothing alike. We went to dinner a few times, but it didn't work out." He continued speaking, but it was apparent to Sara that it was only to hear himself talk. "She wasn't anything to write home about in the looks department, but she was smart. Real smart." He let out a self-satisfied chuckle. "But not as smart as I am. People don't understand that I am always the smartest person in the room. I had to fire her eventually. She spread some rumors, but I got the last laugh. I made sure she couldn't find a job in the hotel industry.

Sara was now standing at the counter and had been so quiet that Gunner had forgotten she was in the room. The instruments rattled on the tray she held, and suddenly Gunner remembered she was there. "I'm sorry, I don't believe that you told me—" and before he could finish the sentence, Sara had left the room and closed the door.

She leaned against the wall, trying to control her breathing. She had to pull herself together. The man who had singlehandedly ruined her career was on the other side of the wall. She took a deep breath and reminded herself that she had a treatment to perform and would do it perfectly, no matter what. She prayed that Gunner would not recognize her. Going to the cabinet, she quickly pulled together a new tray of items for Gunner's treatments and tucked her feelings down deep inside herself. She approached the door and opened it, thankful the lights were low, and he could not see her well. Her hands were the only thing that betrayed her as they continued to shake, making the tray jangle.

Gunner laughed as he heard the tray shaking in Sara's hands. "Do I make you nervous? You and everyone working here should be. Not one of you will still be here when I take over this cruise line," he said, looking at the ceiling. He then turned his head to look at Sara's figure. "Unless, of course, you play your cards right." He let out a self-satisfied sigh. "I can make or break a career," he snapped his fingers, "like that."

Sara placed the tray on the counter. "Now, Mr. Atcher, it's time for us to stop talking and begin relaxing," she said in a soothing voice. "I'm going to place these goggles over your eyes and begin the treatment you so richly deserve. Is the music to your liking?" she asked sweetly.

Gunner nodded. "You don't have an accent; that's nice. That girl I was telling you about had an accent, but you only knew it when she got mad. That's when it came out. I hope this hydrating masque is still working tomorrow. I'm going to the pool at the cruise port and want to look good.

"Shhh, Mr. Atcher, no more talking. I need to smooth out those wrinkles around your eyes and forehead. Wrinkles can be so very telling," she purred.

Sara finished Gunner's treatments and stepped out into the hallway to alert the manicurist that he was ready. In addition to posting the signs on the doors indicating the treatments happening in the private treatment rooms, Mila also believed the technician should come to the guest to keep the element of relaxation flowing. The young woman came in with her tools and began setting up for Gunner's manicure. She had heard about the man and wanted to do a good job, so she took her time first soaking his nails in warm water, trimming his cuticles, and filing his nails. There was a hushed ding, and she took the bowl of hot wax out of the warmer. Testing it, she quickly moved it to the tray table to allow it to cool for a few moments. She decided she would buff Gunner's nails while waiting for the wax to cool.

"Are we almost done?" he sighed impatiently. He wanted to check out the casino before the passengers came back. He had only booked three treatments out of spite to jam the spa's schedule and was now sorry he had. He was irritated that the other technician had left. He had hoped she would perform his manicure so she could feel how strong his hands were. She had never told him her name and had crept out silently when his treatment ended. She had performed his facial expertly and was easy on the eyes. He decided that, for the time being, he would keep her on the spa staff.

The manicurist turned her back to get the buffer from the counter. Gunner decided to hurry things along and plunged his hands into the bowl of wax. He screamed and yanked his hands out quickly. "You tried to burn me!" he howled, jumping out of the chair. He pushed the table away so violently it landed on its side. He frantically tried to peel the hot wax from his hands and fumbled with the doorknob throwing open the door. He stormed into the corridor. "Mila!" he screamed. "Where are you?" He marched down the hall, yelling for her, and opened the door to the lounge. The manicurist stood in the hallway bewildered and saw him go through the door.

Mila was in the lounge apologizing for the unexpected delays and refilling champagne glasses. He marched up to her holding his reddened hands up for her to see. With bits of wax still on them, his fingers looked like

Halloween candles. "As if dealing with that insipid receptionist for a second time wasn't enough and being forced to wait an intolerable amount of time for my appointment, you instructed your manicurist to burn me! Your job with this company is over," he sputtered. "I will demand your immediate dismissal." The guests began looking at each other, visibly uncomfortable at the tirade Gunner was unleashing on Mila. Anna Marie, who had heard the loud voices, dashed into the lounge.

She could feel her temper rising but commanded herself to remain calm. "Mr. Atcher, I am not sure what you are talking about. No one was instructed to burn you, and I am offended that you would believe that. Regarding waiting an intolerable amount of time, I believe you were taken ahead of other patrons who had booked appointments and were here well before you. You have shown boorish behavior," she held her arm out, pointing to the exit. "I'll ask that you leave so our paying customers may find some shred of enjoyment from their spa experience." Simultaneous applause broke out from those who were in the lounge.

He looked around the room, his face reddening. "You have not been listening to me," he said, shaking his finger in her face. A piece of wax flew off, and it landed on Mila's cheek. Gunner came closer to Mila and was inches from her face. She could feel his hot breath. "I will make sure you end up going back to that one-horse circus town you came from in Poland," he said threateningly and stormed out of the lounge.

There was an awkward pause, and Mila, trembling, drew in a deep cleansing breath and turned to those in the lounge. "Ladies and gentlemen, I want to apologize for what you just heard. I wish I could tell you this was a skit for tonight's show in the theater, but it was not. I am embarrassed that you had to witness such bad behavior. I am sure it has undone any relaxation you were feeling. Please allow me to take care of your services today." She gave them a brave smile. "Let's have some more champagne to forget about the last five minutes." She bowed and handed Anna Marie the bottle of champagne she held in her hand. "Again, my deepest apologies." With tears in her eyes, she walked quickly through the door.

There are few secrets on ships, and as soon as Kennedy heard about the altercation in the spa, she rushed to Oaza. Mila had composed herself and was rearranging a shelf in the retail area when Kennedy walked in. Kennedy did not stop to talk and walked directly to the back corridor between the fitness center and the back wall of the treatment rooms hoping it would be empty as going to Mila's office might mean someone would overhear them. Muttering loudly in Polish, Mila entered the hallway in a rage. When she reached Kennedy, she pounded her fist into her hand. "I could kill him, Kennedy. I could shoot him in the heart or stab him! But, no, that would be too quick, and he wouldn't feel it. I know, I could beat him over the head with a pipe. Then he would feel every blow to his pea size brain. He is the most insulting, deceitful man I have ever met. He is a bully and gets away with it because of who he is. It's unacceptable."

A few spa team members had heard Mila and stopped to listen to her outburst. "These are good, hard-working people who give up a normal life to work here. To have a jerk like that come along and threaten everything and everyone, it's not right!" She took a breath. "If he died, would anyone care?" she asked angrily.

Kennedy looked around. There were still a few people standing at either end of the hallway. "Mila, hush," she chided. "You can't say things like that out loud." She darted her eyes toward the staff members lingering at either end of the hallway. "I think you all have somewhere else to be," she said evenly. Then, she turned her focus back to Mila. "You have to keep it together!" she whispered. "Don't you have a yoga class to teach?"

Mila nodded her head. "Yes, in thirty minutes."

"Then you need to lock yourself in your office and pull yourself together before anyone sees how angry you are. You can't teach yoga angry. People are probably already talking about Gunner's tantrum and how you threw him out. We've got to do some damage control and fast."

The passengers began to return to the ship, and Kennedy went first to the pool deck to check that it was ready for their arrival. In her experience, the passengers would race to their cabins and make a beeline to the pool deck. She noticed her two groups of friends had already commandeered a seating area. They had become quite friendly from the looks of things.

"Kennedy," Phil cried out, waving at her frantically. "Come over!"

"We have so many questions—" Dave started in a conspiratorial tone.

Louise interrupted before Dave could finish his sentence, "That man in the spa, your corporate person, is horrible. I've told everyone how he acted toward Mila. In front of guests, too!"

Dave finally got in a word. "But he does look kind of cute." And several people at the table stared at him in shock. "Well, he does," he offered meekly.

Kennedy chose her words carefully. "Louise, I am so sorry you witnessed what happened."

Marilyn laughed. "I'm not. I got a free spa service and champagne. And I feel marvelous," she said in an exaggerated drawl and stretched her arms overhead.

"Leave it to you to find joy in someone else's drama," Dolly said and turned to Kennedy. "Is this the jerk from last night? Tell me quickly. I may die in the next few minutes, and I need to know!"

Phil spoke up before anyone else could. "Is it true the staff is calling him the *goat*?" he asked. "That just cracks me up," he tittered. Everyone at the table turned and looked at him strangely.

"A what?" Dolly questioned. "A goat? As in four legs and eats grass? I may be old, and my hearing may not be right. He's a jerk, but he's not an animal."

Phil snorted. "A goat is someone who is the greatest of all time, get it, G-O-A-T?" He spelled it out for them. "We had one in our New Orleans office. Oh, I was so thankful when he finally transferred. We would be in a meeting, and he would start talking about himself. Blah blah blah, I did this, blah blah blah, I did that, blah blah blah, I'm so smart, blah, blah, blah, I can't believe none of you figured this out, blah blah blah. We couldn't stand him, but we had to be polite. It's the rules of business. All I wanted to do was toss him out the window."

"Oh, you beast," John said, smacking Phil's arm playfully. "What would Miss Manners say?"

Phil put his nose up in the air. "I believe Miss Manners would have walked over, rolled his chair to the window, and politely tipped him out, freeing us from his uncivilized behavior. Then, she would have then suggested we go out for mint juleps."

Kennedy cleared her throat. "I wish I could stay and chat, but I've got to check on the other passengers. Again, on behalf of the company, please accept my apologies."

She walked away and, when John was sure she was out of earshot, said, "Poor dear, I hear he ripped her show and the cast to shreds this morning."

Marilyn looked puzzled. "How do you find out these things?"

"Oh, little birds just flock to me," he smiled cattily and waved his hand. "And honey, don't make that face. It absolutely ages you. It adds at least twenty years."

Marilyn looked as if she had swallowed a bug.

Beth had been following the conversation but suddenly had a baffled look. "How do you get the birds to come to you? I've always wanted to be able to do that," she sighed. "Just like a fairytale princess."

"Beth, it's a figure of speech," Louise snapped. Then, seeing Beth was still perplexed and waiting for John to answer, she quickly turned back to John. "Don't answer her, but as you have little birds, what about the rhinestone cowboy couple from last night? Who are they? What do you know about them?"

John had a smug look on his face. "Well…"

Kennedy hurried to the lobby to welcome the rest of the passengers back. It was a little touch of hospitality she did not mind performing. She prayed she would not run into Gunner, but as it was a task he would probably consider beneath him, Kennedy didn't think she would see him. She had finished listening to one couple's snorkeling adventure and saw the sunburned but happy faces of Terri and Jones Butler. Jones was carrying several packages, and Terri had a small black bag on her arm. Her walk seemed a little unsteady, and when Kennedy got to them, she realized Terri was tipsy.

"Oh, Kennedy," Terri slurred, "we had the best time today, first the speedboat, then swimming with the cute little piggies. I had this wonderful fruit punch while Jones swam with some sharks." She threw her arms around Jones and kissed his cheek. "You know, he's such a daredevil. Then my darling took me to do a little shopping." She reached into the black bag. "What do you think of this?" she asked. She pulled out a black box and opened it.

Kennedy gasped. Inside the box, lying on a bed of white silk, was a large choker necklace made into the shape of an alligator. When you put it on, the alligator's head appeared to be resting just above the wearer's chest while his tail wrapped around the neck. "It's quite unusual," Kennedy said awkwardly. "Words escape me."

Jones preened. "I told you she'd be impressed." He nudged Terri, who almost toppled over in her high heels. Kennedy grabbed her arm quickly to steady her. "Kennedy, just look at those jewels." Jones pointed at the red eyes and the green of the alligator. "Genuine rubies and emeralds," he drawled slowly. In her mind's eye, Kennedy saw the store owner dancing with glee and locking the door after selling the gaudy piece of jewelry, thrilled he had finally unloaded it and at a profit.

Terri stumbled and hiccupped. "I'm sorry, but we can't stay and chat," she slurred. "I need to go to our cabin and take a nap. I'm exhausted." She began to giggle. "And now I need to figure out what outfit I will wear tonight with my new necklace."

"I'm sure you will be lovely," Kennedy said smiling.

"Adios, Kennedy!" Jones waved and steered Terri to the elevators. Kennedy watched them stumble through the lobby, thinking to herself that tonight's dinner should be entertaining.

As the *Helio* departed the port of Nassau, the passengers were in their cabins, preparing for the evening. The itinerary had read: *The Seventies in Song. Turn back the clock as our entertainers sing the classic songs of your favorite 1970s television shows while you dance the night away. For those more daring, prizes will be awarded for the best dressed.* Over her years as a cruise director, Kennedy was sure of a few things. The first night on board was always the Captain's Dinner and the stage show, and the second night required dancing, nostalgia, and costumes of some sort. She was confident there would be at least ten people dressed as a ship's captain and quite a few disco queens. She set off quickly to the Solstice Theater to make sure the cast was ready.

The spa, fitness center, and yoga studio were all connected. When the spa was open, you could enter the reception area and go down a short hallway to the right to access the cardio machines, weight room, and outdoor yoga studio. If the spa was closed, you could access the fitness center from the main corridor. One side of the gym commanded an incredible ocean view as cyclists, joggers, and rowers could pound away on the machines. The other side of the gym had a wall of mirrors and housed the weightlifting equipment, barbells, and free weights. On the other side of the wall of mirrors, a small corridor allowed staff to get back and forth between the spa and the gym. Mila had specifically requested the two-way mirror instead of a wall so guests in the weightlifting section could check their form while working out, and the staff could check on the guests as well as towel and water replenishment without disrupting those in the gym unnecessarily.

Bert, strolling down the corridor, noticed Oaza was empty of passengers. He walked up to Anna Marie at the reception desk and asked if he could take some photos. "Sure," she said glumly. "After what happened today, I hope we have appointments tomorrow." Bert, who had spent most of the day on the beach in Nassau, was unaware of the drama that had occurred earlier. Always eager to hear gossip, he listened while Anna Marie shared what had happened.

"Oh, geez," Bert said. "I better get as many shots as I can. I may also try to take some in the fitness center if it's empty." He turned to walk toward the fitness center's entrance from the spa.

"Only if it's empty!" Anna Marie admonished him. "Do not go in there if there are guests, Bert!" Bert raised his hand in acknowledgment.

Gunner had decided he needed some time in the gym. The irritations of the last two days and the altercation with

Mila in the spa had made him testy and working out would help remove the tension. He had entered the gym from the main corridor so he wouldn't run into Mila or any spa workers. *Besides, I need to keep up my physique. The beauties in Grand Turk will want to feast their eyes upon me.* He entered the gym and noticed at once it was empty. *If this ship had a younger crowd, it would be full*, he thought, looking around the room. *Beautiful people exercising and checking each other out. We can upcharge for the use of the gym and make more money. And because it's my idea, I'll demand that a percentage of that revenue be part of my compensation package. The younger set needs their gym and their coffee. We should take that small café upstairs and turn it into a high-dollar coffee shop. We could even put a satellite space in the spa.* He walked to the weightlifting area and began warming up, watching himself in the mirror.

Sara was still in the spa cleaning up. Walking down the back corridor, she saw Gunner in the two-way mirror. He had begun to work out with the weights. She laughed silently to herself as she noted how Gunner was still self-absorbed.

Sara remembered he couldn't pass a window without checking his reflection.

Gunner stood in front of the mirror. "You are a stud," he said to the mirror and curled his arm upward to admire the muscle. "You have a beautiful girlfriend who worships the ground you walk on!" He began flexing his bicep. He turned to view himself sideways and continued his curls. "You will become vice president of this company and then president, which means a place at the board table." He continued speaking to his reflection. "You will do whatever is necessary to take over this company, no matter who gets in your way. Getting rid of this leadership team is the first step. They will fold like a house of cards by the end of this cruise." He smiled at himself in the mirror.

Sara watched Gunner with disgust. *What did I ever see in you?* When Gunner turned sideways, she chuckled silently, seeing the paunch starting at his midsection. *Things don't seem to be as tight as they once were, Gunner. It looks like life might be catching up to you.*

Gunner huffed and puffed as he began lifting the barbell. "You are so good-looking," he said to the mirror. He grunted. "You are smarter than anyone else. You are the greatest of all time!"

Sara had not realized that Bert was at the opposite end of the corridor, looking at her as she watched the man on the other side of the glass.

The guests began arriving for dinner, and the outfits were varied. Some had come dressed in costume, while others were in regular dinner attire. The Club Diva Boys arrived as the cast of a 1970s show that took place on a cruise ship. They posed for Bert in front of the disco backdrop, and Kennedy was delighted that they had embraced the opportunity to dress in costume. Their outlandish outfits would help to loosen the other passengers up for the show. Steve was perfect as the captain in his white shorts and a button-down shirt with epaulets and white knee socks. To complete the outfit, he had a bubble pipe in his hand. "I didn't want to break the smoking rules," he grinned. He put the pipe up to his lips, and a stream of bubbles came out.

John twirled over to Kennedy. "How do you do? I'm Julie, your cruise director," he trilled in a lavender chiffon dress and golden blonde pageboy wig.

"Oh, and look, we have Gopher, Isaac, Doc, and…" She looked at Phil, wearing a sailor suit and a long, curly golden blonde wig. He had a red rose at his ear. "Charro?" Kennedy clapped her hands. "You don't know what this means to me."

"Honey, you don't know what it means to us to get out and get dressed up, and cuchi cuchi cuchi," he said excitedly, shaking his shoulders.

Kennedy held out her arm. "Please allow me to personally escort you to your table, gentlemen…and ladies," she said, winking at John and Phil.

Kennedy walked back to the podium as the Ladies from Harmony Lakes arrived, also in costume as the cast of a detective show featuring four beautiful women and their male sidekick. "Oh, my goodness, ladies," she exclaimed, "you have outdone yourselves!" She smiled at Dolly.

"Yeah, I got the short straw because I'm short. Hi, I'm Bosley," Dolly said, holding out her hand to shake Kennedy's, "and these are my…angels?" She looked at the four women behind her. "Wow, *that* is going to be a tough sell." Dolly wore a pair of men's plaid pants, a button-down shirt, and a wide tie. "I even got the wig with the receding hairline to make me look authentic," she laughed.

"You look like you just stepped out of the show."

Louise smirked and looked at the others. "I think Kennedy needs to turn the dial on her television. We must be fuzzy." She paused, looking at Kennedy's face. "Oh, you're too young to know what that means. I feel so old now," she said dismally. "I was in my prime in those days. I was fearless, reckless—"

Marilyn interrupted, "And I was as sexy as I am today! Only a select few can pull off reliving those days, my dear, and I am one of them." She fluffed her teased hair and shimmied in her blue sequined jumpsuit.

Kennedy laughed and offered her arm to Dolly. Please allow me to show you to your table," she giggled. Kennedy walked them through the dining room, and there were cheers and wolf whistles for the femme fatales of 1970s television.

Terri and Jones walked up to the podium to be seated. "Oh, Jones," Terri wailed, seeing the Ladies from Harmony Lakes getting attention as they walked through the dining room. "I knew we should have dressed up. Look how everyone is clapping for them. I wanted to be noticed tonight, especially with my new necklace." She pouted and stuck her chest out, stroking the alligator around her neck.

Jones patted her shoulder. "Now, don't you worry, Sweetsie, there is no way anyone could take their eyes off you tonight, especially wearing that necklace. We'll walk around tonight so that people can see it."

Tony had returned to the podium and smiled. "Good evening," he said to them.

Jones extended his hand and held a five-dollar bill between his fingers, "Good evening, I'm Jones Butler. Perhaps you have me on the VIP list for tonight?" He looked at Tony knowingly. "I'm sure you have us at one of your better tables tonight. I want to make sure that everyone can see my beautiful wife and her new ruby and emerald necklace," he said loud enough for those nearby to hear.

Tony stammered, "Y-y-yes, sir, I am sure we can, but I cannot take your money. Will you allow me one moment?" Tony tore his eyes away from Terri's necklace to check his diagram. There was no way anyone would *not* notice Mr. and Mrs. Butler this evening. Terri was in an emerald green silk slip dress, and the alligator necklace Jones had bought her earlier in the day made a bold statement as it appeared to be creeping toward Terri's plunging neckline.

"Hard to take your eyes off her, isn't it?" Jones said to Tony.

"I-I-I apologize," Tony stammered. "I have never seen anyone carry off a necklace such as that one. Please, this way." He motioned for them to follow him.

Jones slapped him on the back. "No need to apologize to me, son. I've been looking at her with my tongue hanging out since the first day I met her at the truck stop where she worked. I didn't realize that she was one of my employees." He looked at Tony and winked. "And that dress certainly stands out, if you know what I mean." Tony escorted them through the dining room, and as they passed the other passengers, a wave of loud whispers followed them to their table. Tony held out Terri's chair. "Now see, honey, not a single person can take their eyes off you. And every woman is as green as your dress with envy." Jones rubbed his hand up and down Terri's naked arm.

Terri sat in her chair and looked dejected. "I guess," she pouted. "But those old ladies got applause, and I didn't." Tony excused himself and shook his head as he walked back to the podium.

Dinner service went smoothly until Gunner, and Mr. Phillips arrived. As soon as the staff noticed Gunner's presence, their anxiety became palpable and heightened. One server tripped over her feet, sending her tray crashing to the ground. Shortly after, two other servers, busy trying to see where Gunner was sitting, walked into one another. Gunner shook his head at the spectacle and motioned for Tony to come over. "Tony, these glasses have water spots on them again. Why were the glasses not polished before the seating?" He held the glass into the light and squinted at it. Tony could not see any spots, but before he could answer, Gunner began speaking again. "I am sure we discussed the need to inspect the dining room yesterday, and here you are, still not following my directions." He sighed and looked at Mr. Phillips. "We should consider the options we discussed earlier today." He looked back at Tony. "Perhaps we should figure out if this job is the right fit for you. Unfortunately, I'm finding that many of you are unsuitable for the jobs you returned to. Time away from the industry has made you rusty, although I wonder if you were any good before. You may leave," he said tiredly, dismissing Tony. Tony walked

away, devastated, and reached in his pocket for an antacid

tablet, and at that exact moment, he felt a sharp pain stab his

stomach, making him wince. Tony had inspected each table

personally, yet Gunner felt the need to point out imaginary

spots on the glasses and bring them to Mr. Phillips's

attention. He sighed, wondering if he wanted to be on

the *Helio* anymore. He loved his work family but wondered

if he should return to Puerto Rico. The constant worry that he

could be fired for a minor misstep was not worth the stress.

The Solstice Theater was set up differently this evening. The

main stage had been transformed into a dance floor, and the

cast was in the balcony seating areas belting out television

tunes from the 1970s. It was an unusual setup, but it worked.

Those who wanted to sit and watch the singers and the dance

floor had a comfortable place to do so, and the stage was

available for those who wanted to dance the night away.

Bert was busy getting candid shots of everyone in the theater. Servers appeared throughout the room with glasses of water and SunRumbrellas. Suddenly, the music changed, and the theme from a popular police show from that decade came across the speakers. Kennedy walked out onto center stage, and the spotlight followed her. Those who had been on the stage dancing stepped down to cool off. Two crew members followed Kennedy, each placing a four-foot-tall acrylic pillar on either side of her. After they left, two more crew members walked out. Each was holding one of the coveted ship's trophies. They placed the trophies on the pillars.

"Ladies and gentlemen, I want to thank you all for being such a great crowd tonight," Kennedy said into the microphone. "Our Seventies in Song night was one of the best we have ever hosted, and it is because of all of you. I want to thank those of you who dressed in costume especially. I am told it takes a special person to relive that decade." The audience laughed. "While I think you are all winners, there can be only two to take home a trophy." The audience let out a soft groan.

There was anticipation as she held the envelopes. "May I please have a drum roll?" A snare drum came through the speakers. "The trophy for our best-dressed man goes to…" She paused, opened the envelope, and smiled. "Our best-dressed man goes to Julie, your cruise director from the *Love Boat*! John, would you like to come up and accept your award?"

In his long gown, John was hilarious as he feigned shock and surprise at winning. He sashayed up the aisle blowing air kisses and waving to the crowd with the comedy of a first-time awards show winner. He pranced up to the stage and pretended to fall dramatically up the steps. When he reached Kennedy, he enveloped her in his arms and bent her backward for a theatrical stage kiss. The audience was already excited, but the flair John brought to the stage increased their enthusiasm, and they made catcalls and whistled. Kennedy was laughing so hard she had to wipe tears from her face. She handed him the trophy and walked over to the side. John, never afraid of the microphone, imitated a famous actress's acceptance speech. "You like me, you really, really like me!" The crowd broke into another round of applause and laughter as he stepped back from the microphone.

Once the excitement had settled down, Kennedy returned to the spotlight, and John was escorted to one of the stage wings by a cast member. "Well, that was certainly…something," she said. "But I'm not sure what. Let's see who the next winner is." She opened the envelope and grinned. "Well, tonight is certainly a strange evening. Our winner for best women's costume is someone you all knew and loved but always felt a little sorry for. Let's hear it for Bosley!" She clapped her hands loudly and motioned for Dolly to come up to the stage.

Dolly was stunned when she heard her name. She couldn't move. A laughing Laura and Marilyn pulled her to her feet and urged her down the aisle to accept her award, but her feet would not move. John noticed that Dolly, the outspoken, brash octogenarian was as still as a concrete statue. The audience watched in fascination as he kicked off his shoes, hiked up his dress, ran down the steps, and up the aisle. He scooped Dolly into his arms and ran back to the stage. Dolly was in a daze until she saw the trophy. Kennedy placed it in her arms, and Dolly hugged it to her body. Then, realizing her small stature, Kennedy handed her the microphone.

"Wow, I never would have thought I would have gotten a trophy for dressing up like a man. Who knew it was that easy?" The crowd laughed. "All I can say is…VICTORY IS MINE!" She raised the trophy over her head. The audience went wild, and the disco music began playing again as confetti cannons went off.

Later that evening, Kennedy knocked on Mila's door. While her night had been a success, her friend's day had been terrible. "Do you think I should start packing my stuff?" Mila asked morosely, motioning Kennedy to come in. "Gunner is intent on getting rid of me after today. Ugh. Is it better for me to go away quietly?" she asked as tears welled up in her eyes.

"Mila Casimir!" Kennedy handed her friend a tissue. "I don't know what happened to my vibrant, proud, gutsy friend, but would you please ask her to come back? I am not sure who this sad sack is." She looked Mila in the eye. "May I remind you that we are the leaders of the *Helio*, and Gunner is not the vice president yet. He's a consultant. He consults. He advises. When we get back to Florida, I'm going to call Alfred, and it wouldn't hurt for you to be on the call as well," she said feistily. "We will not allow someone like Gunner to turn us into spineless jellyfish." She hugged Mila. "You've championed the spa for a long time. You poured your soul into its success. Will you allow a goat to take it away from you?" she demanded. She put a finger on either side of her head and pointed them at Mila. "I say, BAAAAHHHH, BAAAAHHHH."

Mila looked at her, and her lips began to quiver. Then, a laugh escaped, and soon she was doubled over in hysterics laughing at Kennedy's terrible impersonation of a goat.

"Now that I have the real Ms. Casimir back, we need a plan." Kennedy began pacing the room. She pointed to her forefinger. "First, we must come out of this cruise with great comment cards. We cannot give Gunner any chance to throw mud. Second," she pointed to her middle finger, "we, all of us, need a meeting with Alfred. He needs to hear what happened on this cruise. We don't want to appear to be whining, but we need to make him understand our position." She pointed to her ring finger. "Next, we need to find out from Alfred why we didn't know about this guy coming on board. I don't understand why corporate didn't tell us. It doesn't make sense, even for them. They should have told us." She shook her head.

While Mila and Kennedy were formulating a plan, Rosemary and Franklin were in their own discussion on the promenade deck, and both were miserable. "Rosemary, I cannot leave you on the ship alone," Franklin said. "Please come with me. We will pack tonight and get off the ship when we dock. Then, we can catch a plane and go wherever you want." He looked at her earnestly. "We can figure this out together but being on the ship miserable is not worth it. I can retire now with full benefits. The only reason I haven't left yet is because of you."

Rosemary looked down at the deck. "I know, Franklin, but now is not the right time for me." She looked at him sadly. "It broke my heart to hear him say that my staff was not worthy of their jobs. They are my family, and I cannot leave them now. They need someone to protect them, and that is my job. If he fires them, where will they go? No, I can't leave them now."

Franklin shook his head. He leaned on the rail and looked out into the inky darkness below. The wind ruffled his white hair. "Rosemary, I cannot work for a man who belittles others to make himself look good. I can't respect someone who only talks about himself. I grew up on this ship, and we've always looked out for each other. I've watched each of you come on board and grow into your roles. We've become a family and are dedicated to each other, our guests, and our company." They were silent for a few minutes as each pondered their next step. Franklin broke the silence. "I cannot allow Gunner to destroy our team," he growled, pounding the railing.

Rosemary joined him at the railing. She wore a thoughtful look on her face. "I remember something my grandfather once told me when I was bragging about winning a board game. I was being a very boastful girl and hurting my cousin's feelings. He said, 'A lion never has to tell the jungle that he is a lion. The jungle knows. Only the small animal needs to make noise to feel important.'" She turned to Franklin. "That is how I think of Gunner—a small animal needing to feel large. I feel sad for him." She looked at Franklin and squared her shoulders. "I have to stay on the ship until I can find another way to earn money. I still must take care of my family in the Philippines. We lived in poverty until I got a job on a ship and could send money home. I work hard every day for them. I cannot just leave because it suddenly has become difficult." She laughed. "My grandfather would find humor in this situation. He would tell me that Gunner is nothing more than a mosquito flying around, trying to make me think about him and not my goal, and my goal is to take care of the guests, not to worry about some pesky fly."

Franklin looked at her for a long moment as her words sunk in. "As always, you find a way to bring me around." He sighed. "Okay, you win. We will stay until you have a plan." He held out his arms. "And I believe you owe me a dance, Ms. Flores." Rosemary smiled and stepped into his arms. The moon washed them in soft light as the music came out quietly from the speakers. Looking into each other's eyes, they forgot about Gunner and the stress he was causing.

When the song ended, Rosemary whispered two words in Franklin's ear, "Mahal kita."

Sunny Dayz Cruise Line

THE HELIO

DAY THREE

GRAND TURK, TURKS AND CAICOS ISLANDS

ARRIVAL 7:00 A.M.

DEPARTURE 4:00 P.M.

The *Helio* docked in Grand Turk early the next morning, and as the passengers made their preparations for their day, Kennedy, Mila, and the others gathered on the promenade deck.

"So, it seems like we have all had a taste of goat," said Franklin.

"All but Luke and me," Omar replied. "For whatever reason, neither of us has had the pleasure of his company."

Franklin looked at Omar. "Oh, just wait, my friend," he said ominously. "I am sure you will have your turn under the hot lights before we return to Florida, and then you can be ripped to shreds and bloodied like the rest of us."

Kennedy spoke up, "The reason for this meeting is that I would like everyone to write down their interactions with Gunner. I want us to meet with Alfred when we return to Port Canaveral, and these notes will be important. There are a lot of questions we need answers to." She looked at each of her friends. "We have two and a half more days with Gunner, and we need to change our methods and kill him with kindness, especially if we want to remain together as a team."

Mila picked up the conversation. "It will take all of us working together, and Gunner will be suspicious." She bumped Kennedy's hip. "Last night, an incredibly wise woman reminded me that our job is to take care of the guests. Unfortunately, the distractions Gunner is causing us has made us forget the focus of our jobs."

Tony spoke up, "Mila is right! My servers do great work until he walks into the room. He's made me so nervous and jumpy, worrying about what he will say, that I have pressured my team to the point they are paying more attention to Gunner than our passengers." He visibly brightened as he said these words. "I need to remind them and myself to focus on the guests, and we will get back to being the well-oiled machine we are." He exhaled a large breath and kissed Mila on the cheek. "Mila, thank you, thank you, thank you."

Mila blushed. "Well, it wasn't me, it was Kennedy, but I'll take the kiss," she said wryly.

"It appears that there are two wise women in this group," Franklin spoke up. "Rosemary told me the same thing last night. Take care of the guests, and everything else will fall into place."

Rosemary nodded her head. "It's what we have always told our staff," she said confidently. "I reminded each of them of that this morning."

Kennedy looked at everyone. "We need to focus, guys." She looked at her watch. "And I have to run. Don't forget we have a safety drill directly after our staff meeting while the guests are in Grand Turk." Kennedy left, feeling a bounce in her step for the first time in three days. Making her way to the lobby to check on the passengers as they left for Grand Turk, Kennedy was surprised to see Terri and Jones Butler standing in the lobby. Terri wore a white, gauzy dress while Jones sported a white linen shirt, khaki shorts, and a straw hat. "Off to the ponies," he said, walking up to Kennedy, who looked at him quizzically. "Terri wanted a romantic ride on the beach," he explained and winked at Terri. "So, that's what we are going to do."

Terri nodded enthusiastically. "It's so romantic when you ride out into the ocean," she said breathlessly. "It's like a scene from a movie."

Jones looked around the lobby. "I wonder where he is?"

"Who?" Kennedy questioned.

"The little photographer guy. The one who has been taking all the pictures of Terri. He was supposed to meet us in the lobby."

"Bert?" Kennedy asked strangely. She could not fathom why Jones would be looking for him unless it was to take a photo of Terri in her white dress. Jones had bought every photo Bert had taken of Terri so far.

Jones nodded. "Yes! There he is!" He pointed at Bert, who was trudging through the lobby, wearing several cameras around his neck. He wore a large duffle bag like a backpack.

"Okay, I have my gear. Ready when you are," he said breathlessly.

"Bert, what's going on?" Kennedy asked curiously, looking from Bert to Jones.

"Oh, I asked Bert if he would take some romantic photos of us on our horseback ride," Terri replied. "I want to make all the ladies back home jealous of my dreamy trip with Jones. I've seen them in the magazines, and I'm sure Bert can recreate them for us."

Bert looked at Kennedy with anxious eyes and gulped. "Sure can!"

"Well, let's get going!" Jones said enthusiastically. They began to walk toward the gangway. "Now, I've got some photography tips I'd like to share with you, Bert," Kennedy could hear Jones talk as if instructing a student. Kennedy didn't know whom to feel sorrier for—the Butlers, Bert, or the horses.

Vera was the next of Kennedy's VIPs to leave. "I missed you last night, Mrs. Jameson," Kennedy said as Vera walked up to her.

"I abhor the idea of a costume party, but I understand the guests had an enjoyable time." She gave Kennedy a serious look. "I must commend you on an outstanding job so far, Kennedy. The cruise has been as expected with very few bumps, other than that abysmal couple and that odious, boastful man, neither of whom you had any control over. Nevertheless, you've made certain that the passengers are enjoying themselves. I do hope it is reflected in the comment cards and in returning reservations."

Kennedy was in shock. "Thank you, Mrs. Jameson," she stammered. "I will admit that I was worried when I did not see you at dinner last night."

Vera laid a hand on Kennedy's arm. "My dear, I was not going to sit in that dining room with people dressed from the 1970s. There was nothing good about taking a trip down that memory lane." She shook her head. "Living through that decade was painful enough, but to relive the fashions is not something I wanted to ever see again." She shuddered, and Kennedy looked at her questioningly. "I had a flashback to a few questionable clothing choices. Brown corduroy flared short suits and macramé vests." She shuddered again. "Mr. Meier was kind enough to indulge me, and we dined in the Vantage Point Lounge, a place that, I must say, is growing on me." Kennedy must have looked puzzled, and Vera laughed. "With all of your excitement over the disco era, you forgot about him, didn't you?" she said mockingly, arching an eyebrow.

Kennedy quickly recovered. "Oh, Mrs. Jameson, I didn't forget about Mr. Meier, and I am thrilled he was able to escort you again, although I may have to keep my eye on the two of you moving forward," she grinned. "So, where are you off to today?"

"My, but you are a nosy young lady. If you must know, I am off to see an old friend whose salt business I have invested in and to address some business matters with one of my bankers," Vera replied.

Kennedy smiled sadly at Vera. "Do you ever have time to enjoy yourself, Mrs. Jameson?" she asked, concerned.

Vera patted her arm. "My dear, growing the company is my fun, but I also must find ways to grow the profits and do some good in this world. I can't allow my husband's family to get my hard-earned money when I die. Not one of them deserves a cent, other than my niece Inez who works for me," she said crisply.

Kennedy's mouth hung open in shock. "Mrs. Jameson, that's horrible!" she exclaimed.

"No, Kennedy, it isn't," she said without emotion. "They get their quarterly dividend check to ensure they don't meddle in the company affairs. I decided long ago to put my money where it would do good." She sniffed and put her short-handled purse on her forearm. "Which is one of the reasons for my visit to the banker. I support a school here in Grand Turk, and I want to see for myself that they do not need any supplies." She looked at her watch. "Goodbye, Kennedy. I will see you later this afternoon. I won't be long in port today. I have another spa appointment, and I am looking forward to it."

"Goodbye, Mrs. Jameson, have a good time," Kennedy said quietly, absorbing what Vera had shared. Over the years she had known Vera, she thought she had a good grasp on the woman and felt that she was headstrong, difficult, demanding, and abrasive. However, learning about her investments in a local island community made her readjust her thinking. She walked toward the photo wall and ran into the Ladies from Harmony Lakes, who were writing down the numbers of the photos they wanted.

"Oh, look, it's one of you, Mother," Laura said.

"And look, there's one of me with someone who's supposed to be a ship's captain!" Marilyn cooed. "I always did love a man in uniform," she fluttered her eyelashes.

"Marilyn, you would have slept with anything in uniform and still do!" Dolly jeered. "And that includes the town dog catcher." The ladies laughed while Marilyn pretended to be hurt.

Kennedy walked up to them. "Well, ladies, what are we doing today? The Salt Museum? Shopping?"

"Oh, please! That's for the lightweights," Dolly said, her eyes dancing. "ATV riding and zip lining is the order of the day. I've always wanted to do it, and I only have so long to finish my bucket list."

"Mother!" said Laura, horrified. "Could we please not talk about your impending death?"

"Death, schmeth," Dolly retorted. "I won the Sun Trophy last night, which checked another box on my list!" She laughed and pantomimed, making a large checkmark in the air. "We need to start living life, ladies, and I'm going to make sure we do." She turned and looked at Kennedy, who was still shocked by Dolly's announcement of their plans for the day. "You look like you need a drink, kid. You should go check out the pool bar while we are gone!"

The senior staff gathered at ten o'clock for their scheduled meeting in the conference room. "Kennedy, what time is the drill?" Tony asked as he popped several antacids.

"I'll call Safety Officer Tully as soon as we are finished," she replied. "He's heard about our meetings lately and decided against setting a time until we were available, but he wants to get it done as early as possible in case we find any glitches."

"Is the goat, I mean Gunner, coming to this meeting?" asked Franklin. "He hasn't been to the maintenance shop yet to inspect it, and the maintenance requests are backing up. I suppose it's probably too early in the morning for his highness," he said snidely. "Perhaps, as he is not here now, we could—"

Gunner and Mr. Phillips walked in, and Kennedy wondered for a split second if they stood at the door and listened to find the right time to make an entrance. "We could what?" asked Gunner caustically. Franklin glared at him.

"Perhaps, we could do our meeting quickly so we can prepare for the safety drill," Franklin retorted hotly. "Some of us have real jobs to do around here, Mr. Atcher, not find ways to make more work for others."

"Well, Mr. Blaas, as your department failed miserably yesterday, I think everyone should hear about my findings, don't you?" He gave the group seated around the table a sarcastic smile. "Well, I'm sure you already know since no work orders have been completed." He walked to the front of the room. "Settle in, people. We have a lot to discuss this morning."

Gunner turned to Kennedy. "Kennedy, please inform whomever you need to that you will not be released to take part in the safety drill until I dismiss this meeting, and not one minute before. Please also inform them that I will not be taking part in it." He pinched his fingers between his eyes. "It's a mundane staff drill, and I have other things to do. I am well versed in all things safety-related. Speaking of which, when I was the general manager of..." Gunner began to tell another tale from one of his greatest moments while the others sat in frustration.

Omar wrote on his notepad and slid it to Kennedy while Gunner's back was turned. *The captain will not be happy about this.* Kennedy gave him a quick shrug of her shoulders.

"Now, to discuss my visits to the maintenance and housekeeping departments. Simply put, as with the visits to the kitchen and dining room and my review of our onboard entertainment, I find you and your staff lacking. Mr. Blaas and Rosie are aware of their deficiencies, and I am certain they were up late last night preparing for my next visit, which I can only hope will be better than the ones I experienced yesterday."

He continued and turned his stare onto Mila. "As to the spa," he blinked his eyes several times, "suffice it to say that after much consideration, I am going to recommend that we have someone else run it. Mr. Phillips and I discussed it last night, and we will send over our recommendations after this meeting. I was going to wait until we returned to Florida, but the change needs to be made sooner rather than later. I have someone who can take over as soon as we reach Port Canaveral. I haven't decided whether we will close the spa in the meantime or if I will manage it." Everyone faced Mila, who had turned deathly white as the blood drained from her face and the slow burn of rage began to course through her body.

"Which brings me to my next point." Gunner cleared his throat and blinked his eyes again rapidly. "I have determined, and Mr. Phillips agrees, that we must make some changes to the leadership of this team to make this a highly functioning ship. I have not met with a few of you yet, but I will let you know when those meetings will occur." He began to pace the room. "Be assured, people, there will only be one voice the corporate office and the board hears, and in case you forgot, it's mine."

He looked at the stunned group sitting around the table. "I am fully aware that I am not liked on this ship," he said heatedly. "And it pains me to know that you have purposefully poisoned your staff against me." He held up his hand. "Don't try to tell me otherwise. It has been painfully evident by the treatment I have received since I boarded this ship, but what you need to share with them is that when *you* are no longer with this company, if they are lucky and still have a job on the ship, they will have to deal with *me*, and I can make life very unpleasant."

Gunner had his back turned from the group. "I know most of you dislike or even hate me. Guess what? It doesn't matter because not one of you has the guts to stand up to me." He looked at each of them individually. "Believe me when I tell you, I will move on from being vice president to being president of this cruise line very rapidly. If you're lucky enough to make the cut, it would be in your best interest to begin sucking up now." The room was silent as Gunner made his last statement. The only noise was the ticking of the clock on the wall, and his words chilled every person in the room.

He once again turned his eyes on Mila. "I will be stopping by for another spa appointment before I go into Grand Turk. Please make certain that I am taken care of quickly and without the drama, I have experienced in the last two days." Gunner made his way toward the door. "You might want to let your staff know I plan to spend much of my remaining time in the spa to see if anyone is worth keeping."

Gunner looked at Mila. "You may find it easier to begin packing your personal belongings now as you will most likely be removed from the company as soon as we dock in Port Canaveral." He gave her an arrogant smile. "Mr. Phillips, I believe we have a letter to draft," he said as he opened the door and walked out, followed by Mr. Phillips, who gave a sad smile to the group sitting around the table.

The team gathered around Mila. She took in a deep breath and tried to steady her hands.

"I'm going to kill him," said Franklin.

"I'll help," Omar replied. "And we both know where to put the body, so it won't be found."

Mila raised her head stoically. "You know, I love you all," she said, her voice quavering. "I'm just sad that I will no longer be part of such an amazing team. You guys are my family. I'm not even sure of what to do next." She took a ragged breath.

Kennedy drew herself up. "You are not going to do anything except wash your face and stand your ground," she said firmly.

"That's right," Rosemary said, standing beside Mila. "You will run the spa for the rest of the cruise just as you would on any other day. He can't fire you. He can recommend firing you, that is all. I want you to think about something today, Mila, and hold it in your heart. A lion does not concern himself with the opinion of sheep, and Gunner is nothing more than a sheep. Alfred and everyone in the corporate office knows you, and the board of directors knows you. They would not have allowed you to spend money on renovating the spa if they didn't believe in the person that you are. And every person in this room will fight for you." She waved her hand toward the door. "That man is trying to make himself important by making you look small." She looked around the room. "It's time for us to go buy mattresses," she said in a gravelly voice as she tried to impersonate a famous actor who had said a similar line in a well-known movie about the mob. The group began to laugh.

"Rosemary, I think you mean we need to *go* to the mattresses!" Tony laughed, pinching his waist.

Rosemary's grasp on American pop culture sometimes had holes in it, but they all understood what she meant. She shrugged her shoulders. "Go to the mattresses or buy the mattresses; either way, we need to put our plan from this morning into place."

While the team was in their staff meeting, Bert had returned from the Butlers' romantic ride. It had been a painful shoot. The horses were not interested in modeling or following directions, and Terri and Jones thought they were celebrities on a photo shoot. Nevertheless, he felt that with some editing, he had some decent shots to sell them. Dumping his duffel bag in his cabin, he walked to the spa to finish taking the photos he had promised to the corporate marketing department. Hearing rumors of a potential shakeup on the ship, he knew that staying low and keeping corporate happy was the way to go if he was to keep his job.

Gunner arrived in Oaza for his unscheduled appointment. Anna Marie was at the desk and blanched when she saw him. "Anna Marie, before you say something you shouldn't—"

However, before Anna Marie could open her mouth to say that the spa was closed due to the scheduled drill, Mila breezed into the reception area. "Good morning, Anna Marie," she said with false enthusiasm. "I'm going to take care of Mr. Atcher personally." She smiled pleasantly at Gunner. "You don't mind, do you? The staff is busy preparing for the drill, and as director, I should be the one to take care of you. What treatment would you like to try today?"

Gunner was unprepared for Mila's attitude and was confused, wondering what angle she was taking. *Perhaps she's trying to save her job in a last-ditch effort, not that she has a chance, but it'll be fun to see her grovel*, he thought. "I'd like the eucalyptus facial," he replied stiffly. "I believe it will help me relieve the stress and tension I have felt since I stepped on this ship."

Mila nodded her head in agreement. "It is a fine choice, Mr. Atcher. The eucalyptus will invigorate you mentally and physically. I believe you said that you were going into Grand Turk. It may be best for you to go into the men's locker room and change. There are robes you can put on so that your suit and shirt stay fresh." She continued, "Anna Marie will meet you in the lounge with a refreshing spa water while I prepare the room."

Gunner walked into the men's locker room perplexed. He had all but fired Mila in front of her colleagues. He had demeaned her in front of customers and staff, yet she continued to show him graciousness. He didn't understand her behavior. Changing into a robe, he entered the lounge and found Anna Marie holding a shaking glass of cucumber water. He took it from her trembling hands and sat down. Before he had time to finish the water and complain, Mila opened the door to escort him to the treatment room.

Bert was still taking photos of the spa and watched the exchange between Mila and Gunner in the reception area. Although he could not hear what they were saying, it was clear from Mila's body language that she was extending every hospitality to Gunner. *It's none of my business,* he thought to himself. *My job is to take pictures and turn them over, nothing more.* Bert went into one of the treatment rooms to take photographs. Minutes later, he heard loud voices coming from the room on the other side. Unable to control his curiosity, he pressed his ear against the wall.

"Mr. Atcher, please reconsider your position," Mila pleaded. "This spa means so much to me. I poured my heart and soul into it. You can teach me. I can retrain the staff. I can—"

"Miss Casimir," Gunner interrupted. "I am interested in nothing more than my facial," he said in an even tone. "You have been difficult to work with since I boarded. You poisoned your staff against me, and may I remind you," he said dramatically, "you threw me out of the spa, me, your future boss. You are not a very smart woman, are you?" He settled into the treatment chaise. "The decision was not hard at all, and after my facial, I will review the message Mr. Phillips has drafted, he will press send, and you will be gone. Once the others see how quickly I had you removed, they will quickly fall into line. People are fickle. They will do anything to save their jobs. Look at yourself. You are standing here begging for your job." He waved his hand to the tray of products. "Now, if you please, let us proceed with my facial. It's probably the last real spa treatment you will ever give. Perhaps you can find employment doing manicures in some suburban strip mall."

Mila looked at the ground and counted to ten in her head. She took a deep breath to channel her feelings as she went from hopelessness to rage and back to despair. Gunner sat there watching her face, enjoying the torment he was putting her through. "May we get started? I have things to do," he asked impatiently, and Mila nodded. She pressed buttons on the control panel to lower the lights and turn on the music, and then she wheeled the tray over to her chair. Sitting down, she placed the small goggles over Gunner's eyes, wishing instead she could put her fingers on his eyelids and push them into his brain.

Bert was wide-eyed at what he had just heard, realizing the rumors were all true. He went through the mental list of photos still to take, which were still, unfortunately, many. He had wasted time and was now in a crunch. He walked through the corridor between the fitness center and the back of the treatment rooms and saw Sara refilling the refrigerators with water through the two-way mirror. She had parked a cart of towels nearby so she could put them on the tables throughout the room. Seeing the bottles of water and Sara's towel cart gave Bert an incredible idea. He would put a glistening bottle of water and a towel on the elliptical. The moisture on the bottle would reference the sweat of someone looking out at the ocean while they used the machine. "I am a genius," he said to himself, slapping his forehead. "This shot could be the lead for the fitness center web page!" He raced into the fitness center to set up the shot. He put his earphones on. The white noise they played in his ears would help him focus on what he needed to do. He still had many more photos to take, but the inspiration of the one shot was sure to help him finish his assignment.

Mila finished applying the mask to Gunner's face and said softly in a low voice that she needed to dismiss the staff for the drill and would return momentarily. Gunner waved a hand dismissively at her. "Please hurry back as I want to have enough time to visit Grand Turk."

Mila walked into the reception area and clapped her hands together to get her staff's attention. "Everyone, it's time for the drill. You all know what to do. Follow the directions given by the safety team to the letter. Now, please make your way to your assigned areas." The group left chattering, and Mila noticed Sara standing by the reception desk with a cart full of towels. "Sara, why are you still here?" she asked.

"Mila, I have a few last things to finish. It will only take a few moments to complete them. Please? I promise I can get them done quickly and be at my assigned station on time, scouts honor," she smiled, holding up three fingers.

Mila frowned. "Okay, okay, but Sara, hurry. I don't need you to get into trouble. You are an asset to our spa, and we don't want anyone to say anything different."

Sara noticed her boss's gloomy demeanor. "Mila," she said kindly, "why don't you let Anna Marie and I reopen the spa for you after the safety drill? I can see the stress on your face, and you look like you could use some rest. The passengers won't be back for hours, and there won't be much to do until they return. I promise we won't mess things up too badly," she laughed softly.

Mila protested, "No, I can't do that. I have responsibilities, and what if someone needs something?"

Sara gave Mila a patient smile. "Then we will handle it. I promise." She paused for a moment. "And if you are worried about Mr. Atcher, don't be. He told me yesterday when I was doing his treatments that he was going to hang out at one of the pools in Grand Turk." She laughed. "He said he hoped the effects of the hydrating masque he got yesterday would still be in place so he would look good."

Mila nodded her head. "Okay, thanks, Sara. I'll finish Mr. Atcher's facial and go to the safety drill. After that, I'll lie down in my cabin for a while, but I'll be back by three, so I can be here to help with the afternoon's appointments. Promise me that you will finish and get to your designated area on time. Officer Tully will have both of our heads if we aren't where we are supposed to be."

Bert hoped no one would notice that he was missing from the mandatory drill. He found them boring and reasoned there was always someone else to take responsibility if something serious happened. In his opinion, it was just a box to check. He took his time photographing the locker rooms and took a few more shots in the spa's private treatment rooms. Setting up a long shot, he noticed Sara walking toward the locker rooms with an armload of towels. "I wonder if I can do a motion blur with her in it," he said to the empty hallway. "I'll need to adjust my shutter speed. If I can pull this off, the shot will be epic!" He snapped the shutter a few times and looked at the image on the small screen, pleased with the result.

Sara, having put the towels in the men's locker room, walked down the hallway between the back of the private treatment rooms and the fitness center. She pressed her ear against the wall. She could hear Mila speaking to Gunner.

"Mr. Atcher, this completes your facial. I apologize for leaving you so quickly, but I must prepare for my part in the drill. Safety Officer Tully knows you will not be participating. You are welcome to go to the locker room at your leisure," she said in a soft, calm voice.

"Whatever you think you need to do," he said glibly. "Although, if it were me, I would be cleaning out my office and not taking part in some stupid safety drill. It's not exactly like you'll be coming back, is it?"

Mila blinked back tears. She couldn't respond to Gunner because of the lump forming in her throat.

"I, myself, am going to go into port just as soon as possible," he said. "But first, I need to send a certain message to the corporate office."

Mila stepped out of the room and closed the door quietly. She needed to figure out her next steps as the *Helio* would no longer be her home.

Bert had gone into the gym to get a bottle of water from the refrigerator. As he came out of the staff entrance, he saw Sara with her ear pressed to the wall. When she pulled away and walked past him, he took off his earphones and whispered loudly to her. "What were you doing, eavesdropping?"

"No, you idiot," she hissed. "I needed to see where they are in the treatment so I can make sure there are enough towels in the locker room for Mr. Atcher."

Bert looked at her, puzzled. "But didn't I just see you put towels in there?" he whispered loudly.

Sara looked startled for a moment. "Whatever," she muttered and pushed past him with a small stack of the white terry in her arms. "I don't answer to you. Don't you have a drill to be at?"

Bert turned red. "You mean the same one you're supposed to be at?" he hissed caustically and jammed his earphones back in his ears.

After Mila left, Gunner sat in the chair for a few more moments, deciding what he wanted to do next. He could go into Grand Turk, or he could go to Mr. Phillips's room and read the message to be sent. Visions of young women in minuscule bathing suits made the decision easy. He would go into Grand Turk and, when he came back, meet Mr. Phillips, and make any changes necessary to the draft message. He reasoned that Mr. Phillips would still be in his room waiting for him regardless of when he arrived. He got up, left the room, and walked toward the men's locker room. Due to the impending drill, the lights in the locker room had been turned off, and the emergency exit lights dimly lit the room. Gunner entered the darkened room from the back.

Bert thought of one last shot after he had packed up his equipment. He still had his earbuds in his ears. *Oh, getting that shot would be great and could be a series.* Using the blurred image of Sara walking with the towels in her arms and the water bottle shot on the elliptical, the third shot would make it a triptych that would be noticed far more than two single shots, which could be easily overlooked. He had already packed up his equipment but knew he only needed his camera, the right lighting, and a steady finger for the shot. He positioned himself, envisioning the image. The half-open door leading into the men's locker room from the dimly lit corridor was perfect. The only problem was the piece of paper taped on the wall between the locker room and sauna doors. He could just barely see the edge of the paper through the viewfinder. He stepped over to the wall, took the piece of paper down, and stuck it on the wall on the other side of the sauna door. Satisfied, he turned around to get back into position to take the shot and didn't hear or see the paper fall to the floor. He aimed the lens and depressed the shutter button rapidly, praying one of these would be the perfect shot. After snapping the shutter, a final time, Bert felt satisfied with the images he had taken. He turned around, picked up his camera bag, and left the hallway. He went through the employee entrance in the fitness center, grabbed another bottle of water from the refrigerator, and proceeded to take the back staircase to his cabin to wait out the safety drill.

Gunner felt around the wall to turn on the lights. Not finding a light switch quickly, he huffed loudly to the darkened room. "Are you kidding me, Mila?" He strode to the front entry, where the door was partially opened, allowing a thin shaft of light from the corridor to come through. Surely the light switch would be beside the doorframe. "You turned off the lights so I couldn't get ready? What, one last shot?" he said to the empty room.

Suddenly he was hit from behind. As he doubled over, clutching his head in agony, he heard a voice purr. "No, Gunner, Mila didn't do it." Another blow fell on his head. "I did," and he felt something heavy smash again and again onto the back of his skull. Gunner fell to the tiled floor, losing consciousness.

He opened his eyes a few minutes later. Black spots dotted his blurry vision. "Oh, my God, what happened?" He touched the back of his head, which was throbbing with waves of pain. He rolled over to his side, feeling sick. His hand went again to the back of his head, but he pulled it back quickly in agony. "What happened?" he weakly asked again to the empty, dark room. Gunner struggled to change positions and knew he needed to get on his hands and knees and then to his feet. He cried out feebly for help, but as he began to see dark spots again, he realized no one would be able to hear him. They were all at the drill.

Gunner rocked back and forth gently on his hands and knees. Finally, he willed himself to crawl slowly toward the triangle of light on the floor. He succumbed to the dark spots a few minutes later and passed out again just as he reached the door, returning to consciousness a few moments later. He felt the bottom edge of the door and held onto it for dear life. He was dizzy and weak, his body was trembling, and he could feel nausea rising in his throat. His fingers grasped the door like talons as he willed himself into a sitting position. He panted from the exertion and rested for a moment as the dark spots danced in his eyes again. When he finally felt ready, his hand crept up the door, and he began slowly pulling himself up. It was difficult as the door kept moving back and forth, and its motion made his head spin. He tried to make sense of what had just happened. He heard the woman's voice in his head. *"'No, Gunner, Mila didn't do this. I did.'"* His head began to swim again, and he gasped as a wave of pain racked his skull. He leaned against the edge of the door, panting.

Once Gunner had gathered enough strength, he moved his body across the door. The doorknob dug into his belly, and as he stretched his arm across the surface, he finally felt the other side of the door frame. He let out a small cry when his fingers touched it and pulled himself toward the edge and the corner of the wall. He rested his weight against the wall, thankful it was solid and wouldn't move, and began slowly shuffling down the hallway. He waved his left arm up and down the wall like a blind man while his other held his neck to support his head. The constant crashing waves of pain were like nothing he had ever felt before. He had to find help. He remembered that each private treatment room had an intercom beside the control panel in case of an emergency.

When his hand touched a doorknob, he let out a cry. He grasped the knob and turned it with all his strength. Dark spots appeared again from his exertions, and he began to weaken again.

Willing himself to stay conscious, Gunner let go of the wall and felt nothing but air as he blindly searched for the doorframe. Finding it, he clutched his fingers around the frame and pulled himself through the doorway into a darkened room. He put out his hand and spidered it up and down the wall. His fingertips brushed a box hanging on the wall, and he groped the wall to get closer. As his body moved away from the door, it slammed shut with a loud bang.

Gunner was in complete darkness. When the door had banged shut, he had been startled and pulled his hand away from the wall. He placed it again on the flat surface, struggling to find the intercom with his groping fingers. He began pressing the buttons on the box, calling out weakly for help. But there was no response. *They are probably all at the stupid safety drill, but shouldn't someone be manning the switchboard?* Gunner suddenly felt his legs give out and slid to the ground. His head began to swim, and he thought the room was getting hot and wondered why he felt so warm. He lay against the wall trying to retrace his steps, and realized he was in the dry sauna. He had not pressed buttons to the intercom but had turned on the heat. He held his hands out, trying to find something sturdy to help him stand up and get out. Something solid grazed his hand, and he pulled himself onto what he'd realized was the bench. *I'll just sit here for a minute and rest. Then I will get to the door and find help.*

Gunner summoned all his strength and stood up, swaying. He took two steps forward and lifted his hand to wipe the sweat stinging his eyes. The dark room began to spin violently as another wave of vertigo hit him. He fell backward, striking his head on the corner of the bench, losing consciousness once again. He awoke a few minutes later, and although the room was dark, lying on the floor, Gunner could make out a sliver of dim light across from him, feeling sure it was the door. He crawled on his belly toward the light, and when he reached it, he raised a hand like a blind man, feeling the door. His fingers touched the hot metal and tried to turn the doorknob, but it would not open. The knob would turn to the left and the right, but it would not unlatch the door.

Gunner began to panic and suddenly couldn't catch his breath. It felt like an elephant was sitting on his chest. The dark waves started to return, and he tried again to turn the knob frantically to the left and the right. The door would not open from the inside. *Well, this is a blatant safety violation. I will have Franklin Blaas fired for this!* And in that precise moment, Gunner realized he had sealed his fate. He saw in his mind his hand holding the clipboard with the work order that said, "SAUNA DOOR REPAIR –WILL NOT UNLOCK FROM INSIDE." Gunner remembered the fight with Franklin and how he had stopped all work orders from being completed until the maintenance shop had been cleaned. He had planned to tell Franklin at the morning meeting to resume the work orders, but he had been having too much fun needling the big man. After all, it had been merely to show Franklin that he was in charge and held all the power. He realized his ego was why he was now stuck in the sweltering sauna with a head wound.

"Help me!" he cried out feebly. Sweat poured down his arms and face as he tried to pound against the wall with his remaining strength. The room was getting hotter, and Gunner was finding it harder to catch his breath. Then, a loud piercing whistle sounded, and the ship sensors slammed the fire doors shut, including the one in front of the men's sauna. The shrill whistle and crashing of the door had been deafening, but the click of the magnetic lock was the loudest and most frightening thing Gunner had ever heard.

Safety Officer Tully's voice came over the public address system, "THIS IS A MANDATORY DRILL. ALL SHIP PERSONNEL SHOULD BE IN THEIR DESIGNATED AREAS. ALL GUESTS ARE TO REMAIN IN THEIR QUARTERS UNTIL FURTHER NOTICE. I REPEAT, THIS IS A MANDATORY DRILL. ALL SHIP PERSONNEL, PLEASE REPORT TO YOUR DESIGNATED AREA IMMEDIATELY FOR A HEAD COUNT."

"Help me," Gunner croaked, lying on the floor.

An hour later, a siren blared, the magnetic fire locks clicked open as the doors automatically raised, and the staff and crew returned to their normal activities.

By three o'clock, the passengers had returned sun drunk and sandy from Grand Turk. Kennedy and the cast were busy setting up activities on the pool deck.

Terri and Jones Butler found two chaises by the pool. "Sweetsie, do you mind if I go to the spa and get this horse smell off me? I know I went for a swim, but I still feel like I smell like a stable. The sauna will sweat it out of me, and then I can come back and soak up the sun with you."

Terri giggled. "Jonesy, I don't smell anything, but if you want to go into a hotbox, go ahead." She stretched her body out, and Jones watched her, wondering if he genuinely wanted to leave. He sometimes wondered how he had been lucky enough to marry her. She had put up with a lot over the last few years, and now they would be able to enjoy life together. "All I want to do is lie here, get a tan, and drink lots of SunRumbrellas." She sat up, looking for a cocktail server so she could order another drink. "I just love these!" She lifted her glass into the sun. "You don't even taste the alcohol." Jones could see Terri was beginning to get tipsy.

He stood up. "I'll be back but take it easy on those drinks, okay?" He shook his finger at her. "And no going in the pool until I get back."

Terri scrunched up her face, giving Jones a strange look. "And mess up my hair? Jones, sometimes I wonder about you!"

He took the elevator down to deck six and saw the spa workers waiting to be let inside. Anna Marie unlocked the doors, and before she could tell him that the spa wasn't open yet, he pointed and said, "I'm going to the sauna," and made his way to the men's locker room to change into a robc. She shrugged her shoulders and went to the retail area to begin restocking the shelves. Inside the locker room, Jones saw something on the floor that looked like red paint and made a mental note to tell Anna Marie about it when he left.

As he removed his clothing, he got another whiff of the smelly horse he had been riding. He hoped the photos turned out. Jones didn't relish the idea of redoing the photo shoot at the next port of call.

He grabbed a towel from the stack on the table, stepped out of the locker room, and walked a few steps down the corridor, not looking forward to sitting in the dry, hot room. He placed his hand on the doorknob, turned it, and opened the door to the men's sauna.

His scream could be heard all over the spa. Shrieking like a parrot, Jones jumped up and down in the hallway. "H-h-he's in there, and h-h-he's dead or something," he screamed hysterically. "S-s-somebody help! Help!"

Staff members hurried to see what the commotion was. Still dusting and resetting shelves when she heard Mr. Butler's scream, Anna Marie walked quickly to the desk and dialed the ship's operator. Her voice shook as she spoke into the handset, "This is Anna Marie in the spa. I'm not sure what happened, but a man just yelled that someone was dead. Please send someone from security immediately to the spa."

She scanned the cheat sheet of codes taped beside the phone, and her eyes found what she was looking for. "I think it's a code black."

Within seconds the ship's operator called over the radios on a secure channel that only a few had access to. "Code Black in Oaza. This is not a drill." Minutes later, the security team arrived at the spa. Thankfully, there were no passengers in Oaza yet and only a few members of the spa team. They quickly ushered them to the lounge to wait for Omar. Next, they closed and locked the front doors. One security guard promptly walked to the fitness center to secure those doors and the outdoor yoga area. Omar entered the spa looking grim and went directly to the sauna, grabbing a sheet from the linen closet. Then, knowing what may be on the other side of the door, he drew a deep breath and opened it.

Jones had been taken to one of the private treatment rooms so he could gather himself. When Omar entered the room ten minutes later, Jones, seated on the massage table, looked at him with frantic eyes. "Mr. Butler," Omar said softly, kneeling in front of the man, "where is your wife? She should be here with you." Omar's voice was low and soothing.

Jones stammered. "S-s-she's on the pool deck."

Omar stepped outside into the corridor and pointed to a member of his team. "Come here." The man jogged over. "Go find Mrs. Butler quickly. She's in her mid-thirties with shoulder-length brown hair. She'll be lying by the pool. Quietly explain to her that Mr. Butler needs her assistance. Do not say anything else," he commanded in a clipped tone.

Having heard the code called out on her radio and the subsequent radio chatter, Kennedy was worried but could not extricate herself from her duties in the lobby. As soon as she could, she made her way to Oaza thirty minutes later but found the doors locked. Someone had hastily put sheets over the glass doors to block anyone from looking in. As she was about to knock on the door, it opened, and Dr. Craig, the ship's doctor, walked out wearing a stern face. One of the security guards saw Kennedy and motioned for her to come in, and she could hear Jones Butler's voice as soon as she entered. Having gotten over his initial shock, Jones kept insisting quite loudly that he needed to see Kennedy. She could hear his voice rising with hysteria. "I want to see Kennedy, and I want to see her now!"

Omar walked through the door from the back of the spa to the reception area to radio for Kennedy's assistance when he saw her. Relief washed over his face, and he said in a low voice, "I was about to call you. We have a delicate situation, and Mr. Jones needs some help. His wife is here, but would you please see what you can do? I tried to calm him down, but he goes from snapping to hysteria in a split second."

Kennedy swallowed. "But what did happen? I heard the code." She paused, "It means—"

Omar cut her off. "Gunner Owen Atcher is dead, Kennedy. We found him in the dry sauna with traumatic injuries to his head. He got locked in there during the safety drill."

Kennedy's hand went to her mouth in horror. "Who could—"

Omar held up a hand to silence her. "Kennedy, I need you to take care of Mr. and Mrs. Butler. We must take control of this situation and keep the gossip to a minimum." He extended his hand out for her to walk with him. "I need your help." They walked in silence to the private treatment room where Jones and Terri sat.

She took a deep breath and pasted on a warm smile as Omar opened the door for her to enter. "Mr. Butler, this is just awful. How can I help?"

Jones Butler was lying on a massage table with a cloth over his eyes. Terri sat beside him, holding his hand. "Well," Jones snapped, whipping off the towel and jumping off the massage table, "I demand an upgrade. I want a new suite. And I want to know the reparations the cruise line will make to me for th-th-this incident. I cannot believe that I found a b-b-body in the sauna." His voice began to rise again in hysteria. Terri squeezed his hand. "I certainly don't know how I will ever be able to sleep or relax again."

"Oh, Jonesy, I don't want to move out of our room," Terri said. "It's the Owner's Suite, and I love it," she whined softly.

"Mr. Butler, I'm not sure what the company will do," Kennedy said honestly. "We've never had this happen before. The captain will have to call them to see what they will do for something this serious and upsetting." She paused. "In the interim, perhaps dining with the captain and the senior staff and a tour of the bridge will take your mind off today's events?"

"Well," Jones said, wearily sitting back on the massage table, "that's a start. But you should tell the captain that I should not have to pay for this cruise and get a free one and unlimited spa services. It's the very least the company could do." He shuddered. "Seeing that man's body has undone every bit of relaxation I had started to have. I came on this ship to relax and unwind. And now, every time I close my eyes, all I see is him lying there on the floor." His voice began to rise again.

Kennedy spoke quietly and soothingly. "Mr. Butler, I'm sure we can work something out. Why don't you take a moment to collect yourself? I'll wait in the hallway for you and take you to your suite." She had a thought. "I'll have some champagne sent to your room and ask Chef Michèle to whip up something comforting for you to eat. Perhaps a rest before dinner will help." Kennedy exited the room and gave Omar a grim nod.

A few minutes later, Terri and Jones emerged from the treatment room. Jones looked drawn and haggard. His tan skin had taken on a grayish hue. They walked out of the spa slowly with Kennedy, and she ushered them to the elevator. She was thankful that most of the passengers were either still in port or on the pool deck. When they arrived at the Butlers' stateroom, Kennedy turned to them. "Do either of you have your key?" They both looked at her blankly. "I left mine in the locker room with my clothes," Jones said.

"Mine is with my bag by the pool."

Kennedy nodded. "May I?" She produced her master key. "I'll have someone fetch your things and launder your clothing, Mr. Butler." She opened the door for them to enter. "If you don't feel like joining us for dinner tonight, please have me paged, and I will have Chef Michèle prepare a special meal for the two of you."

Jones nodded his head. "I think I just want to lie down and rest," he said resignedly, sitting down heavily onto the round ivory settee.

Kennedy needed to manage her next words delicately, "Mr. Jones, on behalf of the company, I would like to thank you for your discretion in keeping this very unpleasant discovery quiet. I'm sure as a businessman you understand. We don't want our current or future passengers to think of this situation when they hear our name."

Jones took a deep breath and exhaled. Kennedy could tell he was feeling fatigued from his emotions. "As long as I get a tour of the bridge, dinner with the captain, and the other things we discussed, my lips are sealed," he said and made a motion of zipping his lips.

Terri spied her dress from earlier in the day, lying on the bed. "Oh, Jones, do you think the photographer has our pictures ready yet? I can't wait to see them. I bet they are marvelous," she chattered. "Kennedy, do you think you could find out?" she inquired.

Kennedy wondered if Terri realized that her husband had just been through a traumatic experience or if she was simply trying to take his mind off what had happened. "I'm not sure, but I would be happy to find out for you," she said with false enthusiasm.

Kennedy left the Butlers' suite and quickly radioed room service for some appetizers and champagne to be sent up to them quickly. Next, Kennedy sent Bert a text. *Bert, please let me know the status of the Butlers' photoshoot ASAP.*

Bert responded quickly. *I'm working on the spa photos for the corporate office. I'll work on the pictures for Mr. and Mrs. Butler tonight.*

Kennedy texted Bert back. *I need you to stop working on the spa photos. You can do them tonight and tomorrow. Make the Butlers' photo shoot a priority and let me know as soon as they are done.* Kennedy hit send and then typed another message to Bert. *It's urgent!* Bert made a face, shrugged his shoulders, and pulled up the photos of Mr. and Mrs. Butler and their awful photo shoot.

Kennedy had one more chore left to do. She needed to update the captain on the events and explain that he would be entertaining the Butlers with a tour and dinner tonight. *That should go well.*

She knocked on the door of the captain's office. "Enter," he barked. Kennedy walked in and was startled to see Omar sitting at the table with him. "Well, Kennedy," he said, gesturing for her to sit with him and Omar at the table. "How are Mr. and Mrs. Butler? What do we need to do for them?"

"Honestly, sir, they seem to be okay right now. He is obviously shaken up, and she's," Kennedy paused, "well, she's either very oblivious or knows exactly how to manage her husband. Mr. Butler has made several requests, however." Kennedy relayed Jones' demands, and the captain nodded.

"Seems fair," he said. "The corporate office can take care of all of that. I'll make them aware."

Kennedy hesitated for a moment. "There is one more thing. He wants a tour of the bridge and dinner with you and the senior officers tonight. I'm afraid it was my idea."

The captain sucked in his breath. "Well, I suppose I can take one for the team." He shuddered. "I can only imagine what she's going to wear."

Kennedy stood up to leave, but the captain motioned her to sit back down. "Kennedy," he cleared his throat, "we have a few loose ends to clean up. Have you spoken with Mr. Phillips?"

She swallowed hard. "No, sir, I haven't. Would you like me to speak with him?"

The captain nodded. "Omar or I can contact the corporate office for the disposition of the body, but I believe that you should be the one to speak with Mr. Phillips. It will sound better coming from you. Gentler."

Looking down at the pad in front of him, he crossed off a few lines. "There are a few other things you should be aware of. First, Mr. Atcher's cabin has been secured and will only be accessible by Mr. Meier or myself. The FBI will meet us tomorrow morning. Because our next stop is Punta Cana, and we use tenders to ferry the passengers, the authorities will come on an early tender. They will want to question anyone who interacted with Mr. Atcher or was in the spa when he was there. Can you help with the passenger list?"

Kennedy removed her pen and pocket notebook and jotted down a few words. "Yes, of course. Mila and I can get the appointment book and cross-reference it with the passenger list. Mila will remember who was there when Gunner was in the spa, and there were no appointments today due to the drill. The passengers were in port or confined to their rooms for the safety drill."

Omar picked up the conversation. "The spa will be closed while the investigators determine why the door was not able to be opened from the inside and find whatever gave Mr. Atcher the traumatic head injuries he sustained." Omar looked at his pad. "I need you to pull the staff schedules for the entire ship so we can cross reference where everyone was working." He looked at the captain. "Thankfully, it will not be difficult due to the safety drill. Mr. Atcher was killed sometime between when he entered the spa for his treatment and when Mr. Butler discovered the body. So, we should be able to see who was logged in as present by the safety team members."

"What will we tell the passengers about the spa's closure?" Kennedy asked.

Omar was thoughtful. "We'll say there is a plumbing issue that maintenance is working on. The staff in the spa at the time of the incident has been told that they may not speak about the code black."

Kennedy scribbled in her notebook. "Okay, next?" she queried.

The captain and Omar looked at each other and then at her. Kennedy felt uneasy at their stare. "Kennedy, we need you to do a little damage control," the captain said, slowly leaning forward and steepling his fingers. He was frowning. "Gossip has already begun to spread. The crew and staff are already speculating who died. It's well known that Mr. Atcher was neither easy to get along with nor well-liked, as evidenced by his private and public behavior." The captain swallowed and looked Kennedy in the eye. "I need you to find a way to distract everyone." He straightened up in his chair. "Everyone: passengers, crew, and staff. Something completely out of the ordinary and the more outrageous, the better." He looked at her hopefully, "Can you throw something together with the cast for tonight? Something to make everyone talk about anything other than this tragedy?"

Kennedy looked down at her notebook as her mind went in a thousand directions. Finally, she raised her head to meet the captain's stare. "Well, I need a minute to think about what to do, but, yes, consider it done, sir."

He stood up and reached out to shake her hand. "Thank you, Kennedy. You may go. Mr. Meier and I have a great deal to do before tomorrow morning. Please let Tony know to have Mr. and Mrs. Butler at my table tonight." He paused. "Who else is at the table tonight?"

"Vera Jameson," Kennedy winced.

"Oh, lucky me."

Kennedy left the captain's office for Mr. Phillips's stateroom. She knocked gently on his door. "Mr. Phillips," she said and knocked again. "It's Kennedy, the cruise director. I have an urgent matter to discuss with you."

The door opened, and Mr. Phillips stood in the doorway. His hair was disheveled, and his glasses sat crookedly on his face. The bright orange two-piece tropical print short set with black socks and sandals made Kennedy take a step back.

"Yes, may I help you?" he asked, running his hand through his hair and straightening his glasses. Realizing it was Kennedy, he said quickly, "There is nothing I can do."

"Mr. Phillips, may I come in? I have something to discuss with you and would prefer not to do it in the corridor."

Mr. Phillips began shutting the door. "If this is about Mr. Atcher, I am sorry, but I cannot help you. He did not come by earlier to see the message I had composed, but he was very specific about the information to send," he began to close the door.

"Mr. Phillips," Kennedy said softly, "I am sorry to tell you this, but Mr. Atcher is no longer with us."

Spluttering, Mr. Phillips jerked the door open. "What do you mean he is no longer with us? Did he take a plane back to Florida? He was supposed to tell me if he was leaving early."

Kennedy interrupted him, "Mr. Phillips, Mr. Atcher did not get on a plane. He had an accident in the spa, and I'm sorry to be the one to tell you this, but he's dead. The FBI will be—"

He cut her off, "The FBI?" He asked wide-eyed and began speaking rapidly while stumbling backward into his room. "Oh, my goodness, oh, my goodness, oh, my goodness!" He began pacing around the living room area, flapping his arms as he spoke. "What will the board think? I don't know what to do." He looked at Kennedy with questioning eyes, "What should I do?"

Kennedy took the opportunity to step inside and close the door. Mr. Phillips walked in circles. Then, when Mr. Phillips came toward her, she caught his eye, and he stopped. She took slow, deep breaths like she did when Tony was upset, hoping Mr. Phillips would copy her. "Mr. Phillips, as you knew him, do you know if he has any family the corporate office can contact? Is there a next of kin?"

All color left Mr. Phillips's face as the reality of Gunner's death sunk in. He looked around for something to sit on. "Oh, my goodness," he said slowly this time. "I don't feel so well. My heart is pounding, and I feel weak and sweaty."

Kennedy guided him to the sofa. "Mr. Phillips, I need you to lie on the couch." She entered the bedroom, grabbed several pillows from the bed, and returned to the couch to place them under his legs to elevate them. "I'm going to call the ship's doctor, Mr. Phillips. I think he should look at you." She walked quickly to the phone on the desk and dialed the operator. "Please have Dr. Craig come at once to Cabin 839. I have a passenger in shock after receiving some unwelcome news."

Kennedy went into the bathroom, filled a glass with water, and wet a hand towel. "Would you like a drink of water?" He nodded gratefully, and she helped him sit up to take a drink and then placed the cool towel on his forehead. After what felt like hours, there was a knock on the door, and Kennedy walked over to admit the ship's doctor. "Thank you for coming, Doctor. Mr. Phillips has just received some distressing news. He said he felt faint and that his heart was racing. So, I thought it was best to call you." Dr. Craig nodded and looked at Mr. Phillips while Kennedy spoke.

"Thank you, Kennedy. I can take it from here," he said. Mr. Phillips's face had gone ashen.

Kennedy collected her notebook and pen. "Mr. Phillips, if you need anything, please do not hesitate to have me paged." She looked at him with concern. "You've just received some very upsetting news, and we want to make sure you are taken care of."

Mr. Phillips smiled at her shakily. "Thank you, Kennedy, you have been most helpful. You aren't nearly as incompetent as Mr. Atcher made you out to be." He paused for a moment. "I think I'm glad Mr. Atcher and I did not connect this morning to send that message."

Kennedy felt goosebumps go down her arms as relief coursed through her body. "I am as well, Mr. Phillips." She looked at Dr. Craig, who was frowning at her. "Okay, I'm going!" she mouthed and left the cabin.

Kennedy stood in the corridor. She wondered why Mr. Phillips would make a statement about Gunner flying back to Florida. It didn't make sense. She blew out a breath. "I can't think about that right now," she said to the empty hallway. "I need to pull off something out of the ordinary." As she walked down the corridor, she tapped her finger on her lower lip, and inspiration struck. She went quickly to the kitchen and found Chef Michèle and his sous chef, Ano. They were in the beginning stages of preparation for the evening's dinner. They looked up at her quizzically when she entered. "Hi, guys, I hate to do this, but I need as many snacks as you can gather on the pool deck as soon as possible. It doesn't have to be anything elaborate. Bar snacks will be fine. I'll get Tony to help set up some tables." She breezed through the dining room and shared with Tony what she needed, and he quickly found some servers to help him. Before she left the dining room, she called around for Luke and was told she could find him at the pool bar. She dialed the number and was thankful he answered.

"Great, I found you! We need to change to complimentary happy hour drinks for the next two hours, captain's orders." He began to protest. "Luke, I'll explain later, I promise. Complimentary happy hour drinks for two hours," she repeated. She raised her radio and asked the cast and the ship's audio-visual team to meet her on the pool deck by the bar. When everyone arrived, she quickly explained that she needed a party atmosphere on the deck as soon as possible. "I have food coming, and there will be a free happy hour for the next two hours." She pointed to two of her cast members. "Ladies, I know you hate doing this, but I need line dancing started. Will you help?" They nodded. She blew out a large breath and looked at her small ensemble. "As soon as things are underway, meet me in the Solstice Theater in one hour. I have some arms to twist, and by the time I'm done, we will have a short time to pull off a major miracle."

She walked around the pool deck and saw her friends relaxing in the chaise lounges, soaking up the sun. She walked over to them, wearing a dazzling smile. "How are my favorite guys today?"

"Hey, what's going on?" Phil sat up from his lounge chair. "Everyone looks freaked out."

Dave rolled over and pulled down his sunglasses. "Rumor is that somebody died. Is it true?"

Kennedy held up her hand to interrupt the barrage of questions coming her way. "Guys, I have a huge favor to ask. I have never needed you more than I need you right now. Will you meet me in the Solstice Theater in fifteen minutes? I'm in a jam."

Seeing the glimmer of anxiety in Kennedy's eyes, John looked from her to the group and then back at Kennedy. He lowered his rhinestone sunglasses and nodded. "Of course, my dear," he said solemnly. "We will be there with bells on, whatever you need."

Kennedy was walking toward the elevators when she saw the Ladies from Harmony Lakes by the ping pong tables. "Oh, Kennedy," Marilyn cooed, waving at her. "Can we talk to you?" Kennedy pasted on a smile and watched as the group hurried toward her. "We've just heard an awful rumor," Marilyn said. "Some of the passengers are saying someone died. Is it true?"

Kennedy gave Marilyn a puzzled look. "Marilyn, that's the most preposterous rumor I've heard today. We had a safety drill while everyone was in Grand Turk. I think people are confused. Everything is fine. Listen, I hate to run off, but I am late for a rehearsal. I'll see you all tonight," she said hurriedly and walked quickly into the corridor to take the elevator down to the theater.

"Humph," Dolly snorted, looking at the deck that had suddenly become remarkably busy with staff and crew members. "I think something did happen. Besides the gossip, just look." She pointed her hand around the pool area. "They are setting up tables with food and free drinks, and there are a lot of people up here encouraging us to have fun. To top it off, Kennedy just gave us the bum's rush. That tells me there is some kind of coverup!"

Laura let out a heavy sigh. "Oh, Mother, you always think things are more dramatic than they really are. It's those mystery books you read. They are warping your mind." She pulled her arm. "Let's find a table, have some free drinks and appetizers, and do your favorite thing, people watch."

Marilyn pouted. "I bet that tacky woman will be out here wearing some tiny bikini to make all the men look at her," she said petulantly. "No one will pay any attention to me."

"We can ask if someone can fall into your lap again," Beth said, giggling. "That got you a lot of looks."

Dolly perked up thinking about Terri and Jones Butler. "If they aren't at the pool, they'll definitely be at dinner. I wonder what outfit she will wear tonight."

They found an empty table and sat down. "Whatever she is wearing tonight, I'm sure it can be bought in a Frederick's of Hollywood catalog," Louise said dryly as she pulled a magazine out of her tote bag and settled down to flip through it.

"Isn't that the catalog that you get, Marilyn?" Beth piped up loudly. "I think I saw that catalog on your coffee table before we left. You had a bunch of pages turned down.

I had no idea you shopped at the same place. What a small world."

Marilyn put her sunglasses on and pretended to look around the pool deck. "Hush, Beth," she whispered loudly, "or I'll change your vitamins with sleeping pills and leave you in port tomorrow."

The Club Diva crew was waiting for Kennedy in the theater. She faced them and took a deep breath. "I need you to perform tonight as your Club Diva personas," she said in a rush.

"What?" Steve asked.

"How?" Phil questioned.

"Now?" Don demanded.

Dave pulled down his glasses. "Why?"

Kennedy saw a hint of excitement in John's eyes. He turned to his four friends. "I believe, ladies, that Kennedy did not stutter. She needs the divas, and she needs them tonight. It doesn't matter why." He turned, facing Kennedy again, and said softly, "She needs us. Is that correct, dear?" She nodded and looked at them with hopeful eyes. John swooped her into a bear hug. "We would be delighted to perform, Kennedy."

"Oh, thank you. Thank you!" she cried in relief and hugged each of them quickly. "I cannot thank you enough. How can I ever repay you?"

Robert gave a small chuckle. "John will make sure you repay him somehow, don't worry. He will hold this over your head, and I foresee that you will be performing at Club Diva anytime you are in town."

They sat down, and Kennedy pulled out her notebook and pen. "So, where do we start? What do you need?"

John spoke up. "We need to see your costume room first. We can't make up the show list until we know what characters we can be." Then, he turned to the others, "You need to think about what you might have with you that we can use."

Kennedy jumped up. "Let's go," she said joyfully."
They trooped across the stage to the back, and Kennedy opened the door to the costume room. Wigs, costumes, makeup, hats, and other props littered the shelves and racks of clothing. They entered, each going in a different direction. As they began looking and holding up items, their excitement began to build.

"What do you think?" Phil asked. "Can I pull off the goddess of pop in this?" He held up a long, black, curly wig and a black leather jacket. "I could pair it with my black running shorts."

Don rushed over. "It's perfect!" He looked at Kennedy thoughtfully. "Kennedy, do you have a male cast member who could impersonate Mick Jagger? I mean, really do the Mick moves?" he asked. Phil looked at him quizzically. "I could wear the Charro wig from the seventies party, John's dress, and imitate the divine Ms. Bette Midler," Don answered excitedly. "They did a great duet!"

John sauntered up from the back of the room, carrying a sequined dress and a blonde wig. He cocked his hip to one side dramatically. "Move over, ladies. Dolly is in the house! Oh, this is such fun. What else do we have?"

Thirty minutes later, Kennedy had the preliminaries to review with the cast and the audio-visual team so John and the others could perfect their costumes. They had agreed to reconvene in one hour for a dry run. The audio-visual team suggested that the show could be taken up a notch by hosting it on the pool deck instead of the theater to add to the excitement.

"You are sure about this?" Kennedy asked, and they all nodded enthusiastically.

Mila, discouraged from her conversation with Gunner, was halfway to her designated area for the safety drill when she suddenly stopped. She heard Gunner's words replay again in her head, telling her that she should be cleaning out her office instead of going to the safety drill. He was right. What would it matter if she went? She was obviously out of a job when they docked in Port Canaveral. With a defeated sigh, Mila turned around and began walking to her cabin, wanting to be alone instead of in a room full of chattering people. She entered her cabin and first silenced her phones and radio. Mila looked at the bed. She could pull out the two large suitcases and begin packing, but the thought of putting clothes in the suitcase and looking at them for the next two days depressed her. Next, her eyes went to the legal pad on her desk. She should begin making notes for Anna Marie, so there was a smooth transition. As bright and capable as Sara was, Mila reasoned she could help Anna Marie keep things going until Mila's replacement arrived.

A few hours later, having filled up the legal pad with detailed notes, she went back to Oaza and found that someone had put fabric over the glass doors. She pulled on the handle but found the doors locked and began to bang on them, not understanding what was happening. She was furious. Sara had promised to reopen and take care of things until Mila returned. The notes had taken her longer than she had expected, but there was no reason for the doors to be locked. The spa should have opened an hour ago. The door jerked open, and a security guard blocked her path. Realizing it was Mila, he motioned for her to enter, shut the door, and locked it quickly behind her.

"What's going on?" she asked in bewilderment. "Where is my staff, and why is the spa locked up? Why is security here?" As she asked each question, her tone grew more panicked.

"Go directly to your office and wait for Omar, Mila," the guard said with authority. "He's been trying to find you, but you didn't answer your phones or radio."

"I was—"

"You probably shouldn't say anything, Mila," the young man said. His tone softened. "Just go to your office, please?" he pleaded.

Mila, bewildered, walked slowly through the spa looking this way and that. None of her employees were there, and the security guards she passed would not look her in the eye. She walked through the door and down the hallway to her office.

A few minutes later, Omar knocked softly on her door. "Mila?" he said and stepped into her office.

"Omar! What the hell is going on?" she asked anxiously. "Someone locked the doors to the spa, none of my staff are here, and one of your goons told me to go to my office and wait for you. What is going on?" she demanded.

"Mila, I need you to be calm," he said quietly, sitting in the chair across from her.

"Calm?" she replied angrily, standing up. "You shut down my spa without telling me? Thanks, friend! I've got paying customers who have appointments right now!"

"Mila!" Omar barked, and she looked at him with startled eyes. "I need to share some information with you, and I need you to be calm and not interrupt me. Now sit down." He looked down at one of his polished black shoes. "It would be best if you listened and didn't speak right now." He took a breath. "Gunner Owen Atcher was found dead in the spa this afternoon. Mila, he was attacked. Bludgeoned. We found him in the men's sauna, and the last person to see him was you."

Mila's face turned ashen, and her mouth opened, but nothing came out. Instead, her mind whirled in a thousand directions. She may not have liked Gunner, but the loss of his life was never something she had wished for.

Omar sighed heavily. "Mila, I have no choice but to confine you to your cabin until we can ascertain your whereabouts, especially as you were the last person seen with him."

"I don't know what to say," Mila said, still in shock. "The door to the sauna—"

"Don't say anything," Omar interrupted. He softened his tone. "Right now, the less you say, the better. Let's go," he said and stood up. He opened the door, and they stepped into the narrow hallway. He ushered her through the door into the reception area, and Mila could feel the eyes of Omar's team on her as she and Omar walked through the silent spa. One of them quickly opened the door, and Mila and Omar walked down the corridor of deck six to Mila's cabin on the same deck. Mila had gone through a myriad of emotions since she had arrived at the spa—anger, shock, confusion, sadness. She had been in a fog when Omar told her about Gunner's death, but now, seeing a guard posted outside her cabin door, her anger snapped her to attention.

"You must be joking," Mila stopped in the corridor and looked at him in disbelief. "You are serious!"

Omar rubbed his hand over his face. "Mila, let's go inside so that I can explain."

"Oh, believe me, there is a lot of explaining that you need to do," she retorted. They entered her cabin. She threw her clipboard onto the bed and turned to look at Omar, her arms crossed.

"As I said in your office, I am very sorry, but I need to confine you to your cabin until we reach Punta Cana and the authorities are on board," he told her in a matter-of-fact tone. "There are too many questions that have come up, and you were the last person seen with Mr. Atcher. Someone also said they heard the two of you speaking in loud voices behind closed doors."

Mila sat down on the bed, stunned, "Wh-what? Who heard us?" she stammered. "What did they say they heard? Talk to me," she cried out.

"Mila, I cannot say anymore. I'm sorry." He looked at her gravely. "Right now, I am not your friend. I am the director of security of the *Helio*, and an incident occurred on the ship. A man died, and the death could be construed as foul play." He sat down heavily in the chair across from her. "My biggest problem right now, in addition to a dead body, is that we have not been able to account for your whereabouts during the safety drill, which is when we think Gunner died. Everyone else attended the drill except you and Bert, and he was taking photos with a time stamp on them, so we know where he was. You didn't check in at the drill, and you didn't answer your phones or the radio. Therefore, we have no official log of where you were after you reentered

Gunner's treatment room and when you arrived back at the spa." He shook his head slowly.

"But—" Mila stood up, beginning to tell Omar her reason, but he held up his hand to silence her.

"Mila, please do not say anything." He drew a deep breath. "It's bad enough that you and Mr. Atcher have been seen and heard having very loud, unpleasant, and threatening conversations in public by members of the ship and passengers."

"What about the passengers who had appointments and the staff? What has my staff been told?"

"The passengers have been told that the spa is closed temporarily due to a plumbing issue, and the few staff members that were present at the time of the code black have been instructed not to discuss it with anyone."

"What will they be told about me?" Mila felt hysteria rising in her voice. She got up off the bed.

"That you are under the weather," he replied.

Omar stood and took both of Mila's hands in his.

"Now, please, I beg of you. While I am trying to figure out what happened, please stay in your room and do not try to leave. If you do, I will have to confine you to one of the cells on the lower level. I am trying to do what is in your best interest, Mila." He took a deep breath and looked into her frightened eyes with sympathy. "I am confident we will have this matter cleared up in the morning." He walked to the door, opened it, and left the room. When the latch on the door clicked, Mila suddenly felt the gravity of the situation.

Mila grabbed for the chair, suddenly feeling dizzy as her mind whirled. Gunner had died inside the men's sauna. But she couldn't understand why he would go in there. The men's sauna was out of order. She remembered she had spoken with Franklin and turned in the maintenance request for it. Anna Marie had made an out-of-order sign, and Mila herself had hung the sign on the wall beside the door so that everyone would see it. She chastised herself for not putting a chair or a cabinet in front of the entrance to block it and wondered why Gunner didn't see the large sign in red letters.

As for her absence from the drill, Mila had every intention of going to her designated station, but she had been so upset at hearing Gunner's words that she just wanted to be alone. She remembered turning off her phones and the radio. At first, she had decided to pack, but that had depressed her. Thinking about her staff, she sat at her desk and filled a legal pad with notes for Anna Marie and Sara. Surely, if she showed the notes to Omar and explained the rationality of her actions, he would understand.

Mila closed her eyes. She suspected there was another reason for her confinement, but Omar had been kind enough not to mention it. Many years ago, long before she had met Kennedy, Mila had shared her story with him. She told him about her family's ties to organized crime in Poland, her former lover who, in addition to being an up-and-coming fighter, practiced on Mila in drunken rages and did *favors* for some known criminals in Las Vegas. Omar was also aware of her missing ex-husband, who shortly after Mila filed papers for their divorce had been reported missing but was never found. Sighing deeply, she stood up and began pacing the room, wondering about Gunner's death and who had been angry enough to kill him.

After Omar left Mila's cabin, he radioed the rest of the team to meet him quickly on the promenade deck. While it was outside standard security protocols, he knew he would spend valuable time answering their countless questions if he did not share what he knew and why he had confined Mila to her quarters. Their concern, while well-meaning, would hamper his investigation. It was easier to tell them together, so they heard the same thing. While waiting for them, he looked at the waves, wondering if this would end his budding relationship with Kennedy. They seemed to be on the same page, but he worried her relationship with Mila and his job would cloud both Kennedy's feelings and her judgment. He didn't believe Mila had killed Gunner, but it didn't look good for her either.

"What's going on, Omar?" Franklin asked as he and Rosemary walked up the steps and over to the railing where Omar stood.

"Let's just wait for the others," he said. "I'd like to tell you all at once so that everyone hears the same thing at the same time."

Franklin pushed against the railing. "I can't say I'm upset that he's dead."

"Don't say another word, Franklin. I mean it," Omar snapped. "I may be your friend, but I am an officer of the law right now." As Omar finished his words to Franklin, Kennedy and Tony reached the trio, followed by Chef Michèle and Luke.

"Hi, has anyone heard from Mila? I can't find her, and she's not answering calls or texts. It's weird," Kennedy said anxiously.

Omar looked at the worried faces around him. "That is why I asked you all to come up here," he said gravely. "Gunner Atcher is dead, and Mila is a suspect. She is confined to her quarters until tomorrow when the FBI arrives." He drew in a breath. "We suspect foul play, and to protect her, she will stay in her cabin until the authorities have the opportunity to investigate. The spa and the fitness center will be closed until further notice. If anyone asks, there is a plumbing issue that maintenance is working on. The staff in the spa at the time of the code black have been given strict instructions that they may not say anything to anyone."

Kennedy opened her mouth to speak, and Omar held up his hand. "Kennedy, please let me get this all out. I shouldn't be speaking to any of you, so I ask for your complete silence on this matter." They nodded in agreement. "As you know, Mila and Gunner have been seen and heard arguing in public. He said things to her in staff meetings and at the spa. She has said things about him that were heard by passengers and members of the ship. We all know what he said this morning in our meeting." His voice took on a flat tone. "The last time he was seen alive, she and Gunner were seen entering a private treatment room." He grimaced. "While they were in the room, a spa team member heard loud voices coming from inside. A passenger found Gunner's body in the men's sauna, which is in the spa, minutes after

Anna Marie unlocked the doors." He splayed his hands in front of him. "There is nothing I can do at this time. The captain and I agreed that the best way to protect her is to keep her confined to her quarters. If anyone asks, tell them that Mila is under the weather."

Omar saw Kennedy's stricken face. "It was either her cabin or one of the cells in the lower hold, and I couldn't do that," he said softly. He looked around at the group. "Tomorrow morning, Mila, as well as many of you, will be questioned by the FBI. I will let you know when and where the questioning will occur." He cleared his throat. "One thing that is not in Mila's favor is that she did not check in during the drill as the rest of you did. Because of these things, she is, unfortunately," he sighed, "a prime suspect."

Kennedy's eyes welled up, and her nose began to run. "Omar, you know she didn't do this. Mila is a kind and gentle soul." She shook her head. "If she finds a spider, she puts it in a glass jar with holes in the top and releases it in port so that it doesn't die. She even feeds them if we are on a sea day!"

Omar handed her a handkerchief so she could wipe her eyes and nose. He looked at the team imploringly. "Confining her is for her protection. Now, I am sure, like me, you have much to do before dinner, and I will remind you to please keep this information to yourself." Everyone nodded in agreement, and Omar took both of Kennedy's hands into his and squeezed them. "I need you to be strong, Kennedy. You can't fall apart. I need you to put your personal feelings aside and think of the passengers," he said. "I promise you I will do my best to find out who did this. It is for that very reason I am keeping Mila confined." Kennedy dropped her hands and nodded slowly. She began to walk away, feeling the weight of the world on her shoulders. Omar looked defeated as he watched her leave. He had hoped she would understand, but at this moment, it seemed she did not, and what had budded between them would simply wither on the vine.

Kennedy walked back to her cabin to change for the evening before going to the theater for the impromptu rehearsal. She wished more than anything she could talk to

Mila. She had so many questions. When she arrived at the Solstice Theater, the room was a beehive of activity. The audio-visual team was putting their equipment on carts to set up on the pool deck. The cast and several Club Diva members were walking through dance steps, and it seemed as if everything was under control.

"Kennedy," John trilled, wiggling his fingers at her, and hopped off the stage, "I don't want you to worry about a thing. We have the show under control. We've worked out the music, the lighting, and the video screen with the audio-visual staff—such lovely guys. If I could steal them away, I would. That Christopher is a dreamboat, those curls!" He giggled girlishly.

"That sounds great," said Kennedy flatly. "How is the costuming and the cast? Do you need anything from me?" Tears threatened to come down her face, and John looked at her and pulled her into a hug.

"Sweetie, you look like hell, like you've lost your best friend," he whispered into her ear. "Tell Auntie Joan what's wrong."

Kennedy wiped her eyes and shook her head. "I can't, John, but will you give me something to do so I can focus on the show and not my worries?"

He pulled back and looked at her questioningly. "Are you sure?" he asked, and Kennedy nodded her head and sniffled. John gave her a sly smile. "Before I tell you what I need you to do, would you like to see the final setlist?" he asked excitedly. "I must admit, having only a few hours to throw this together has been invigorating."

Kennedy forced a smile on her face. "I would love to see the list, Auntie Joan."

Opening: "Lady Marmalade" full ensemble

"Get the Party Started" Dave

"9 to 5" John

"Believe" Phil

"Beast of Burden" Don (and male cast member?)

"I Say a Little Prayer for You" Steve, Dave, John

"Material Girl" Robert

"Dancing Queen" full ensemble

Kennedy looked at John, stunned. "John, this looks amazing," she exclaimed breathlessly. "Can we pull this off? And don't worry, I have the perfect cast member for Mick Jagger, swinging hips and all."

He motioned for the others to join him. They jumped off the stage and formed a circle around her. "For you, doll, we can do anything, and the cast seems to be as excited to do this as we are," Robert said.

"The audio-visual guys are the ones fueling the fire. They are very excited," Steve was quick to add.

"But we have neglected one thing," Don said sadly.

"You see, our shows are a little like a carnival," Phil added. "And this one even more so."

Dave moved behind her. "So, we need one thing," he said and grinned. "We need a ringmaster." He pulled a black sequined top hat from behind his back and placed it on her head.

"Think you can keep us in line?" John smirked and tapped the hat on her head.

Kennedy felt a surge of happiness wash over her and grinned. "Gentlemen, I would be pleased to run this three-ring circus," she said, beaming.

John clapped his hands. "All right, everyone, let's take it from the top," he said, motioning for everyone to get on the stage. He pointed his finger at Chris, who ran the audio-visual team. "Ready, dreamboat?" Chris nodded his head. He looked at Kennedy. "Just improvise as you can, dear," he said. "We need you to introduce each song and diva." He clapped his hands together. "Oh, this is going to be so much fun!"

Kennedy straightened her shoulders, winked at John, and walked saucily up the steps and onto the stage.

The dining room was abuzz. It had been a strange day, and the whisperings behind menus and hands were like crickets chirping before a storm. Suddenly a hush fell across the room as Vera Jameson, dressed in an elegant, long black fitted gown with sheer sleeves, entered the room on the arm of the captain. Her diamond bracelet and chandelier earrings danced in the lights. When they arrived at his table, the officers stood immediately, and the first officer pulled Vera's chair out and stood behind it. "Well, everyone, good to see you this evening. May I please introduce Mrs. Vera Jameson to all of you? She is one of our very special guests." He took his place and rubbed his hands together. "It appears that we are all here."

Vera pointed her head at two empty chairs. "Aren't we missing two?" she asked. "Who else will be joining us?"

The captain held up a finger, feigning a discussion with the first officer. "Yes, we will need to address that first thing tomorrow morning," he said importantly, making a stern face. He turned to Vera. "I'm not sure, Mrs. Jameson, but I am certain they will be a delight."

Tony appeared at the table bearing drinks, and the captain looked at him gratefully. "Mrs. Jameson," Tony said, placing a champagne flute with brown liquid and an orange peel in front of her. "Vera's old-fashioned compliments of Luke," he said with a smile.

"Well, this is a charming surprise. After all my cruises and tips on this ship, Lucas has decided to name a drink after me," she said dryly.

The captain lifted his glass in Vera's direction. The officers raised their glasses as well. "To Mrs. Jameson," he said.

Vera enjoyed the burn of the bourbon as it slid down her throat, and she looked around the room. Her eyes went to the entrance, and she suddenly began coughing as she saw Jones and Terri Butler walking behind Tony toward the captain's table. She took a drink of water and turned to the captain. "Are you certain you don't know who is sitting in those two seats tonight?"

"Would you believe me if I said I had temporary amnesia?" he offered weakly.

She smiled at him through gritted teeth. "How I wish this were two hundred years ago because if it were, I would have you keelhauled," she said, arching an eyebrow. The captain shuddered. He had a vision of Vera standing on the deck of a clipper, making sure the knots of the ropes tied around him were tight before throwing him overboard to be drug under the ship.

Terri and Jones entered the dining room to a roar of whispers, as they had on previous evenings. They followed Tony to the captain's table, and it seemed that every guest had something to say to someone at the table near them. Terri's dress was a showstopper. Made of red satin, it hugged every curve and had a neckline that plunged to her navel. Looking at her was like seeing a car accident. You didn't want to look, but you felt compelled to see as much as possible. She glided beside Jones, dressed in a black and red brocade dinner jacket and black pants.

"Do they think they are the king and queen of the prom?" Louise whispered behind her hand to Laura.

"Holy Moly!" Beth exclaimed loudly as it was hard to be heard with the noise created by the other passengers who were all talking at once. "Not any prom I ever attended. If a girl had worn that, she wouldn't have been allowed in the gymnasium."

Dolly was bouncing in her seat. "Have any of you noticed her necklace? She's wearing a snake around her neck. You know there was a burlesque dancer who used to dance with a snake around her shoulders! Very exotic."

"Mother!" Laura hissed. "Enough!" Then she turned and looked questioningly at her mother. "How would you know about a burlesque dancer and a snake?"

"Kitten, I had a life before I became a mother," she said with a wry smile and winked.

It did appear that a bejeweled snake was draped around Terri's neck. And while the ensemble was garish, the passengers would have been disappointed if she had worn anything else. They approached the captain's table, and the officers and the captain rose at once to greet the newcomers. Tony held out Terri's chair, and she slid delicately into her seat, trying not to strain the seams holding the dress together. The dress was not made for sitting but for standing and being photographed. Vera took in Terri's outfit from the side of her eye. She wondered, if Terri sneezed, would the dress split at the seams, or would her breasts pop out? The mental image made her chuckle inwardly. She leaned over to the captain and whispered in his ear. "Well, I suppose Victoria has no more secrets, does she, Captain," and she laughed wickedly.

The captain choked on his glass of water and cleared his throat. "Good evening, Mr. and Mrs. Butler. Let us get you some drinks immediately." He motioned to one of the waitstaff, who came over quickly. "Please, another round for the table and whatever Mr. and Mrs. Butler are drinking."

Vera chimed in, "And keep them coming." She winked at the captain and added sarcastically, "I expect it will be an entertaining evening." Shortly after the drinks arrived, Vera turned to the Butlers, feigning interest. "Mr. and Mrs. Butler, I understand you are staying in the Owner's Suite. That's quite prestigious. How do you like it?" The captain kicked Vera under the table.

Terri became animated. "Oh, Mrs. Jameson, we just love it. I don't know what I love better, the zebra print carpet, the round couch, or the black and gold bathroom. Did you know that the tub is in the middle of the bathroom? We've asked Kennedy, you know, the cruise director, to help us get the name of the decorator. We want them to replicate our stateroom into our new home," she gushed.

Jones sat up a little straighter. "It's more of an estate," he said, bragging. "When I sold the company, I knew we needed to get ourselves something to show off our success but also worthy of the name we wanted."

Vera had an idea of where the conversation was going, and she couldn't resist pushing the envelope. She ignored the captain's bug-eyed stare. "Oh?" she purred, "what is the name of your little pied-à-terre," she asked. She realized from the look on Terri's face that she didn't know what Vera had asked. "What is the name of your charming little abode?"

"Tara!" they said in unison. "Get it? Butler? Tara? From the book?"

Vera blanched. "How very charming," she said, and several others at the table smothered laughter behind their napkins. Then, thankfully, the servers arrived with the first course, and everyone was suddenly busy attending to their salads.

Suddenly, the lights in the dining room went out, and brassy trumpet fanfare began to play. Then, the lights started to come up slowly. As if by magic, the room was now filled with dancers wearing colorful tropical headdresses and costumes, dancing enthusiastically to the music emanating from the speakers. Steve, the quietest member of Club Diva, pranced and shimmied from the entry of the dining room to the microphone which had mysteriously appeared in the center of the room. Steve's costume was perfect for the song. Dressed in an outfit to make Carmen Miranda jealous, he wore a tropical fruit basket headdress on top of the golden blonde wig Phil had worn the night before. A short, yellow-fringed dress and platform heels completed his ensemble, and he danced up to the microphone kicking his legs behind him as he shook his maracas and began to lip sync the decades-famous song, "Conga." At the same time, two shirtless male cast members played bongos, and several female cast members wearing similar fringed dresses blew toy trumpets, mimicking the loud, brassy blasts of the song.

"What on Earth is going on?" Marilyn asked, looking around the room and fanning herself with her hand.

"I don't know, but I am not missing the show tonight!" Dolly said, bouncing in her seat.

The room was abuzz with excitement, and suddenly a table of guests near them got up and began to form a conga line. Another table joined them to the delight of Kennedy and the others watching from the back. The captain turned his head one way and then another, trying to find Kennedy.

When he saw her near the podium, he gave her a wink and a nod. Kennedy hugged herself. They had pulled off step one of the diversion. The lights snapped off when the song's last note played, and the dancers and Steve vanished. The lights came back on, and Kennedy was suddenly standing in front of the microphone wearing her traditional long black skirt and sequined top. However, she was now sporting a sparkling top hat that sat on her head at a jaunty angle.

"Ladies and gentlemen," she belted out in her best ringmaster voice. "Thank you for allowing us to interrupt your dinner to give you a prelude to tonight's entertainment. Unfortunately, our normally scheduled show in the Solstice Theatre has been canceled." There was a small groan of disappointment. Kennedy held up her hand. "However, we have a special treat for you tonight. Please join us on the pool deck after dinner for a show you won't soon forget!" She snapped her fingers, and the room was again plunged into darkness. When they came back on a few seconds later, Kennedy had disappeared.

"Well, I'm not often at a loss for words, Captain, but I believe I am speechless," Vera said in awe. "What is going on?"

The captain smiled, turning back to Vera. "My dear Mrs. Jameson, I have no idea. It must be that pesky amnesia acting up again. You will have to go to the pool deck with everyone else to find out." He placed a forkful of salad in his mouth.

Kennedy and the team sprinted through the back passage to the Solstice Theater. "We rocked it!" Steve hollered, giving high fives to the cast and audio-visual crew.

"Did you see their faces? Those people have no idea what just hit them," someone said excitedly.

Kennedy was elated. "Okay, everyone, quick victory lap, but we need to settle down and get ready to pull off part two," she said with some anxiety.

"Don't you worry, my dear," John said theatrically. He placed his arms around Don and Robert's shoulders.

"You are with the Club Diva Boys, and we never give a bad show."

After such an exciting disruption, the dining room took on a more festive air. Tony was smiling, the servers were not bumping into each other, and not once during the dinner service was a tray of glasses knocked over.

Terri turned to Vera. "Do you go on cruises often? This is our first one, and I love it. Especially now, as the company is going to give us a free one and unlimited spa treatments," she babbled. "Maybe you could give me your phone number, and we could book our next cruise together! Wouldn't that be great?" She clapped her hands together, and Vera suddenly had the image of a toy she had been given as a child. It was a monkey that banged cymbals together. She hated the toy and made sure it stayed at the bottom of her toybox.

Vera smiled uncomfortably. "Oh, my dear, I am so sorry. But, unfortunately, I never know until the last minute if I can get away due to my line of work," she said quickly.

"That's okay," Terri replied. "Jonesy and I aren't working anymore and can go at the drop of a hat, can't we, honey? So, what do you do that you are so busy?" she asked in a breathless voice.

"Funerals," Vera said flatly, hoping it would steer the conversation in another direction.

"As in dead people?"

Vera nodded.

"Oooh," Terri said solemnly. "You should talk to Jones because he found a—"

"Mrs. Butler," the captain interrupted, "what are your plans tomorrow in Punta Cana?" He was unable to continue to steer the conversation at the table as an older couple had come over to speak to him.

"Whatever Jones wants to do," Terri chattered, looking at everyone at the table. "For the rest of the cruise, whatever Jonesy wants, he gets. Normally it's about me, but after finding the, you know, B-O-D-Y, it's all about Jonesy now." She squeezed his arm.

"A body?" Vera asked, showing mild surprise.

Jones nodded his head. Vera had watched Jones during dinner and seen the man down drink after drink. "There he was, lying on the floor, blood everywhere. This whole thing has made me appreciate life more." He gulped the drink in front of him. "At any minute, any one of us could go just like that!" He slurred and tried to snap his fingers, but he could not do it. "I'm going to do things I always wanted to do—skydiving or parasailing, and I want to ride a bronco. Or, maybe do that running of the bulls." Jones was quiet for a moment and then suddenly began to speak again, "I mean, to see him lying there on the floor, dead. I will admit it. I'm not too proud. I lost it," he said shrilly, and a hysterical giggle exploded from him.

Everyone at the table turned and looked at Jones. "I mean, who would expect to find a body in the sauna? It's crazy. I only went to the sauna to get the horse smell off me." He looked at Vera, and she saw that his pupils were dilated. "I've never seen a dead body before, have you?"

The closed sign Vera had seen on the spa's doors when she went for her appointment and the rumors she had heard earlier in the day clicked into place. Jones Butler had found the body of the man who had died in the spa.

"Oh, Jonesy, she knows all about B-O-D-I-E-S. She does funerals," Terri answered him.

"You do?" Jones croaked, blinking his eyes rapidly.

Before Vera could say another word, the captain, loudly clearing his throat, stood up. "I believe it is time for us to go on our tour of the bridge." One of the officers offered his arm to Terri and said, "Mr. and Mrs. Butler, I believe you will enjoy the technical aspects of how the ship runs."

The captain turned to Vera, who was still seated at the table. "I hope you enjoy your evening, Mrs. Jameson. Mr. Tully, our safety officer, will escort you wherever you wish after dinner. I would suggest you get a table poolside. It promises to be a most…inventive show."

Vera frowned at him.

"Unless, of course, you wish to spend more time with the Butlers this evening." He nodded his head toward Terri and Jones. "We would be thrilled for you to join us," he teased.

Vera shuddered at the thought. "No, Captain, I think I will beg off. Dinner has been most enlightening." She smiled and nodded her head at him.

Kennedy looked behind the curtains hastily put up by the maintenance and housekeeping departments. Tables and chairs from all over the ship had been gathered and placed on the promenade and pool decks. The pool deck was full, and people took the steps up to the promenade deck to find additional seats. It appeared that every person on the ship—passengers, staff, and crew was there to watch the show. She saw Dolly and the other Ladies from Harmony Lakes. They had found seats in front, and Kennedy wondered if they had left dinner early to get them. "Good to have some friendly faces in the crowd," Steve said over her head, noticing them. They pulled their heads back inside.

"Steve, you were amazing tonight," Kennedy said, still in awe of his performance. "You are always so quiet around the group, but tonight you owned the dining room."

A blushing Steve shrugged his shoulders. "Growing up, I always wanted to be on stage," he grinned. "Only I wanted to be the femme fatale wearing the amazing costume, not the boring hero or the best friend, and that wasn't possible in my small hometown. Then, I met Phil in college in the drama club. We were doing traditional Shakespeare, and the men played all the women's parts. I had the best time that semester. Then, Phil took me to his home in New Orleans, which was an education unto itself." He grinned. "After graduation, I got accepted into law school in Florida and moved there. Phil was studying for his CPA exam and said he could study just as easy in Florida as in New Orleans and moved in."

He ran a hand through his thinning hair. "Neither of us knew anyone in Florida, and there was such freedom," he said wistfully and laughed. "That summer was crazy. We scrounged for any job we could get and ate a lot of spaghetti. Then, one afternoon I was delivering a pizza to Club Diva. I walked in while John and Don were practicing, and I was starstruck. There's no other word for it." He looked at Kennedy, and she nodded understanding. "A few days later, after many conversations and a few shots of tequila, Phil and I went in and asked if we could audition. The rest, as they say, was magic. We found a home and a family. I worked there during my four years of law school and loved every moment," he said with a sigh. "You see, Kennedy, I'm not a small, balding man wearing glasses in a brown suit preparing wills and land deeds on stage. On that stage, I'm a presence, a diva. I can let out that crazy person inside who loves to strut, flaunt, and be outrageous."

Kennedy nodded. She knew what he meant. "I know the feeling, Steve, but after watching you tonight, you should give up the law and go back to performing. You said you were starstruck when you went into the club, I was starstruck watching you perform."

He shook his head. "It's not time yet, but maybe soon. Although, I will admit that performing tonight felt an awful lot like putting on your favorite pair of shoes that somehow got lost in the back of the closet."

The Ladies from Harmony Lakes sat in their seats excitedly awaiting the show. All of them but Beth had deduced that somehow the charming young men they had been having fun with on the cruise were performers and would be putting on a show, and having seen Steve's performance in the dining room, they had a good idea.

The backstage area was a flurry of excitement. John clapped his hands together to get everyone's attention. "All right, ladies and gentlemen, is everyone ready? It's showtime!"

Dave's tanned face turned pale. "Oh, my goodness," he squeaked and began shaking his arms. "The butterflies are back!"

The spotlights began dancing crazily on the stage, and music started playing through the speakers. The drumbeat was hypnotic, and excitement was building in the audience. The crowd craned their necks to see what was about to happen.

Kennedy placed her sequined top hat on her head. She had changed out of her black skirt and now wore a pair of tight black shorts over a pair of black fishnet hose. She had found a pirate jacket in the costume room to go over her sequined top. The large chandelier earrings and rhinestone bracelet she usually wore for her cabaret show winked in the lights. The look she had cobbled together was eccentric and perfect for her ringmaster role. "Go time!" she whispered to herself, and John squeezed her hand. She swaggered onto the stage, and the spotlight followed her. "Ladies and gentlemen," she said into her microphone theatrically. "Welcome to our little soiree! It is with great pleasure that I introduce...for one night, and one night only…Club Diva!"

Without warning, smoke began to appear on the blackened stage, and the opening beats of the chosen song began to play. The spotlight shined slowly on each of the six beautiful women on stage. Each outrageously dressed woman lounged seductively on chaises and chairs the cast members had scrounged from all over the ship. After displaying each diva one by one in the spotlight, it returned to Phil, who was lying on a tufted chaise lounge in his long black wig and leather costume. He jumped up, singing, and began to strut across the stage. With his hip pops and flamboyant manner, he made you believe he was indeed the goddess of pop. Suddenly, the stage was flooded with light as Dave, John, Robert, and Don joined Phil in the song, and when it was time for the chorus, the *Helio's* cast members began to dance with them, and the audience was captivated. The first song ended, and the lights went out quickly. The audience went wild with wolf whistles and thunderous applause. The backstage area became frenzied as staff and crew members worked quickly to remove furniture and set the stage for the next song.

Kennedy walked out onto the stage. She yelled into the microphone. "Did I hear we need to get the party started? I need some applause!" She exited the stage clapping her hands and laughing as Dave appeared in the spotlight wearing a spiky white wig, black leather ball cap, a hot pink tube top, black sequined jogging pants, and a ridiculous amount of gold necklaces. Dave's outfit had been one of the easiest to put together, as the pieces had come from the cast's street clothes.

"He looks like a tiny female version of that man who wore all of the jewelry," Louise said. "Remember that show?" She thumped the table with her hands to the beat of the song.

"The dancers with her are darling. I can't believe Kennedy or the boys kept this from us," Laura said.

The evening continued. John dazzled the stage dressed as Dolly Parton in a sequined evening gown and mile-high hair. Phil followed next, singing, "Believe."

"His outfit is one of Cher's most memorable ones," whispered Marilyn in awe as Phil walked out to the opening lines of his song in a pair of fishnet hose, black shorts, and a black leather jacket. He placed the microphone in the clip of the mic stand and pushed back the long black tresses of his wig behind his shoulders while he waited for his moment to sing.

While Phil was singing, the captain came backstage and tugged on Kennedy's jacket. She turned around quickly. "Well done," he said, smiling. "Not a single person on this ship is thinking about what happened earlier today. But I must know, how on Earth did you pull this off?" he asked.

Kennedy grinned. "Well, sir, you asked for a diversion and something outrageous. So, I waved my magic wand, and poof, here we are," she said mischievously.

"I don't know whether I should be relieved or terrified. You are to be commended," he said sincerely.

Kennedy nodded. "Thank you, sir, but it was a team effort. Every member of the ship has a part of tonight's show." She could see that Phil's song was ending. "If you will excuse me, I need to introduce the next act. It's time for Bette Midler and Mick Jagger to perform."

"Goodness," the captain said mockingly, "I had no idea we had such celebrities on this cruise. Carry on," he winked at her and saluted, and she ran onto the stage.

"We're not even close to being finished, folks," Kennedy hollered to the audience. "Please give it up for the Divine Miss M!" The curtain raised, and the cast was in the background mimicking a backup band playing an assortment of musical instruments. Don paraded out in the garish wig Steve had worn earlier in the dining room and John's dress from the costume night. Halfway through the song, one of the male cast members wearing a pair of dress pants and a shirt unbuttoned to his naval suddenly got up from the table he had been sitting at and began dancing in the aisle. The audience broke into frenzied applause as he swaggered to the stage and joined Don in the duet.

The show was coming to a close. While the others quickly changed into their costumes for the finale, Robert went out to perform his song.

"Okay, is everyone ready for the finale?" John asked. He turned his head, looking for the *Helio* cast. "We're counting on you to guide us. The finale is your song, not ours." Phil, Dave, Don, and Steve burst out laughing. "Well, I suppose it is ours," he said as he placed a hand on his sequined hip and fluffed his blonde wig.

"We're ready, boss," they whispered and gave him a thumbs up. The cast was having a marvelous time, and tonight had been a rush. They were doing something extraordinary, and it was exciting.

Kennedy walked out again onto the stage. "Well, ladies and gentlemen, I am sad to say this magical evening is coming to a close." The crowd booed. It had been an electrifying night for everyone. "But don't be sad yet!" She strutted back and forth on the stage, and music began to play loudly. "Now, you may have heard this the other night in the Solstice Theater, but I don't think you saw it performed quite this way." The music swelled, and "Dancing Queen" played through the speakers. Kennedy placed the microphone in the clip on the stand and began clapping her hands over her head. Every member of the ship: maintenance workers, servers, cooks, and housekeepers, walked either onstage or stood around the sides of the audience, clapping their hands over their heads to the beat. "We invite you to stand up and dance with us as I give you, one more time, Club Diva!" she yelled into the microphone.

Later in the Solstice Theatre, the entire group sat around the room. Empty bottles of champagne and glasses littered the stage. Pieces of costumes, shoes, and wigs sat in piles next to their owners. The high of the evening was winding down. Kennedy was sitting on the stage, and she looked around the room. "Guys, I can't thank you enough," she said. "I never imagined when I asked for help earlier today that we would pull something off like this."

"Yeah," one of the cast members said morosely, "our shows are going to blow now. The passengers will want Club Diva, not the *Helio* performers!" Everyone laughed.

"Which brings me to your payment, Miss Reeves," John said, standing up and walking over to her. "Don't pack away your outfit. I believe we will need an emcee from time to time when the club reopens, and you, my dear," he picked up her hand and kissed it, "will be expected to pay the piper."

Kennedy smiled warmly. "With pleasure. Oh, John, one more thing," she said, "the captain was thrilled with the show tonight and wondered if you guys would want to do something on the last night of the cruise. But only if you wanted to," she added quickly.

Phil had been pouring another glass of champagne for himself. He was still wearing his wig, but it now sat crookedly on his head. He put his hand on his hip. "Tell the captain we would be pleased to come out of retirement one more time for him, but," he poured the last bit of champagne into his mouth and flipped his wig back, "we're going to need a lot more champagne!"

Kennedy's radio beeped, and with regret, she pulled herself away from the group. She needed to catch up with her team to see where things stood with Mila. As she walked to the meeting spot, her worries came back with each step, and when she reached the deck, Kennedy saw the long faces of her friends. She put on a brave face. "What's the latest?"

Franklin shook his head and took her hands in his. "First, let's talk about that show. It was amazing! I can't believe those were men! How did you know about them?"

Kennedy answered, smiling. "They've been taking our cruises for a long time and were there for one of my first performances, and I was terrible. So, they took me under their wing and, ever since, have been giving me advice on my shows, outfits, makeup, and shoes." She chuckled lightly. "It's like having a team of backstage mothers." She paused. "But enough about the show. Is there anything new about Mila?"

Omar walked up to the group as the words came out of her mouth. He looked at them sternly. "I believe I told all of you that there was to be no congregating or gossiping, and yet I find you all here trading information." He pulled a hand over his face. "Guys," he sighed, "you're making my job harder."

Tony spoke up, "Actually, Omar, we were talking about Kennedy's show. We haven't talked about Mila…yet," he said awkwardly. "Did you happen to catch the show tonight?"

Omar tried not to smile, but he couldn't contain it. He broke into a wide grin. "I did, and it was a most intriguing performance. I don't think I have ever seen a show with so many celebrities." His smile left and was replaced by a stern look. "However, I must ask that you all go to your rooms. And no further chatting," he admonished them and then turned to Kennedy. "I will personally escort you to your cabin so there can be no further discussions." Kennedy took his proffered arm. "Please be available for your interviews tomorrow. I have sent messages with the times and location."

The others left, and Kennedy and Omar began to walk the deck. "I know you are anxious. Unfortunately, there have been no new developments." He patted her arm. "Mila is still confined to her quarters, and the officials will arrive tomorrow morning to conduct interviews."

Kennedy suddenly felt exhausted. "Omar, I know she didn't do it. Mila just couldn't harm anyone, not even Gunner."

"I know," he said softly. "But to help Mila, we must follow the protocols, and unfortunately, that means she must be confined to her room. I'm doing this for her protection, Kennedy." They continued to walk in silence. Kennedy thought how nice it was not to talk and simply enjoy the peacefulness.

They finally arrived at Kennedy's cabin, and her hand was on the doorknob to go in. Omar put his hand over hers and spoke. "Kennedy," Omar said solemnly, "before we say goodnight, I need to ask you an important question."

She looked into his deep brown eyes. "Of course, Omar, what is it?" she asked, worrying about the question and how it might pertain to the investigation.

He smiled softly and showed his beautiful white teeth. "Where did you procure such an unusual outfit? I don't recall ever seeing it. Nor have I ever seen you dressed so…" he paused, "I am at a loss for words…so wickedly." He looked at her. "I am a big fan of this particular ensemble." He kissed her hand and touched her nose. "Goodnight, Kennedy, sleep well," he said and turned on his heel. She watched him walk down the corridor humming a song from the show with his hands behind his back.

Kennedy was stunned as she walked into her cabin and hugged herself. She realized that her cheeks were hurting because she was smiling so hard. She wished she could call Mila more than anything to share what had just happened. But unfortunately, that thought quickly turned what should have been a joyous moment into one of anxiety and sadness.

Sunny Dayz Cruise Line

THE HELIO

DAY FOUR
PUNTA CANA, DOMINICAN REPUBLIC

ARRIVAL 7:30 A.M.

FIRST TENDER 9:00 A.M.

LAST TENDER 6:00 P.M.

DEPARTURE 7:30 P.M.

The *Helio* anchored off Punta Cana early the following day. A tender arrived at eight with three FBI agents and a few members of the Dominican National Police. Omar and the captain met them and quickly led them to the spa. The area was still out of service, and only those on a specific list were allowed entry by a security team member. The private treatment rooms had been set up for interviews. Omar hoped that the early hour and having the interviews in the spa would help to quell any busybodies. While two FBI agents met with Omar, the third one and the members of the national police team examined the sauna and then the men's locker room.

"Has anything been moved in this room?" one of the policemen asked.

"No, sir," Safety Officer Tully answered. "When the body was found, our security team immediately locked down the spa and its adjacent areas. We had been performing a safety drill earlier in the day, and the spaces had just been reopened to the guests when Mr. Atcher was found."

The officers walked around the room. One noticed a pile of towels in a cart in front of the fire extinguisher cabinet. "Is there a reason this is here?"

Tully turned pink. "Absolutely not, sir, and as the ship's safety officer, it's my job to check the extinguishers daily." He shook his head in frustration. "I have told the spa workers countless times that they can't put anything in front of the extinguishers. I will make a point of writing up the person responsible."

The officer moved the cart away, and they all stared at the empty cabinet. "Was there an extinguisher in here yesterday?" one of them asked.

Tully felt his face turn bright red in embarrassment. "Yes, I have a checklist I initial each day for every location. So, I'm not sure why it isn't in the cabinet."

The FBI agent turned to him. "Would you please get your log?" He looked at the other officers. "We need to find the missing extinguisher. It may be what was used to cause the trauma to the deceased's head. Excuse me. I need to find my boss."

Franklin was being interviewed by one of the FBI agents. "Can you tell me about your interactions with Mr. Atcher, please, Mr. Blaas?" she asked.

Franklin took a deep breath and blew it out. "I'll be honest. They weren't good. I tried to be cordial, but the guy had a way of getting under your skin like a tick. He was rough on the senior staff – especially the women. It made you wonder if he had something against them just because of their gender. He dismissed Kennedy, Rosemary, and Mila from the room during the first meeting. I'm embarrassed I didn't stand up for them, but I was in shock. I've never encountered someone like that. You would think he would want to observe one cruise before trying to make changes. But, instead, making people miserable and talking about himself was all he did while on the ship."

The FBI agent wrote down a few words in her notebook. "Would you please tell me specifically what happened while he was on board?"

Franklin let out a deep sigh. "Let me begin with our first meeting," and he shared the three days of meetings and individual visits with the agent.

"Mr. Blaas, can you help me understand why the sauna door would not unlatch from the inside? It is a safety violation."

Franklin nodded. "Yes, ma'am," he answered, "you are correct. It is a safety violation, and Mila gave me the work order." He looked down at his hands. "Mila was...is our spa director. She gave me the work order two days ago. She had noticed the problem and asked that it be repaired quickly. I told her to put up an out-of-order sign until we fixed it. Unfortunately, the goat, I mean the deceased—"

The agent looked up quickly from her notebook. "The goat?" she queried.

Franklin blushed, embarrassed, and looked at his feet. "We called him the goat," he said sheepishly. "You know the greatest," and she joined in with him, "of all time!"

"Oh, my goodness, I guess every industry has those," she chuckled. "We had an agent in Pittsburgh like that. I had forgotten the term. But let's go back to the sauna door. Why wasn't it repaired?"

Franklin was blunt. "Mr. Atcher and I had a disagreement in the maintenance shop the day before, and he declared that there were to be no work orders completed until the area had been thoroughly cleaned and inspected by him."

The agent looked at Franklin quizzically. "That sounds a bit odd. Aren't you all adults? It sounds vaguely like my mother telling me in the third grade that I couldn't do my homework until I had cleaned my room. It was my understanding that he was consulting on this cruise."

Franklin nodded in agreement. "From the first day on the ship, he kept telling us that he would be the new vice president and that if we crossed him, we would be removed from our jobs." He raised his hands in the air and let them drop defeatedly. "I wanted to quit, but I couldn't leave my team."

The agent closed her notebook. "Mr. Blaas, that clears up why Mr. Atcher could not open the door from the inside, and this completes our interview. I ask that you not share our conversation with anyone while the investigation is underway."

Franklin left the treatment room and saw Rosemary coming out of her interview. Her eyes were wet, and she dabbed them with a tissue. The FBI agent was patting her on the back. "Please don't worry, Ms. Flores. We know you were not to blame. Your presence and the presence of all of your staff are accounted for at the safety drill. We only wanted to get your impressions of the deceased." At the word deceased, Rosemary began crying harder. She saw Franklin and walked over to him quickly. He put his arms around her and enveloped her in a bear hug. "I'm so sorry," the agent said.

"She'll be okay. She's just very worried," Franklin replied and walked Rosemary with his arms over her shoulders through the spa's reception area. They passed

Kennedy and Chef Michèle, who were next to be interviewed.

"I don't know what else I can tell you," Kennedy said regretfully. "He was just an awful person, but none of us wished him dead. He threatened our jobs, berated us openly…" she felt a sob working its way up her throat and paused. "It was just a horrible situation," she said softly, shaking her head.

The agent was thoughtful for a moment. "What were your impressions of his interaction with the ship's executive chef? I understand that after their meeting, the chef got very volatile."

Kennedy inhaled slightly and then bit her lips together. She looked the agent in the eye, "Chef Michèle can overreact, but that is his public persona." She smiled ruefully. "The only thing he has ever taken his aggression out on, to my knowledge, is a chicken breast," she said with a giggle. "Oh, I'm sorry that was inappropriate."

Now it was the agent's turn to chuckle. "Not at all. I always know when my wife has had a difficult day. On those nights, she serves a mushy chicken piccata for dinner because instead of flattening the chicken breasts, she beats them to a pulp." He stood up and shook her hand. "Thank you for your time, Ms. Reeves. It seems this cruise has not been easy, between Mr. Atcher's behavior and having to keep the passengers happy and entertained. You have been under a lot of strain and have my sympathies." He paused before opening the door. "I heard there are some celebrities on this cruise. Who are they?"

Kennedy gave him a sly smile. "I'm sorry, I'm not at liberty to say. Strict company policies about privacy. I'm sure you understand."

The agent nodded and opened the door, and Kennedy stepped out of the room.

She quickly left the spa and headed to the lobby. The passengers were queued up to take their tenders into Punta Cana. She walked around, reminding them to allow plenty of time to get back as the tenders could only hold so many guests per trip. "The ship leaves at seven thirty tonight, so please make every effort to be at the tender station no later than six o'clock," she told them. Walking through the lobby and visiting with several groups, she came upon the Ladies from Harmony Lakes. "Well, ladies, our last port of call for this trip. Shopping, I'm guessing?"

Dolly snorted and furrowed her brow at Kennedy. "Wrong, wrong, wrong, Kennedy, but after last night's amazing show, I forgive you. Tell her what we are going to do, Laura," she said, smirking and crossing her arms.

Laura let out a tired sigh. "It appears that my mother is still working on her bucket list, and we are taking surfing lessons at Macao Beach." She turned around and looked daggers at Marilyn. "Somehow, Mother and Marilyn connived and booked the excursion without telling any of us, and I am a trifle irritated with both of them."

"Hey!" Dolly cried, "I've only got a few years left, and it's another thing to check off the list."

"And I'm doing it for other reasons, Kennedy," Marilyn cooed. "When we go on the next cruise, hopefully, your handsome brother will be there, and I'll be able to show him my moves if you know what I mean." She gave Kennedy a theatrical wink.

"Good Lord, Marilyn, you don't want the poor boy to go blind when he sees you in a wet suit!" Dolly jeered.

Louise threw Kennedy an apologetic look and began herding them across the lobby. "Ladies, we need to get on the tender," she said. "And Kennedy, amazing show last night. We had no idea that the guys would be performing. They never let on about the show, not one peep. I don't know how you kept it hidden under your hat!"

Kennedy swallowed and smiled. "I like to keep a few surprises up my sleeve. I can't have you bored on the ship, leaving a negative review." Beth had been standing there quietly, but she looked strangely at Louise and Kennedy.

"Come on, you old bags, let's go!" Dolly yelled across the lobby. "I'm not getting any younger!"

"Well, you heard her," Laura gave Kennedy an apprehensive look. "And if we don't catch up…well, I don't want to think what sort of trouble she'll get in. The retirement home is looking better and better. Goodbye, Kennedy. We'll see you this afternoon."

Kennedy waved them off and looked around the lobby. She was concerned about the Butlers. In planning and executing the diva show last night, she had been unable to check on them. She suddenly saw them step off the elevator. "Kennedy! I'm so glad we found you. I still cannot believe that show!" It completely took my mind off finding the…" Jones looked around and whispered loudly behind his hand, "you know, B-O-D-Y."

So, where are you two lovebirds off to?" Kennedy asked.

Terri spoke up, "Well, since yesterday was my day, and then the terrible thing happened, today is all about Jones. We are going snorkeling and taking dune buggies out on the beach," she chirped in her sing-song voice. "I just know that being underwater with the fish will be like being in a giant aquarium. I wonder if we will see an octopus or a whale. That would be cool," she said wide-eyed.

Kennedy was not sure what to say, so she changed the subject. "Did you receive your photos?" She had slid them under their door between dinner in the main dining room and the diva show.

"Oh, Kennedy, they were amazing!" Terri trilled. "I'll have to show them to you later, but they were so romantic." She turned to Jones. "Weren't they, Jonesy?"

Jones smiled indulgently at his wife. "They were perfect, just like you, Sweetsie. I think I'll have the one of you lying on the palm tree over the water in your tiny bikini enlarged and put in my office." He put his index fingers and thumbs out as if placing a picture on the wall. "It will be the first thing people see when they walk in. Now, we have to go, or we will miss our tender. See you later, Kennedy."

Watching Jones and Terri depart, Kennedy decided that there was someone for everyone. *You just have to find them."*

A whisper in her ear startled her. "Ugh, those dreadful people, I've been hiding behind a potted palm, hoping they would leave soon. I need to wait a bit and get on the next tender. Being stuck with them is not going to happen," Vera said hotly. "Sitting with them at dinner last night is two hours of my life that I will never get back."

"And hello to you as well, Mrs. Jameson," Kennedy remarked. She had wished she had seen Vera skulking behind the plant. "What will—"

Vera cut her off. "First things first," she said intently. "I understand that dreadful man, Gunner something or other who accosted me right here on the first day, is no longer of this Earth as my late husband would say. Is it true?"

"Mrs. Jameson," Kennedy pleaded.

"Don't you, Mrs. Jameson me, young lady," she whispered hotly. "I know people, remember?" she arched an eyebrow at Kennedy. Kennedy nodded slightly. "Well, he was ill-mannered and uncouth. Is that little man that trailed after him like a puppy still on board?"

Kennedy looked around to make sure she couldn't be overheard. "Mr. Phillips? Yes, but we have him under a doctor's care. The news yesterday was hard on him. The doctor has suggested that he stay in his room and rest until we return to Port Canaveral. You don't know him, do you?" Kennedy asked nervously.

"Why?" Vera barked.

"Well, you are fairly connected with the board of directors, and he *is* one of the board members and has the notes from the visit. I'm afraid they don't paint a pretty picture of us. Gunner was going to have Mila fired and replaced. He threatened my job and others as well," she said anxiously, wringing her hands.

Vera looked at Kennedy and said in a harsh tone, "Stop wringing your hands like some helpless nincompoop, Kennedy." She softened her words seeing the stricken look on Kennedy's face. "You will all be fine. I'll see to it. I've known all of you long enough to know that you are the cream of the crop, hence why the corporate office selected the *Helio* for the first cruise. And don't worry about Mila; she will not lose her job. I will make sure of that. After the transformation in the spa, the company would be foolish to let her go." She looked at her watch. "Now, I cannot be late. I need to be on the next tender. I have a tee time at Corales at the Punta Cana Resort, and I need to see a man about some cigars." She waved her fingers at Kennedy and walked away.

Vera's goodbye lifted Kennedy's spirits. "I need to find..." Before she could say her friend's name, Kennedy's hopes plummeted, which had been sky-high only moments ago. Mila was still confined to her cabin and would be having her interview shortly. Worrying about getting fired was now the least of Kennedy's worries.

Omar was walking to Mila's cabin while Kennedy saw the passengers off. He had hoped that she would be prepared and well-rested for the questioning she was about to undergo because she had been confined to her cabin and had not had contact with any of her friends. Unfortunately, when she answered the door, Omar could see at once that she was neither well-rested nor prepared. She looked terrible. Mila had not brushed her hair, and she looked as if she had rolled out of bed to answer the door. He stepped into her cabin.

"Mila," he said sternly, "you need to pull yourself together. There are three FBI agents in the spa right now who want to question you about Gunner's death. They have heard about the altercations between the two of you and more. I know you are innocent, but you need to prove it to the FBI agents." He pointed to the bathroom. "Go in there and make yourself presentable. I will wait outside in the corridor," he said sternly. "You have fifteen minutes."

Ten minutes later, Mila opened the door. She had pulled her hair back into a chignon and was dressed in a pair of white gauze pants and a black sleeveless tunic. "Let's go," she said in a flat voice, looking directly ahead.

"Just tell the truth, Mila," Omar said quietly.

"Unfortunately, telling the truth may put me in worse trouble."

Omar ushered Mila into the spa and took her to the private reception area. It was the largest area in the spa that still had privacy. Mila and Omar stood up when the three agents entered. "Please have a seat," one of the agents said, and everyone took a chair. "Ms. Casimir, we want to ask you some questions about your interactions with the deceased. We understand there were some verbal altercations."

Mila nodded and answered slowly. "We had some difficulties, and Mr. Atcher threatened my job on more than one occasion."

The female agent spoke up. "Is it true that you were the last person to see Mr. Atcher alive?"

"Mila, you don't have to answer that," Omar said, and the female agent shot him a sharp look.

"Mr. Meier, perhaps it is best if you stepped outside." Omar blew out a breath and stood up, nodding curtly at the three agents, and gave Mila what he hoped was a look of encouragement. He hated himself for speaking out. He had wanted to be in the room to provide Mila with some friendly support.

Mila watched her friend leave and raised her head. "I don't know if I was the last person to see him. I can tell you that Mr. Atcher requested a facial before going into Grand Turk. As my staff needed to participate in the ship's drill, I stayed behind to perform Mr. Atcher's facial."

"Did you explain to him that you needed to take part in the drill?" one of the male agents asked. "I find it odd that he was not a part of the drill."

Mila laughed softly. "Mr. Atcher felt he did not need to participate in the drill. In an attempt to make amends and beg for my job, I decided to perform his treatment personally. And, I will add, he didn't care that I needed to participate in the drill as he had effectively fired me. He even suggested it would be more logical that I not go to the drill and clean out my office."

"And did you?" the female agent asked.

The questioning continued for another two hours, and by the time Omar was summoned to collect Mila, he could tell she was worn out, emotionally and mentally. He leaned over toward her and whispered quickly, "Don't say a word until we're halfway down the corridor."

When they were out of earshot, she began to cry softly. "Omar, they think I killed him. They know about everything—even Dimitri. I thought I had escaped that when I left him," she looked at him with exhausted eyes. "They kept asking me the same questions over and over. If I was the only one in the spa when the drill started and why I wasn't accounted for on the safety drill list? I left the spa intending to go to the drill, but I was so upset that I went to my room to begin packing. Sara may have still been there. I had given her permission to finish up a few things, but she promised me she would go to the drill."

Omar stopped in his tracks. "You never told me that! Did you tell the FBI? Did you tell them Sara was in the spa after the others left?"

Mila answered him tiredly, "Honestly, Omar, it didn't occur to me, and I tried to tell them, but they kept asking me about what happened when I threw him out of the spa the day before and what happened in the meetings." Mila was beginning to get frantic. "They asked me about my threat to kill Gunner. Omar, it was a moment of passion! He had just threatened me, but they didn't seem to understand or care about that. It was okay for him to bully and belittle me continually, but I seem to be the one on trial." Her voice rose in hysteria. "Omar, I don't know what to do."

Omar took a moment to collect his thoughts as they approached her cabin. He nodded at the security guard. "Go into your room and do not come out until the captain and I have had a chance to visit with the agents and find out what will happen next," he said solemnly. "Stay in your room. No visitors," he snapped and quickly walked away. Mila walked into her cabin and locked the door. She sat down woodenly in the chair at her desk and stared at the door waiting for Omar to return.

Omar walked back into the spa. "Well, what are the next steps?" he asked, clapping his hands together.

The captain had a troubled face. "Omar, I have been speaking with the authorities. Mila is to be held in her cabin under guard until we return to Port Canaveral. When we arrive, we will be met by the authorities who will take over. Mila will need a lawyer immediately." Omar was stunned.

One of the agents spoke up, "Captain if you will direct us to our tender, we will be on our way." He nodded at Omar. "Goodbye, Mr. Meier. As the captain said, please keep Ms. Casimir confined to her room until you reach Port Canaveral. We will get in touch with our team there and send over our documentation from the investigation."

Omar's heart was heavy as he rapped on Mila's cabin door. When she opened it, she began crying when she saw the somber look on his face. "Mila, I am so sorry." He took her hands in his. "The authorities have concluded that you are to be confined for the duration of the cruise. When we reach Port Canaveral, the FBI will take you into custody for further questioning."

Mila gripped the doorway for support. "But I didn't kill him, Omar," she protested, and a fresh wave of tears coursed down her face.

"Do you have an attorney I can call to meet you? Do you want me to call your family? How can I help?"

Mila looked down at the ground and slowly began shutting the door. "There is nothing for you to do, Omar," she said in a hoarse voice. "This is something I have to face alone."

"Absolutely not!" Franklin bellowed, banging his fist down on the conference room table. "Mila will not face this alone. I'll take a leave of absence while this gets sorted out. The company can do without me for the next cruise; if not, who cares? I'll retire. Mila is our family, and she will not face this alone." Omar had just shared the update with the team.

"Oh, my poor, dear, gentle friend," Rosemary said softly. She looked up at Omar. "If you know she didn't do this, why aren't you helping her?"

"I tried, Rosemary!" he protested. He sighed and sat heavily in the chair, dragging his hands down his face. "I know, you know, we all know that she is innocent. But unfortunately, too many people heard their arguments, and too many staff members heard Mila say she could kill him and specifically said she wanted to beat him over the head. And, I might add, he died in a room with a faulty door in the spa she runs."

"But that wasn't her fault!" Franklin roared again. "She put in the request, and that jerk stopped all maintenance requests from being performed because he was mad at me." Then, shaking his head back and forth, he moaned and said sadly, "She's being punished because of what I didn't do." Franklin dropped his head into his hands.

Kennedy had been quiet. Some people, when faced with tragic news, cried or got mad. Kennedy was the kind who went into planning mode. Ironically, she had learned this by watching her mother. When there was a crisis: an accident, hurricane, fire, or other devastating event, Lolly made a plan and put it into action. She stood up. "Okay, first things first," she said, looking at the group. "Omar, since you are the only one who can go to Mila's room and talk to her, you need to let her know we have this under control. I'll call my father and ask him to retain the best lawyer he can find for Mila and have that person waiting at the dock when we arrive in Port Canaveral. He's an attorney and should have contacts or know someone who does."

She turned to Franklin. "We need to keep up the ruse that the spa and possibly the gym are having plumbing problems. We'll leave the curtains up so no one can peek in. Could you walk in and out of the spa a few times today and tomorrow with your tools? We'll issue refunds or gift certificates to passengers who had appointments." She looked at Chef Michèle. "Will you please put together some food for Mila? She won't feel like eating, but she needs to keep her strength up. Maybe some comfort food?" He nodded his head, thankful for something useful to do. Kennedy continued, "Since most of the spa team thinks the spa has a plumbing issue and Mila is under the weather, I'll recruit them to help with activities today and tomorrow. It will help with the plumbing issue rumor." Kennedy looked around the room. "We need to convey to everyone that nothing is wrong. We need to smile so hard our cheeks cramp." She was thoughtful for a moment. "I'm forgetting something."

Tony slapped his hand to his head. "Isn't tomorrow a sea day? Those are the longest days," he lamented. "How will you keep the passengers busy and away from the spa? Even if they don't have appointments, you know they will rubberneck to see what is going on."

Chef Michèle, who typically said nothing in meetings and never offered to do anything out of the ordinary, said in a deep voice, "I can offer a few cooking demonstrations tomorrow. Easy things they can make at home. Maybe my friend Luke could offer a couple of mixology classes?"

Kennedy was taken off guard. "That would be lovely, Michèle." She looked at Luke. "Would you offer some classes as well? It would help keep people occupied."

"Sure, anything to help," he said.

"Great, let me know how many classes you can teach and when? I'll post the information."

"Is tomorrow night the traditional dance party? It's a shame we can't have your friends for that show. It could lighten the mood," Franklin offered.

"You never know, Franklin," she said mysteriously. She turned her full gaze on him. "Maybe you will get on stage too? I hear you were a heck of a disco dancer in your prime." Franklin threw Rosemary a withering look, but Rosemary was suddenly fascinated by an imaginary spiderweb in the corner of the ceiling. "Okay, everyone," Kennedy smiled brightly, "we've got a lot to get done. Let's do it for Mila," she said encouragingly.

Later that afternoon in Punta Cana, the Ladies from Harmony Lakes were sitting on the benches awaiting the tender to take them back to the ship when John and the others strode up.

"Ladies, it's good to see you," John said, pulling down his white rhinestone sunglasses. He looked at Dolly, who was wearing a loud tropical print shirt over a wetsuit and gave her a wink. "Nice outfit, Dolly."

"Oh, it's our celebrities!" Marilyn cooed. "You were so wonderful as Dolly Parton last night," she said, batting her eyes at John, who suddenly looked interesting to her. "I always thought I could play her in a movie. You know we have so many similarities," she preened.

Dolly knit her eyebrows together as she looked at Marilyn. "The only similarity I know is that Dolly Parton based her persona on the town tramp, and you are the town tramp!"

Laura turned red. "Mother!" she hollered in embarrassment. "That is enough! You are in time out until we get back to the ship."

The men could not help chuckling. John laughed the loudest. "I do love Dolly Parton. My two favorite quotes by her are, 'It costs a lot of money to look this cheap', and 'it's a good thing I was born a girl. Otherwise, I'd be a drag queen'."

Louise nodded her head at Marilyn. "I believe Marilyn's favorite is, 'If I see something sagging, bagging, or dragging, I'm going to have it nipped, tucked, or sucked'."

John slapped his knee, and the others began holding their sides laughing.

Marilyn looked daggers at Dolly and Louise and then primly turned to Dave. "I think you were just darling in your outfit. Where did you find it? And all those necklaces, it's a wonder one of them didn't fly up and give you a black eye." She turned her head to Phil, sitting on her other side, and playfully slapped his arm. "And you in your black fishnet stockings and leather jacket! Where did you get that wig? You were the epitome of Cher! I've seen her in concert, and I swear it was like she was right there in front of us!"

Beth had a puzzled look on her face. "But…" No one heard her.

"Do we know how long we will have to wait before the next boat arrives?" John asked. "I am dying to get back to find out what happened."

"Exactly what *did* happen?" asked Louise raising an eyebrow. "We saw Kennedy come over to you by the pool, and you all left a few minutes later. The next thing we knew, you were on stage."

Beth exclaimed loudly, "Wait a minute, do you mean that Dolly and Cher weren't on stage? But we saw them!"

Louise looked at her friend pitifully. "No honey," she began to explain, "the boys were… never mind," she waved her hand. "Before Mount Everest was discovered, which was the highest mountain in the world?" She turned to the rest of them. "It will keep her busy for a while. Now spill it!"

Laura put her arms around Beth, who was concentrating hard on Louise's question. "Sweetie, I think we'll make an appointment with the optometrist when we get home. I think you need new glasses."

John looked around. "Well…" He leaned in and told them everything they had heard from the cast.

The good thing about a day in Punta Cana was that it was a long day, and the passengers returned exhausted from their excursions. Dinner was subdued, and many passengers felt disappointed. The other nights had all been exciting. There was no parade, no impromptu conga line, and no outlandish costumes as the Butlers had elected to take dinner in their room. Terri had suffered some bumps and bruises from a dune buggy ride.

"It was wild, though," Jones said, sharing the information with Kennedy when she stopped at their cabin to check on Terri. They had stepped out into the corridor, so they wouldn't disturb Terri, who was sleeping. "We got to see parts of the DR that you wouldn't normally see," he said excitedly. "The dune buggies were great, but I got a little out of control, and Terri got banged up." He looked remorseful. "I feel bad, I've bought her something in each port, but she was so hurt all I wanted to do was get her back to the ship."

Kennedy smiled warmly at Jones. "I am certain that she will feel much better after a hot soak, some dinner, and some sleep. Should I send the ship's doctor by to see her?"

Jones shook his head. "No, but thank you. I feel like I should get her something, though. I'm the reason she didn't get to go shopping."

Kennedy was thoughtful. "The Sunburst Boutique on deck eight has some lovely items, and you could surprise her tomorrow morning at breakfast with something." He nodded his head. As she turned to leave, she remembered she wanted to share the additional activities available the following day. "Oh, and before I forget, tomorrow is a sea day, so there are lots of things planned. We have cooking demonstrations, mixology classes, dance lessons, and more."

Jones was quiet, thinking hard about his next words. "Kennedy, what is going on with the…you know, the thing I'm not supposed to talk about?"

Kennedy had hoped Jones would not bring up the situation but decided honesty was the best policy. "The authorities came on board and have started an investigation. If they decide they need further information, they will contact you at home; however, your interview with Mr. Meier was very thorough, and I hope they will not have to bother you and allow you to put this unpleasantness aside."

Jones nodded. "Thanks, Kennedy. I know that when we rebook, I only want to be on a cruise that you are on.

Terri and I really like you. Plus, we want you to visit us after the renovation. We want you to see how we took our stateroom and brought it home." Kennedy tried to keep from laughing. She had a mental image of the stateroom's decor inside their home and the enormous photo of Terri in her bathing suit in Jones's office. "We could even set you up with one of my brothers or cousins. Terri has a bunch, too! You'd be the belle of the ball. Do you like to hunt deer or go fishing?"

Kennedy had to extract herself from the conversation before she was on a plane to Mississippi. She looked at her watch. "Oh, my goodness, it sounds lovely, but I just saw the time, and I have got to get ready for the show tonight. Mr. Butler, I hope you both have a restful evening, and again, if Terri needs anything, please let one of us know."

Just like dinner, the evening's show was subdued. It wasn't that the cast did anything wrong. They were perfect. Usually, beach music night was a passenger favorite and was always done before a sea day as it was easier on the cast, who would be up early the next morning helping with the activities on the decks.

"Perhaps it was just all of the excitement from last night," she told the cast, who looked crushed.

Sunny Dayz Cruise Line

THE HELIO

DAY FIVE
SEA DAY

Bert was busy at his desk early the following morning. He had some edits to complete on the spa photos before he would need to be on the pool deck to take pictures. A day at sea equaled the opportunity to take many photos, and Bert was motivated. A part of his paycheck came from the number of purchased prints and today was the last day the passengers could decide which photo they wanted from the thousands he took. Bert took a large gulp of coffee. The images from the spa and fitness center he had taken the day Gunner had died were up on his screen, and he began reviewing them, removing the ones that were junk and making improvements on others he wanted to keep.

Two hours later, bleary-eyed from staring at the computer screen, Bert came across the men's locker room photo. "Part three of the triptych," he said, straightening up in his chair. "Maybe I can sell them online and make some extra cash." Perplexed, he looked at the screen and enlarged the photo. As he stared at the image, his heart began to pound. The screen appeared to show two silhouettes in the partially open door.

Bert clicked back and forth through the photos. To his knowledge, only he, Sara, Gunner, and Mila had been in the spa. Bert remembered thinking it was odd that Sara had still been in the spa and not at her drill location but reminded himself that he, too, had ducked out of the drill. Clicking his mouse furiously, Bert found the photo he had taken of Sara with an armload of towels going into the locker room. He recalled that shortly after that photo, he had caught her with her ear pressed against the wall, eavesdropping on Mila and Gunner. When he confronted her, she brushed past him, informing him she needed to put more towels in the locker room. A thought struck him as the memory of seeing Sara staring at Gunner through the two-way mirror in the back corridor came to mind.

Knowing that rumors were running rampant on the ship about Mila, Bert began to feel uneasy, and sweat broke out on his forehead. He got up from his chair and walked quickly out of his cabin on a mission to find Kennedy.

Kennedy was on the pool deck helping the cast and the spa technicians get ready for the day of activities while sleepy passengers began staking out claims for a chaise lounge around the pool. She stopped to see Luke as he supervised his team making vats of SunRumbrellas.

"Any news?" he asked with solemn eyes.

Kennedy shook her head. "Nothing new," she sighed. "Mila's still confined to her room until we reach Port Canaveral. I spoke to my father, and he promised to have an attorney at the dock to go with her for questioning. I would feel better if one of us could go with her and not a stranger, but our next group of passengers arrives at two o'clock."

Luke looked down at the glass he was polishing. "I still can't believe she would do it."

Kennedy's head snapped up, and she looked at him strangely. "She didn't do it, Luke."

He looked at her. "I know, but you have to admit it looks bad. She does have a checkered past."

Kennedy looked at Luke in a fury. "Luke, we all have a past. We all ran to life on a ship for one reason or another. It became our safe harbor from whatever we were fleeing. Do you remember why you turned to bartending on a ship?" she demanded.

"I'm sorry, you are right," he said apologetically.

Kennedy still irritated with Luke, got up from the barstool she had been sitting on. "I've got to check to make sure Chef Michèle doesn't already have Tony popping antacid like candy. He volunteered to do some food demonstrations today, and Tony is helping him."

Luke stopped polishing the glass in his hand and put it down. "Chef Michèle and volunteer, two words I never thought I would hear together," he said, surprised.

"No," she offered, softening her tone, "but stressful situations sometimes bring out the best in people."

Kennedy left the pool bar and went to the Vantage Point Lounge. She found a laughing Chef Michèle and Tony going over the list for the demonstration. "Well, you two," she said brightly, "this looks like a terrific setup." Two long tables had been set up so the audience could watch Michèle cook while also taking in the view of the ocean behind him. "What are we going to demonstrate?"

"Curried shrimp, avocado salad, and my famous pineapple upside-down cake," Michèle replied with a toothy grin. "Something simple they can make at home with ingredients they can find in any grocery store."

Kennedy spied a tub of ice with several bottles of wine in it. "And that?" she pointed to the tub. "Aren't we doing a food demonstration? It looks more like a wine-tasting class," she asked wryly.

Tony cleared his throat. "W-w-well, we thought we would ask the guests questions, and if they got the answer right, Chef would reward them with a glass of wine."

Kennedy crossed her arms and smirked. "That sounds great, guys. Will those who attend get to taste what you are making?"

Tony nodded his head enthusiastically. "Yes, at the end of the demonstration, my staff will bring plates to each person to sample along with recipe cards." He stopped and slapped his forehead. "I forgot to print the cards."

Kennedy smiled at the two men. They were an unlikely pair. "Chef, Tony, it looks like you have it under control. I wish I could watch the show. Your demonstration looks like a lot of fun!" She turned and left for her next stop.

She was walking down the deck when she heard her name called out frantically. "Kennedy!" Bert hollered, and she turned around abruptly. "I've been looking for you everywhere," he shouted. "Stay right there!" When he reached her, he bent over, putting his hands on his knees, trying hard to catch his breath. "I need to show you something right away," he panted.

"Bert, I can't," she began. She still had so much to do. She looked at him. Something told her that whatever Bert needed to show her was important. "What's wrong, Bert?"

Bert looked around. There were several passengers and members of the ship nearby. "Not here," he said, shaking his head, "I need you to come to my cabin. I need to show you some pictures I took in the spa."

"Bert!" Kennedy said with exasperation. "I don't have time right now to see your photos."

"Kennedy," Bert interrupted. "I need to show you something now!" he said forcefully. "It's about Mila." He looked at her pleadingly. "Anna Marie told me everything."

Kennedy blinked several times and then grabbed his arms. "Bert, what is it? You have to tell me now!"

He shook his head. "You need to see these photos, Kennedy. Please come to my cabin. I'll meet you there." Bert took off in the direction of his cabin, and Kennedy radioed the cast to tell them she would be delayed and to rehearse without her. She took the back steps down to the lower deck to Bert's cabin.

Ten minutes later, Kennedy knocked on his door, and Bert yanked it open, beckoning her to come in quickly. "The day we were in Grand Turk, I was taking photos of the spa."

"Okay," Kennedy said slowly, wishing Bert would get on with it. She had a lot to get done.

"This morning, I was editing them. I had this cool idea for a triptych. The first was this one." He pulled up the image of the water bottle on the elliptical.

Kennedy could feel her impatience growing but forced herself to listen.

"Then I had this amazing idea and took these. Look at the timestamp." The image showed Sara walking with an armload of towels to the men's locker room. In the first shot, you could see the figure was Sara. The image showed a blurred figure where Sara had been, but it was taken seconds after the first. Bert continued, "A few minutes later, I caught Sara, the new spa tech, eavesdropping on Mila and Gunner in the back corridor between the fitness and treatment rooms. You know, the hallway with the two-way mirror. Sara had her ear pressed against the wall. When I confronted her, she pushed past me and said she needed to put more towels in the locker room."

"Okay," Kennedy said slowly, not understanding what Bert was trying to say. "I'll talk with her. She shouldn't have been eavesdropping, but since this is her first cruise, she may not understand the rules."

Bert looked at Kennedy in exasperation. "But that's just it." He jabbed the image on the screen. "She had already put towels in the locker room when I saw her in the hallway. Something doesn't make sense. Why would she need to put towels in an empty locker room twice? We didn't have anyone in the spa because of the drill." He began to get excited and scrolled through the images. "This was supposed to be the last of the triptych."

Kennedy peered over his shoulder and saw the long hallway with the partially open door to the darkened locker room. As she looked closer, she saw two silhouette's and one was holding something at the back of the other one's head. She sucked in her breath.

"Look at the timestamp. There's something else that doesn't make sense, Kennedy, something I probably should have told you. At the time, I didn't think it was a big deal, but now—"

Kennedy tore her eyes from the image on the screen. "What, Bert? What?"

Bert swallowed. "I caught Sara staring at Gunner the other day when he was working out. She was staring at him through the two-way mirror. It was weird. It was as if she knew him."

Looking back at the image on the screen, Kennedy swallowed hard. "Bert, I'll be back," she said, walking to the door. "Don't show anyone those pictures. Can you print them out? I need to check something out before we show them to Omar."

Bert called after her, "Did I do something right, Kennedy?" But she was already gone.

On her way to her cabin, several passengers stopped Kennedy asking if the divas would be performing again, how to find the cooking demonstration, or what other classes were available. Kennedy was in a hurry but answered each question politely, trying not to rush them but wanting desperately to get to her cabin. When she finally reached it an hour later, she frantically logged onto her computer. The ship's internet was painfully slow when out to sea, and she made herself wait patiently for the connection. It was like waiting for Alfred's message all over again.

When she was granted access, she typed in the name Sara West and clicked on the images tab. A page of photos popped up with people named Sara West. One picture stood out. The one Mila had shown her the day she had interviewed Sara. The eyes, nose, and mouth were the same, but the hairstyle was different, and she appeared to be a little heavier in the picture. The woman on Kennedy's screen had brown hair with honey blonde highlights cut at an angle, framing her slightly round face and parted in the middle. The Sara, who worked in the spa, was about forty pounds lighter and had an angular face and white hair cut in a pixie, which she spiked up. The difference was dramatic, but Kennedy was sure it was the same person. She clicked on the photo and quickly scanned an article in a hotel magazine entitled

"Thirty Under Thirty." It gave a brief spotlight on young hotel managers on the rise.

Then Kennedy saw something that made her gasp. On the page's right side, the article showed a column featuring the mentors of the young managers. Gunner Owen Atcher's face smiled back at her. "It could be a coincidence," Kennedy whispered and thought back to how Sara had come to be on the *Helio*. She remembered her phone call with Mila and Mila's second-guessing herself because Sara had seemed to be too prepared, eager, and qualified. There had been no reason not to hire her.

Kennedy went onto a well-known social media page and typed Gunner's name. She stared at the screen seeing photographs of Gunner and various women, including several of Sara. Kennedy pursed her lips and turned off her computer. She needed to find Sara and have a chat before she went to Omar with Bert's photographs.

While Kennedy was learning about Sara's background, Sara had gone to Omar's office and asked if she could go into the spa to straighten up and reset the retail products so the next cruise would be ready for guests when they docked. "I think I heard someone say there was a tight turnaround," she added. "I'm supposed to be on the pool deck with the passengers, but I'm getting a little overwhelmed by only seeing miles of ocean all around. I don't know if I am cut out for working on a ship and not seeing land."

Omar was distracted by the amount of paperwork created from the visit by the FBI yesterday. He was not sure who Alfred would be able to find on such short notice to run the spa in Mila's absence, but he didn't want the person to walk into a disaster. "Yes," he said with some resignation looking up from the pile of papers on his desk, "you may work in there, but remember to keep the door locked behind you and allow no one inside." He rummaged around on his desk and handed her Mila's set of keys.

"Yes, sir," Sara said and then paused. "May I also straighten up the fitness center? I know it is out of order as well, but someone should check to make sure it is presentable. I don't know if anyone else thought about it. The spa staff got recruited to help with the passengers."

Omar nodded his head slowly. "Yes, of course, you may also take care of that area. Mila is lucky to have someone as conscientious as you on staff. I do hope you will consider staying on the *Helio.* You get used to only seeing the ocean, and it's only on sea days," he offered. Sara smiled and told him she would think about it. After she left, Omar chided himself for not questioning her whereabouts during the drill. Because Sara had been a last-minute addition to the employee roster, she had not been on Safety Officer Tully's printout for the drill, and why Omar had missed seeing her name on the list until Mila had mentioned it. He needed to pin down where she had been. He thought he could catch her before she got too far away, but suddenly his phone rang. The captain wanted to see him on the bridge.

Kennedy was not able to search for Sara right away. Her duties as cruise director meant she needed to interact with the guests on board, and part of those duties on a sea day was to visit the areas where events were happening. She stopped by the Vantage Point Lounge and was stunned to see the bantering between Tony and Chef Michèle. Generally, Michèle barked, and Tony cowered, but today they were standing in front of the passengers laughing and joking with each other and the audience. Tony and Michèle were each holding a glass of wine. She looked at the tables and noticed every guest also had a full glass of wine in their hands, and the servers were standing nearby to refill them. "Lots of correct answers?" she mouthed to Tony, and he grinned and nodded. She shook her head. This cruise was getting stranger by the minute.

Hurrying from where the culinary class was being taught, Kennedy made her way to the mixology class Luke was teaching by the pool. As Luke showed off his famous five-martini pour, Bert was there taking photographs. The five-martini pour was a great trick and always got Luke a round of applause and sometimes a few dollars when a passenger would bet Luke that he couldn't do it. The passengers watched as Luke set up five martini glasses, three on the bottom and two on top. Then he poured gin and vermouth into five shakers. Stacking them carefully on top of each other, he picked up the tower and, holding them over the pyramid of martini glasses, began filling them simultaneously. The passengers clapped excitedly, nodding to each other.

"Okay, you've watched me," he said and pointed to tables with glasses, shakers, and water pitchers. "Now, see if you can master my trick."

Kennedy walked over to him and whispered, "I thought you were going to teach them to make a drink."

"I was, but they wanted to learn this instead. And *this* trick," he said, pointing at the passengers trying to imitate his earlier moves, "is something they will remember long after they have left." He laughed, "Making memories, isn't that what you preach, Kennedy?"

She rolled her eyes at him. "You win."

"Hey, Kennedy," she heard someone yell, "check this out!" Dolly was pointing and jumping up and down. "She's going to be a hit back at Harmony Lakes!"

Beth stood at the table, expertly pouring water from five shakers into the pyramid of martini glasses. Those in the class stood around her in awe and began clapping while Bert snapped the shutter on his camera. "This is a typical Friday night back in Oklahoma," she said as she slowly poured the rest of the contents of the shakers into the glasses. "This is just like slicing a champagne bottle with the sword."

Kennedy walked over to stand by Louise, who was watching Beth and shaking her head. "It seems that ditzy waters run deep," Louise said in shock.

Kennedy saw Anna Marie helping in the mixology class. "Do you happen to know where Sara is?" she asked. "I was looking for her but haven't seen her out here with the rest of you."

"She left to find Omar. She wanted to ask if she could reset the spa for the next cruise since it's closed, but that was a little while ago," Anna Marie replied. "Kennedy, have you…" Kennedy shook her head, and Anna Marie began blinking rapidly to fight back the tears welling in her eyes.

"No crying, Anna Marie," she said quietly and squeezed the young woman's arm. "This is all going to work out, I promise."

Needing a break from taking photos of the guests as they relaxed or played games on the pool deck, Bert snuck into the spa from the back stairs to take a few last shots. When he went through the photos earlier, he noticed that a few of the private treatment room images had not turned out as well as he had hoped, and he wanted to reshoot them.

Kennedy walked quickly around the pool deck and spied the Butlers lying by the pool. Terri jumped up when she saw Kennedy, to the delight of the men around her.

"Kennedy, I have to show you what Jonesy gave me this morning," she said, thrusting out her hand. On her finger was a pave sapphire and diamond ring made into the shape of a dolphin's tail. "You know, he has surprised me every day with some piece of jewelry, and because I was a knucklehead and got hurt, we didn't get to go shopping yesterday in Punta Cana," she said breathlessly. "I was so sad, but I told myself it was okay, especially after he found the…" she paused and whispered loudly, "the B-O-D-Y. And this morning we were walking along the promenade, and he said," she looked at Jones with adoration, "well you tell her what you said, Jonesy, it was so sweet."

Jones stood up and put an arm around Terri's shoulders. "I told her that if she ever wanted to know how much I loved her, she only needed to count the number of waves in the ocean."

Terri wiped her eyes. "Isn't he the most romantic man?"

Kennedy nodded, winking at Jones. "I wish I could stay and chat, but there is something I need to attend to, but don't forget about the classes," she called over her shoulder.

Kennedy skipped down the outside steps that ran between the decks. She intended to get into the spa from the fitness center's access off the main corridor, hoping that her access card would get her inside. Walking down the corridor, she spied Omar and quickly slowed down. He was talking on his radio. "What are you doing here, Kennedy?" he asked in a clipped tone while he put his radio in his jacket pocket.

"Oh, nothing," she replied innocently. "I was on my way to the game room and must have gotten turned around." She shrugged her shoulders. "I've got so much on my mind."

Omar stared at her, wondering why she was lying. "You aren't perhaps going to visit a friend on this floor, are you?" he asked pointedly and crossed his arms. "You and I both know Mila is on this deck."

Kennedy blinked and answered him honestly. "No, absolutely not, scouts honor," she said, holding up two and then three fingers. "You said I couldn't see her, and I'm following the rules."

His eyes bored into hers. "I'm not convinced. I also said that the spa and fitness center were off-limits, and that includes to you!"

Kennedy nodded her head. "Of course, Omar, I would never think of doing anything like that," she gulped and looked at her watch. "Well, I've got to run and check on the game room. It's on eight," she gave him a weak smile and continued to walk quickly down the corridor. She pointed to the elevators. "See, I'm taking the elevator to the game room," she called out to him and pressed the up button.

When she got in the elevator, she pressed the button for deck eight. When the doors opened, she went quickly down the hallway and through a door marked private, taking the employee staircase down to deck six. She opened the stair door and used her access card to enter the room Mila used to store the yoga equipment. Next, she went through another door and entered the back of the fitness center. She saw Sara straightening up the room. "Sara," she said quietly, not wanting to startle her, "can we talk for a moment?"

Sara turned around quickly and saw it was Kennedy. "Sure," she said hesitantly, "but I need to keep working if that's okay."

"That's fine," Kennedy said and followed Sara over to where several pieces of gym equipment sat. Sara sprayed a bottle of disinfectant on them and began to pick them up one by one to wipe them off. "I wanted to talk to you about something."

Sara looked up at Kennedy. "What?" There was a hint of nervousness in her voice.

"Mila should be the one to have this conversation, but she's under the weather."

Sara looked at Kennedy and raised her eyebrows.

Kennedy continued. "You should be careful about eavesdropping. I heard you had your ear pressed against the wall when Mila was giving a treatment yesterday. I'm sure you were only trying to see where she was in the session, but you should be careful. It can get you removed from the ship for something like that. We take privacy very seriously."

"Who told you that? The photographer guy? What a jerk."

Kennedy nodded. "Just be careful, okay? And don't blame Bert. He wasn't trying to get you in trouble."

"Okay," she said with a sigh.

Bert was making his way down the staff hallway and noticed Kennedy and Sara in the fitness center through the two-way mirror. He couldn't hear what was being said and, thinking about what he had shown Kennedy, felt in his pocket for the recorder. He turned it on and walked to the staff entrance where he could hear them better.

There was an uncomfortable silence; the only noise was the music coming from the overhead speakers. "It's a shame that the spa is closed," Kennedy said finally, and Sara nodded as she continued to wipe down the weights. "I wish you could have seen it before Mila renovated it. The change is dramatic. She's done an amazing job."

Sara gave a little shrug. "I saw some photos that Anna Marie showed me. It was a big change." Sara kept a steady rhythm going as she spoke, spraying disinfectant on the piece of equipment, wiping it off, and putting it away.

"Did you know she's been on the *Helio* for fifteen years?"

Sara didn't say anything but kept to her task.

"Why are you down here?" Kennedy asked curiously. "Aren't you supposed to be up on the pool deck with the passengers helping the cast and the other spa techs?"

Sara looked up at Kennedy. "I asked Omar if I could come in and straighten up the fitness center and restock the spa's retail area. Anna Marie said there was a tight turnaround tomorrow before the next cruise took off, and I thought I would get it done."

"That was a good idea."

Sara continued. "Besides, being up on the deck was making me nervous. All I could see was the ocean. I'm not used to that and started to feel a little panicky. I don't know if I am cut out to work on a ship. I need to think about it. Only seeing miles of ocean can make you feel trapped." She gave Kennedy a long look. "And I know about Mila. It's hard to keep a secret on this ship. I was here when they found the body. I heard in the crew bar that she's under house arrest until we get back to Port Canaveral. I'm just surprised. She was always so calm. I guess you never can tell about a person."

"Sara, Mila wouldn't purposefully hurt someone," Kennedy said defensively.

"No, but I can understand how she might feel. Mr. Atcher was quite a jerk to her," Sara answered. "You can only take so much from someone like that until you just want to explode."

Kennedy paused for a moment. This was the break she had been waiting for. "How well did you know Mr. Atcher?" she asked innocently.

"I knew Gunner like the back of my…" Sara stopped and sucked in her breath. "H-h-how did you know?" she stammered.

"I did a little checking on your background today after I was told you were seen eavesdropping on Mila and Mr. Atcher during his last treatment. And something kept bugging Mila. It seemed to her that you were trying rather hard to get on the *Helio* and this particular cruise. I told her she was wrong and that you were only eager to get the job." Kennedy looked at Sara directly. "So please, answer my question. Did you know Mr. Atcher? It's a bit of a coincidence that you were both on the ship at the same time."

Sara blew the breath she had been holding out. "Yes, I knew him. I knew that lying jerk." She slammed a hand weight down and picked up the next one. "I was being fast-tracked by a hotel management company. I went from being a front desk clerk to the corporate office in a flash and had a career path in front of me. I met Gunner when he joined the company, and we started dating. He was charming, good-looking, and had money and power." She pursed her lips together. "I started to help him out here and there when he could not produce something new to show the higher-ups. At first, it was no big deal. You'll do anything for someone you are in love with." She stopped for a moment as if remembering something and then picked up a kettlebell. "I had been working on a project about hotel linen. It was sure to impress the corporate team, a way to save thousands of dollars, and I had been working on it on my own for months. I had spent hours on the project and showed my findings to

Gunner when I was finished. A few days later, I asked him if he would help me get it on the agenda to present at the next monthly meeting. I'll never forget how he laughed at me. 'I already presented it, babe,' he said, 'and I got a huge bonus!' Then he tapped my nose and said, 'Thanks for doing the hard work.' I stood there in his office stunned. He had passed off my work as his own, and it didn't bother him. That was what ended our relationship. So, I left work, went to his apartment, gathered my things, and left the keys on the counter. I couldn't be with a man that would take credit for someone else's work." She wiped away an angry tear and placed the kettlebell on the shelf.

Kennedy was momentarily stunned. She wasn't sure what she had expected to hear, but her heart went to the young woman. "Oh, Sara, you must have been furious. I cannot imagine how that felt."

Sara picked up another kettlebell, wiped it off, and placed it next to the other one. "Oh, it got worse. I had to work with him every day, sit across from him in meetings while he sat there staring at me smugly." She walked back over to the pile of equipment and stared at it. "Word got out that we had broken up. You know how fast gossip can travel. Everyone knew. People would ask why we broke up, and I would tell them that we didn't work out but were still friends and how I appreciated Gunner's mentoring. He was still my boss. Then, one night, several of my co-workers and I went out for drinks. I drank too many margaritas and told the head of marketing what had really happened. A few days later, Gunner began to make my life difficult. Suddenly, I stopped receiving meeting invites and was left off emails. My name was there, but somehow the spelling had been changed and now had an 'h' at the end."

Sara began wiping off one of the weight benches. "I wanted to go to human resources, but let's face it, I had broken the rules by sleeping with a senior member of the company, and they were not going to be sympathetic. Plus, he was the darling of that group if you can believe that." Kennedy nodded; she was sure Gunner could turn on the charm when he wanted something.

Sara took a deep breath. "In addition to the linen project, I had also been working on a new manual with updated cleaning protocols aimed at making guests feel safer in our hotels. Unfortunately, our company required all projects to be available for viewing at all times by the higher-ups so they could check on your progress. This meant Gunner had full access to my files." She sat down heavily on the bench opposite Kennedy. "Transparency, great, isn't it?" she said wryly, shaking her head. "I had heard through the grapevine Gunner was being pressured to come up with something along the same lines but had nothing to show." She began to speak fast. "I decided it was the perfect time to go to the CEO and expose Gunner for the sleazeball he was. I made an appointment with his secretary under the guise of wanting to discuss my future. I planned to wow him in the meeting with the new cleaning protocols, marketing, and rollout plan. I thought I had covered all of my bases." Sara trailed off. The only sound was her heavy breathing.

"The next morning, security told me to report to Gunner's office immediately when I arrived at work. I was not to go to my office." She looked at Kennedy. "That's when I knew he had been tipped off. "I walked into his office and saw all my personal belongings sitting in a box on a chair." She wiped away the tears that had begun to fall. "He stood there and told me I was fired. When I asked why, he said …" she chuckled sadly, "I'll never forget this, 'You just aren't working out as we had hoped, Sara, you aren't producing anything to wow us. As a young junior manager in the corporate office, you should be coming up with innovative ideas,' and he patted a large binder on his desk. It was the binder from my office that contained my notes for my cleaning protocols project. Then, he walked over to the door and shut it. He wanted to make sure no one else heard what he was about to say. I must have gone through a hundred emotions in those five seconds."

"He walked back from the door to his desk and sat down." Sara mimicked Gunner's voice. "'You were stupid, Sara. You tried to tattle on me. Let's face facts, I'm a senior level vice president, and you are nothing more than a junior level manager.'" Sara looked up at the ceiling fighting back fresh tears. "Kennedy, this was a man who had told me he loved me and wanted a life with me, a family." Kennedy saw that the young woman was in agony, and Sara continued her sad tale.

"But the insult to the firing was still to come." She wiped her eyes with her sleeve. "Gunner sat down at his desk and slid a legal document toward me, telling me it was in my best interest to sign it." Sara stood and began to pace. "I guess he could see how angry I was because he held up his finger and waved it at me. 'Be careful, Sara,' he said, 'don't try to go to anyone about this. When you told the head of marketing, nothing happened. That's because I'm sleeping with her. Oh, and going to human resources isn't going to help either because I have the director eating out of my palm. One romantic dinner with her and your complaint will mysteriously disappear. So, it looks like you are out of options, Sara. And if that isn't enough, I'll remind you that I have some very compromising photos of you that I am sure you wouldn't want to be seen. Sign this document now, or with one push of a button, I will ruin you professionally and personally by accidentally sending the photos to everyone in my contact list. The choice is yours.'"

Kennedy shook her head slowly, realizing Gunner had been a monster long before he set foot on the *Helio*. Sara shrugged. "What could I do? I signed the paper, took my box, and left the building. I couldn't have my reputation ruined. I needed it to get a job. What other choice did I have? Later that day, I learned Gunner had removed my name from the cleaning manual and presented it to the CEO and, soon after, the company's board of directors." She picked up a kettlebell from the pile, wiped it off, and walked over to put it up. "I heard that his little friend in marketing sent a press release to the industry magazines, and the title of the press release was the 'King of Clean'" she called over her shoulder and walked back over to Kennedy. "And with it came his large bonus and the accolades."

She let out a heavy sigh. "All the hours of research and writing during my off time, and he took it away in the blink of an eye. The icing on the cake came when I was trying to find a job, only to learn that I had been blackballed.

Gunner must have been concerned that I would say something. I would submit my application, go through the initial process, and in a few days, I would receive a rejection letter from the human resources director telling me thanks but no thanks. Honestly, that was why I turned to work in the spa. I thought I could at least start in an industry where my stupid mistake wouldn't follow me. I didn't realize that it would help me in the end." She looked Kennedy in the eye. "So, in answer to your question, yeah, I know Gunner."

Kennedy had been sitting on the weight bench in complete shock. Sara had begun to wipe off some small dumbbells that lay in a pile. Kennedy noticed they looked like the ones she had in her cabin. "But how did you know about the cruise ship?" Kennedy asked.

"Oh, that was easy," Sara said, giving Kennedy a slight chuckle. "Gunner's social media pages are public. Anyone can see them." A smile lifted the corners of her mouth. "But Gunner could never keep a secret. Playing poker with him was like playing cards with a little kid. As soon as the cards were dealt, you knew exactly what kind of hand he had by looking at his face." Thinking back to Gunner's body language, Kennedy had to agree with Sara. He was easy to read.

Sara continued, "He began making mysterious posts about having secret talks about a new job. It wasn't hard to figure out where when he was suddenly a fan of the Sunny Dayz Cruise Line and began posting comments about them and referenced a big trip he was taking. From there, it was a matter of waiting. I put my application in with the corporate office, passed their tests, and hounded them until I got an interview with Mila, and here I am." She took two five-pound dumbbells and placed them in the rack. "I will admit," she said, turning around and picking up a smaller weight, "Everything happened so fast, and I hadn't made a solid plan on how to do it."

"Do what?" Kennedy asked.

"Kill him," Sara said offhandedly as she returned to the bench where Kennedy was sitting. "I had hoped for something more satisfying like making him fall overboard, but the situation just presented itself."

Kennedy thought back. She had wished a similar fate on Gunner.

"Mila made sure everyone was gone for the drill, and I convinced her I would leave as soon as I had finished my work. I waited for him in the locker room. It was convenient that the lights were off for the safety drill. It made hiding easier. I was afraid that snoopy Bert would never leave. He was spending so much time setting up a shot that I started to worry I would lose my nerve and my window of opportunity." She rolled her eyes. "Gunner went into the locker room, and I came up behind him and beat him over the head with the fire extinguisher I had taken out of the cabinet earlier when I put the first load of towels in the room." She let out a sigh of irritation. "I didn't realize how heavy those fire extinguishers in the cabinet were. If I had known, I would have found a smaller one." Sara knit her brows together and looked at Kennedy. "I was disappointed when I found out he didn't die from the blows to the head in the locker room. Thankfully, the sauna finished him up. So, there you have it."

Kennedy was so mesmerized by the confession that she didn't notice the small three-pound dumbbell in Sara's hand. With all of her strength, Sara quickly swung the weight at Kennedy.

The dumbbell connected with Kennedy's temple, and she fell to the floor unconscious. Sara dropped the weight and turned to run out of the room, but before she could take three steps, Bert ran in and tackled her, dragging Sara to the floor. He pinned her to the ground with his hands. "Snoopy?" he said as she tried to fight back. "I was doing my job! And those photos are going to win me awards!"

As Bert came in from one side to tackle Sara, Omar charged from the opposite direction. He had watched Kennedy get on the elevator and saw it go to deck eight. Satisfied, he checked Mila's cabin and confirmed that the guard he had posted was still there. As Omar began to walk from Mila's cabin to the gym, his radio chirped. Putting it to his ear, he heard it was nothing more than his team's shift change. He listened for a moment and then turned the volume down. He walked up the small hallway from the main corridor to the gym to ask Sara where she had been during the safety drill and heard Kennedy's voice as he started to open the door. *I cannot believe her! She lied to me!* he thought angrily. He was about to walk in when he heard Sara's voice and listened in fascination to the conversation. After Sara had told Kennedy how she had bludgeoned Gunner with the fire extinguisher, Omar began to walk into the gym and saw Sara's arm fly toward Kennedy with the dumbbell. Too far away to stop her, he watched Bert from the corner of his eye run in and tackle her.

"Code Red," Omar quickly barked into his radio, running toward Kennedy. "I have a code red in the fitness center. I need the ship's doctor at once," he yelled. Omar was torn between his desire to go to Kennedy and his need to secure Sara, but he knew his duty. He scanned the room for something to tie Sara's hands with and saw two jump ropes hanging on a wall. He grabbed them and ran to where Bert had Sara pinned to the ground. "Let's get her up and tie her hands together," he said. He looked at Bert and nodded his head at Kennedy, lying unconscious on the floor. "Bert, will you…" Bert nodded and moved quickly over to Kennedy, kneeling beside her.

"I don't know what to do, Omar," Bert said in a scared voice. His friend was lying there, not moving.

"I've called for help, and the doctor should be here soon. Just stay with her."

Sara snorted, and Omar glared at her. "Sara West," he said officially, "I am placing you under arrest for the murder of Gunner Owen Atcher and the aggravated assault of Kennedy Reeves." He barked orders for his security team to come to the fitness center at once. "Bert, without you, Kennedy may have been hurt worse," he said. "What were you doing here?"

Bert beamed. "Finishing the spa photos so Mila would have them in case she got canned. And that's not the half of it." He held up the small recorder he had been using on the cruise. "I have the entire confession." I've been using it to remind myself which passengers were which."

They both looked at Kennedy as she began to rouse. "Owww…what happened?" she asked, trying to get up.

Omar forced Sara to sit on one of the weight benches, and Bert gently pushed Kennedy back onto the floor. "Don't move!" Omar barked at Sara. He knelt beside Kennedy. "You need to stay put and lie there quietly. I know it will be hard but try." He handed Bert a towel from the bench to put under her head. "You got clocked in the head with a dumbbell, and you've got Bert to thank for saving you." He stood back up and glared at Sara. Kennedy smiled weakly at Bert and squeezed his hand.

The security team arrived quickly, making a great deal of noise. Omar pulled one of them aside and whispered in his ear. He nodded at Sara. "Take her down below to the cell," Omar said tersely. "And someone get the FBI on the phone so that I can update them." He watched as two guards hustled Sara out of the room.

He knelt beside Kennedy once again. She grimaced and turned her head to him. "How did you know I was here?"

Omar laughed and smiled. "I didn't. In all honesty, I thought you went up to deck eight to check on the game room. When I heard your voice in the fitness center, I was on my way in to yell at you, but then I heard Sara's voice. I heard the whole thing. What were you thinking?"

"Girl talk?" Kennedy offered weakly. "And you," she turned to Bert and made a face as waves of pain went from her cheekbone to the top of her head, "why were you here?"

"Finishing up the photos of the spa. I saw you two talking through the two-way mirror. And being nosy, I crept to the other entrance to listen."

"It's a good thing he did, too," Omar said sternly. "She could have done to you what she did to Gunner."

"Well, she didn't," Kennedy said, struggling to get up. Omar pushed her shoulders back down. "Owww," she cried out as her head touched the towel. "If you two would just let me sit up, I can put some ice on my face. I'm fine, I promise, and I have a—"

Omar and Bert mimicked her simultaneously, "A million things to do." She smiled at the two of them and then winced again in pain.

Dr. Craig arrived and examined Kennedy. "I'm fine, Dr. Craig," Kennedy said, flinching as he touched the bruise that was beginning to form. "It's nothing. Oh boy," she said as a wave of dizziness hit her.

"Black spots before your eyes?" Dr. Craig asked mildly. She tried to nod her head, but it hurt too much. "Look, I know you are busy and have things to do, but I need you to stay still so I can examine you," Dr. Craig said. "You've had a terrible hit to the head, but I also know you. So, can we make a deal?" he asked, shining a flashlight into Kennedy's eyes. "If I can make sure that you have no immediate neurological damage, I'll allow you to direct what needs to be done tonight, but," he emphasized, "you have to sit still, and someone will need to be with you the entire time."

Mila's gentle voice was a soothing balm in Kennedy's ears. "I'll take care of that, Doctor Craig. I won't let her out of my sight," she said, and Kennedy burst into tears.

"Owww, it hurts to smile," she cried and looked at her best friend. "And I have so much to tell you!"

A few hours later, having told the story several times to the captain, her friends, and formally to Omar in a statement, Kennedy was ensconced in a comfortable chair in the Solstice Theater, watching the performers as they practiced for the last show. Omar had called her father and explained that there would be no need for an attorney for Mila. At Kennedy's insistence, he did not tell him about Sara's attack on her. Rosemary, Franklin, Mila, and Tony scurried to do whatever running Kennedy needed. Chef Michèle brought a raw steak for her face, commenting that it was a waste of a perfectly good piece of meat.

Kennedy marveled at how the evening's last show was coming together. The captain had found the Club Diva Boys on the pool deck and brought them to the bridge. After explaining what had happened to Kennedy, he asked if they would perform with the cast for the last show as a personal favor to him. John, Dave, Steve, Phil, Don, and Robert quickly agreed.

"We should do the same costumes we did for the last show. It will cut down on time," John said. They were on the stage with the cast walking through the show. John clapped his hands. "Okay, one more time from the top."

A few minutes later, the doors to the theater burst open, and everyone stopped in their tracks as Vera Jameson marched down the aisle with the captain in hot pursuit behind her. "I cannot believe that I had to demand to see the captain in order to find you, Kennedy," she said hotly as she stormed down the aisle toward Kennedy. "Honestly, I have been looking for you everywhere, and I need to speak with—" When Vera reached Kennedy sitting in a chair near the front row, she saw she was holding a steak to the side of her head. Then she saw the outlines of a large, dark blue bruise around her temple. "My dear," Vera said, dropping to her knees. "What happened to you?" she asked tenderly, pushing Kennedy's hair back.

Kennedy smiled crookedly. "Just a little mishap in the fitness center. I'm fine."

Vera looked at her squarely. "You aren't fine, but that is not why I am here. I have been trying to find you to tell you that I got in touch with my college roommate today. Emily's been on a trip to see some Greek ruins." She waved her hand. "Emily didn't know anything about a new vice president of the company, and after a few phone calls, I think we figured it out." She drew in a breath and plunged forward. "Mr. Phillips's seat is up for re-election this year, and he enjoys the perks he gets for being on the board. So, he thought it would help him keep his seat if he had a consultant bring back a false report citing that the *Helio*, the best ship in the fleet, was in trouble. Gunner would present the board with two options. They could pay him a substantial amount of money to consult or name him vice president of operations, which is quite different from being the company's vice president. I'm certain that Gunner promised Bart a hefty finder's fee, either way. When Bart booked the two cabins for Gunner and himself, whoever put in the reservations marked them bs VIP and complimentary as Bart is a board member."

Kennedy squeezed Vera's hand. "That explains why we didn't have any information from the corporate office. They didn't know. Thank you for looking out for us, Mrs. Jameson. It means the world to me."

Vera looked back at her in mock horror. "I didn't do it for you. I simply didn't want to break in a new group." She raised her head to look at Rosemary, Franklin, Mila, Tony, and the captain. "I have you all just the way I like you." She gave them a sly smile. "A little afraid and willing to do anything to keep me happy."

Kennedy grinned. "Oh, so we mean nothing to you. We're nothing more than your minions."

"Precisely," Vera said, rising. As she turned to leave, she winked at Kennedy.

The last show of the cruise was a success, and the team sat together for the performance. Kennedy sat in the center of the row with Omar on one side and Mila on the other. Vera Jameson and the captain were seated behind her with Rosemary, Franklin, Bert, and Tony. Kennedy felt herself in a cocoon of happiness.

During the show, Omar's hand slid over and took hers. Kennedy and Mila looked at each other from the corners of their eyes and smiled slightly. The last song of the show made Kennedy cry. The cast paraded down the aisle, singing about being a family while confetti cannons went off from the balconies and the stage. Kennedy looked around at the familiar faces: Dolly and the Ladies from Harmony Lakes were dancing in front of their seats beside Jones and Terri Butler while the Club Diva Boys blew kisses to Kennedy from the stage. She looked up at the lights and thought to herself, *we are a family, just an unconventional one,* and she smiled.

Sunny Dayz Cruise Line

THE HELIO

DAY SIX

ARRIVE PORT CANAVERAL, USA

DISEMBARKATION BEGINS AT 9:00 A.M.

The party in the theater went on until the wee hours. Kennedy had turned in shortly after the show per Dr. Craig's orders, and Mila went along, promising Dr. Craig that she would wake Kennedy every hour to check for a concussion. Kennedy now stood in the lobby bidding the passengers goodbye.

Bert had sidled up to her at one point and whispered loudly that Jones Butler had coaxed the captain into dancing with Terri Butler, and he had pictures to prove it. "He cuts quite a rug," Bert said, "I almost think he's better than Franklin."

Kennedy looked at him, startled. "Have you seen—"

Franklin strode up. "Who is better than me?" he asked as Bert hurried away,

"The captain apparently," Kennedy said, bemused. "We may need to have a dance-off," she smiled sweetly.

Franklin huffed loudly. "I came to see how you are, but it seems the knock to your face did not affect your smart mouth."

"Has anyone seen Mila? I haven't seen her for a while."

"She's been in the spa getting everything set for the next cruise," Franklin answered. "There are some therapy sessions going on as well. Anna Marie is a mess." He stopped and smiled. "It seems like we are all in need of a little healing."

The first goodbyes of the cruise were with the Ladies from Harmony Lakes. After explaining to them that the injury to her face was from tripping up some stairs, she thanked them for coming on the cruise.

"Kid, you sure throw one heck of a party," Dolly said. "If I'm still around next year, I'll be here with you."

Laura hugged her. "We did have a lovely time. Thank you for everything, and don't listen to my mother. She has plenty of years still left in her."

"Lots of buckets still to check off," Dolly cackled.

"Pray for me, Kennedy," Laura said.

Marilyn was the next to hug her. "Let me know when your brother comes back," she said huskily. "I want to show him my surfing moves."

Louise smirked. "Do you honestly believe that sweet young man wants to see an old bag like you in a bathing suit?" she asked incredulously. "There isn't enough time in the world to make you twenty again."

Marilyn squared her shoulders, put her nose in the air, and began to march away. She looked over her shoulder. "Maybe not," she said hotly, "but some men prefer a seasoned woman with knowledge."

"Oh my," said Louise hurrying after her, "I guess I need to apologize, or she will pout for days. Thanks again, Kennedy, and don't worry, we will fill out those surveys, all tens!"

The Butlers were the next to leave. Terri was wearing a gold-colored dress that came to mid-thigh and strappy sandals. Kennedy wondered how she would get to their car in her four-inch heels but realized it was not her problem.

"Kennedy," Jones drawled, "that's quite a bruise on your face. How did you get it?"

Kennedy was quick to answer. She had been offering the same excuse all morning. "Oh, clumsy me, fell up the stairs."

Jones drew a cigar out of his pocket, saw the stern look on Kennedy's face, and put it back in his pocket. "We just want to thank you for such a marvelous time. You outdid yourself. Sweetsie and I want to give you a token of our appreciation." He placed a ten-dollar bill in her hand.

"Oh, Mr. Butler, thank you, but I cannot accept a gratuity," she said smiling and handed him back the bill. "It's just a part of what we do."

Jones was thoughtful as he put the bill back in his wallet. "Well, remember, we want you and the others to come out to the house once Terri remodels it. We can't wait to show it off to you." He lowered his voice to a loud whisper. "Now, one more thing. Since we have the free cruise coming up for not talking about the B-O-D-Y, can we book that trip directly through you? I want to make sure we get what we agreed on for my zipped lips. You know it was a traumatic experience for me."

Kennedy smiled graciously. "Mr. Butler, when you and Terri are ready to come back, just send me a message, and I will take care of your trip personally." She handed him her business card.

"Well, you are all right, Kennedy," he drawled, "shame you don't want to meet any of my brothers. Are you sure? They'd like a self-sufficient girl like you."

Omar walked up, joining them. "I believe Ms. Reeves is spoken for, Mr. Butler," he said quietly. "Good luck to you both. Vaya con Dios."

"Hi," Kennedy said, smiling at Omar, "did you get everything taken care of?" she asked cautiously.

He nodded his head. "Sara was led off the ship early this morning and taken in for questioning. They will see if they can use Bert's taped confession to get a statement they can use in a court of law. They are also using his photos." He placed a thumb and forefinger on her chin, turned her face to look at the bruise, and winced. "They also have the sworn statements from you and Bert and the photographs of your lovely but bruised face, which should help."

Kennedy looked at Omar. "So, we don't have to do anything else?"

He shook his head. "I took care of everything," he patted her hand and smiled widely. "I am the director of security, after all, and we aim to please."

Kennedy giggled. "Thank goodness, because—"

"I know, I know," he interrupted, "you have a million things to do."

"Well, I do," she said, laughing, "I just hope the next group doesn't have the drama this group had."

"Speaking of drama, I believe your divas are coming up behind you," he said quietly and excused himself.

"Darling, we don't want to leave. We want to stay on the ship with you. Can't we be part of the cast?" John cried.

Kennedy looked at each of them with love. "Gentlemen, I cannot thank you enough for everything you did."

Phil squeezed her hand. "What are you talking about? Thanking us? Because of you and getting to perform, we have decided to bring the show back!"

Kennedy was shocked. "What do you mean? What about your jobs?"

Don quickly answered, "We can do our jobs from anywhere as long as we have a computer. If this crazy year has taught us anything, it's how to adapt."

Steve pulled her into a hug. "If it hadn't been for this cruise, we wouldn't have realized how much we miss working together. We envy what you have here."

Dave continued, "Last night after the show, we were taking off our makeup and putting away the wigs and costumes, and we realized how much we miss performing and each other," he said, looking warmly at the group.

Robert interjected, with his hands on his hips, "Which means, girlfriend, you have a three-ring circus to control when you are in town!"

"That's right!" John shouted, jumping up and down and clapping his hands. "You promised, and I never forget when someone makes a promise to work for me for free."

Kennedy looked at them mischievously. "Well, since we are talking about working for free," she drew out six pieces of paper. "I suppose none of you are interested in these vouchers for a free cruise, compliments of the captain and the corporate office."

They looked at her in stunned silence. "What are you talking about, Kennedy? We did what we did because we love you," said John earnestly.

Kennedy couldn't contain her happiness. "Let's just say the captain made a call, and you are now guests of the company on your next cruise, spa services included."

John looked at her tenderly, taking in the large bruise on her face. "Take care of that pretty face and that handsome director of security, huh, kid?" he squeezed her hand and winked. He patted his head to find his rhinestone sunglasses and put them on. "Bye darling," he said theatrically and waved to her, "we are off to plan and connive." She watched them walk down the gangway, talking a mile a minute as they made plans for their next cruise and the reopening of Club Diva.

Kennedy was perplexed. The lobby was empty, and she had not seen Vera Jameson pass by her. She saw Billy the bellman walking by a few minutes later as he prepared for the next group of passengers. "Billy, did you happen to see Mrs. Jameson leave?"

"Ugh, did I ever," he said, frowning. "Do you remember how it was when she arrived?" he asked exaggeratedly. "Well, she was the same leaving. I had to take her stuff out to her limo, and when she wasn't scolding me about getting scuffs on her luggage, she was yelling at the short little guy who came on board early with the other one." He clapped his hands over his mouth. "Sorry!" He looked around to make sure no one could overhear him and said in a loud whisper, "She made him get into the limo, and I heard her tell the driver that they were going to someone's office and that the little man had a lot of explaining to do." Billy shook his head. "I wouldn't want to be him."

"Me neither," Kennedy said and silently thanked Vera for taking care of Mr. Phillips.

Kennedy looked at the empty lobby. "Well, Billy, we'd better prepare for the next group of passengers. They should arrive in a few hours and—"

Billy interrupted her, "And you've got a million things to do?"

She grinned. "Maybe just a thousand today."

AUTHORS NOTE

WOW! Wasn't that a great cruise? Thank you for reading *A Boat for a Goat!* I hope you enjoyed meeting Kennedy Reeves and her friends as much as I loved bringing them to life. The next book in the series, *A Cruise for Sous,* finds Kennedy in charge of a cooking competition when the corporate office enters into a partnership with a regional television network as they search for their host chef. Secrets and scandal are the spices of this cruise. – MJ Mac

Facebook – MJ Mac

Instagram – MJ_Mac_Author

ACKNOWLEDGEMENTS

The author gratefully acknowledges the assistance of many, many people who helped bring this dream alive: Dan McCarragher, for his patience, love, and support as I started this journey; my beta reader team (Kristy, Denise, Orson, Kathy, Marcia, Nelda, Ann, and Paula) as they patiently read the first draft and offered *loving* critique; Heather Clancy for telling me to, "just write the damn book"; Michelle Krueger, my fabulous editor who polished a very rough diamond. The author also acknowledges Gettys Images, Pixabay, Weape Studio, and Dharma Type for the use of images and fonts.

ABOUT THE AUTHOR

Before embarking on a writing career, MJ Mac was a "Jill of all trades" in corporate America for forty years. MJ was a master juggler in her three-inch heels and lipstick, pulling the ropes from behind the curtain to seamlessly make magic happen. In 2021, a story about a cruise director, her co-workers, and their zany passengers began to formulate in her head. MJ traded in the corporate world of useless meetings, meetings about meetings, high heels, and suits for the sand, flip flops, and a sarong so that she could pursue writing full-time. MJ and her husband Dan (her biggest supporter next to their adorable albeit scruffy dog Elvis) are living their best life on the beach, where she spends her time plotting what drama Kennedy and her friends will find next.